giant

Mollie Ray

faber

FIRST PUBLISHED IN THE UK AND USA IN 2024
BY FABER & FABER LTD
THE BINDERY, 51 HATTON GARDEN,
LONDON EC1N 8HN

ARTWORK AND DESIGN BY MOLLIE RAY
PRINTED AND BOUND IN EUROPE
ALL RIGHTS RESERVED
© MOLLIE RAY, 2024

THE RIGHT OF MOLLIE RAY TO BE IDENTIFIED
AS AUTHOR OF THIS WORK HAS BEEN ASSERTED
IN ACCORDANCE WITH SECTION 77 OF THE
COPYRIGHT, DESIGNS AND PATENTS ACT 1988.

A CIP RECORD FOR THIS BOOK IS AVAILABLE
FROM THE BRITISH LIBRARY.

ISBN 978-0-571-37419-9

2 4 6 8 10 9 7 5 3 1

Printed and bound in the EU on FSC® certified paper in line with our continuing commitment to ethical business practices, sustainability and the environment. For further information see faber.co.uk/environmental-policy

FOR LOUIE*

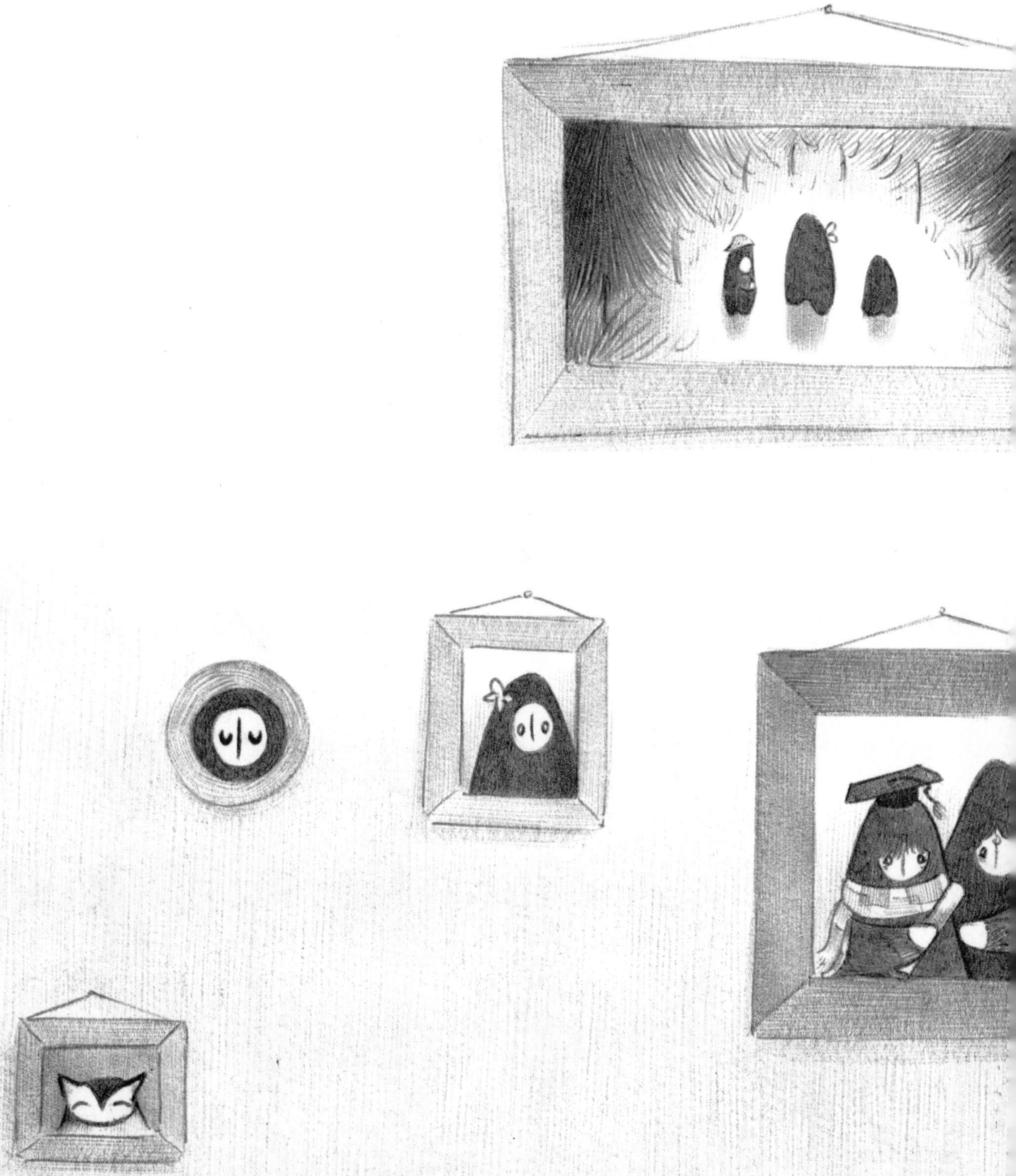

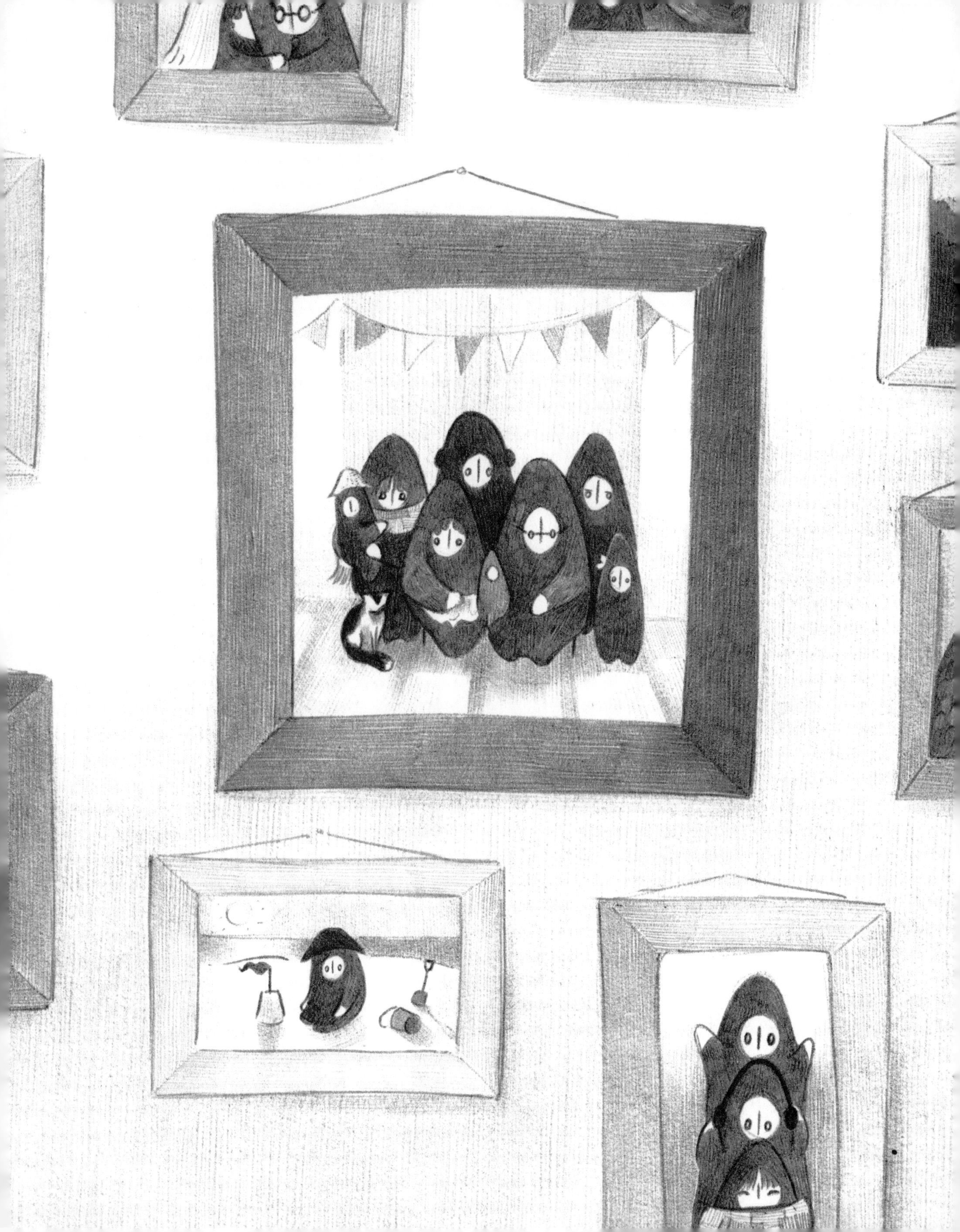

CHAPTER ONE

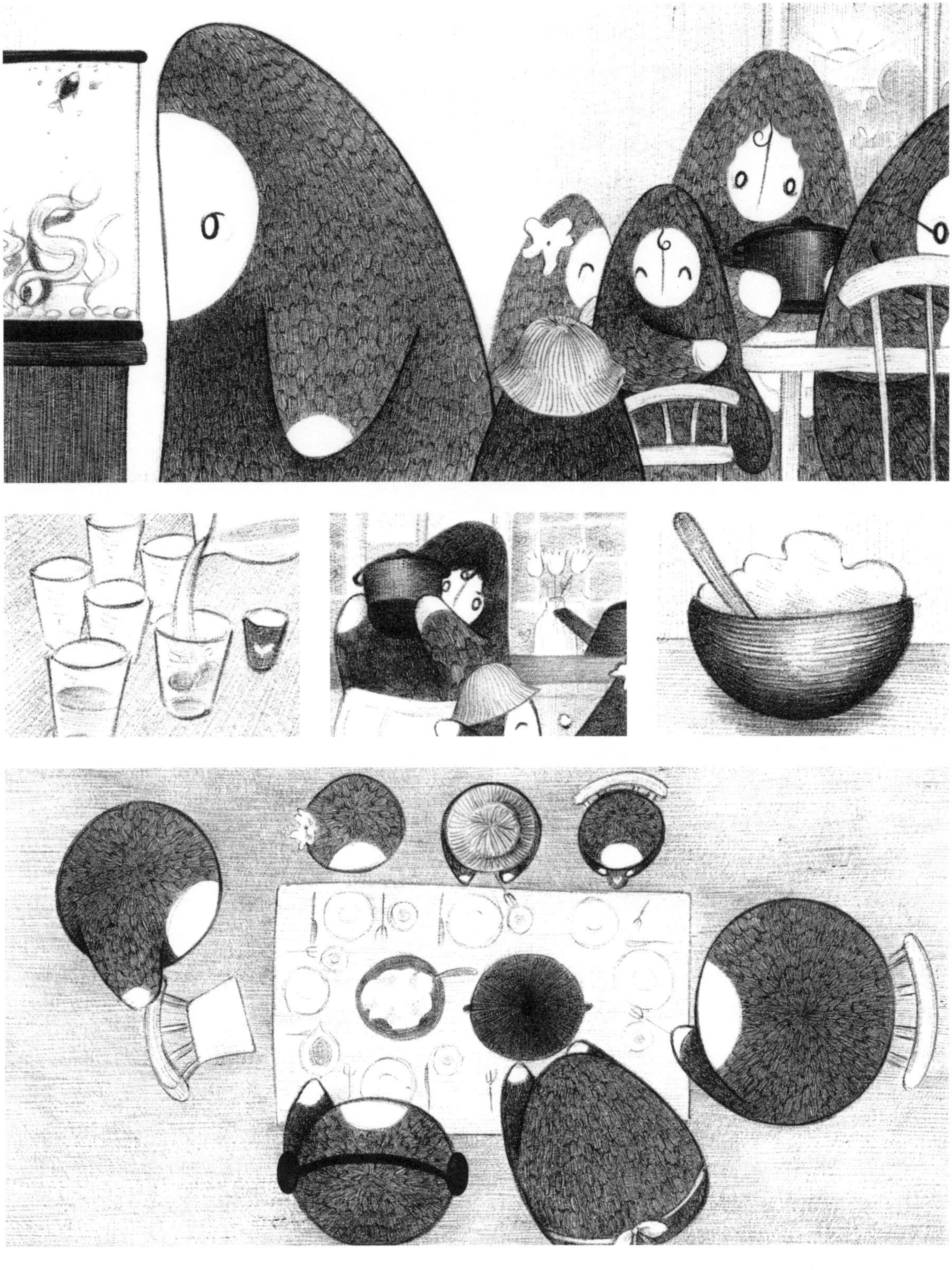

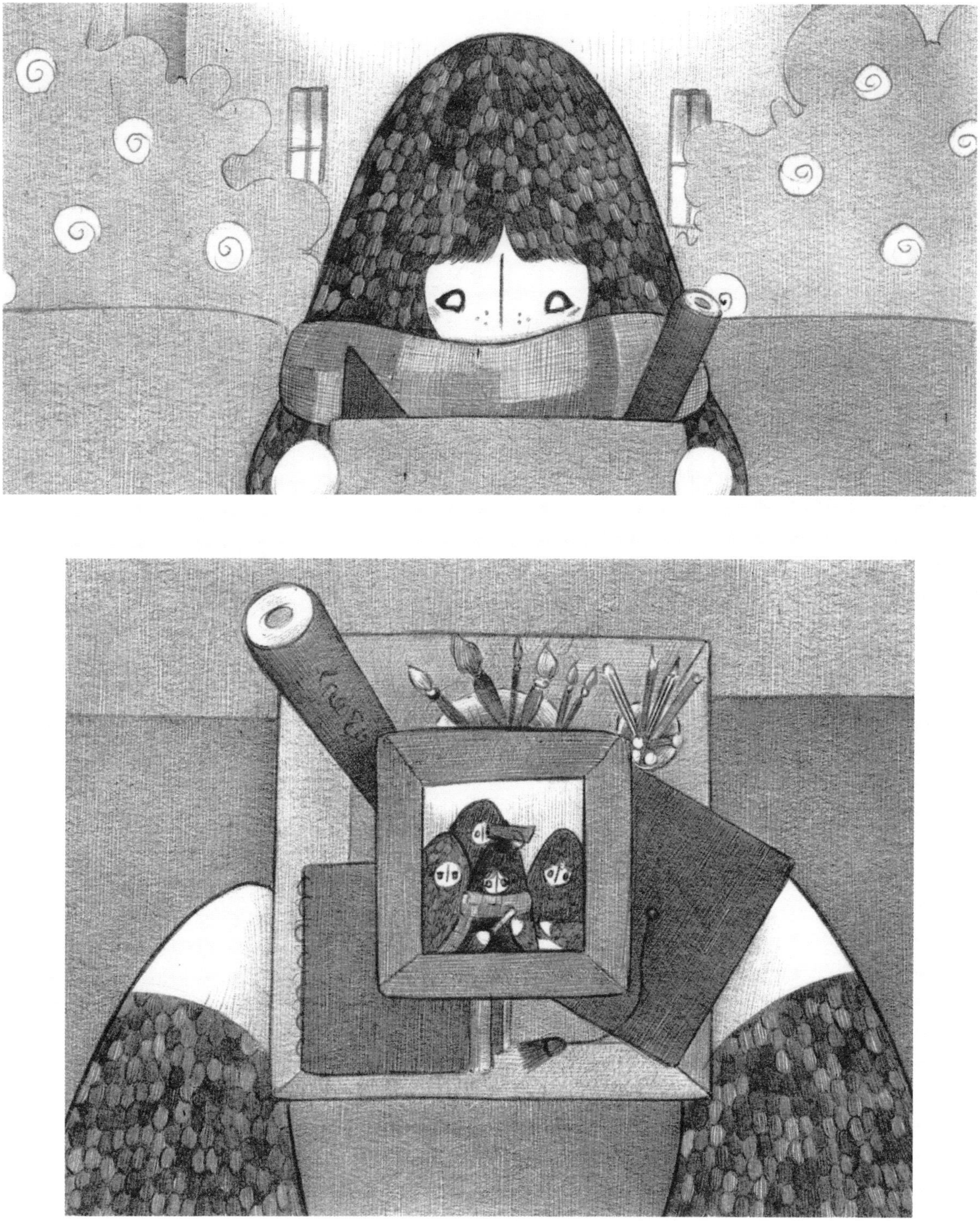

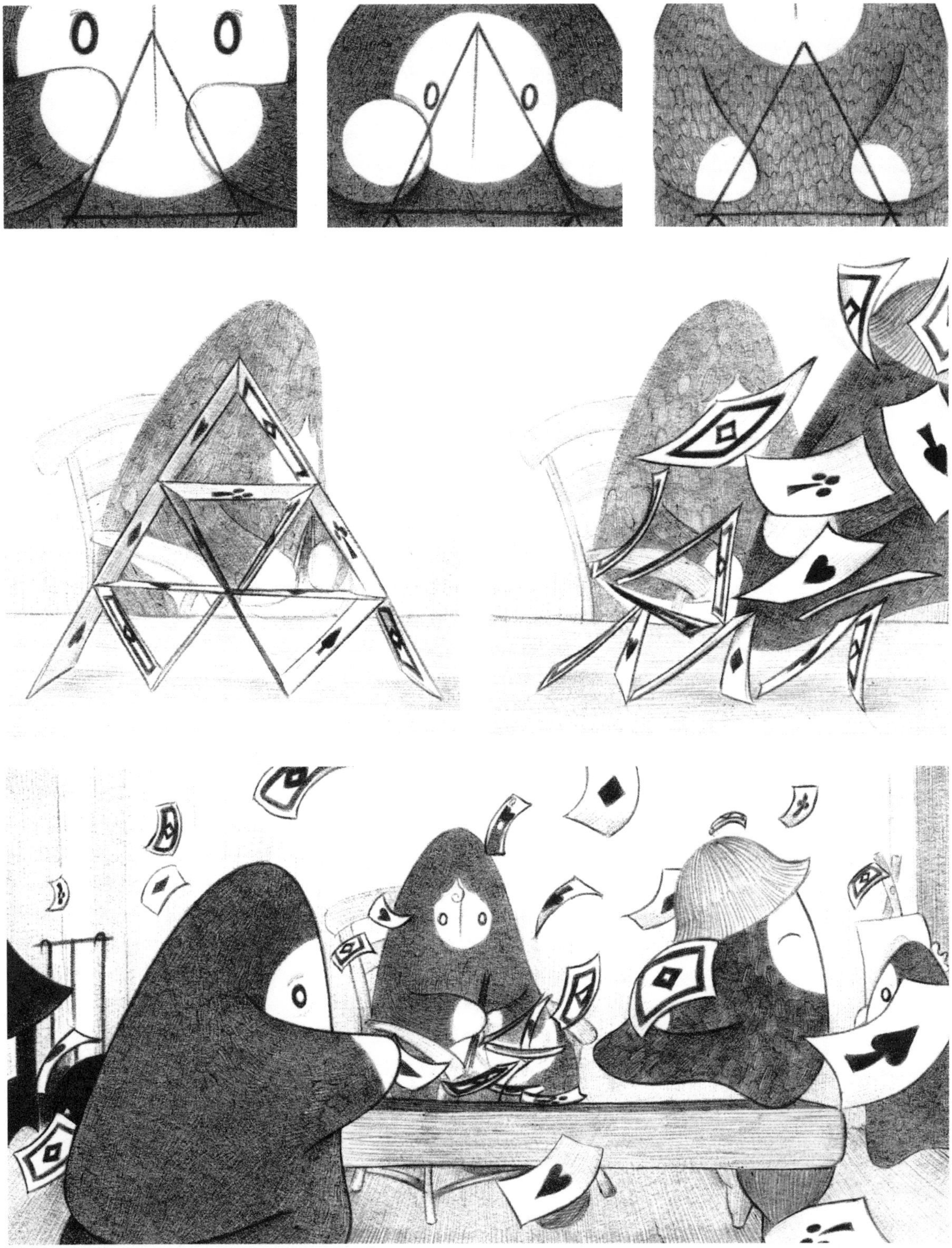

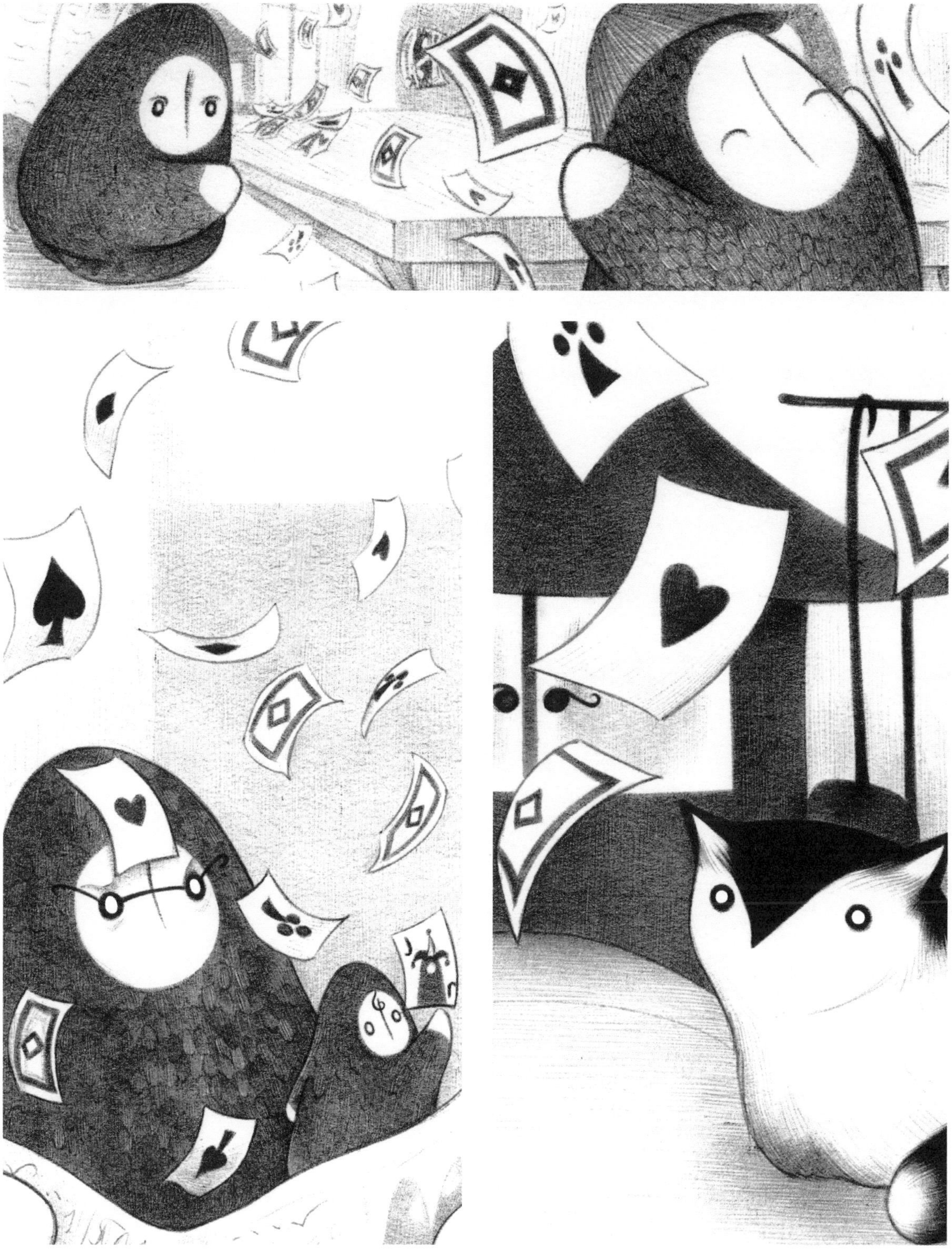

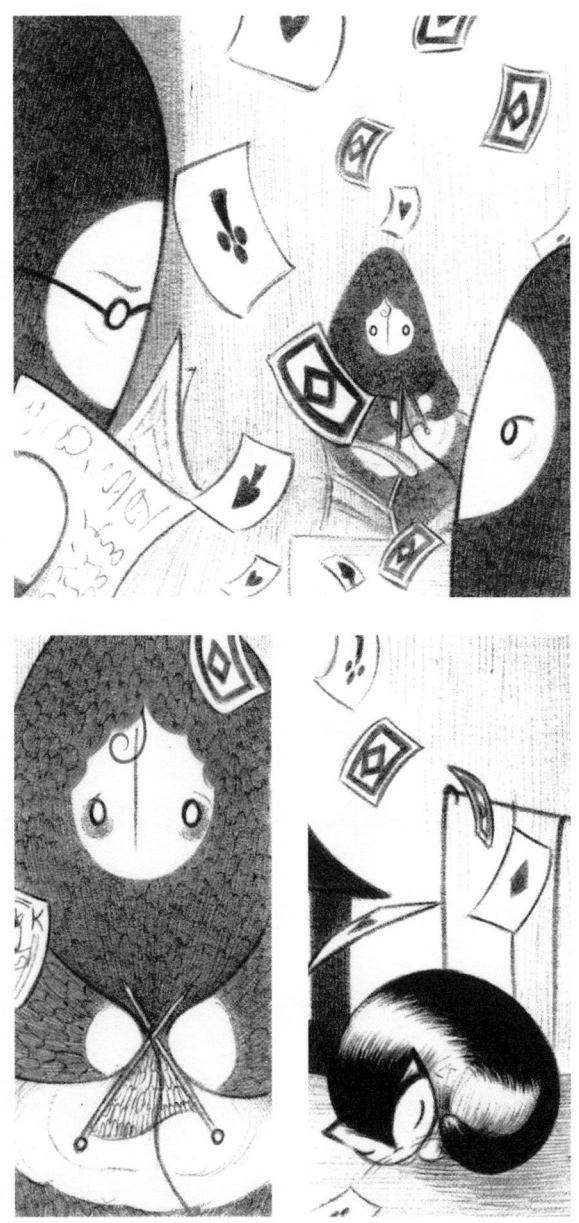

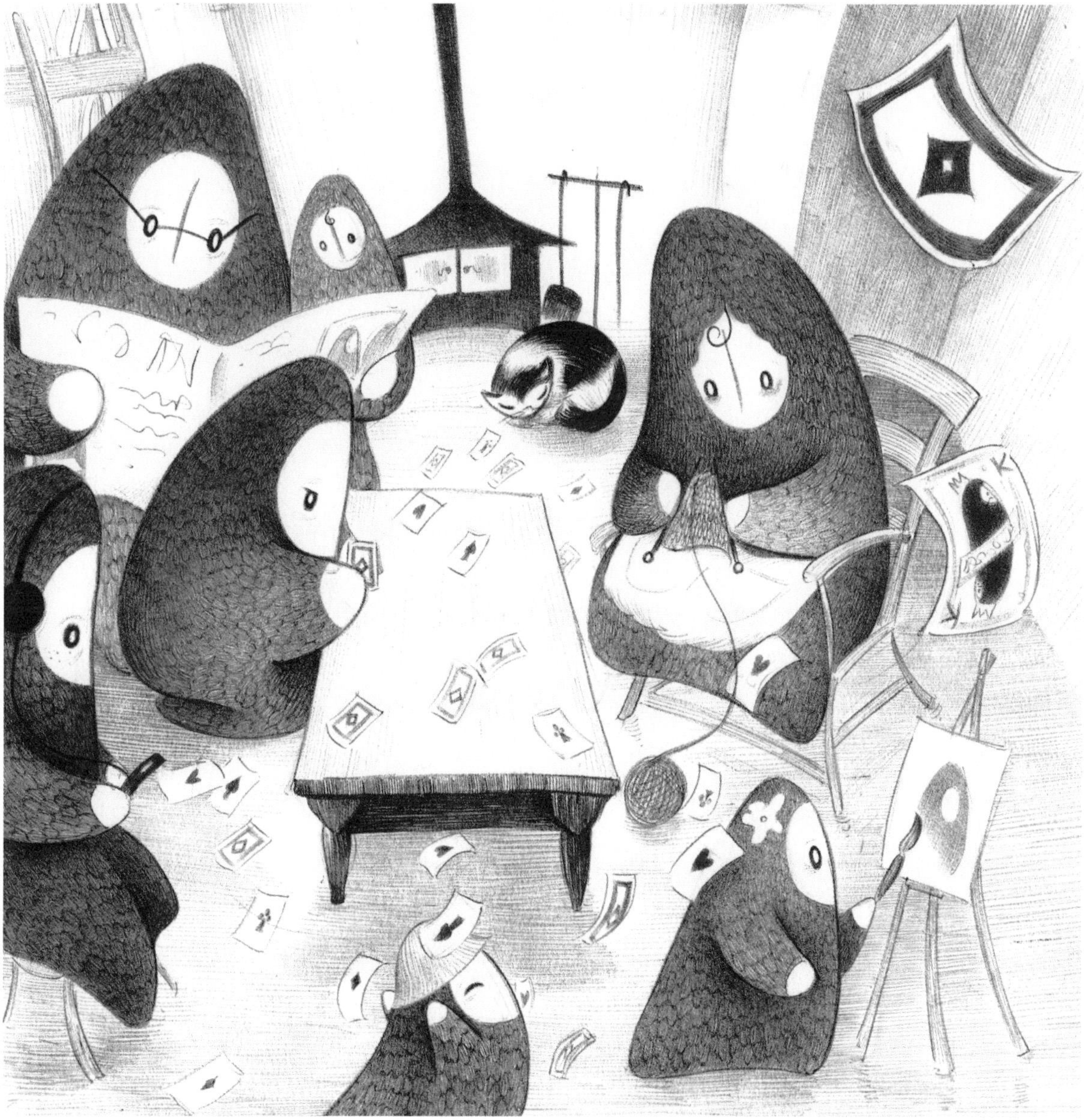

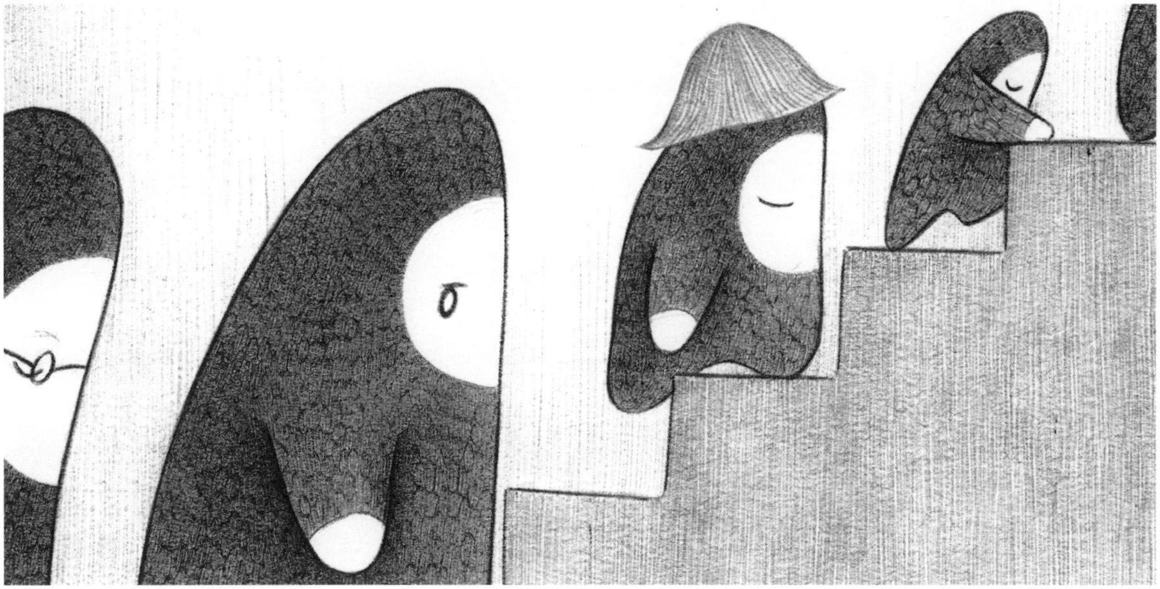

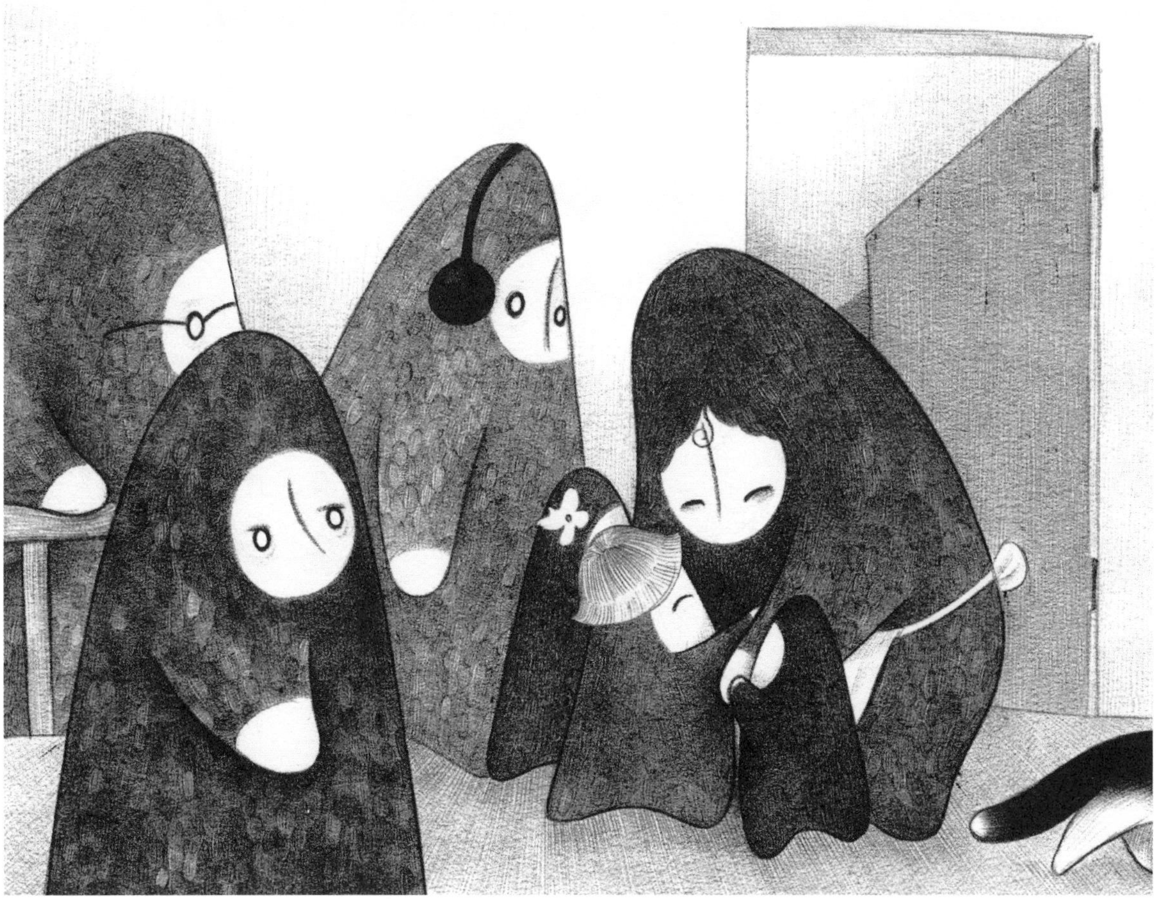

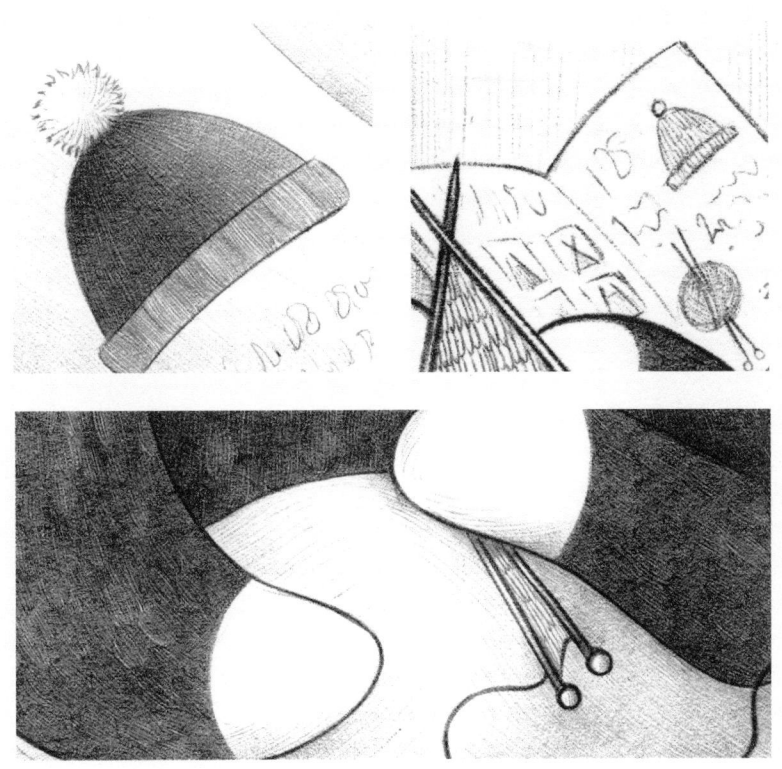

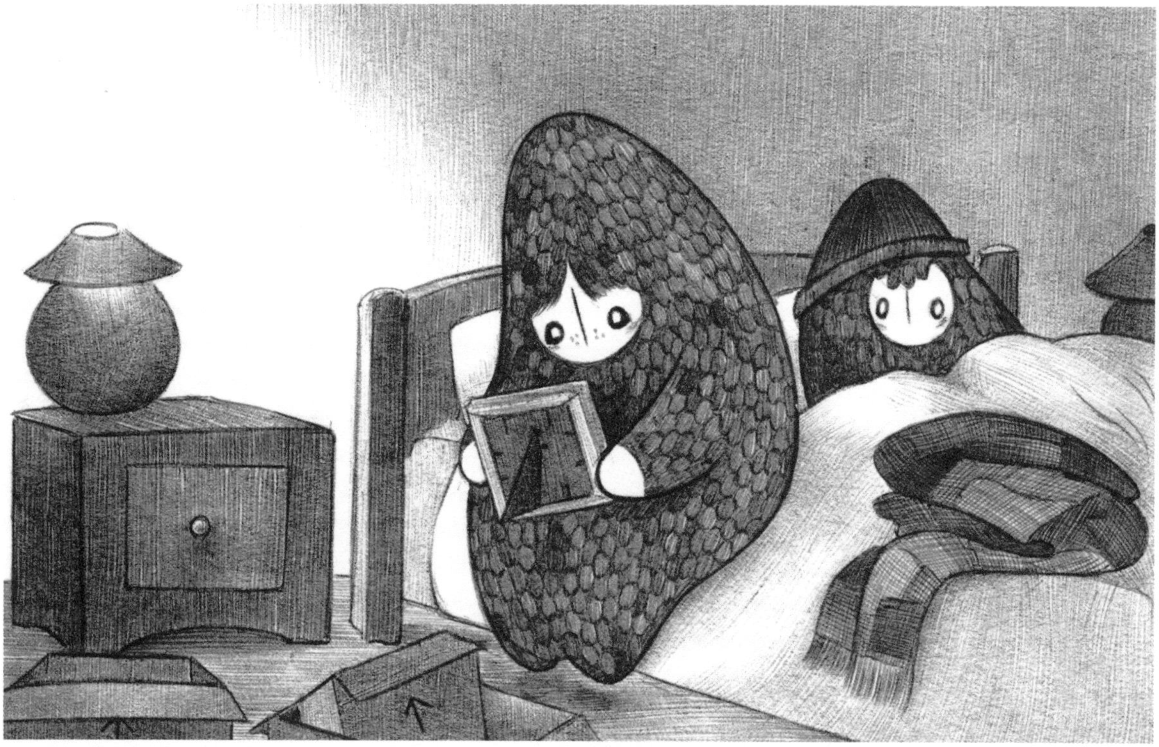

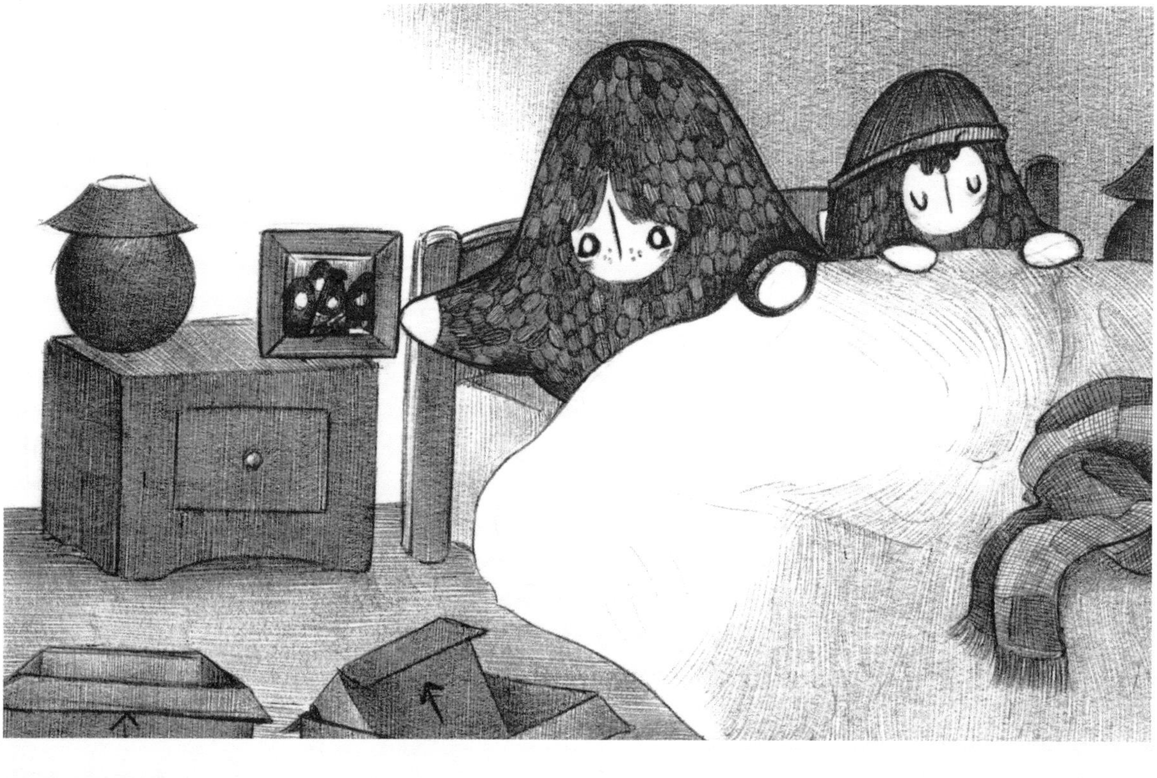

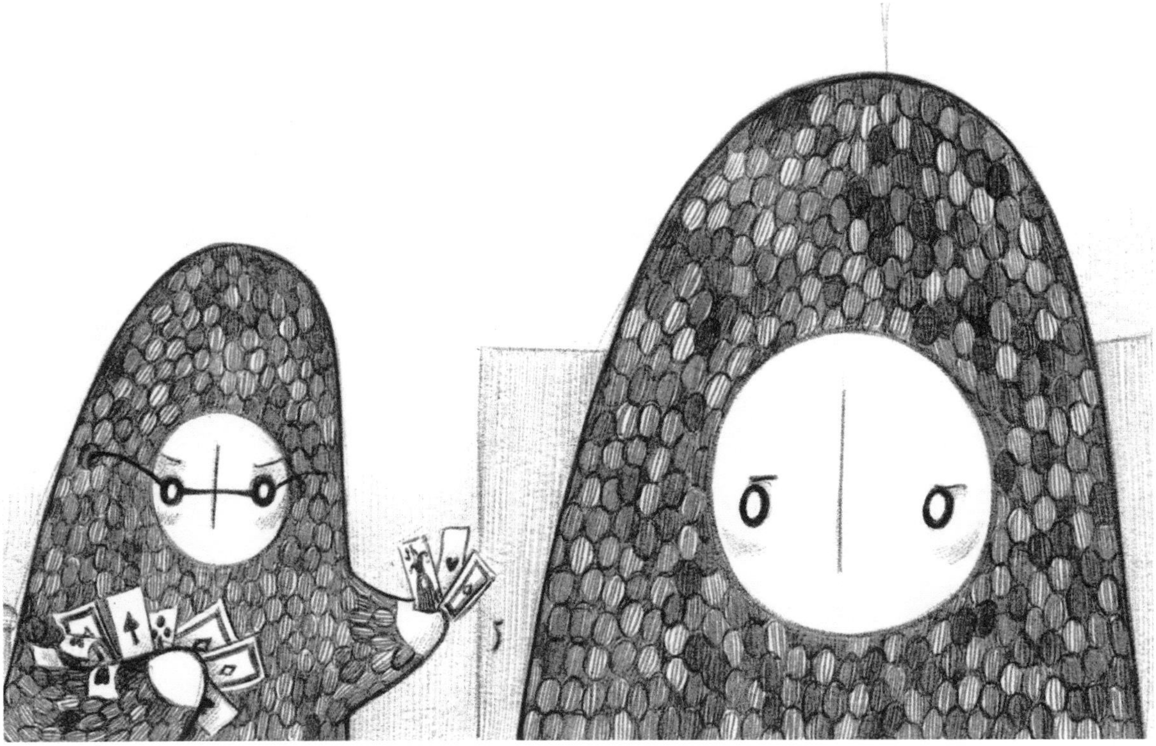

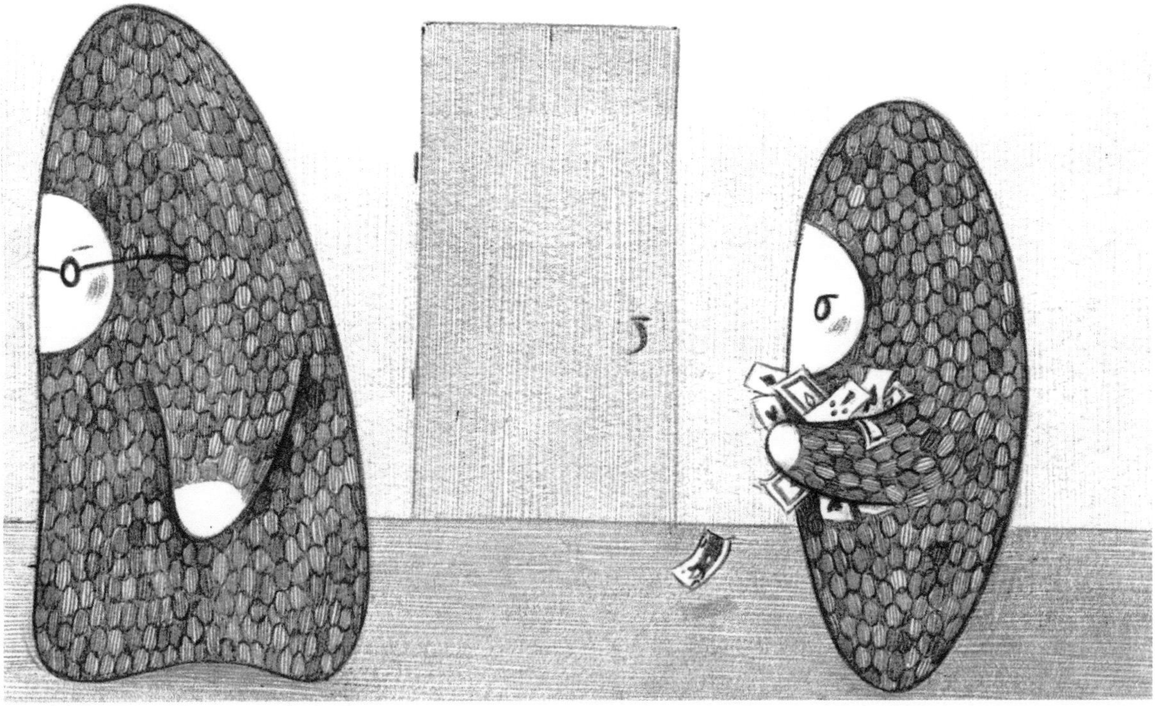

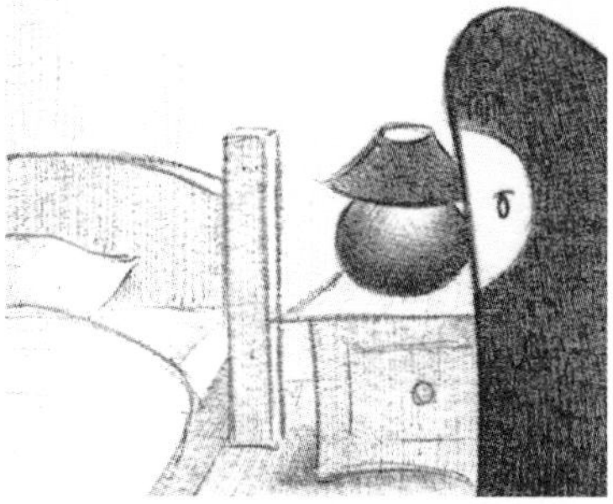
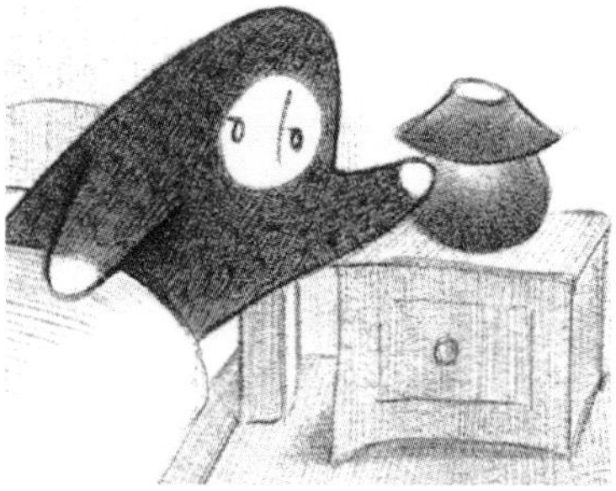
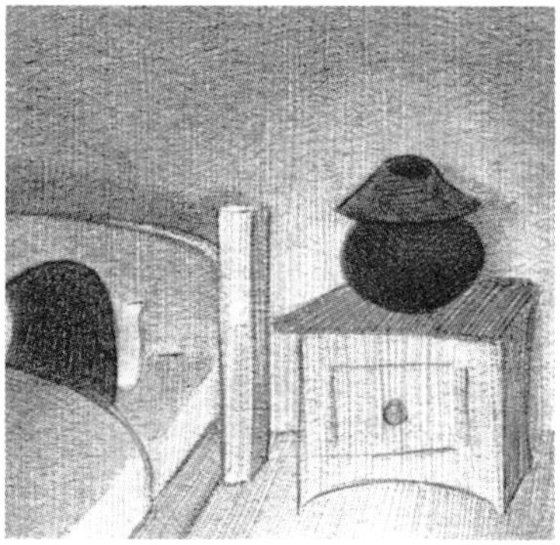
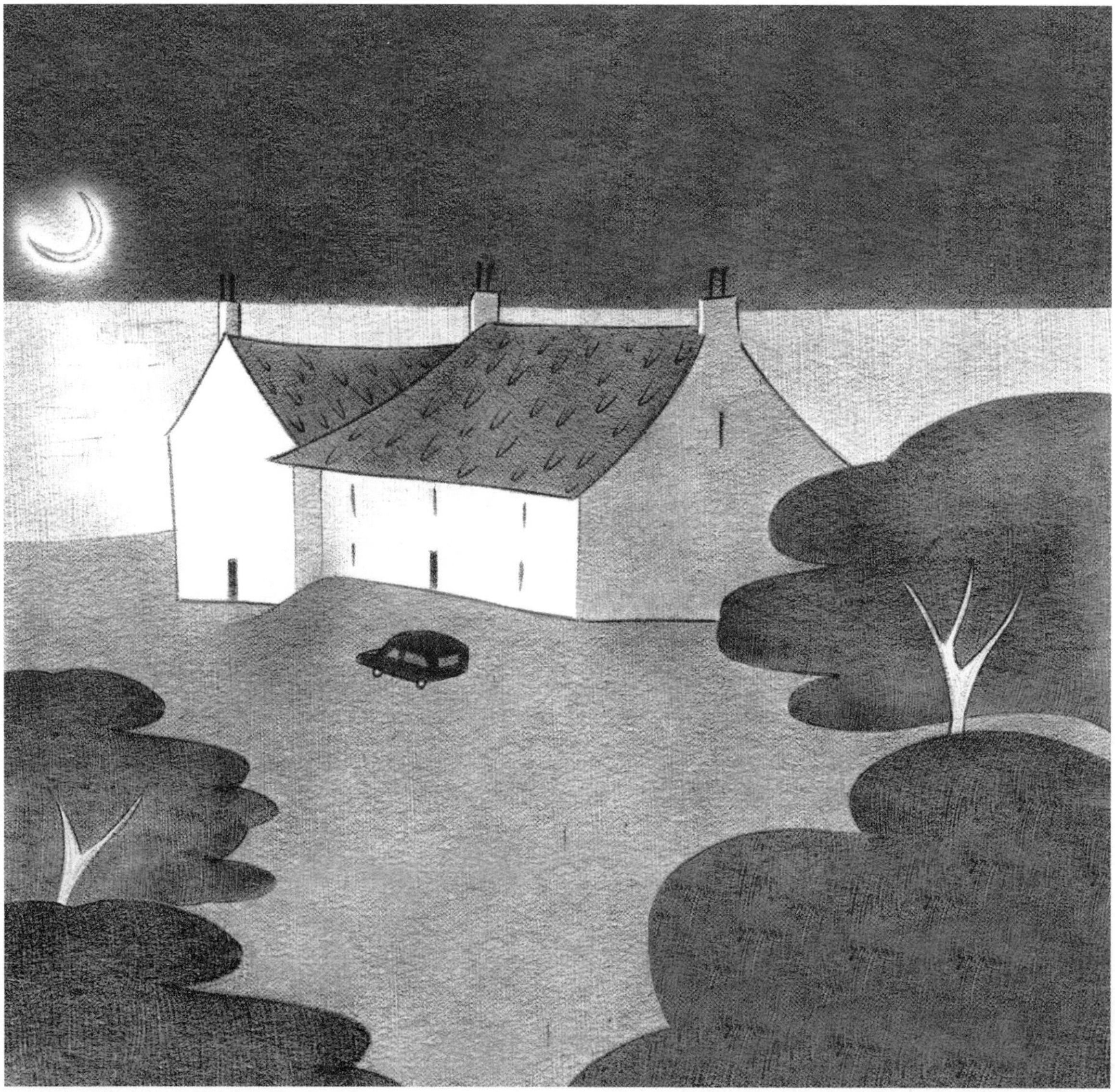

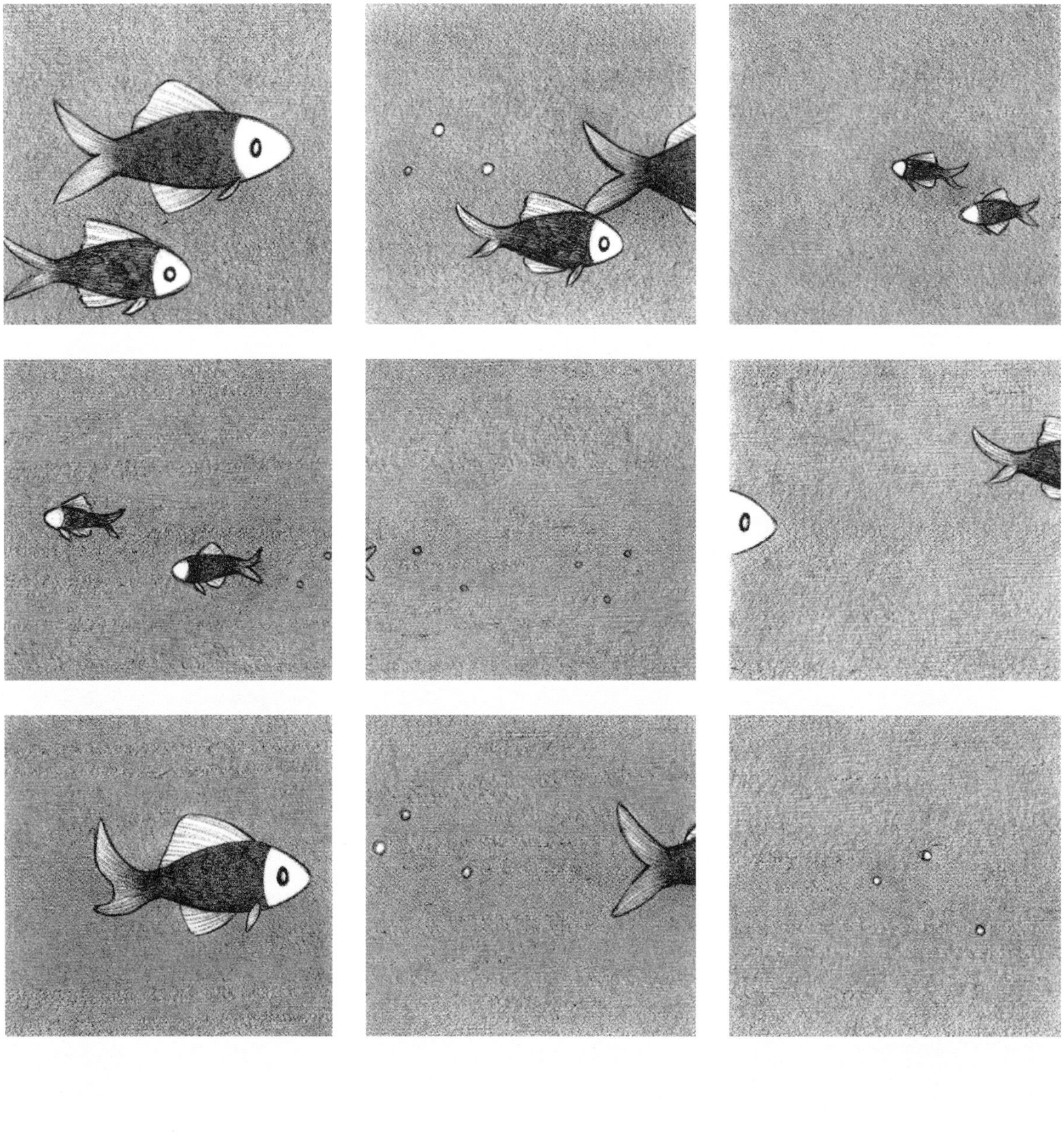

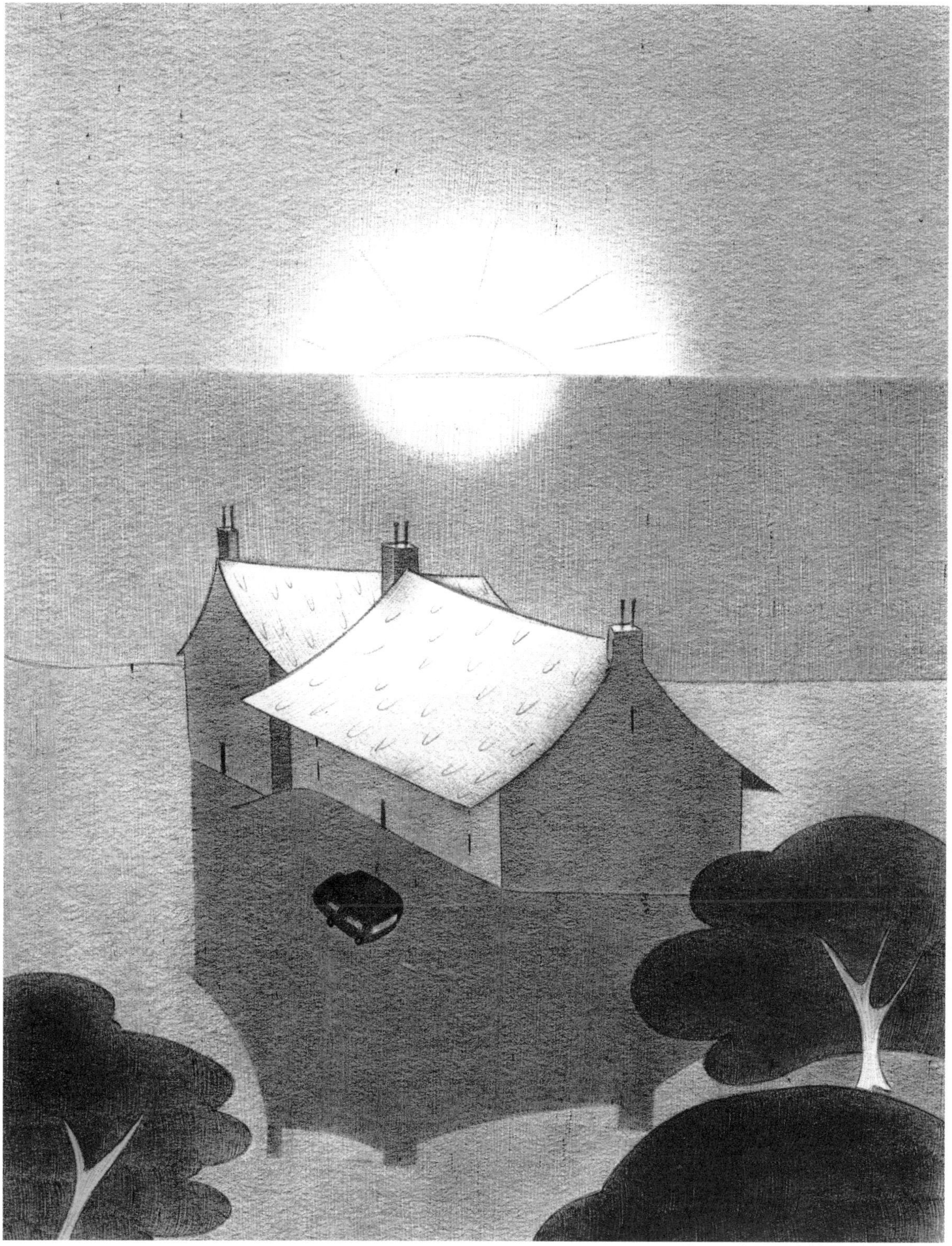

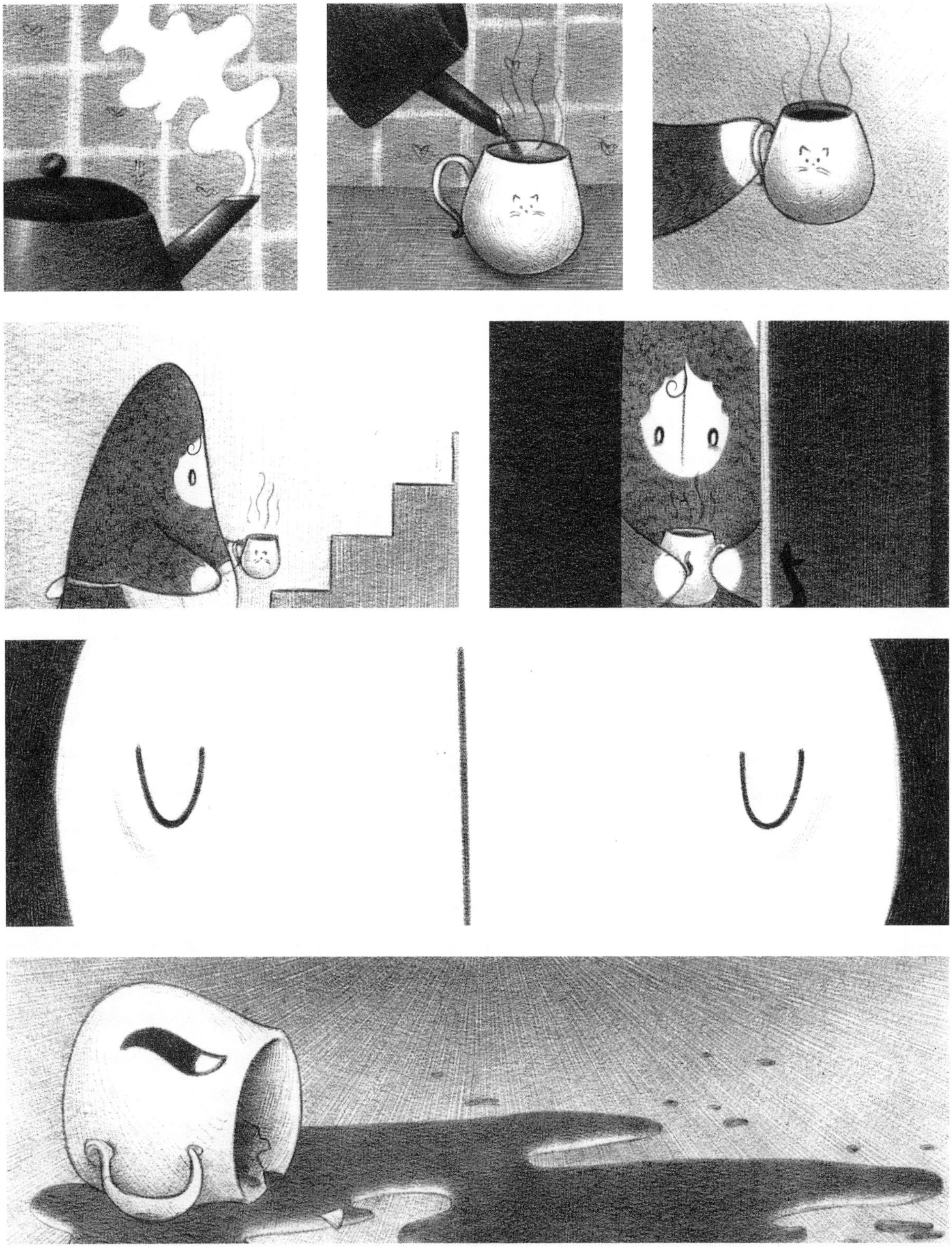

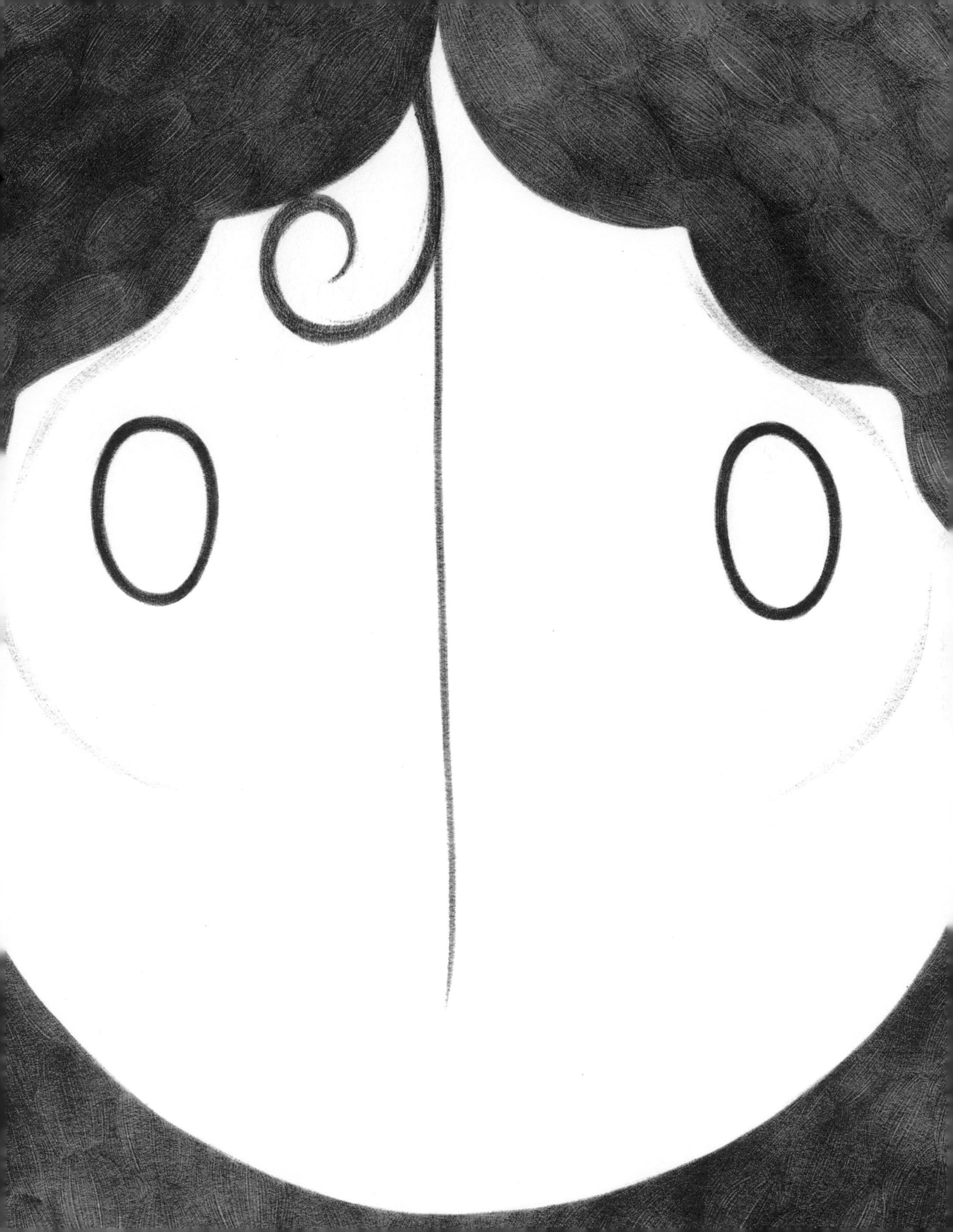

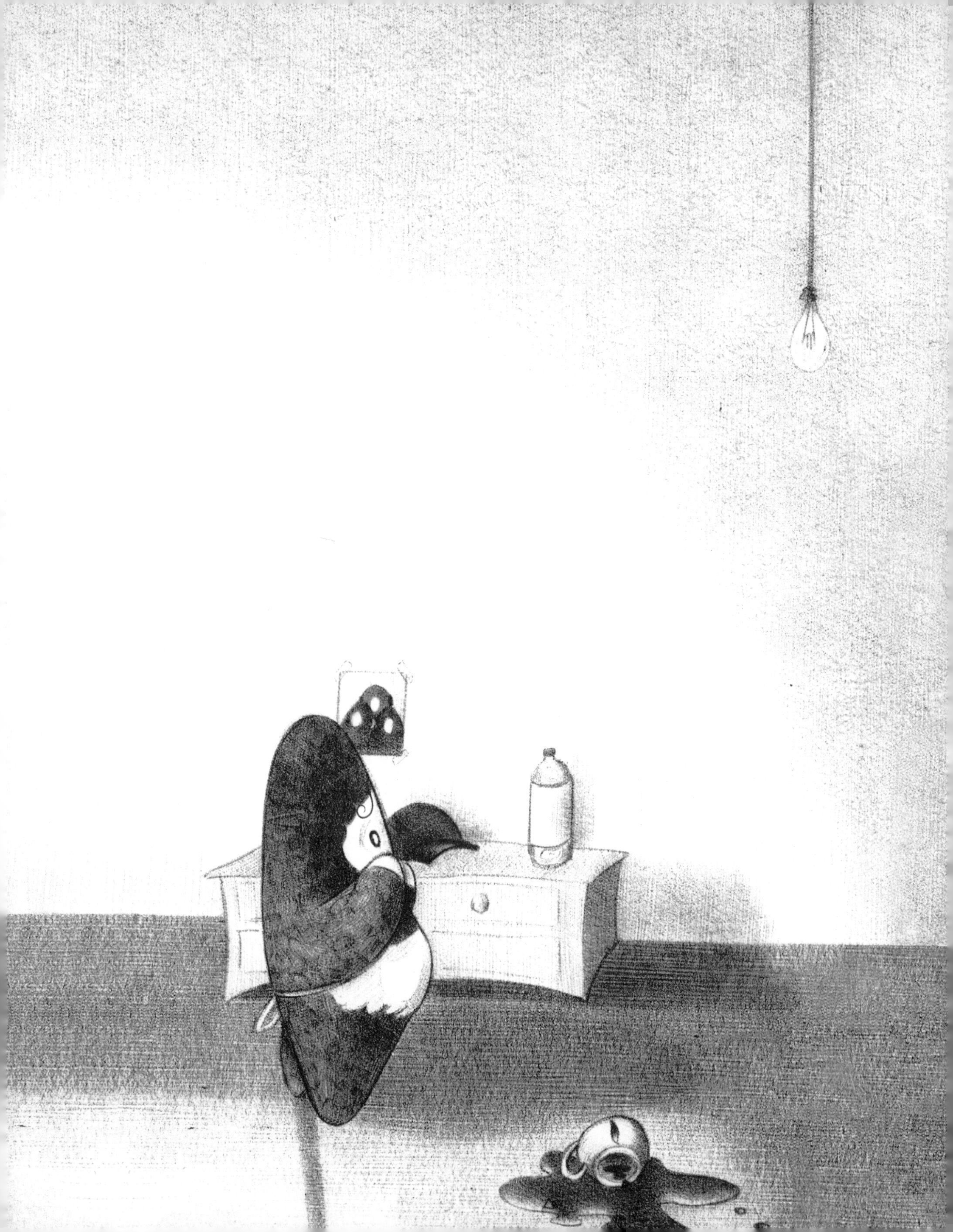

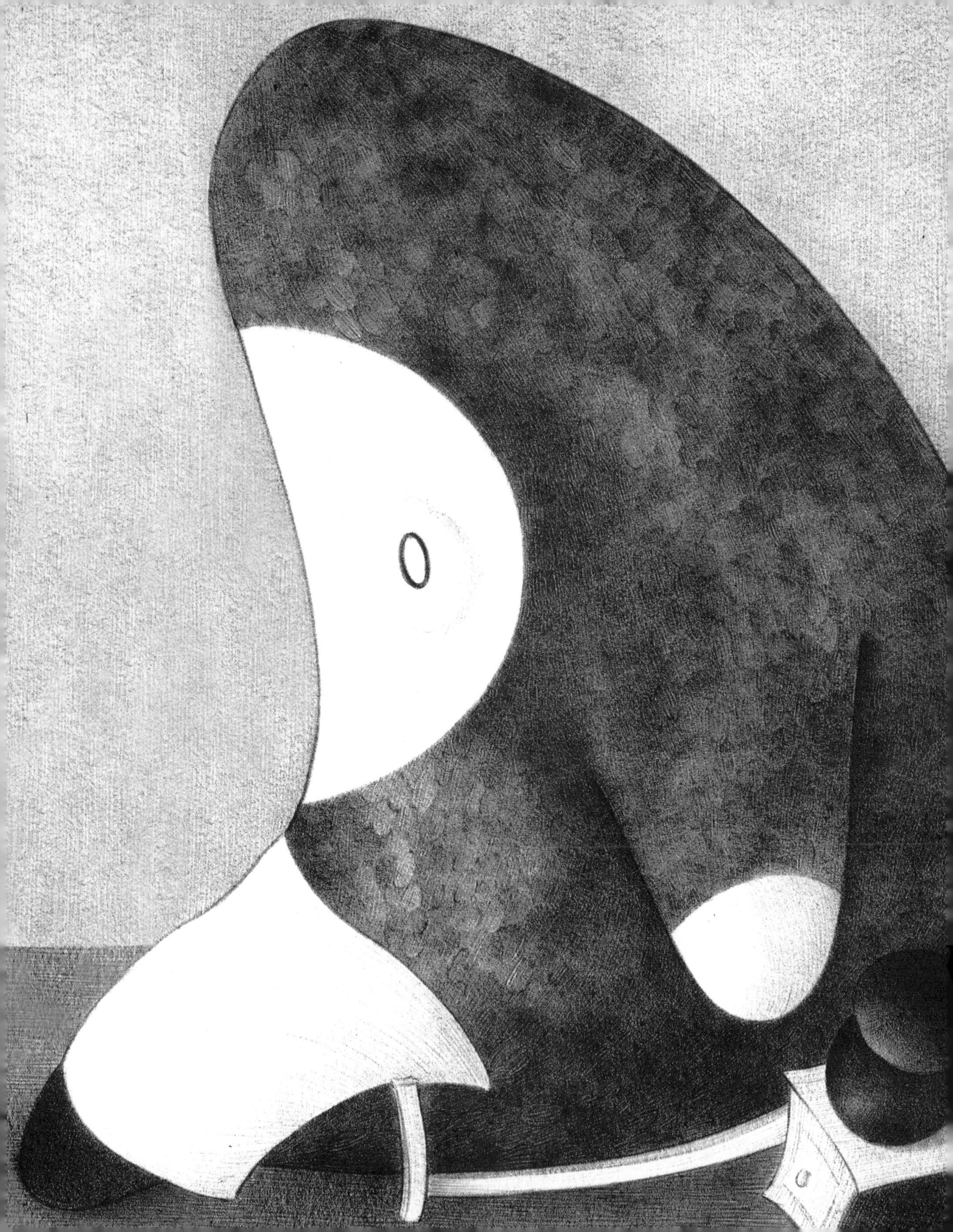

CHAPTER TWO

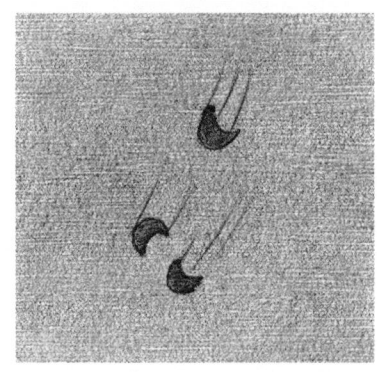

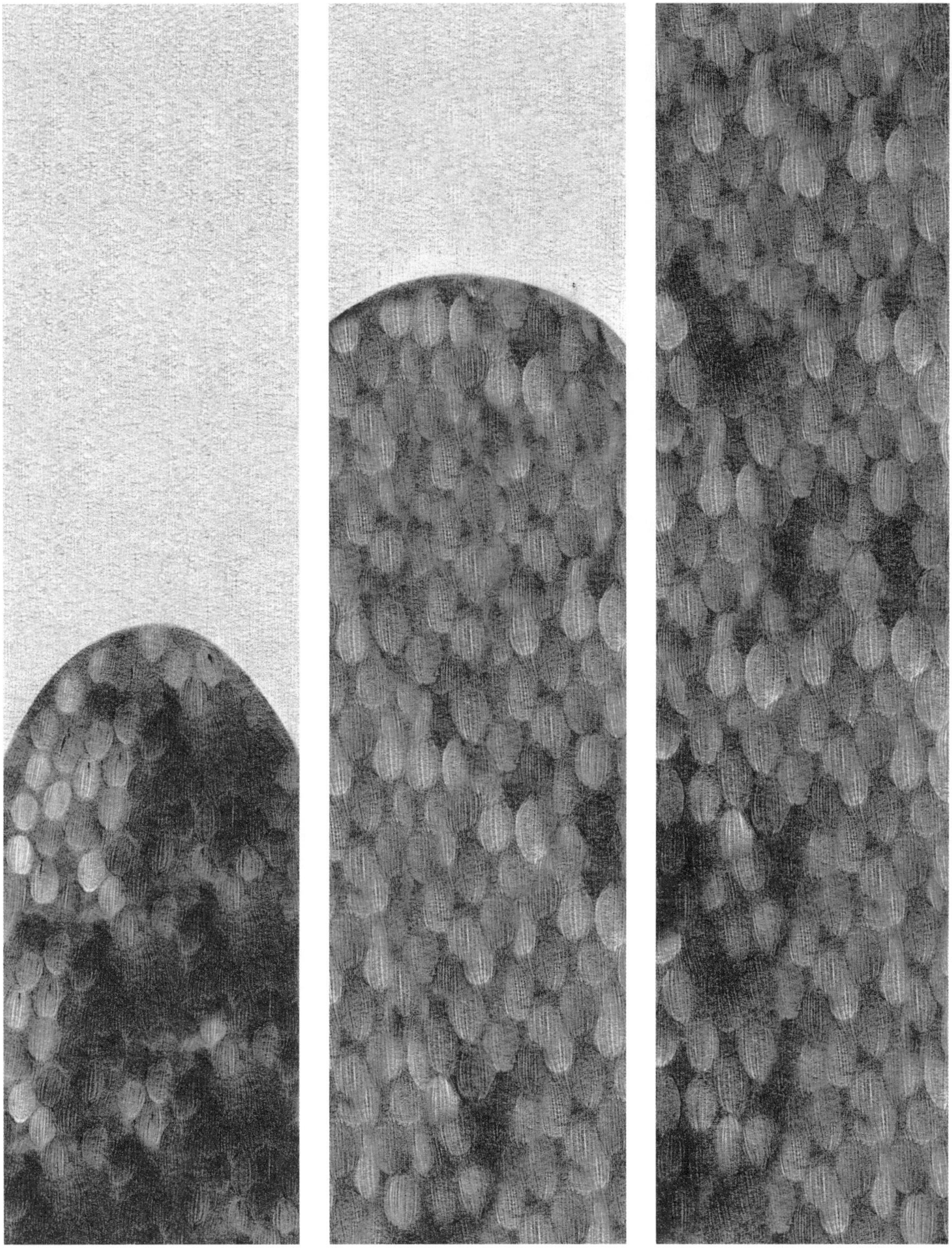

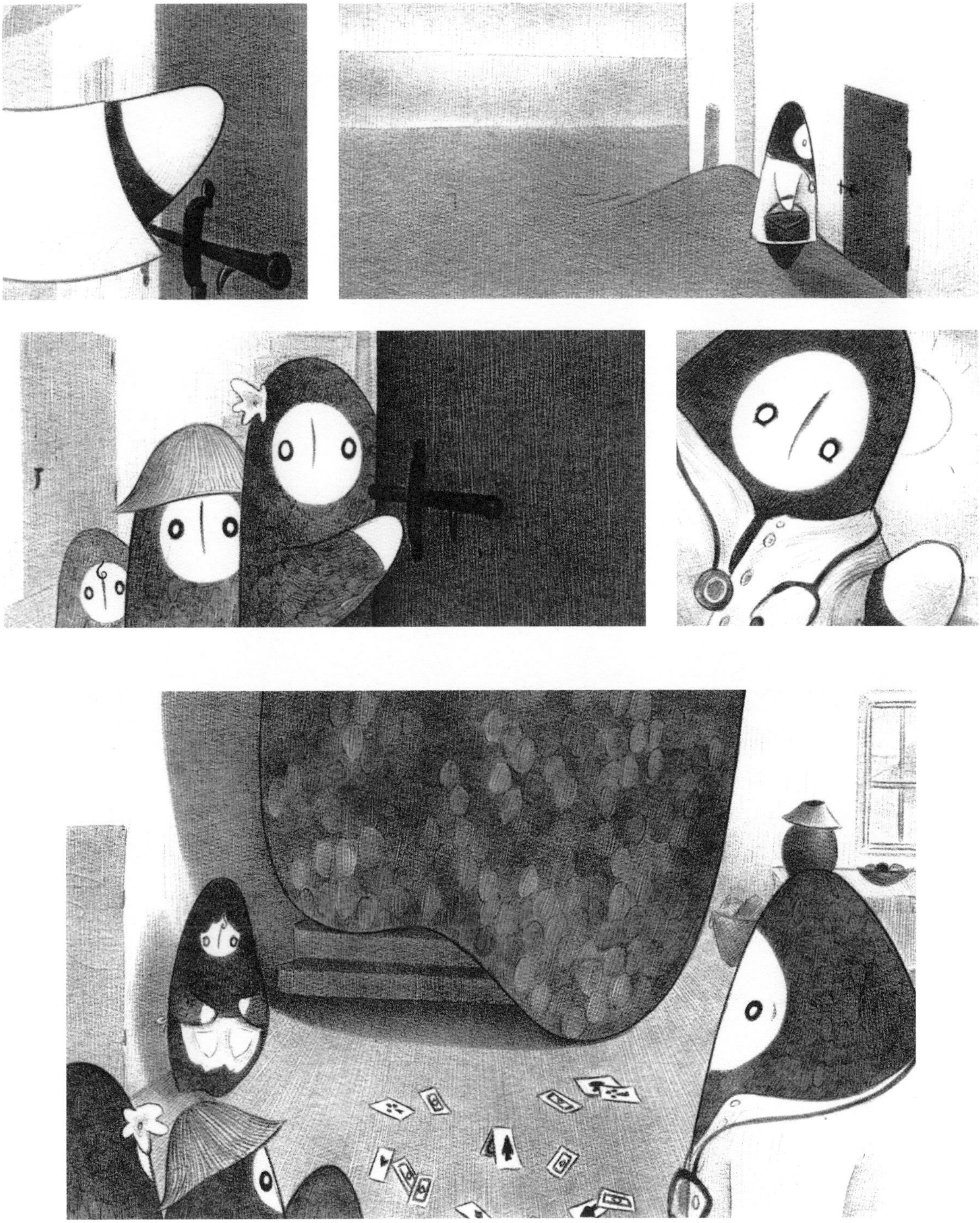

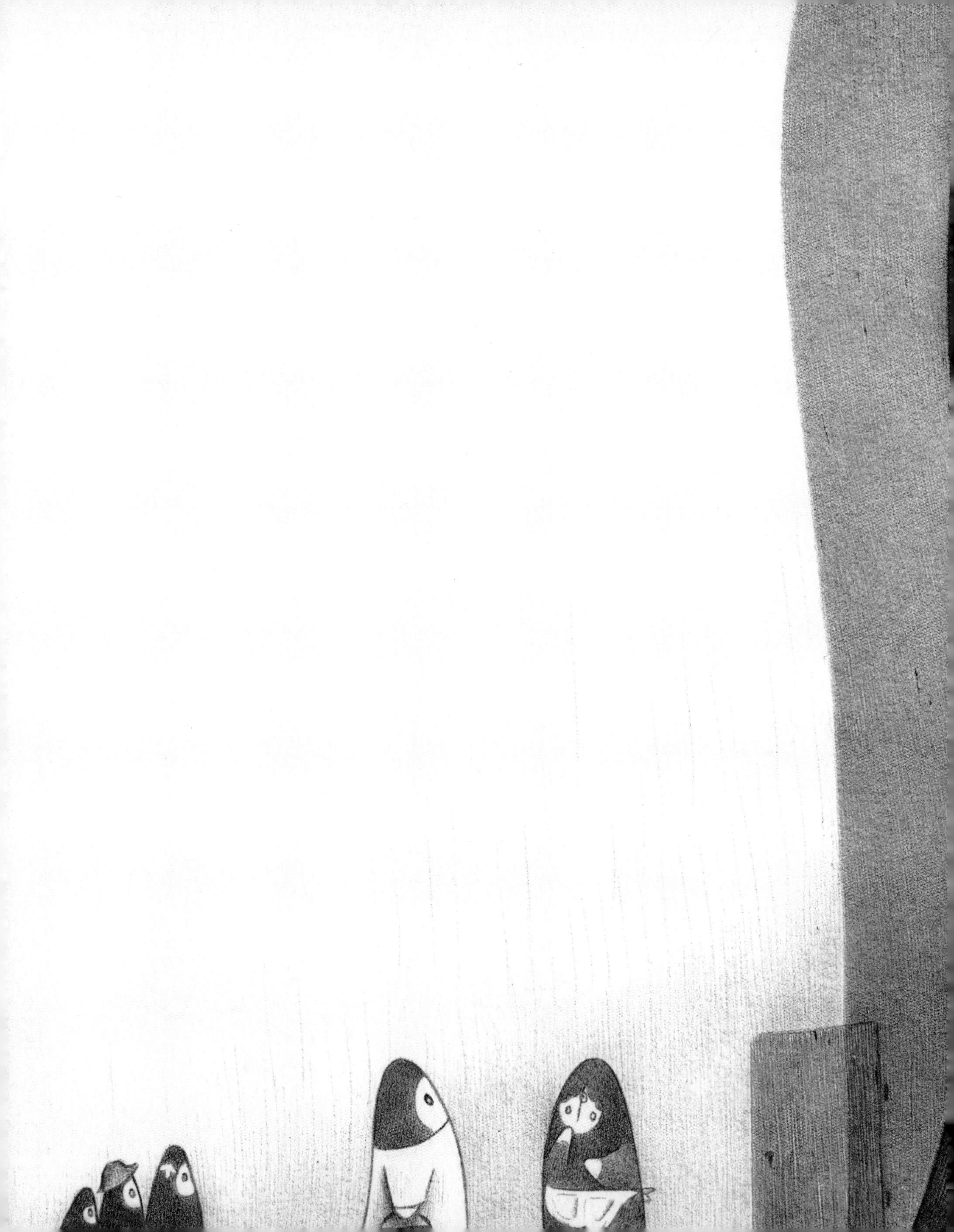

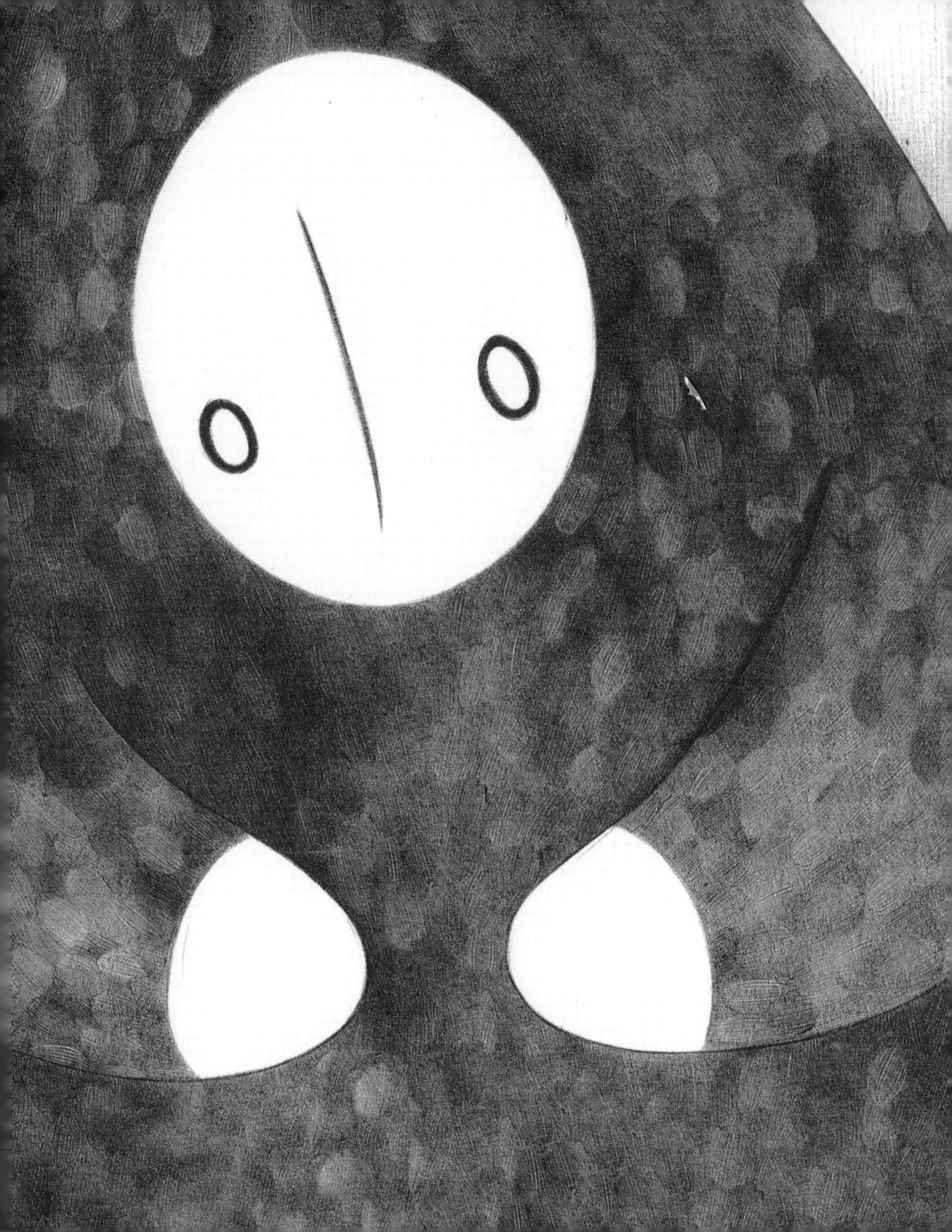

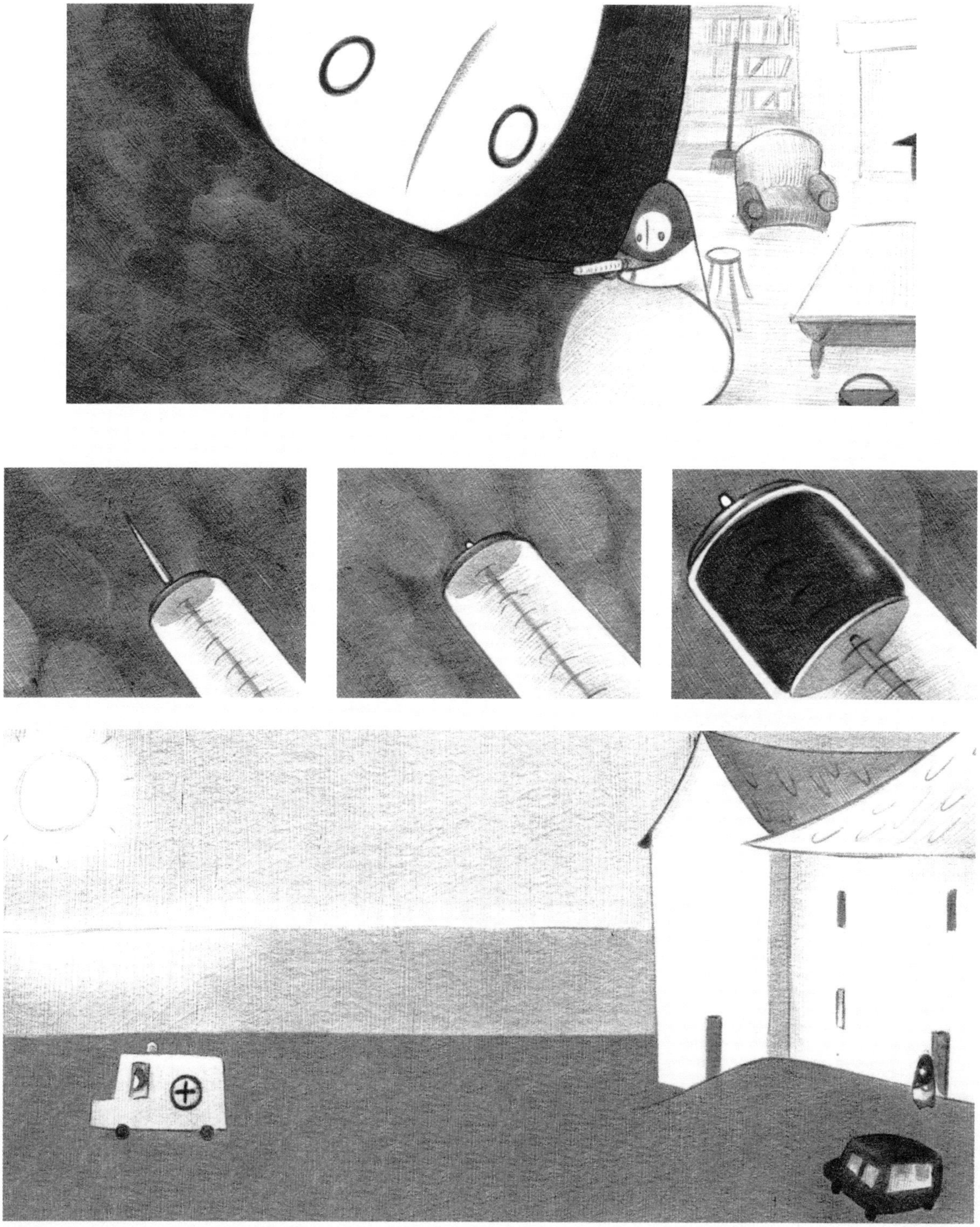

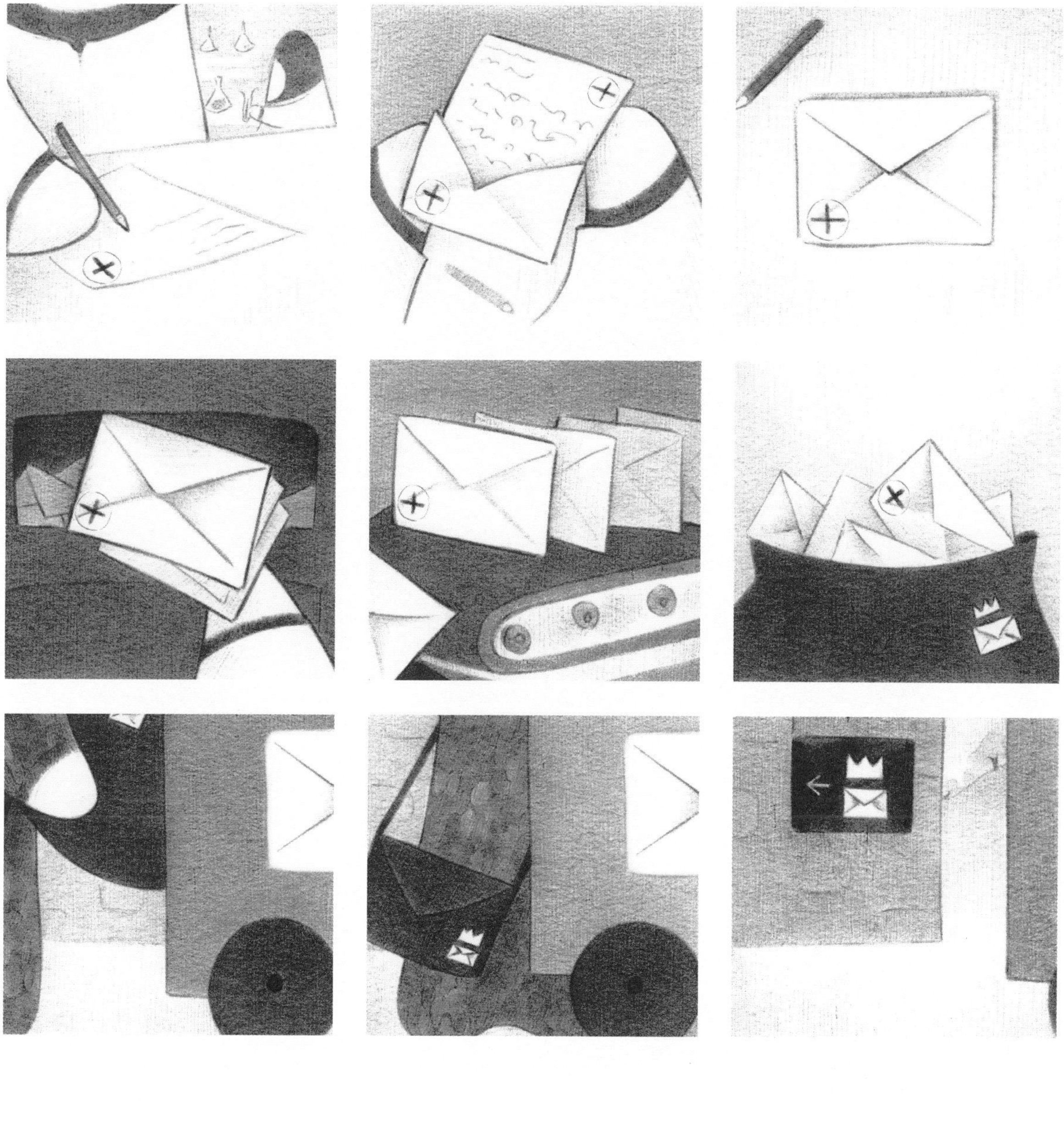

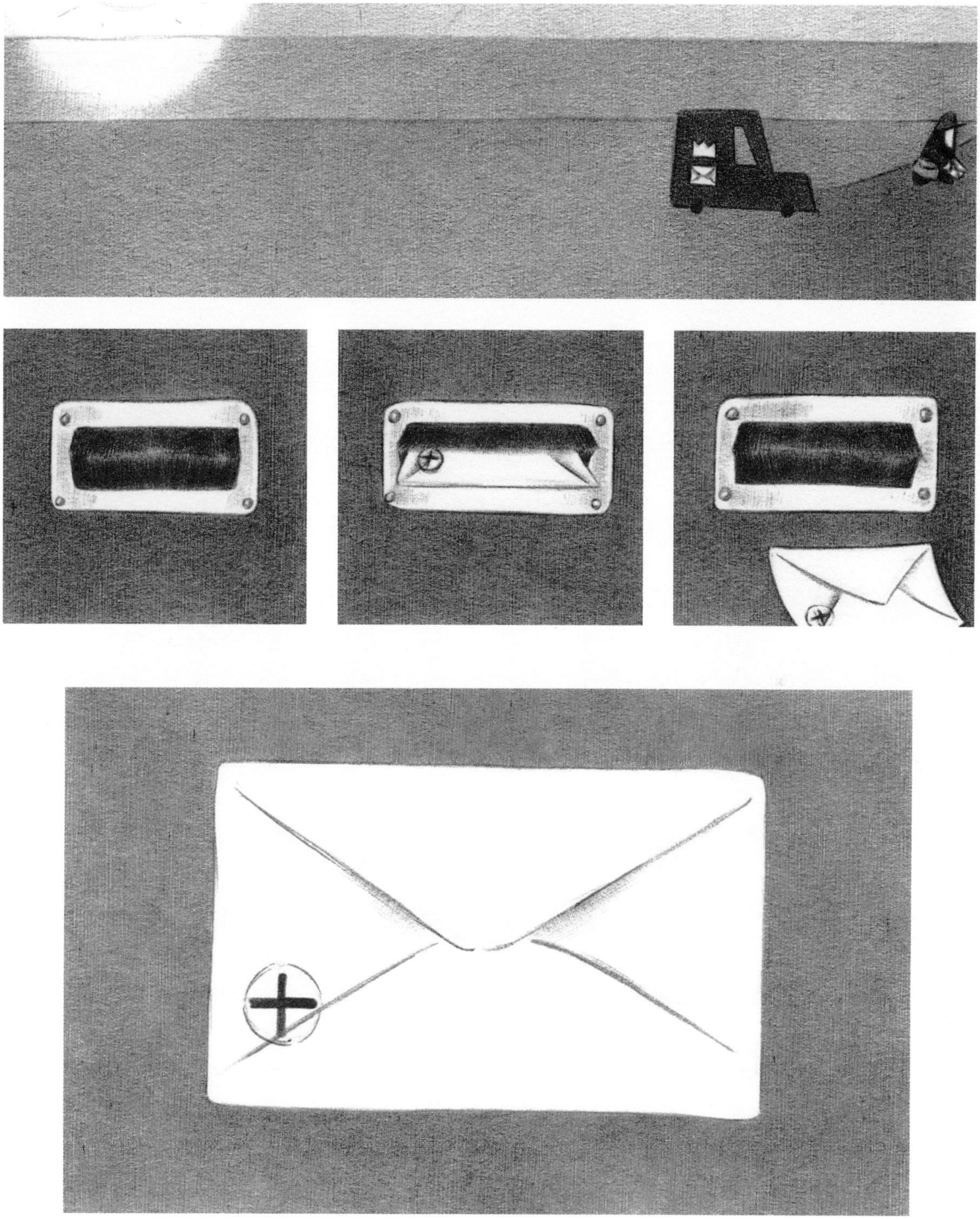

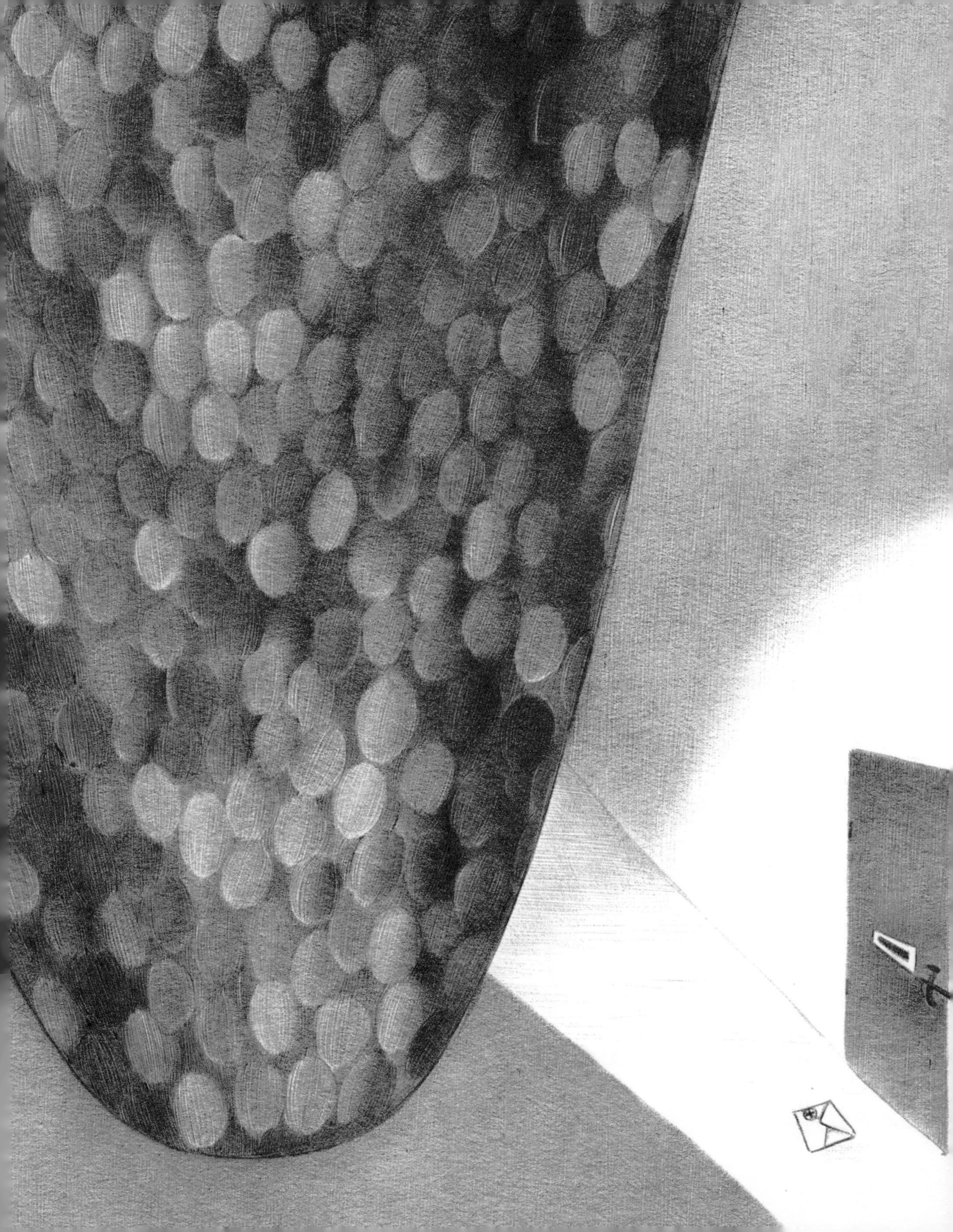

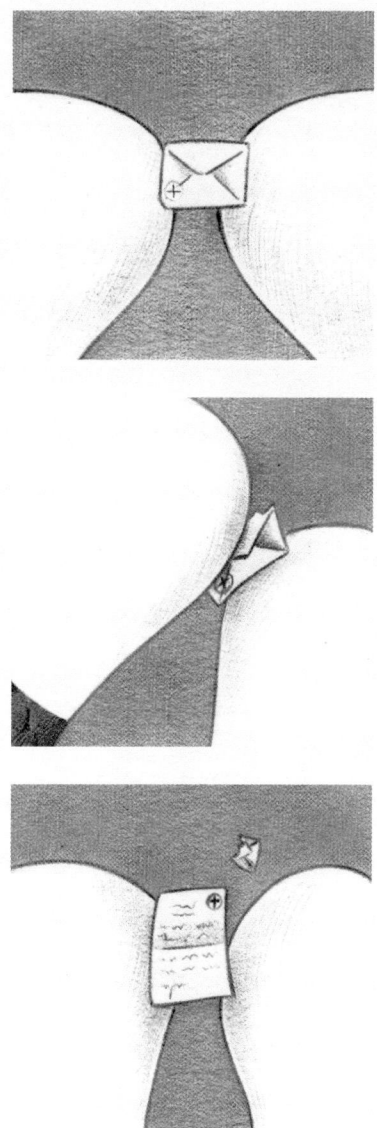

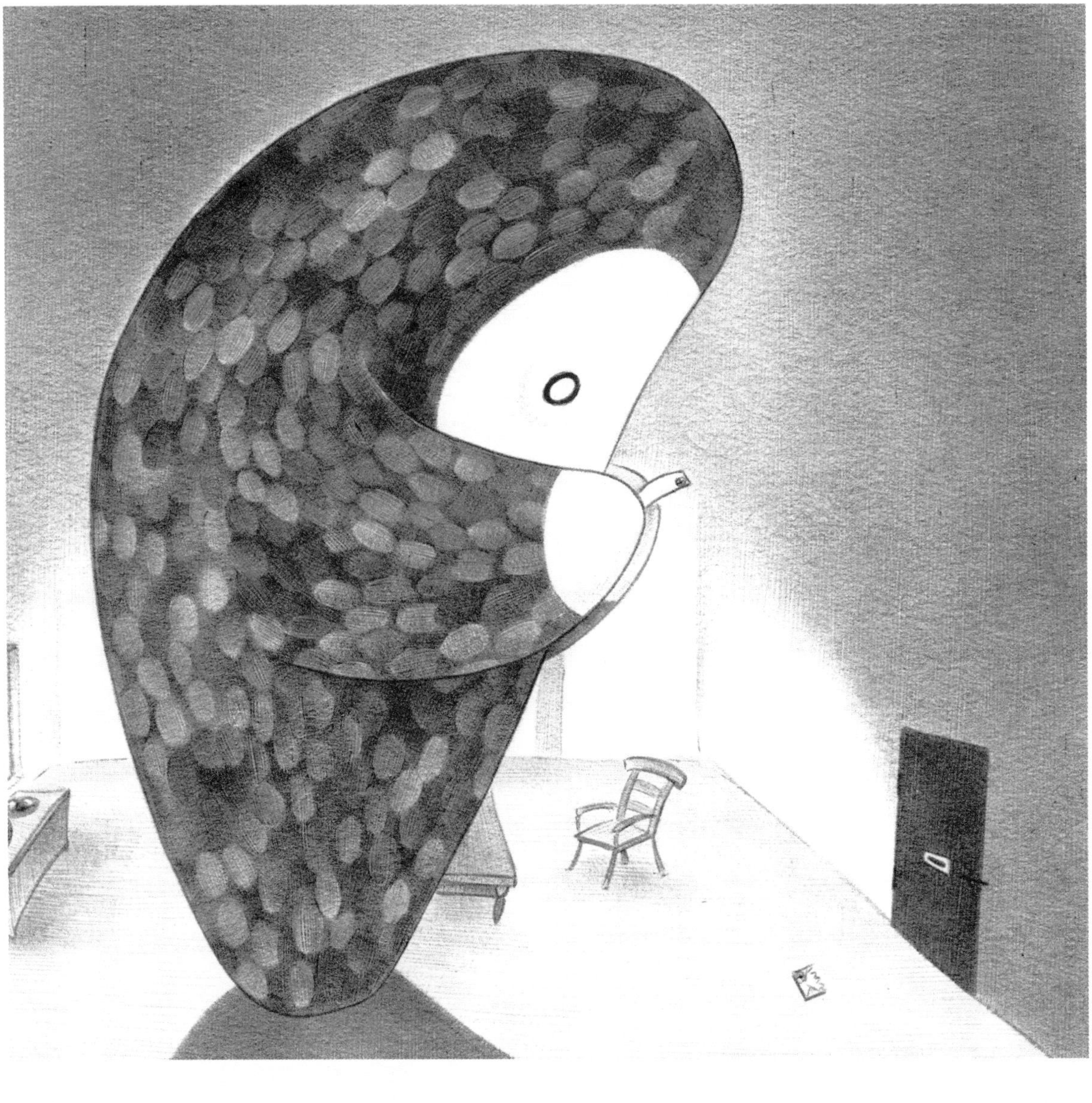

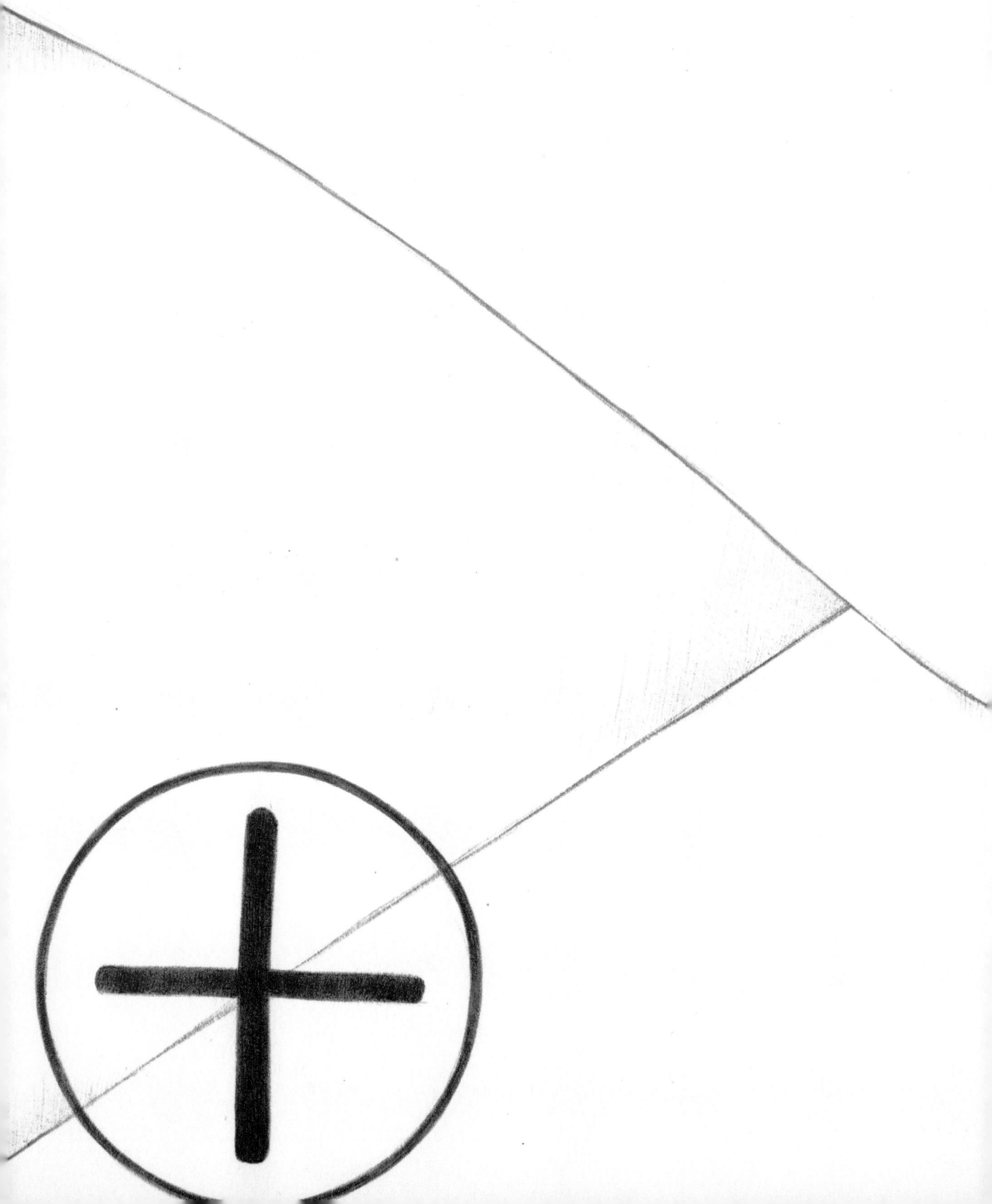

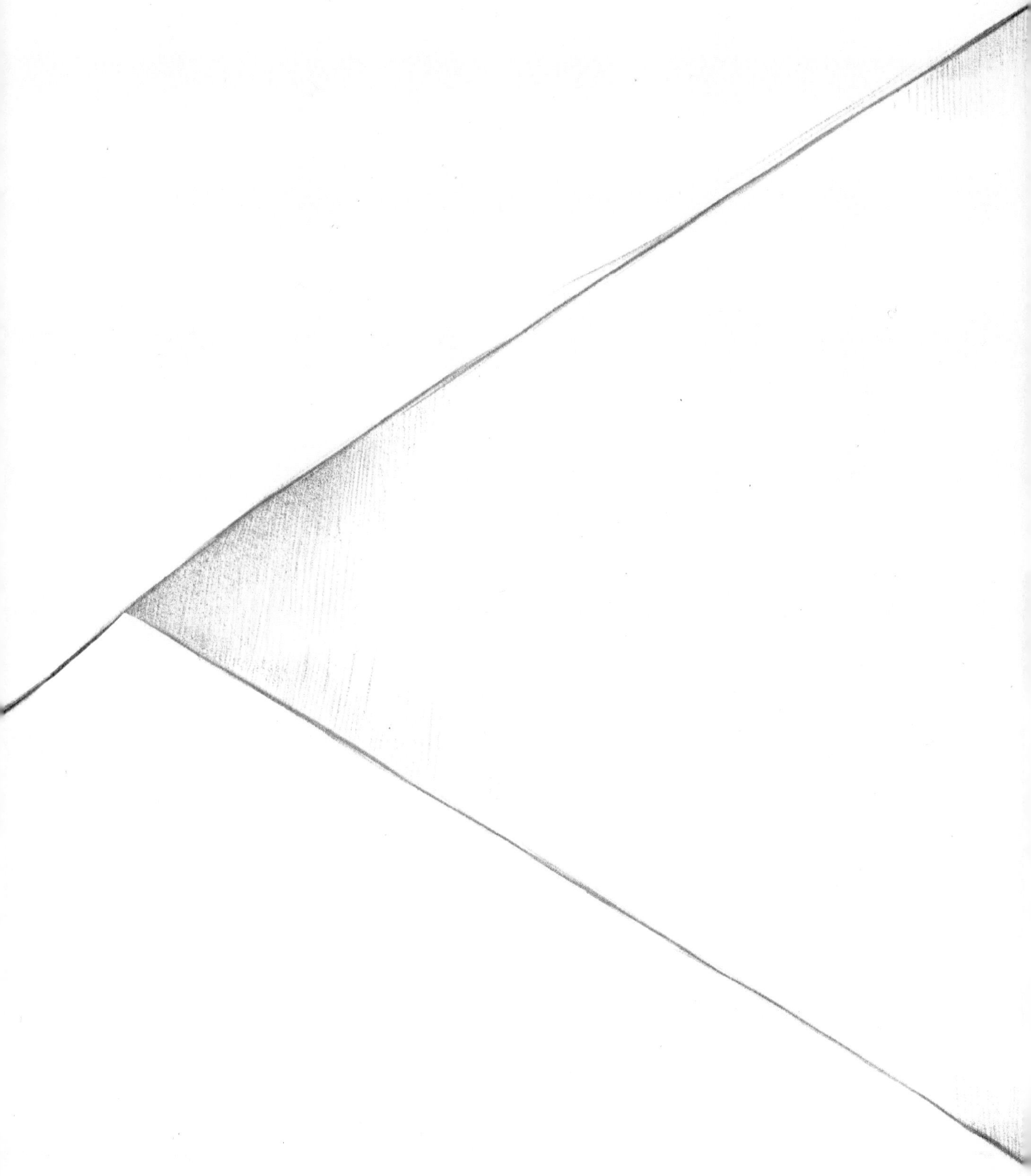

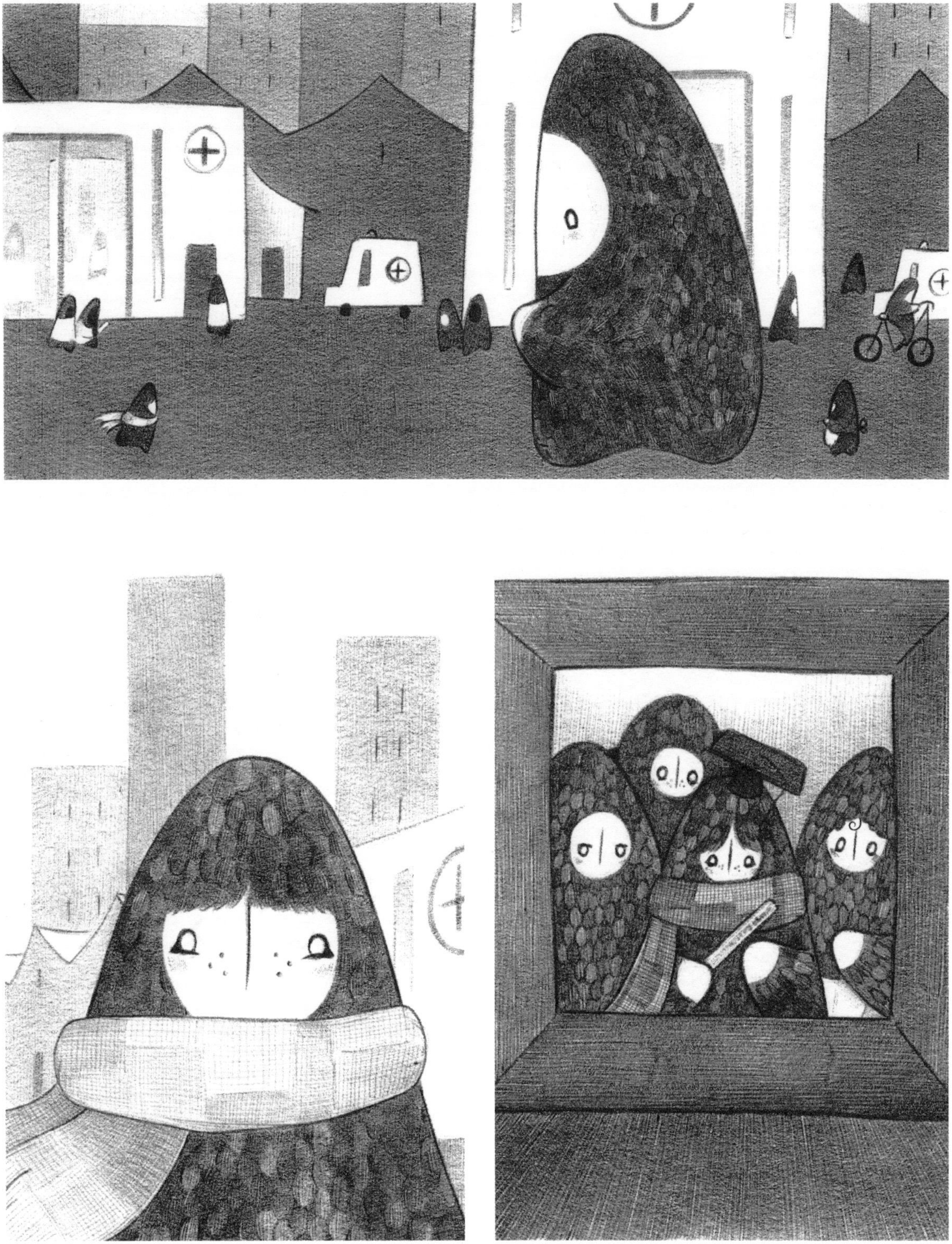

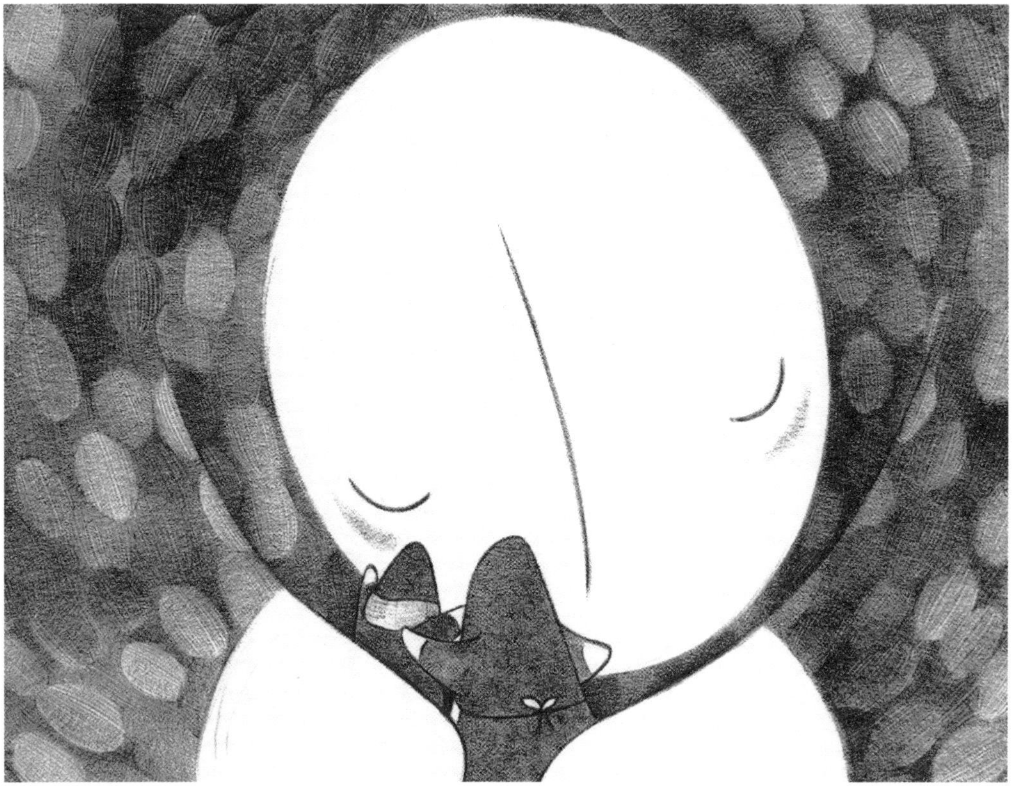

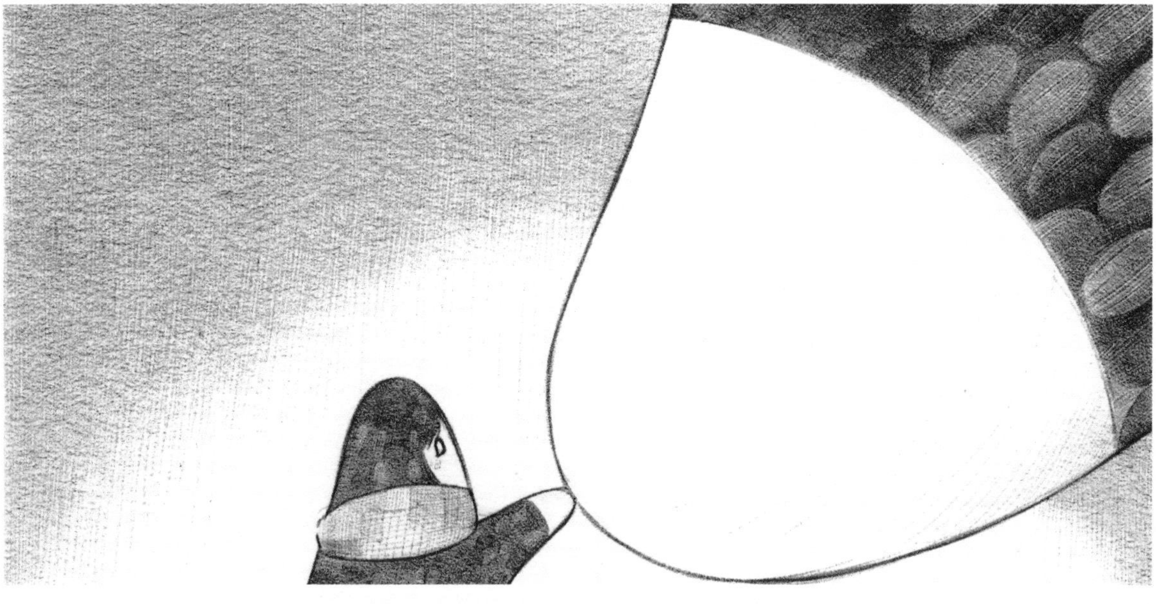

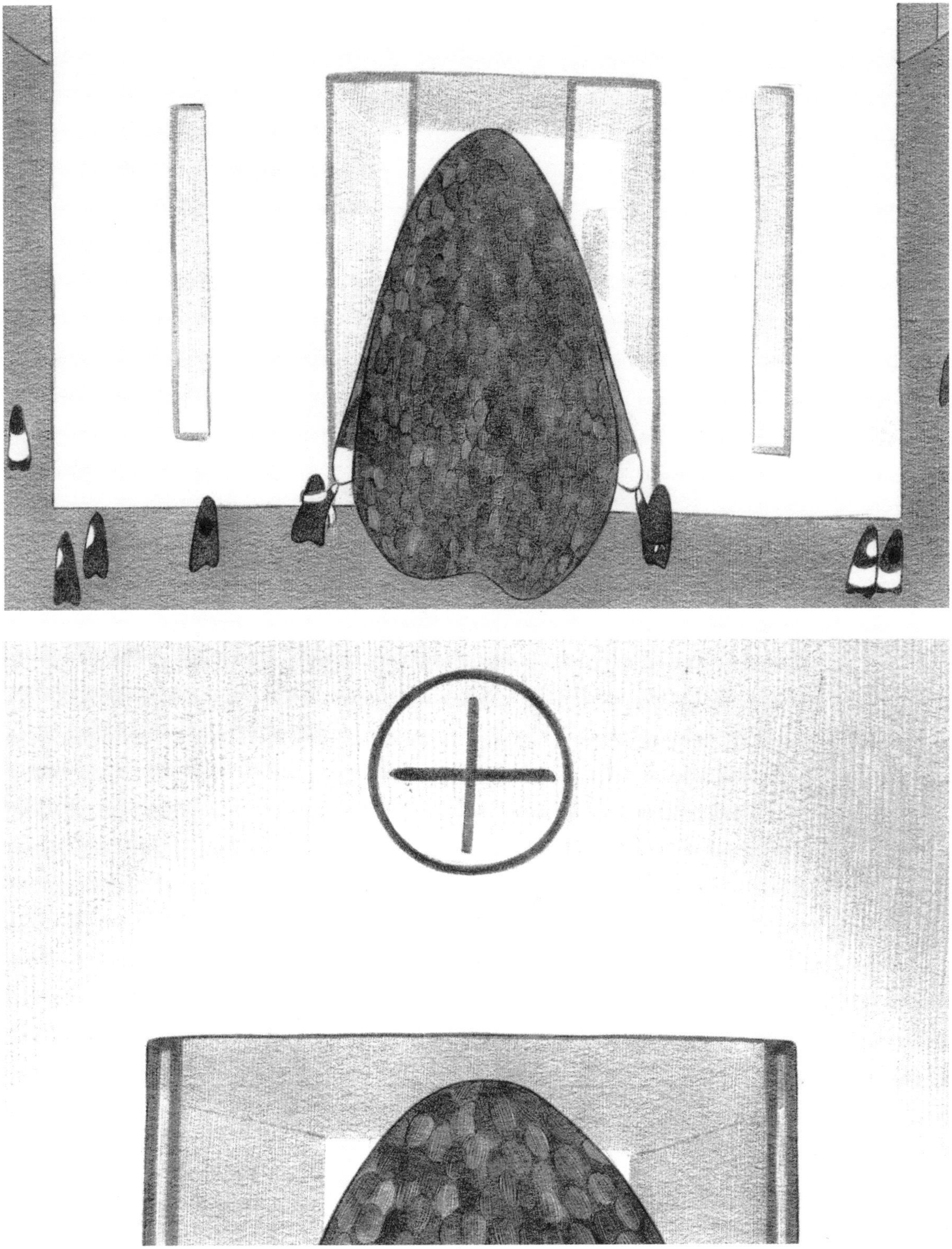

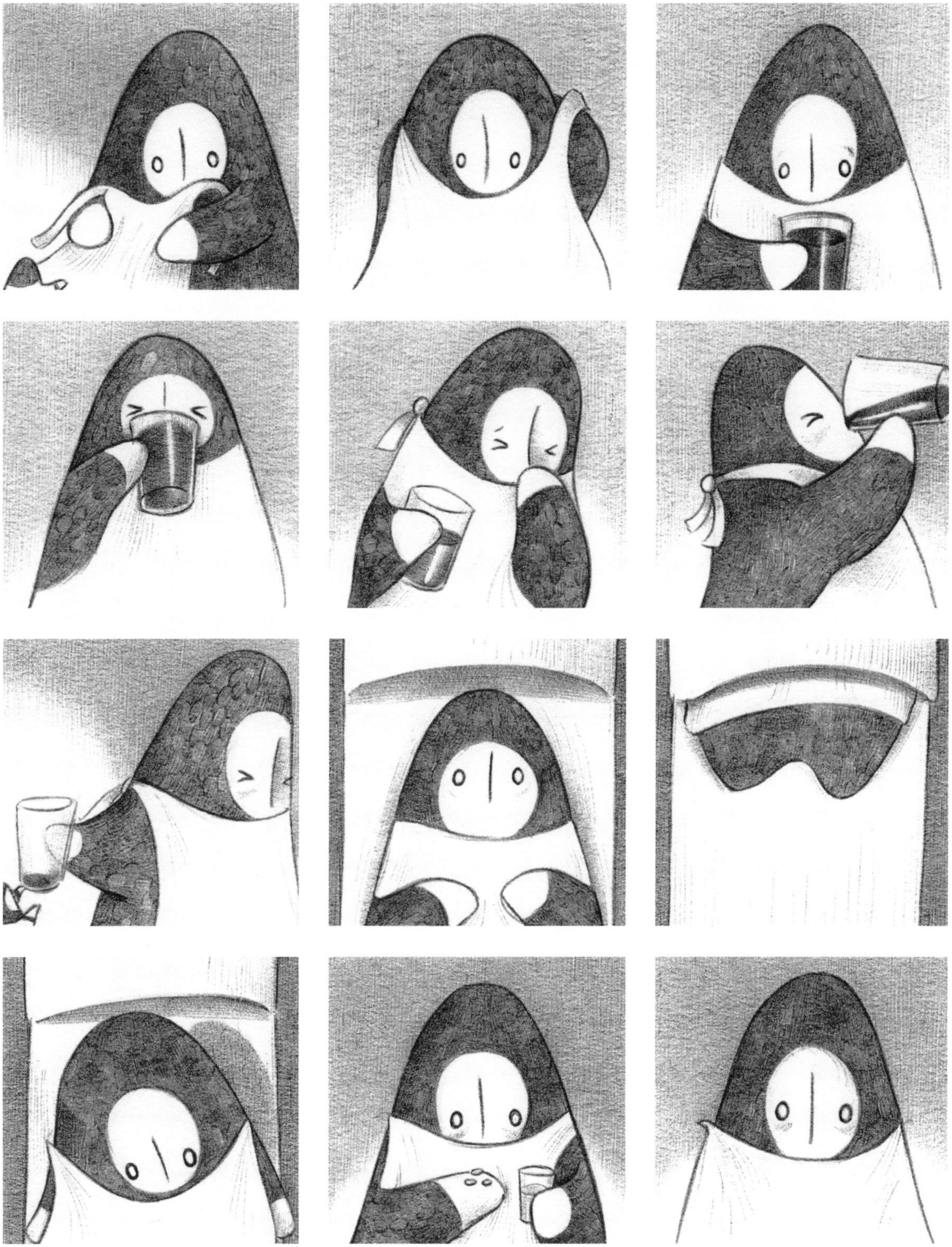

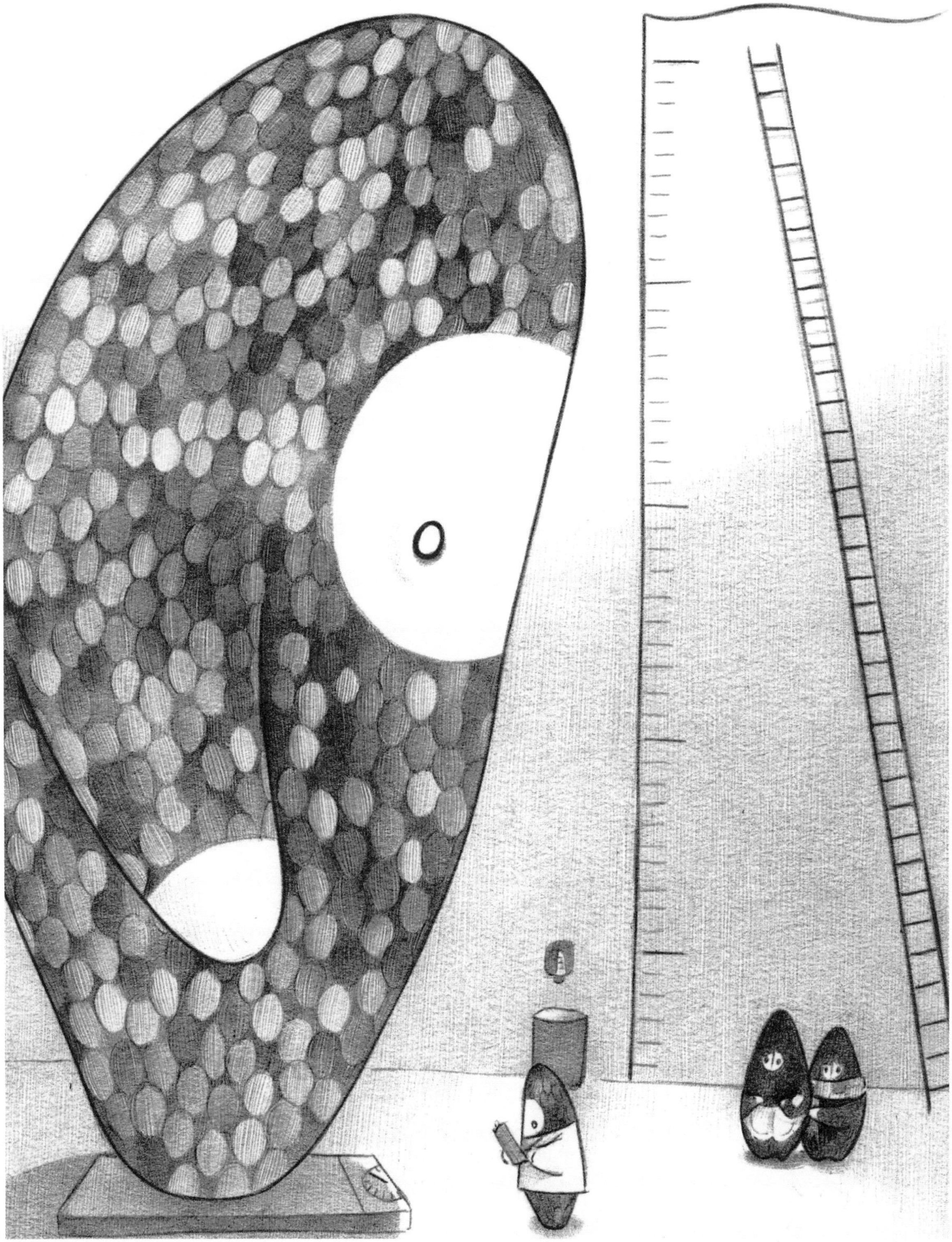

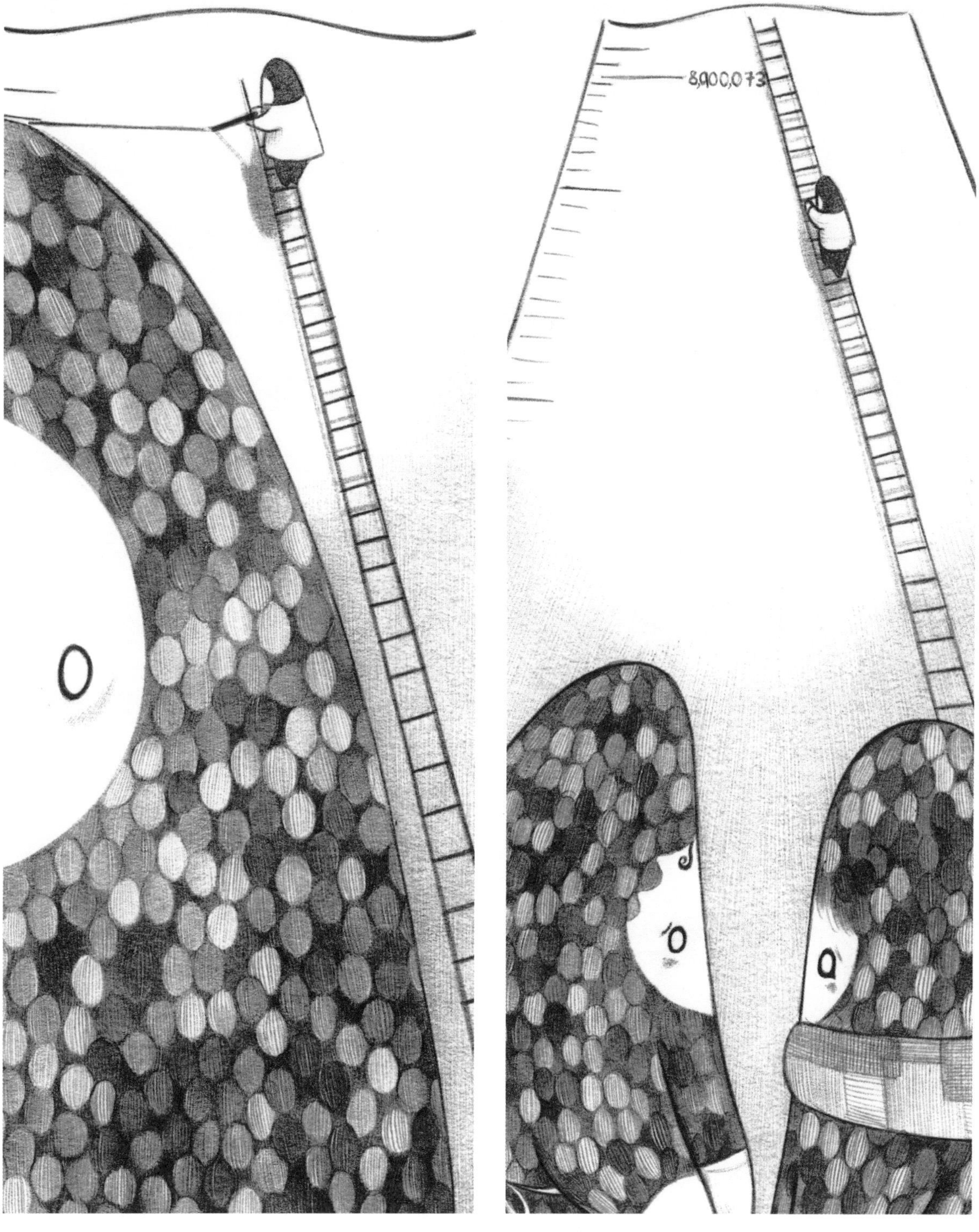
8,900,073

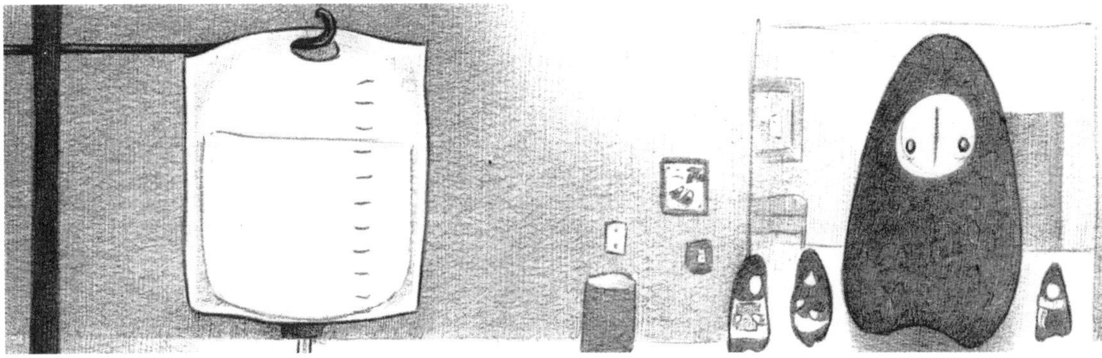

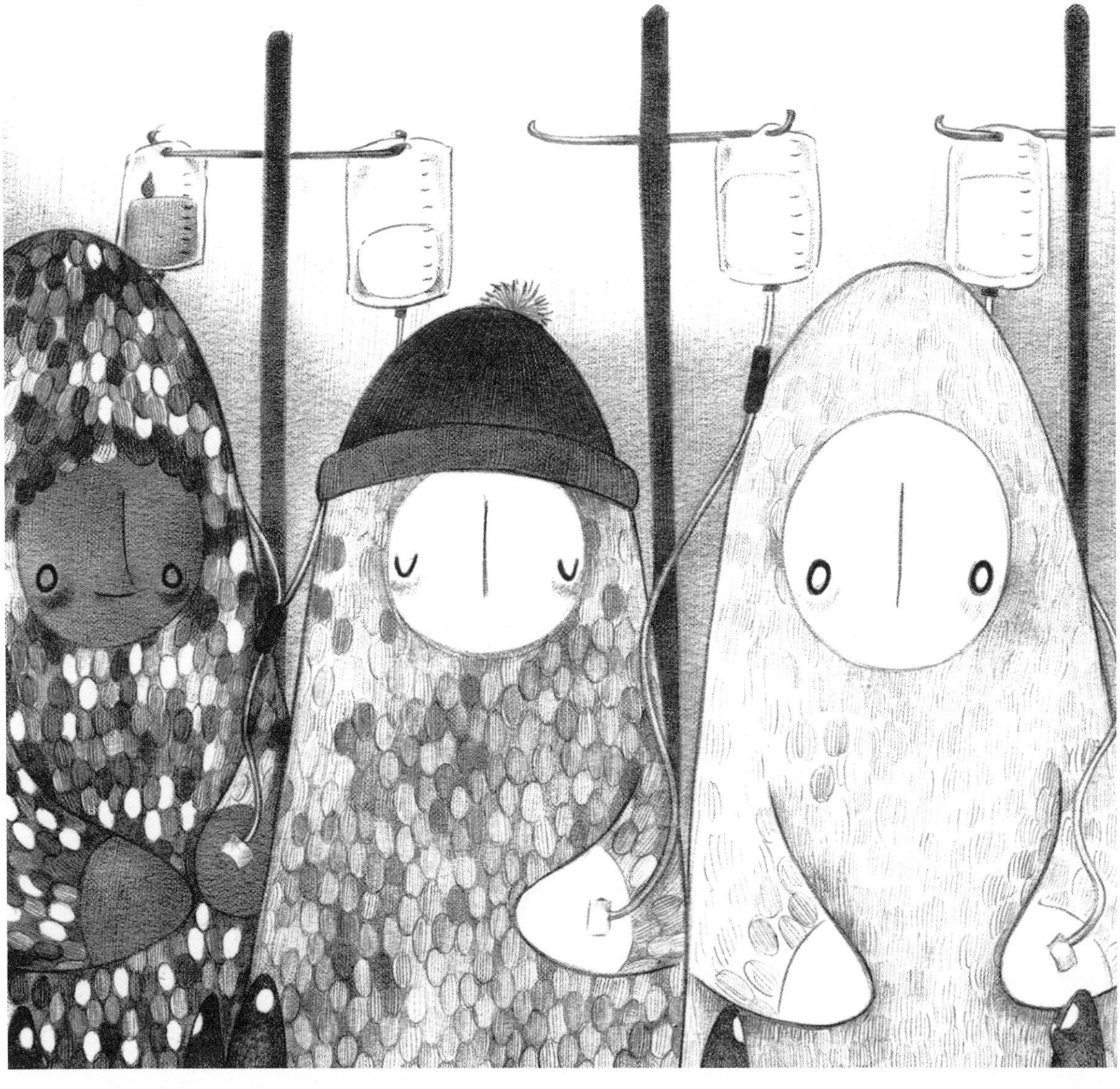

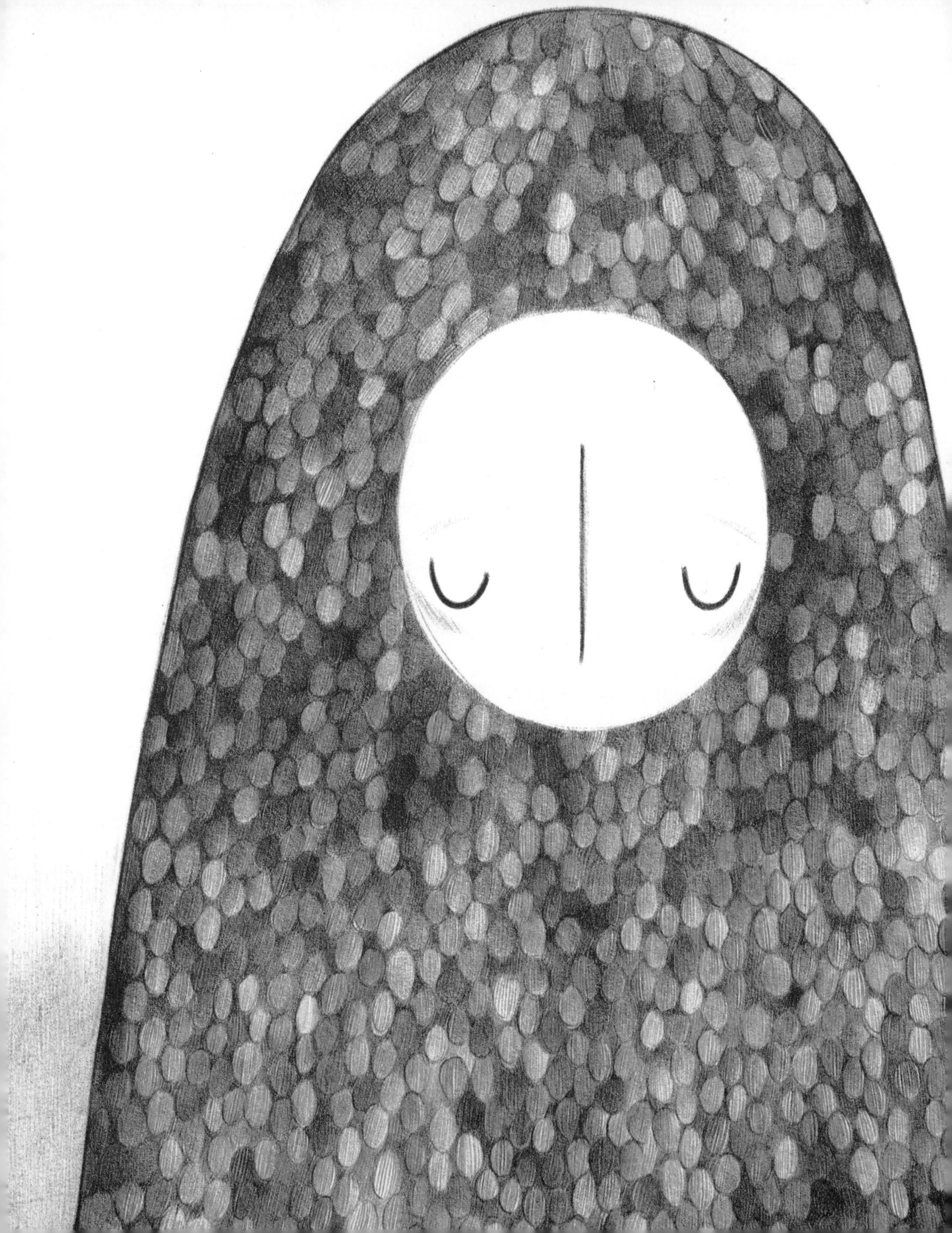

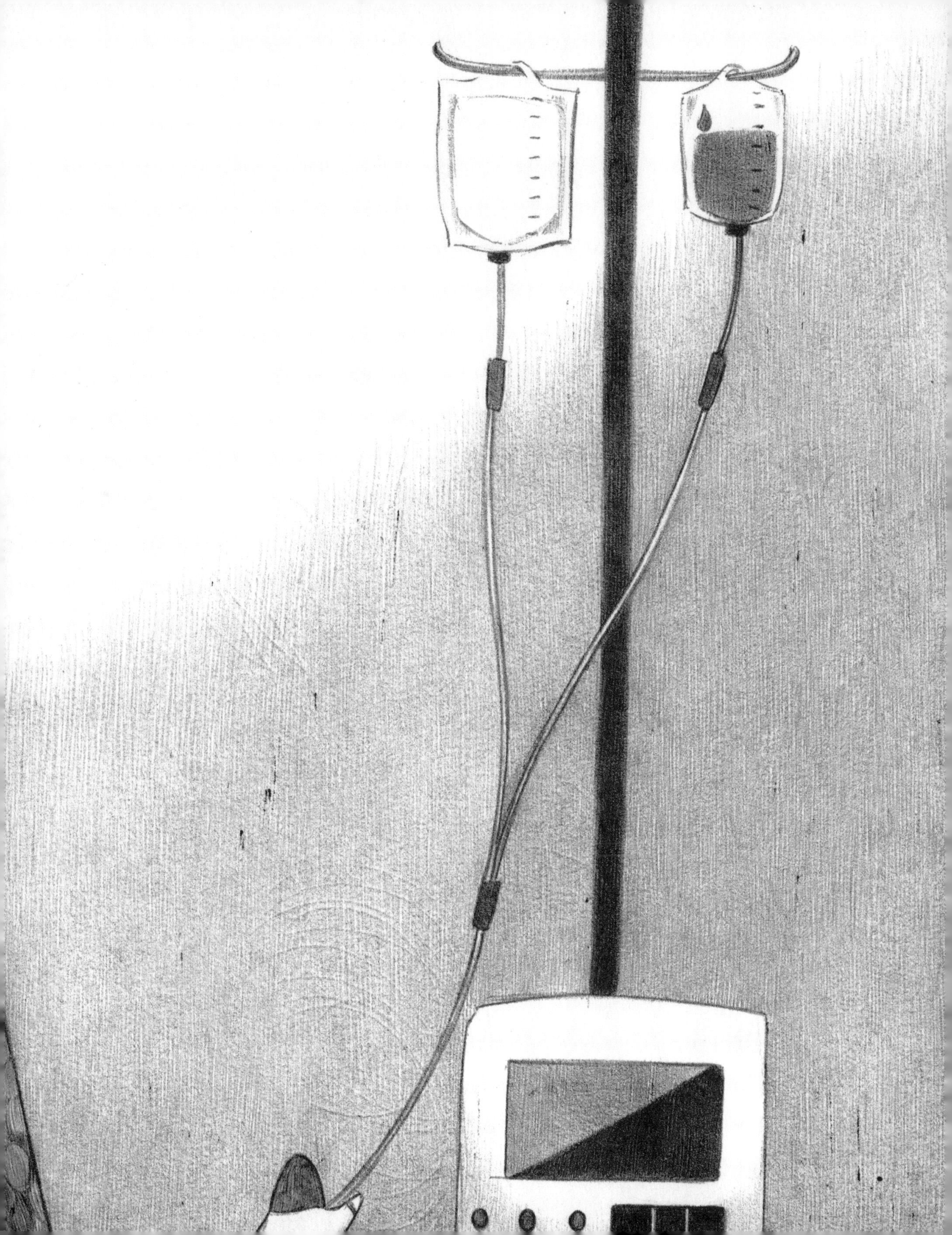

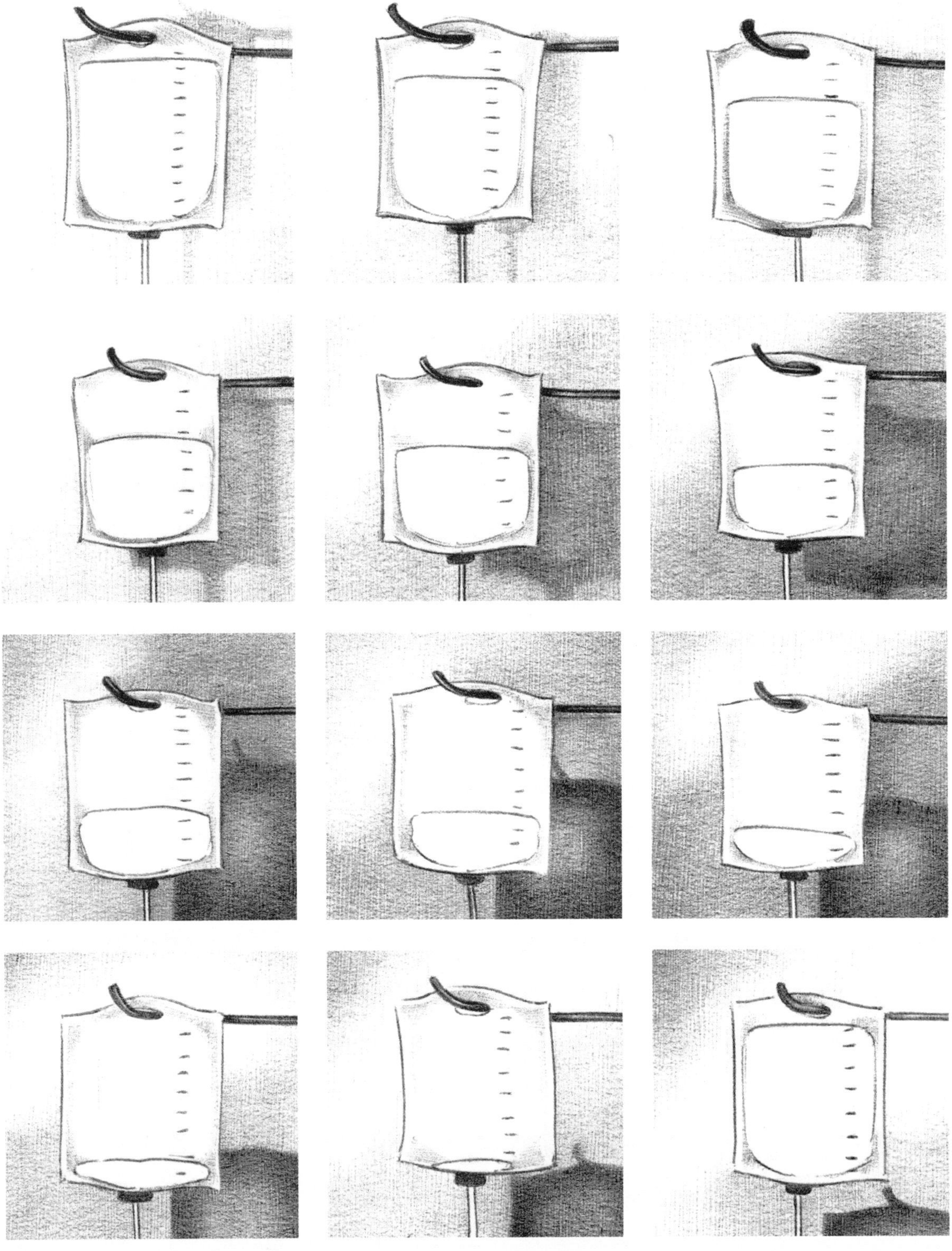

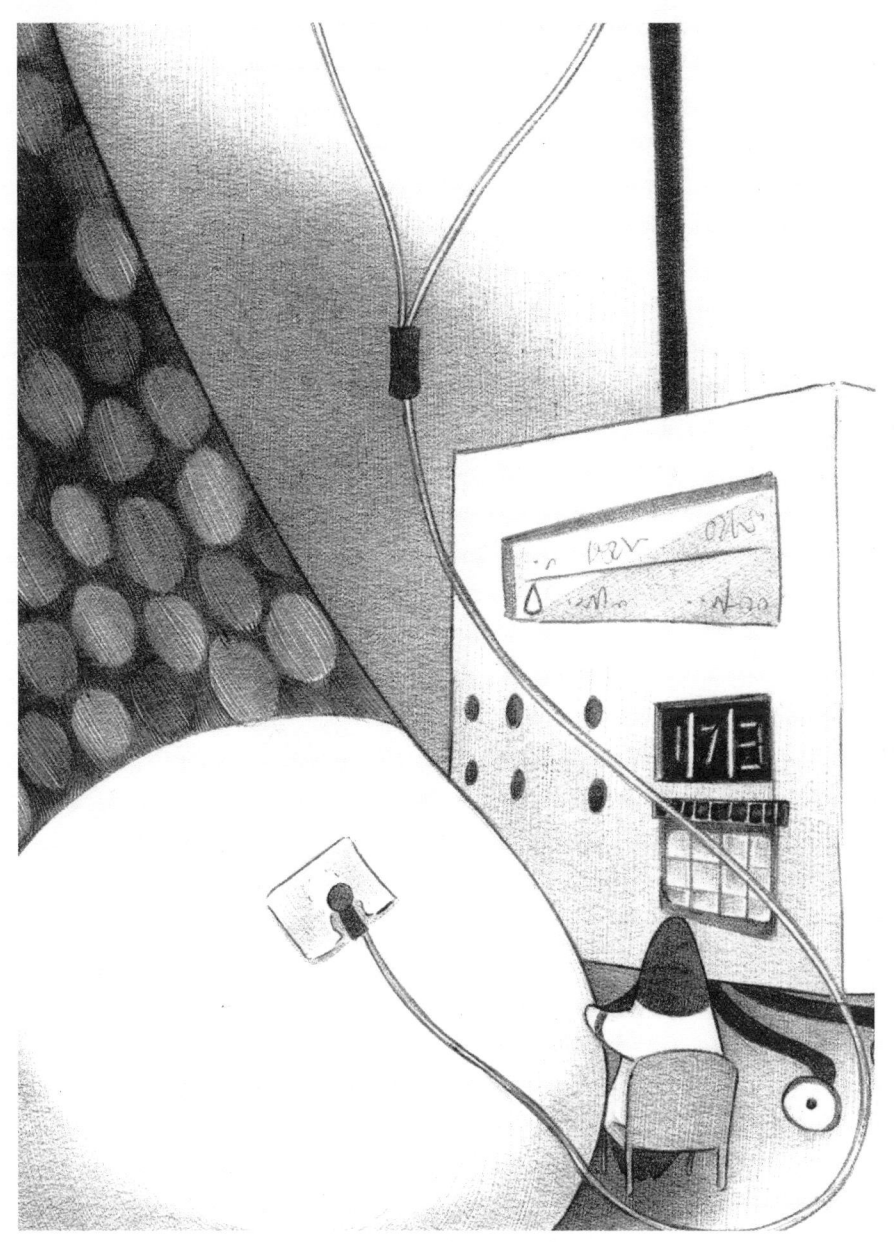

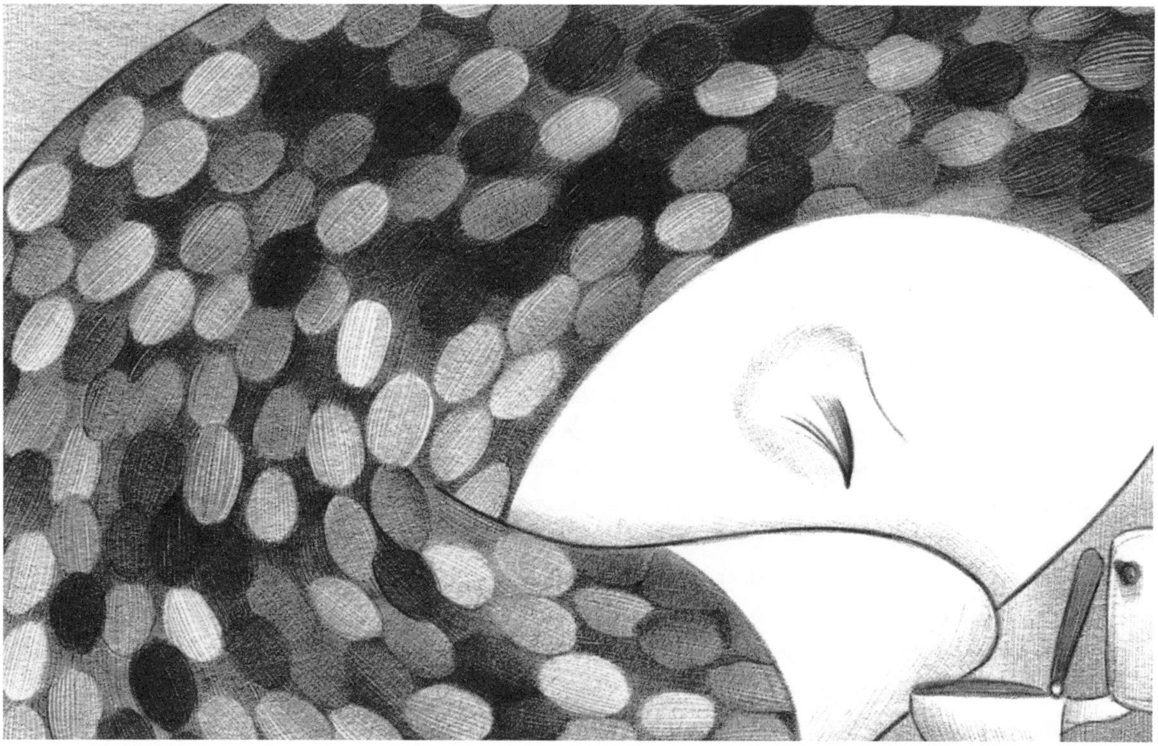

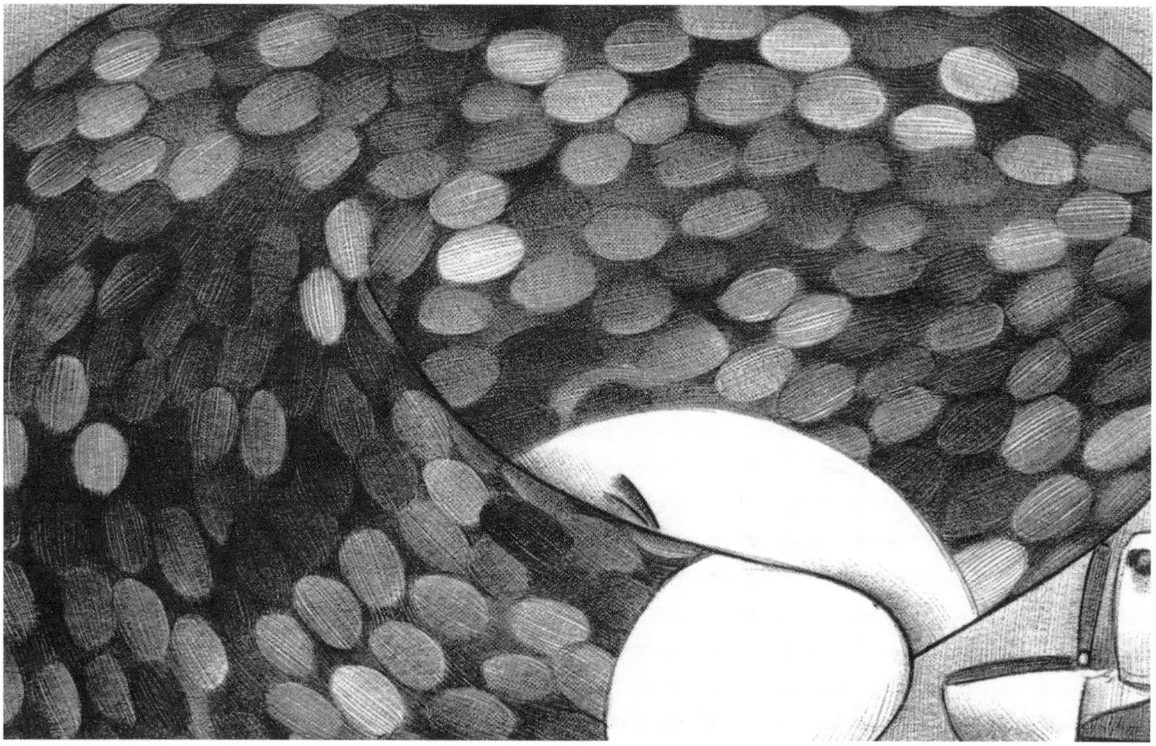

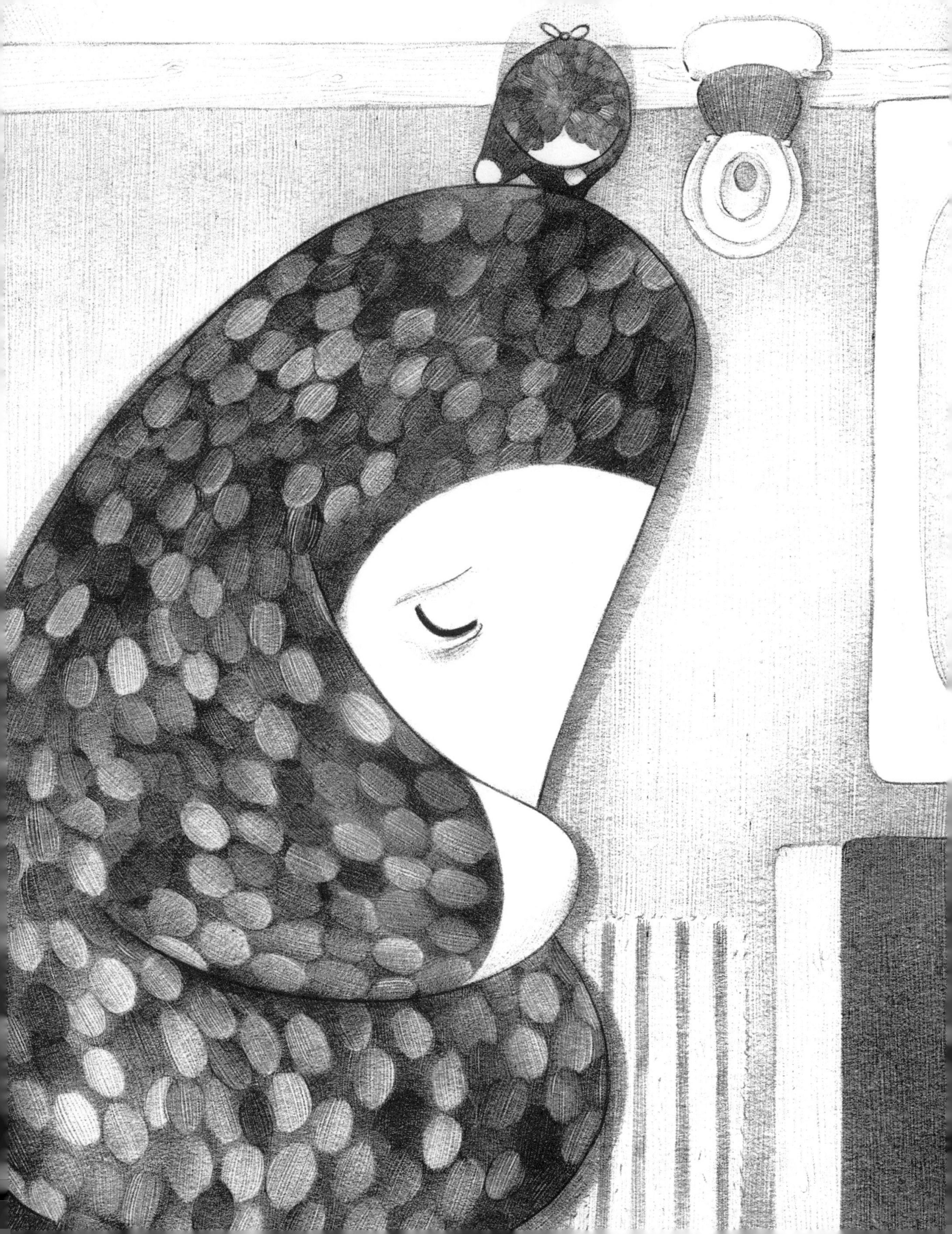

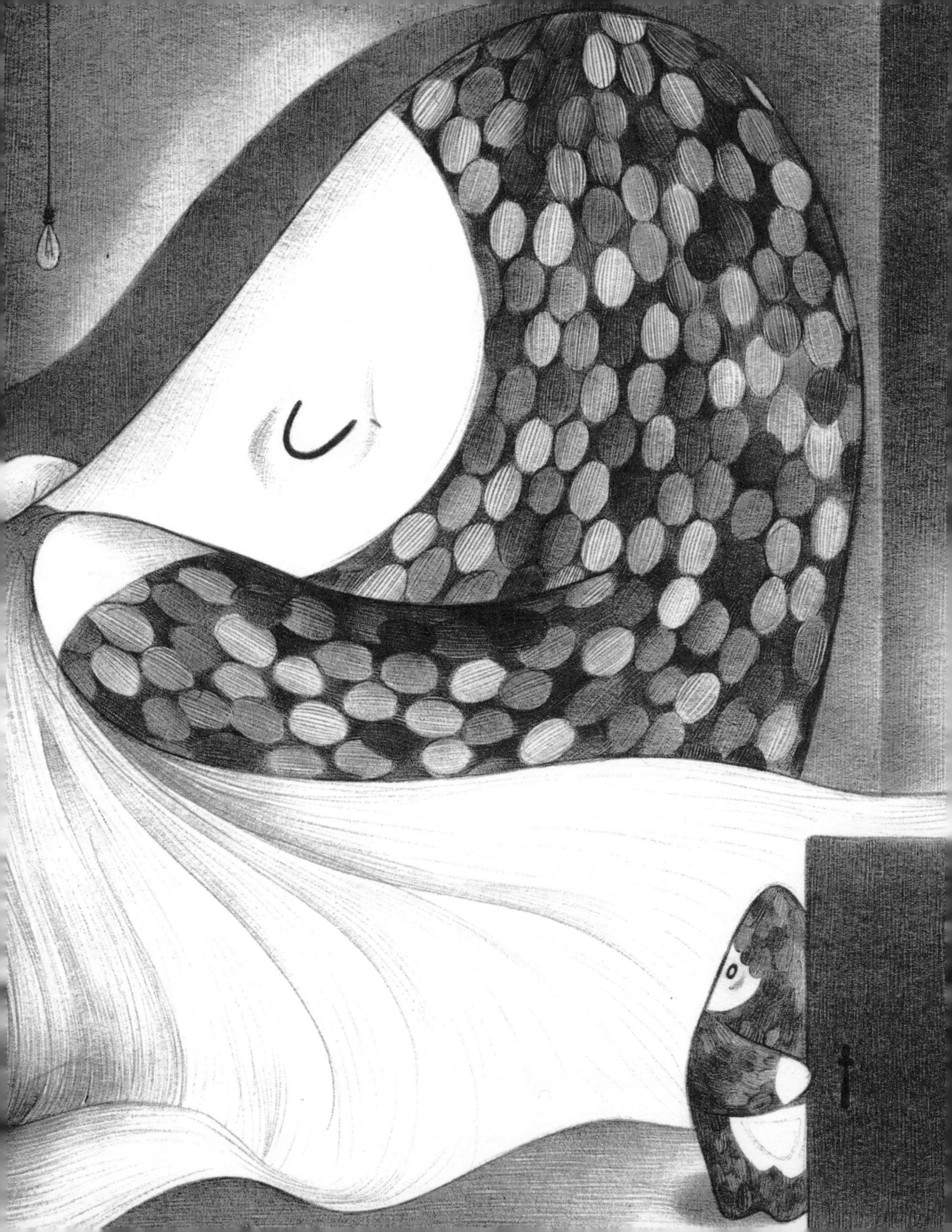

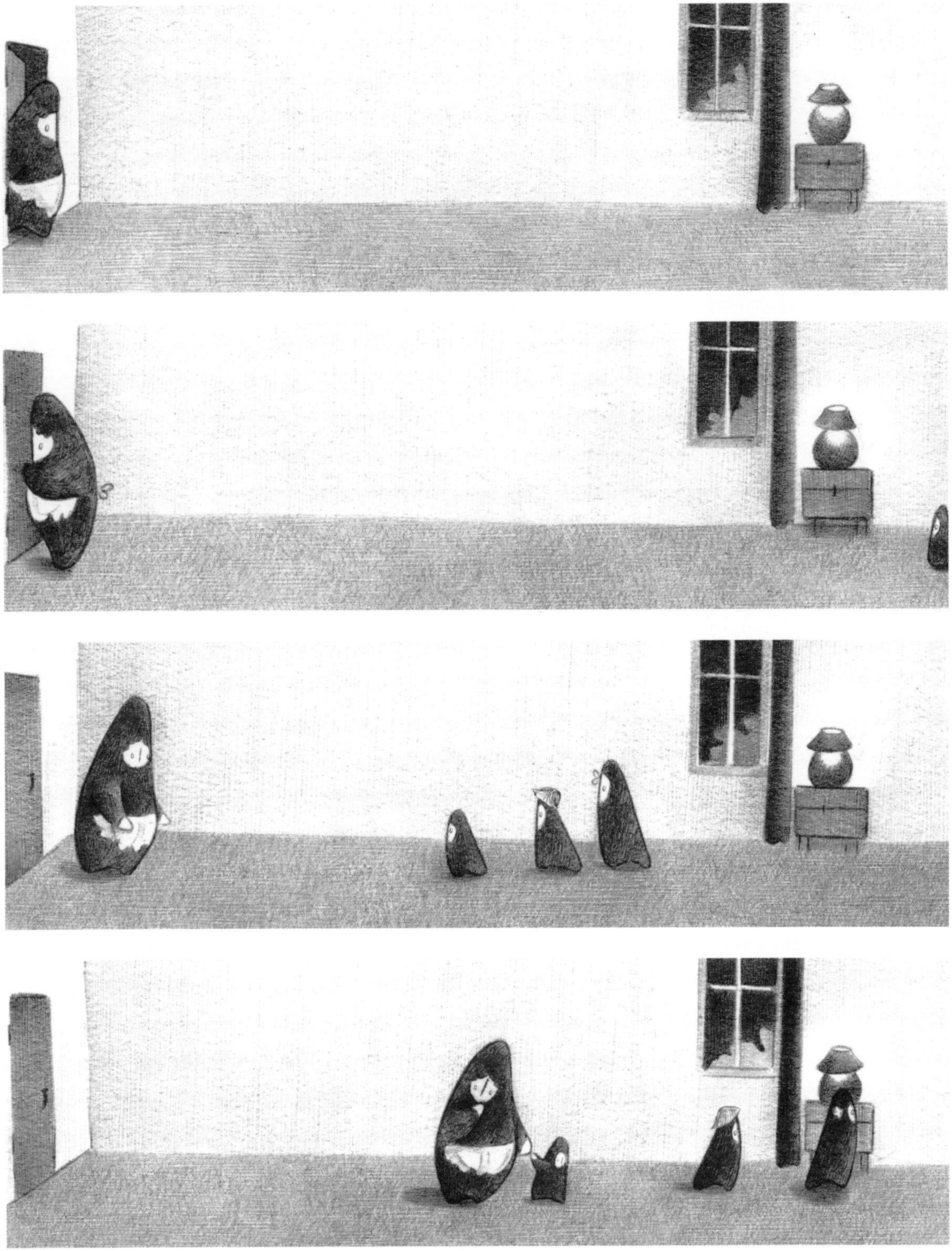

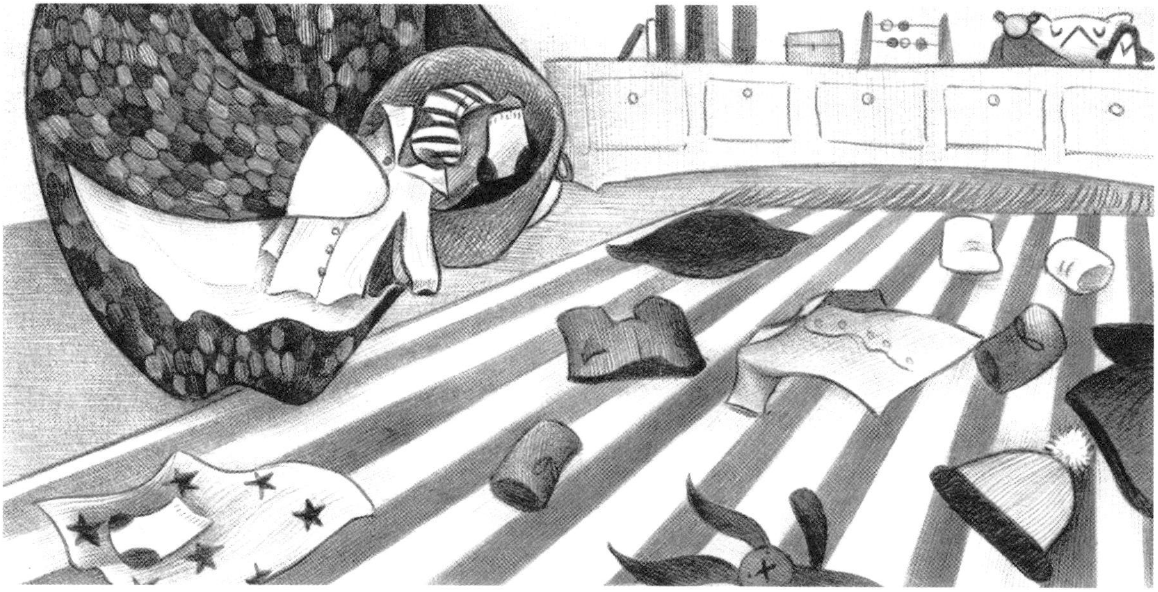

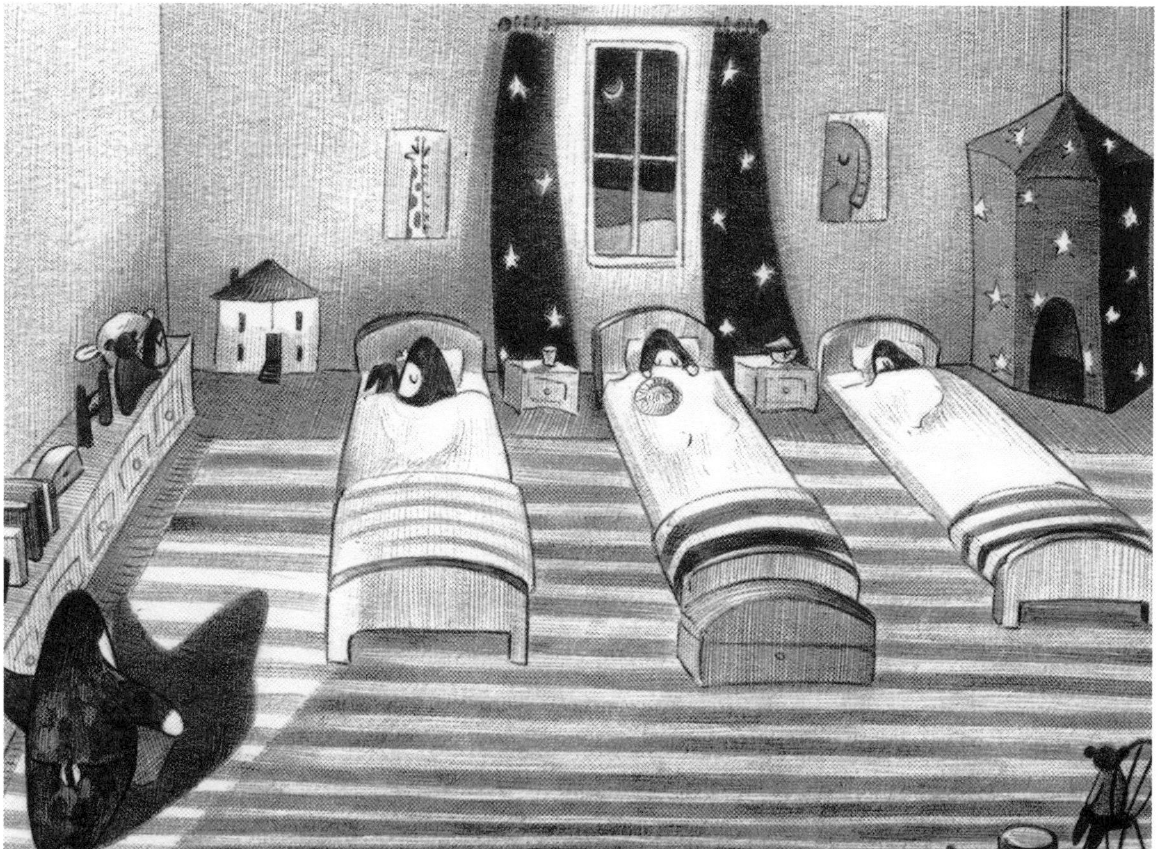

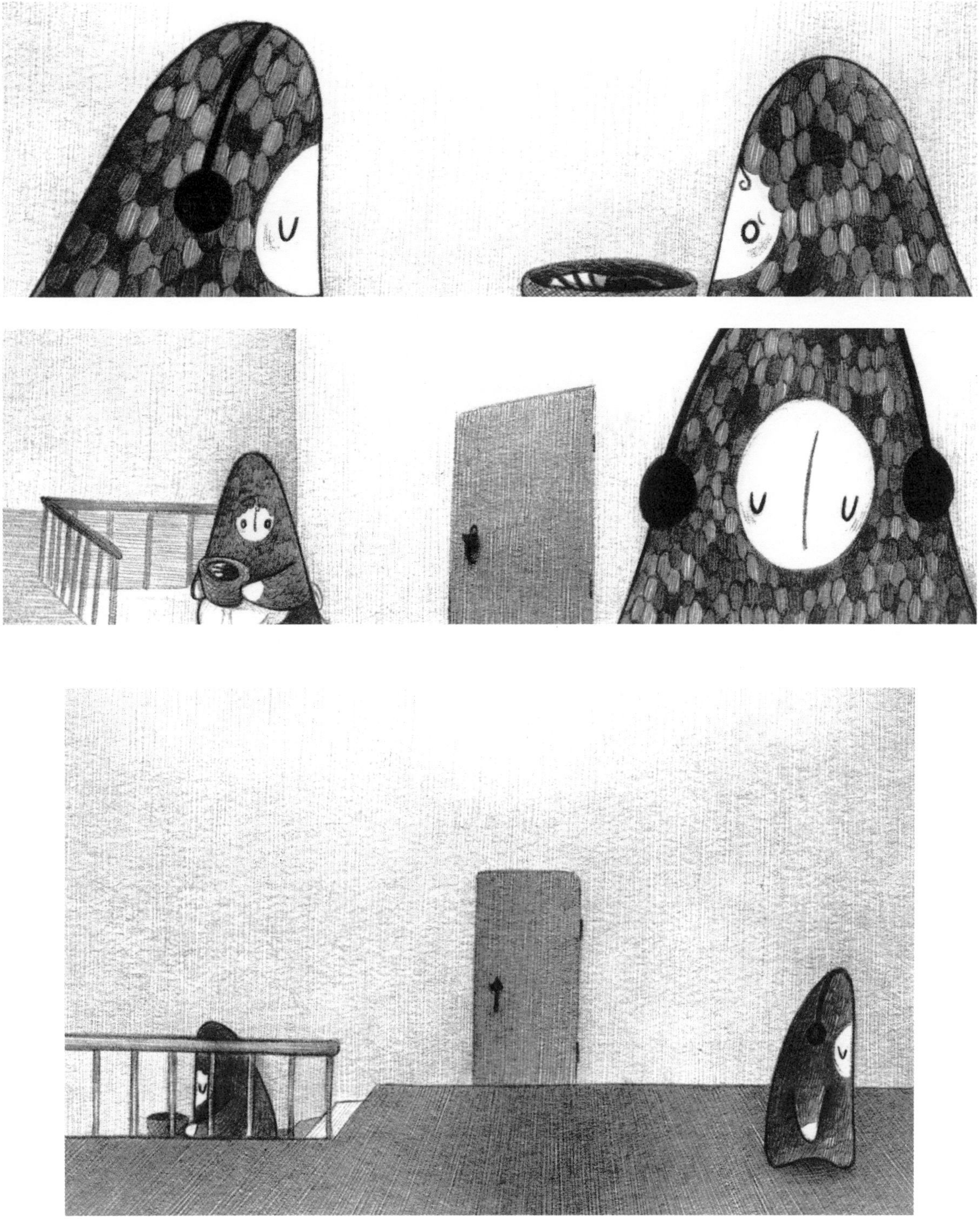

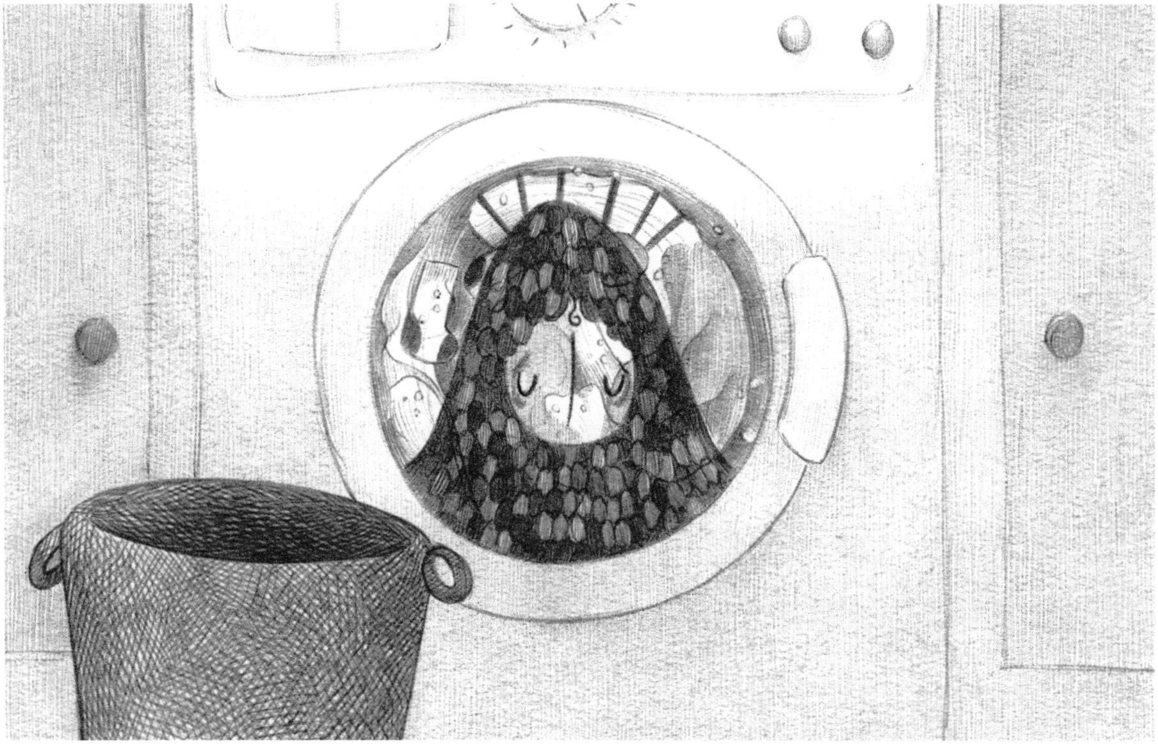

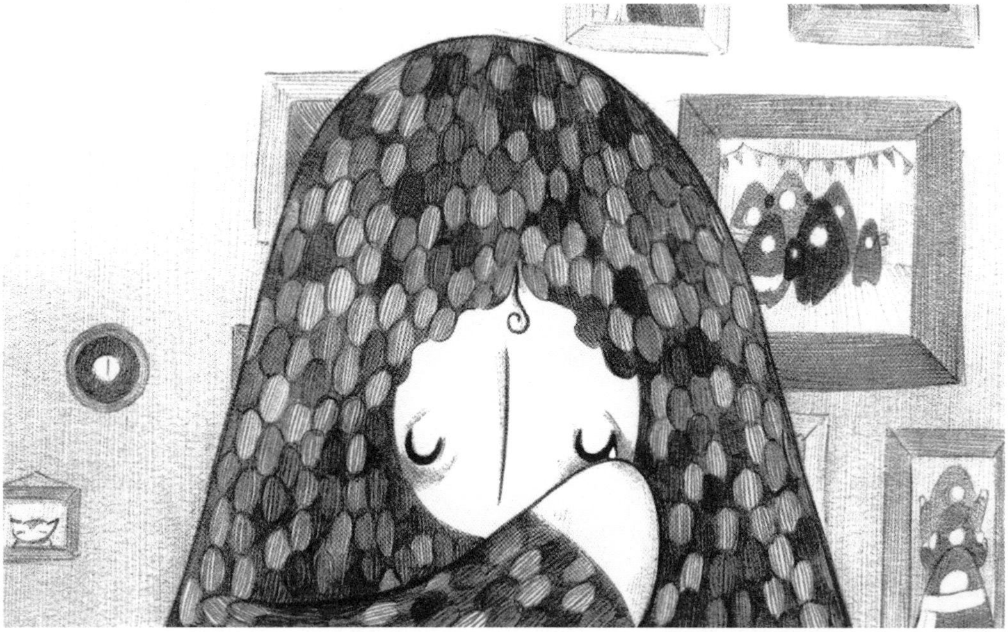

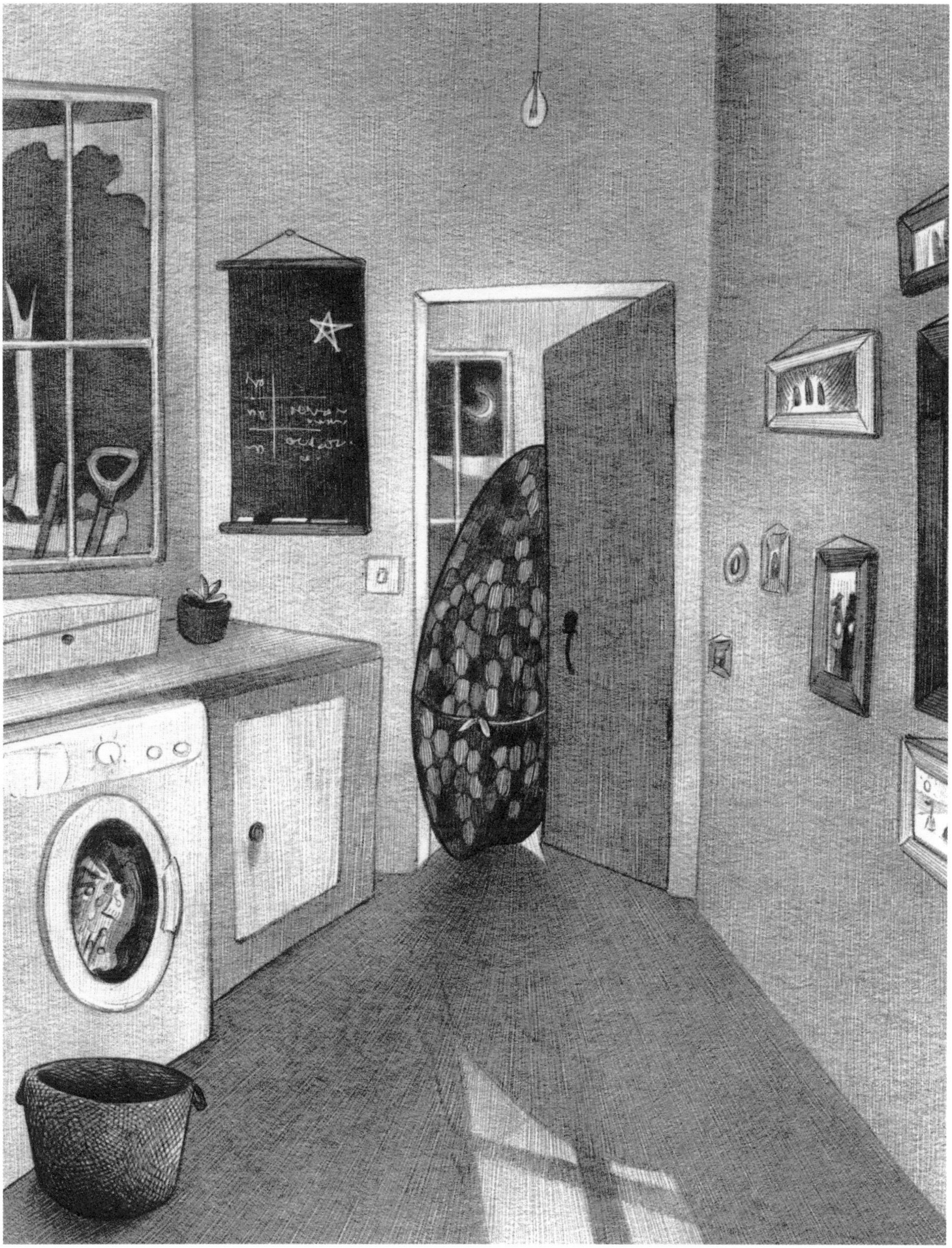

CHAPTER THREE

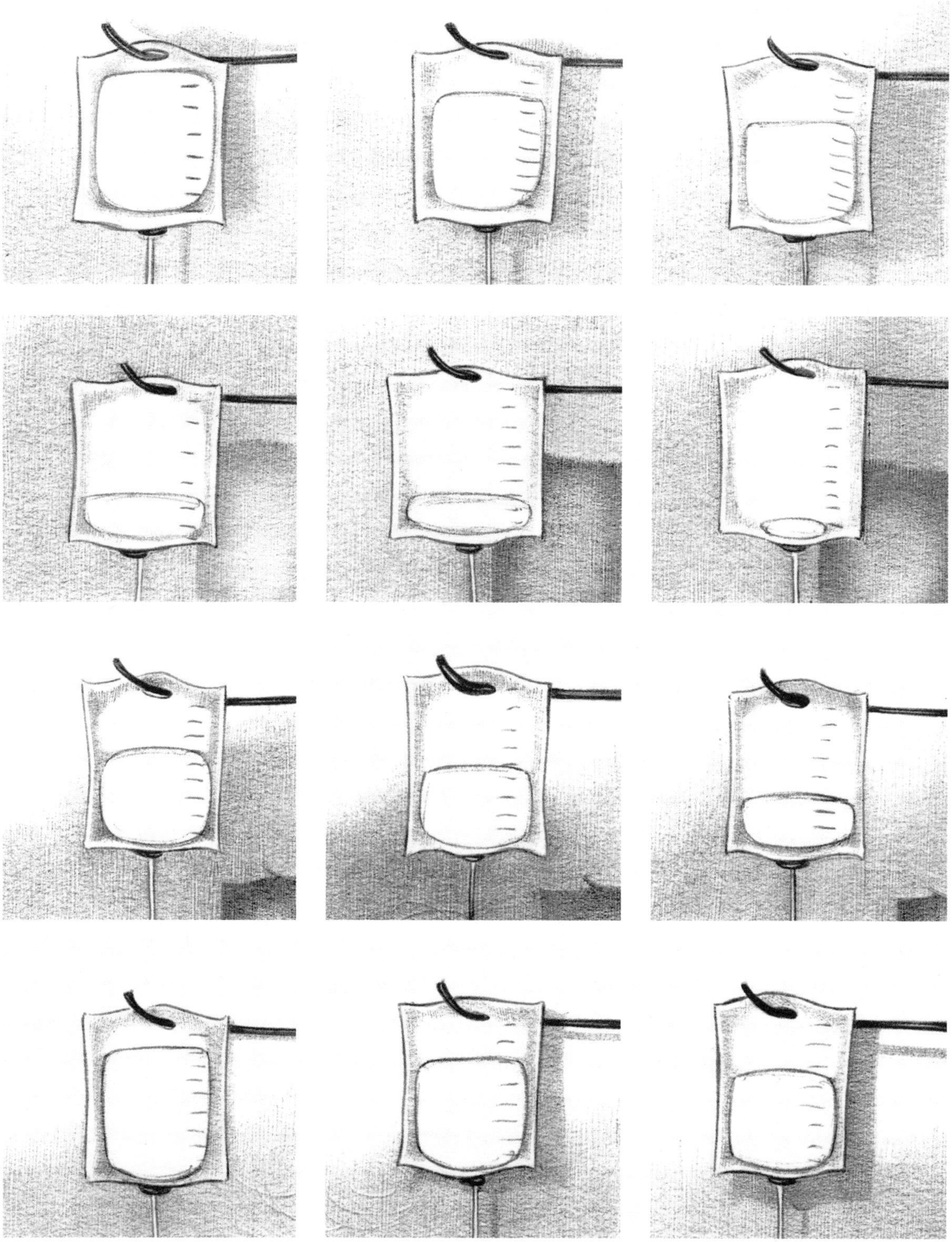

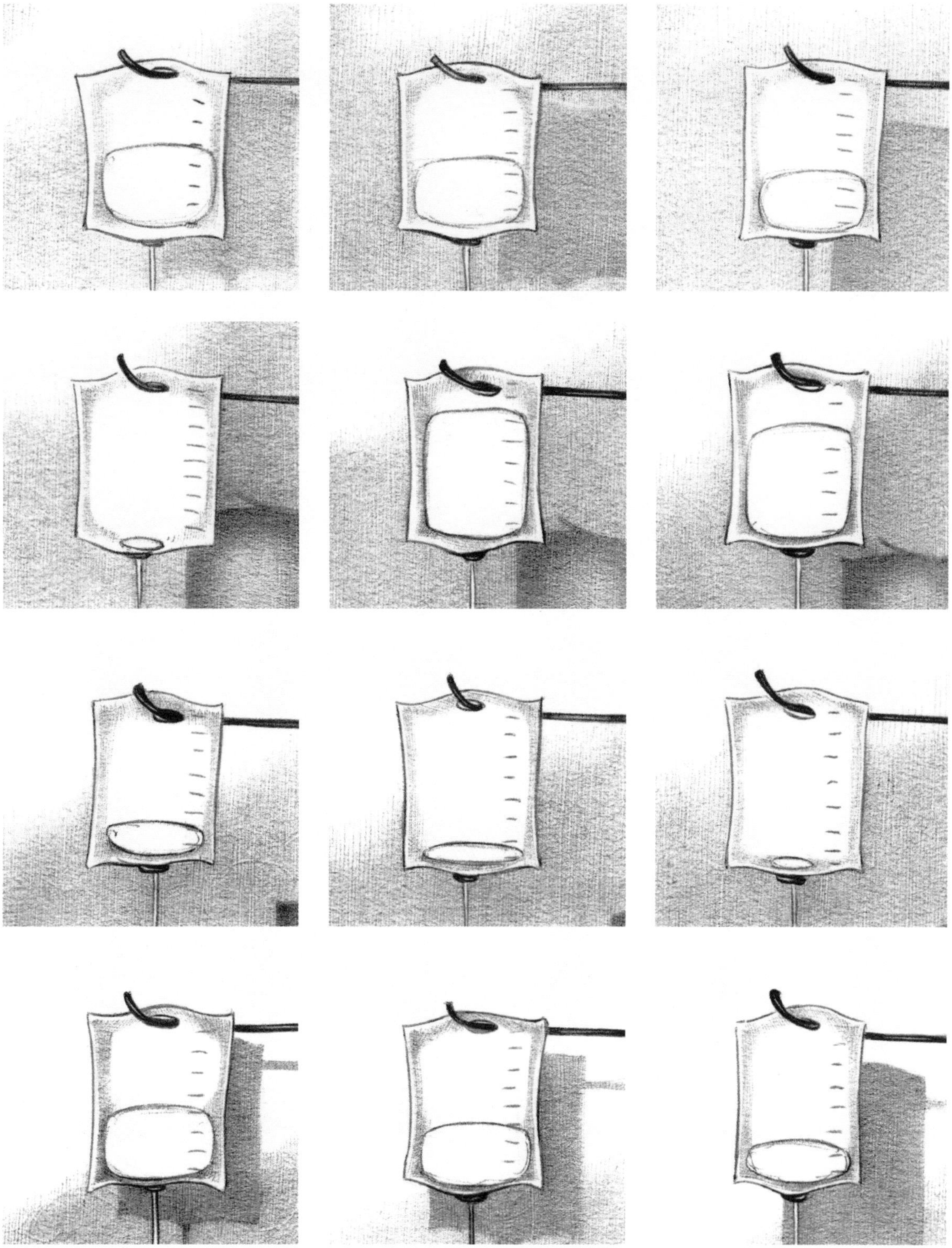

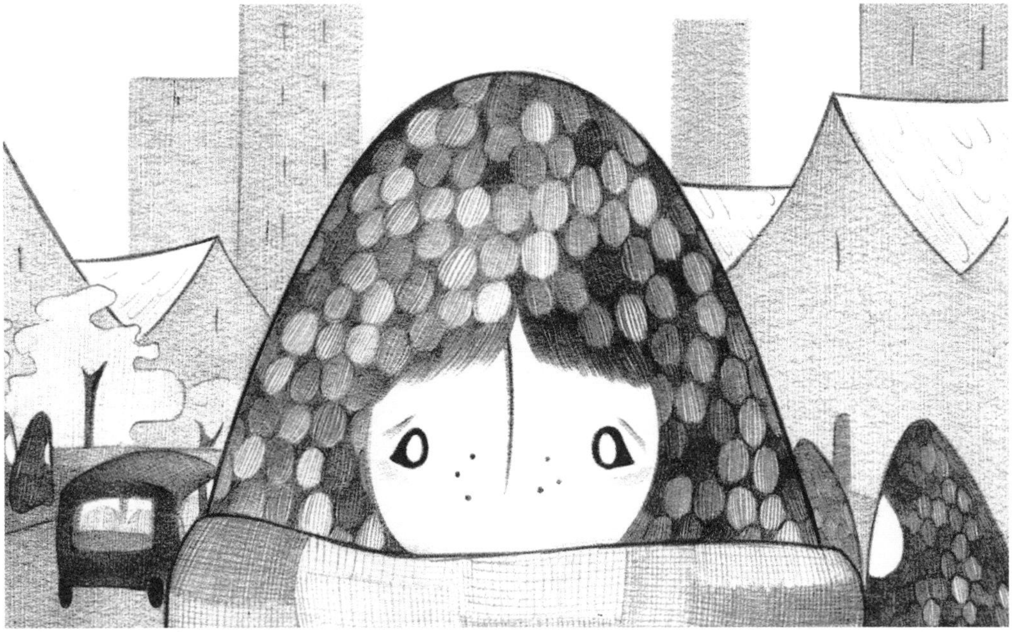

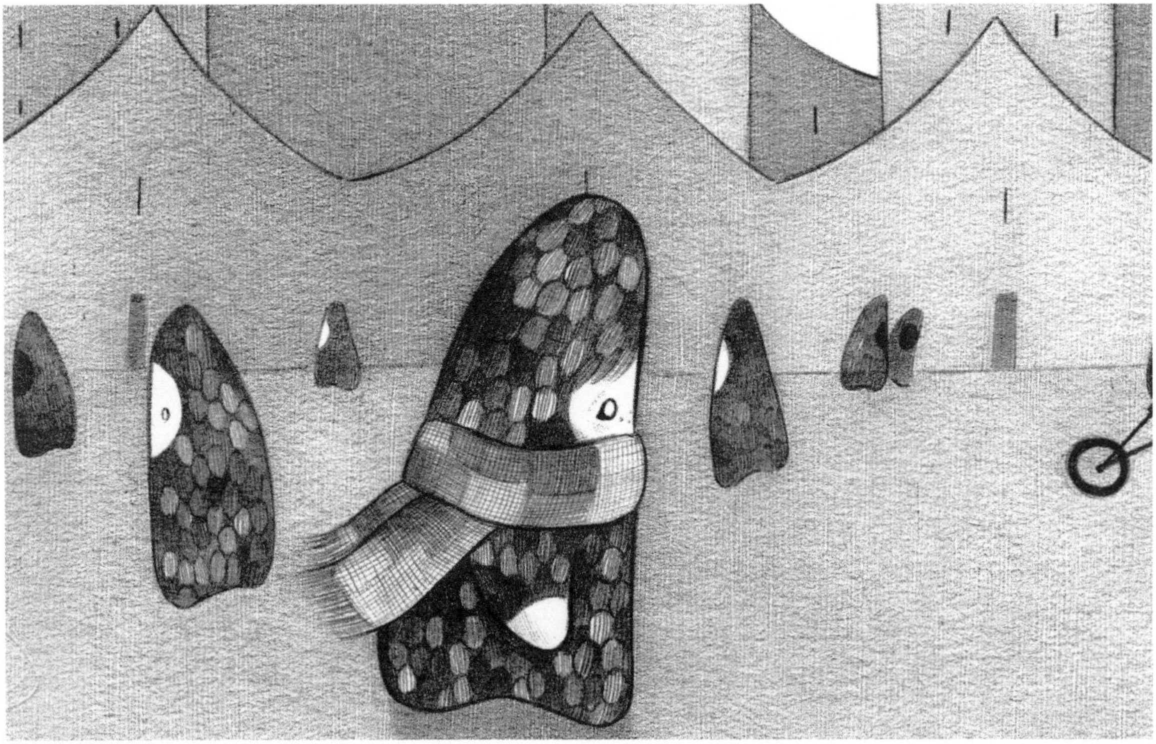

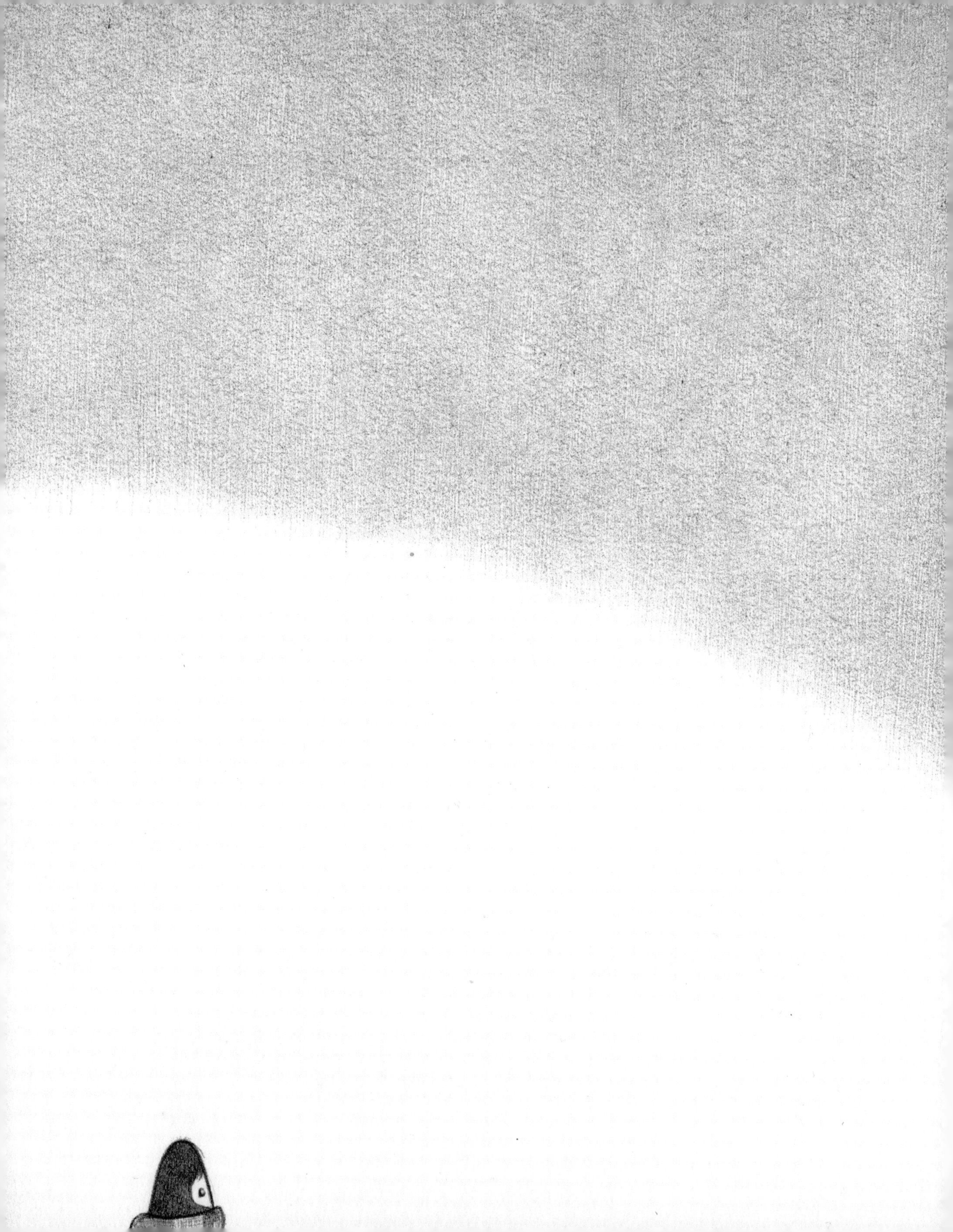

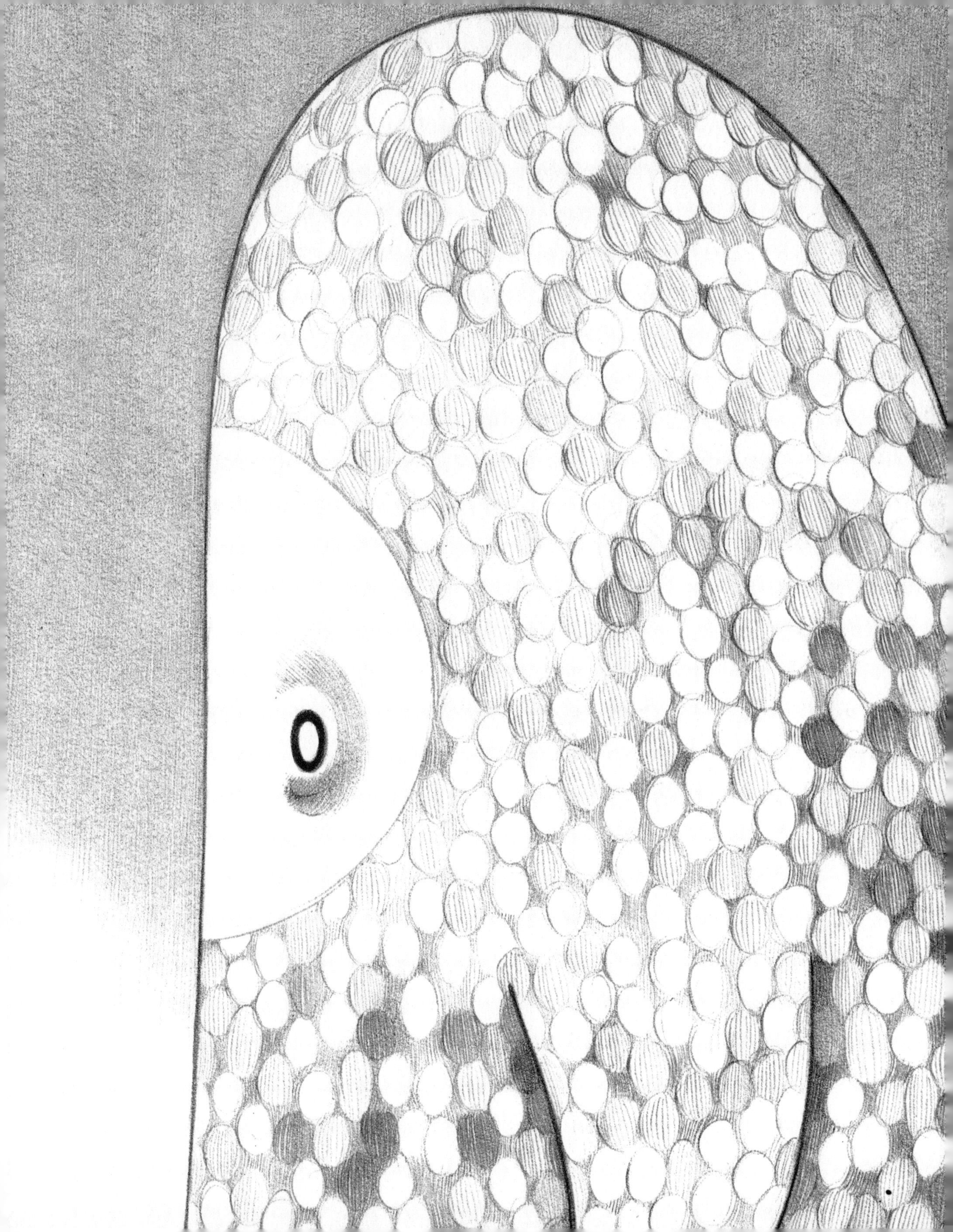

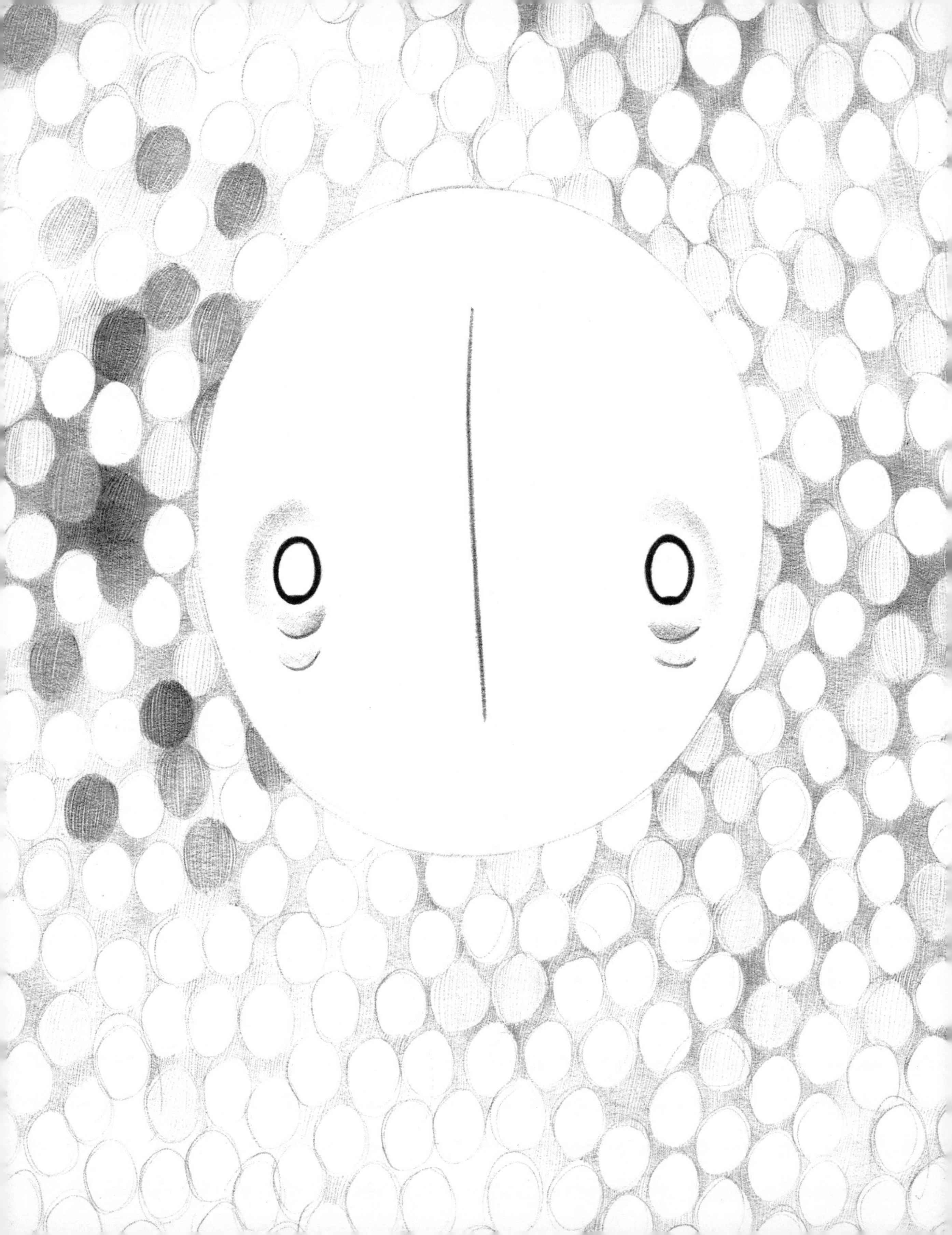

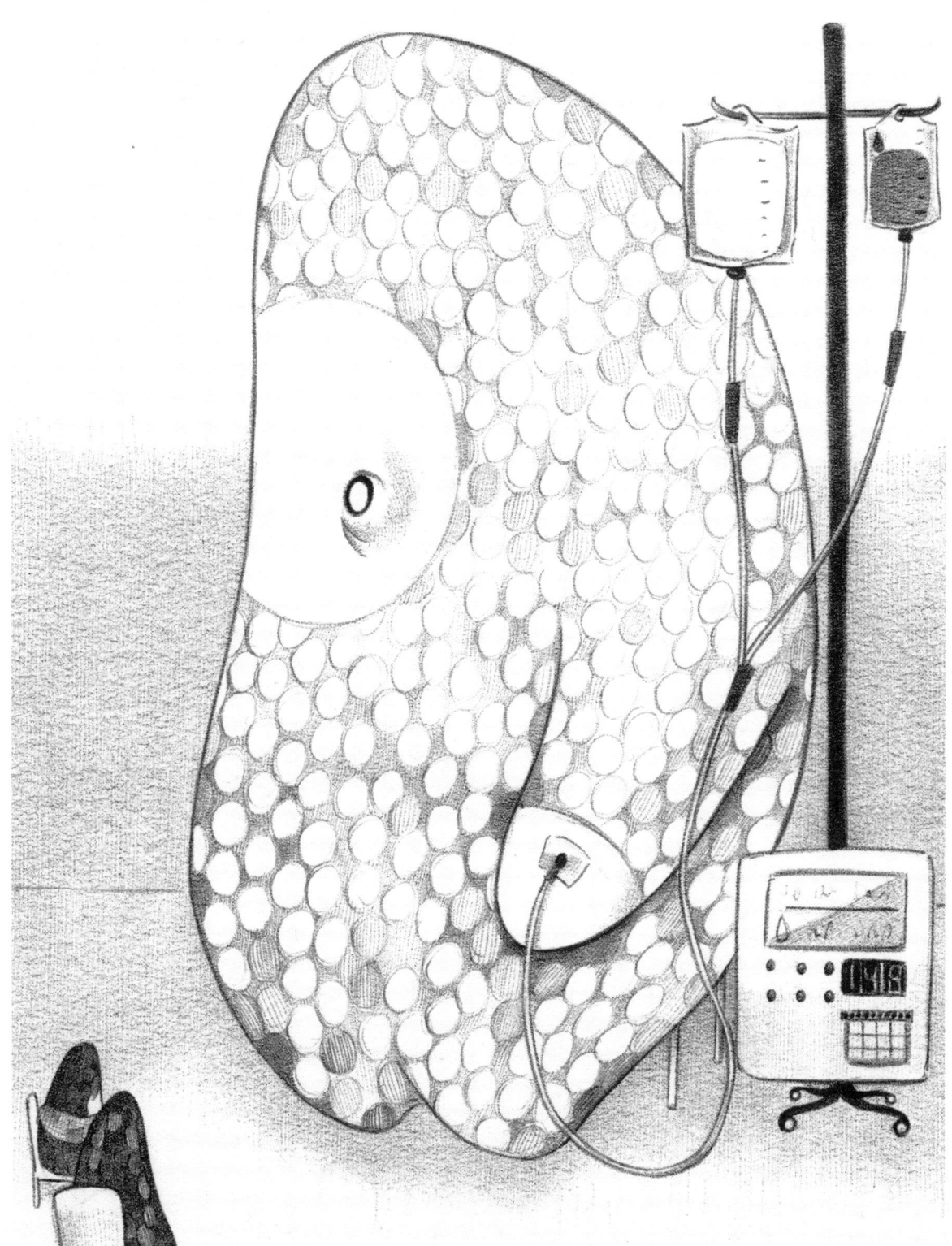

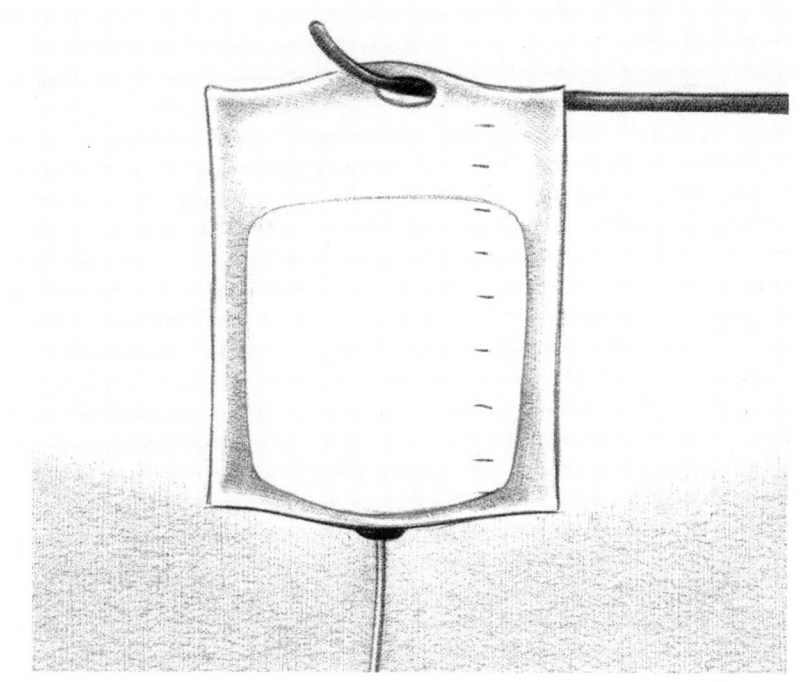

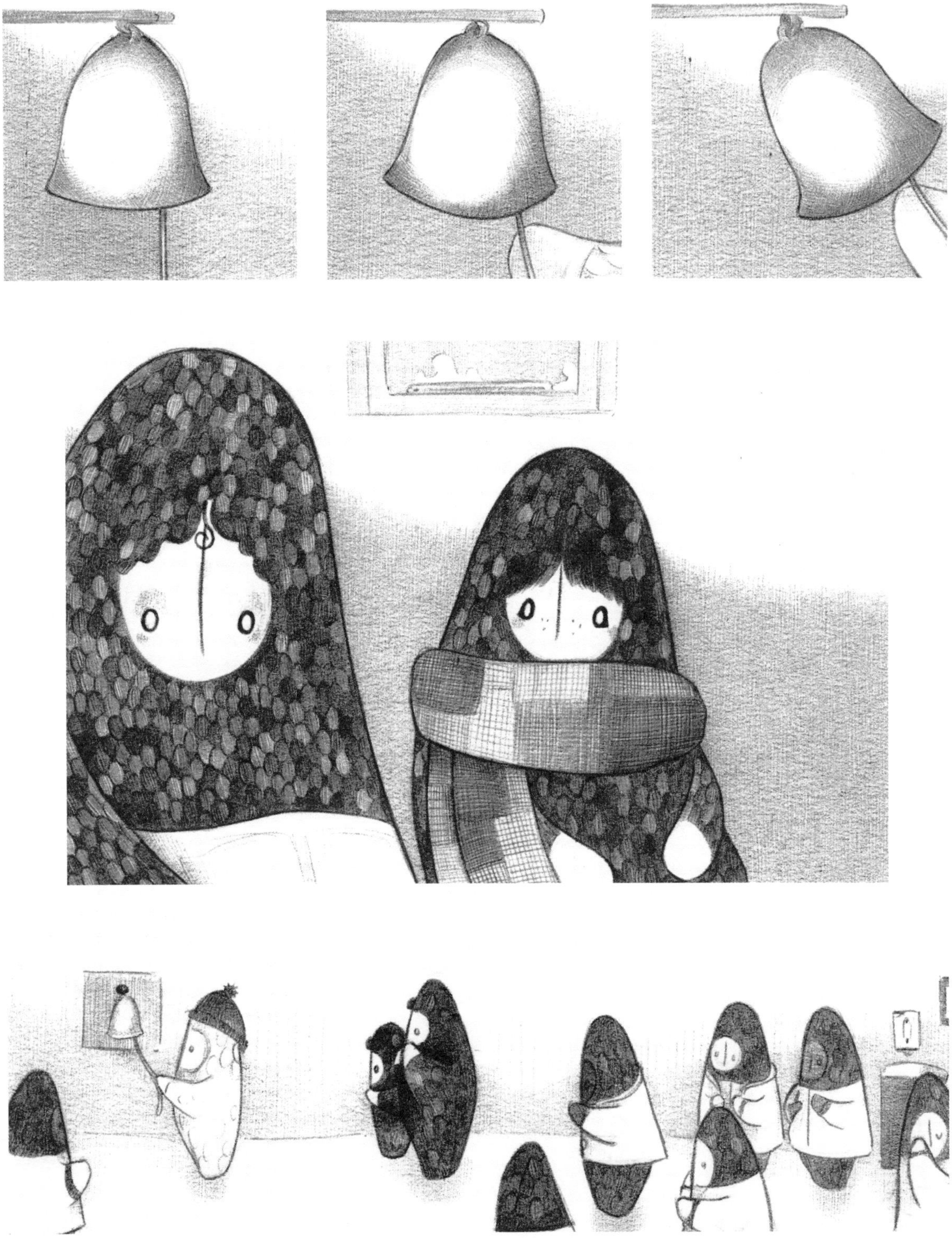

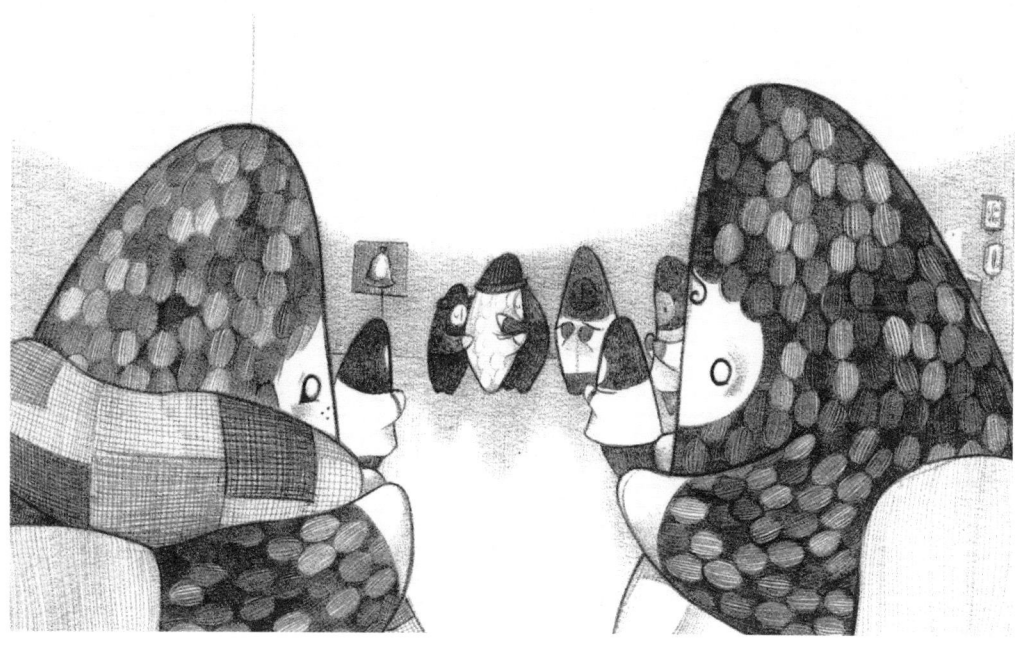

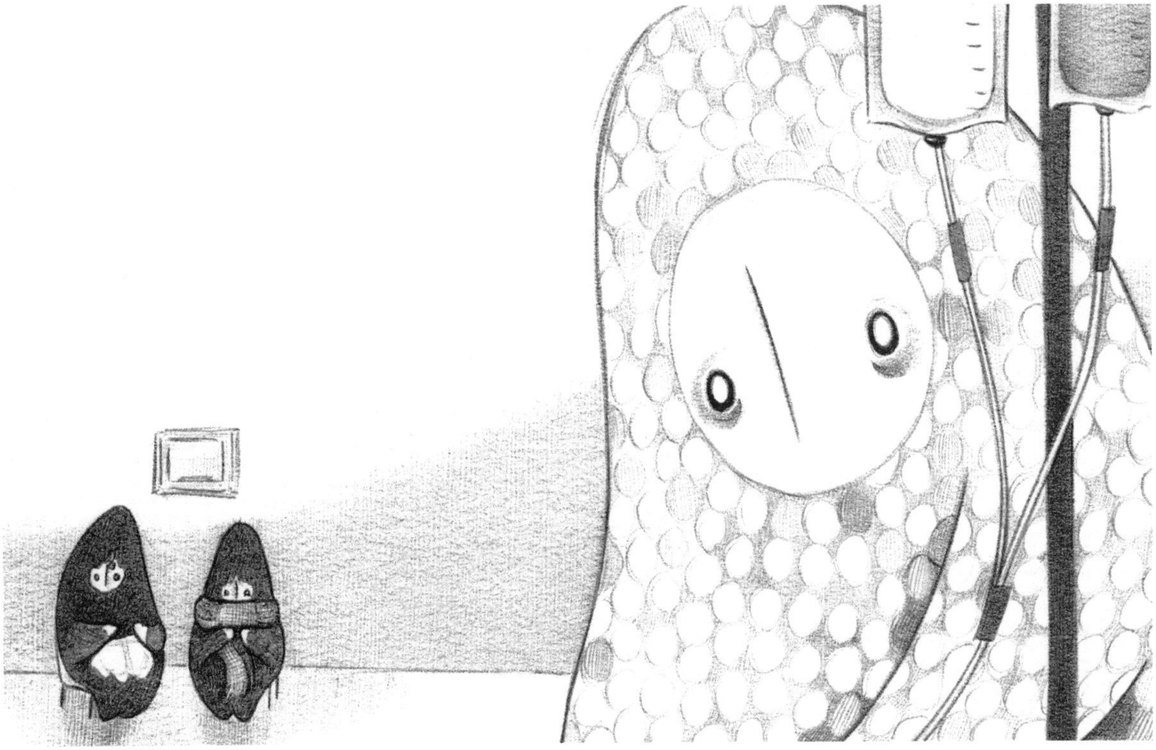

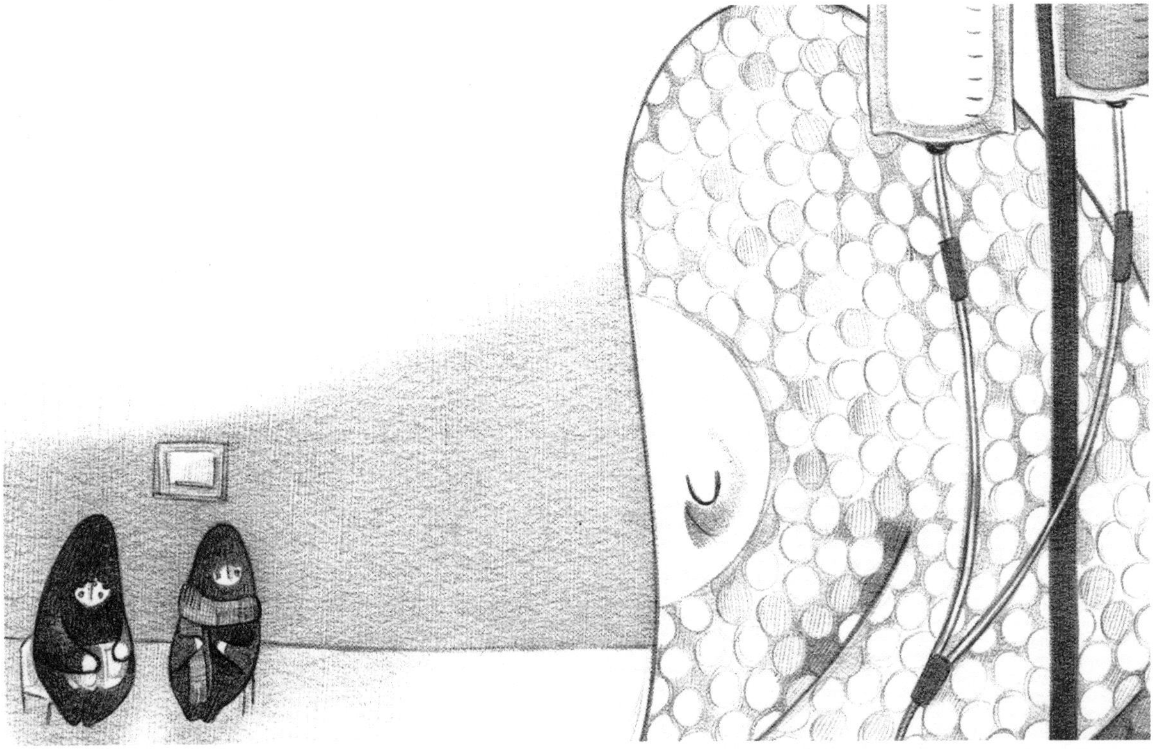

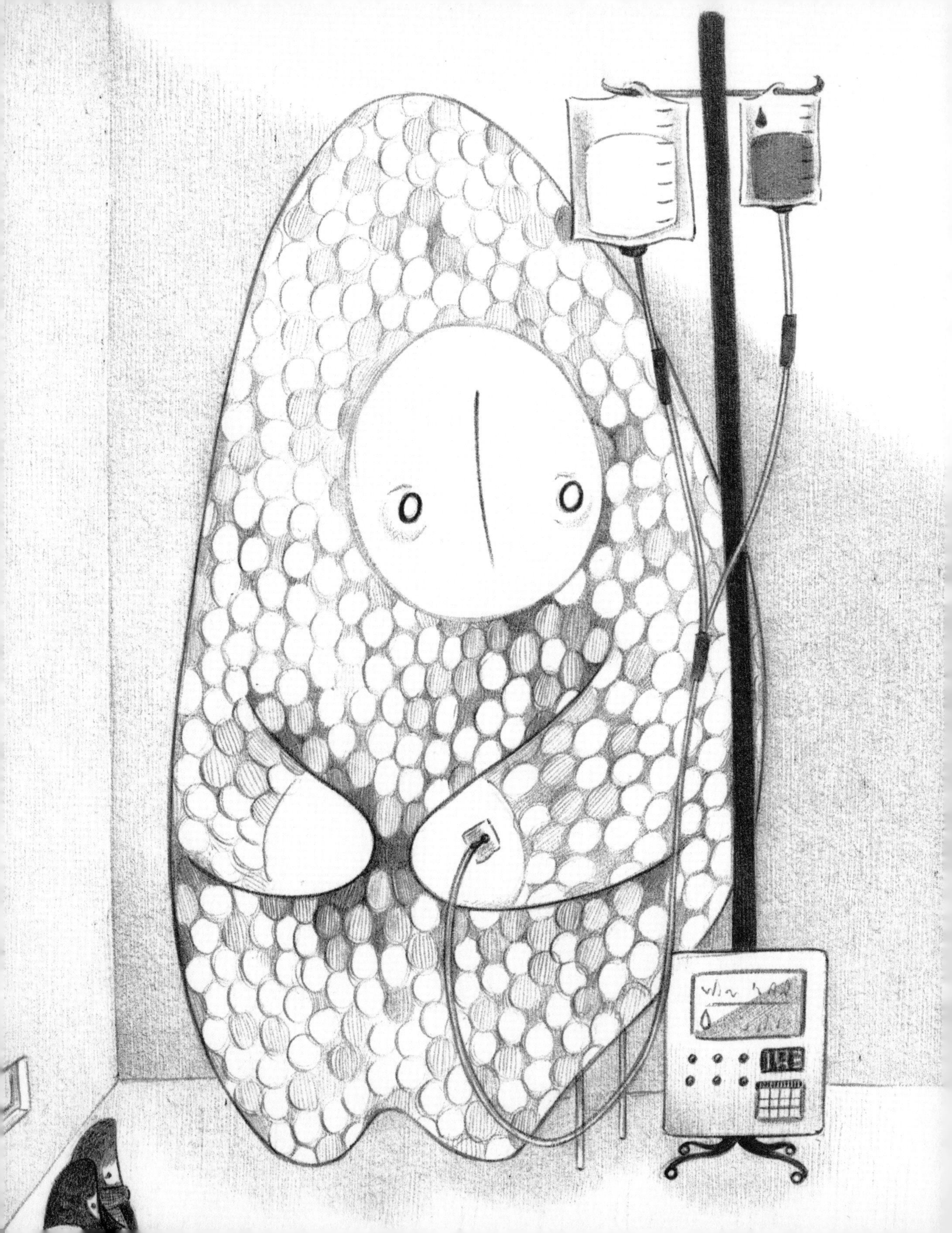

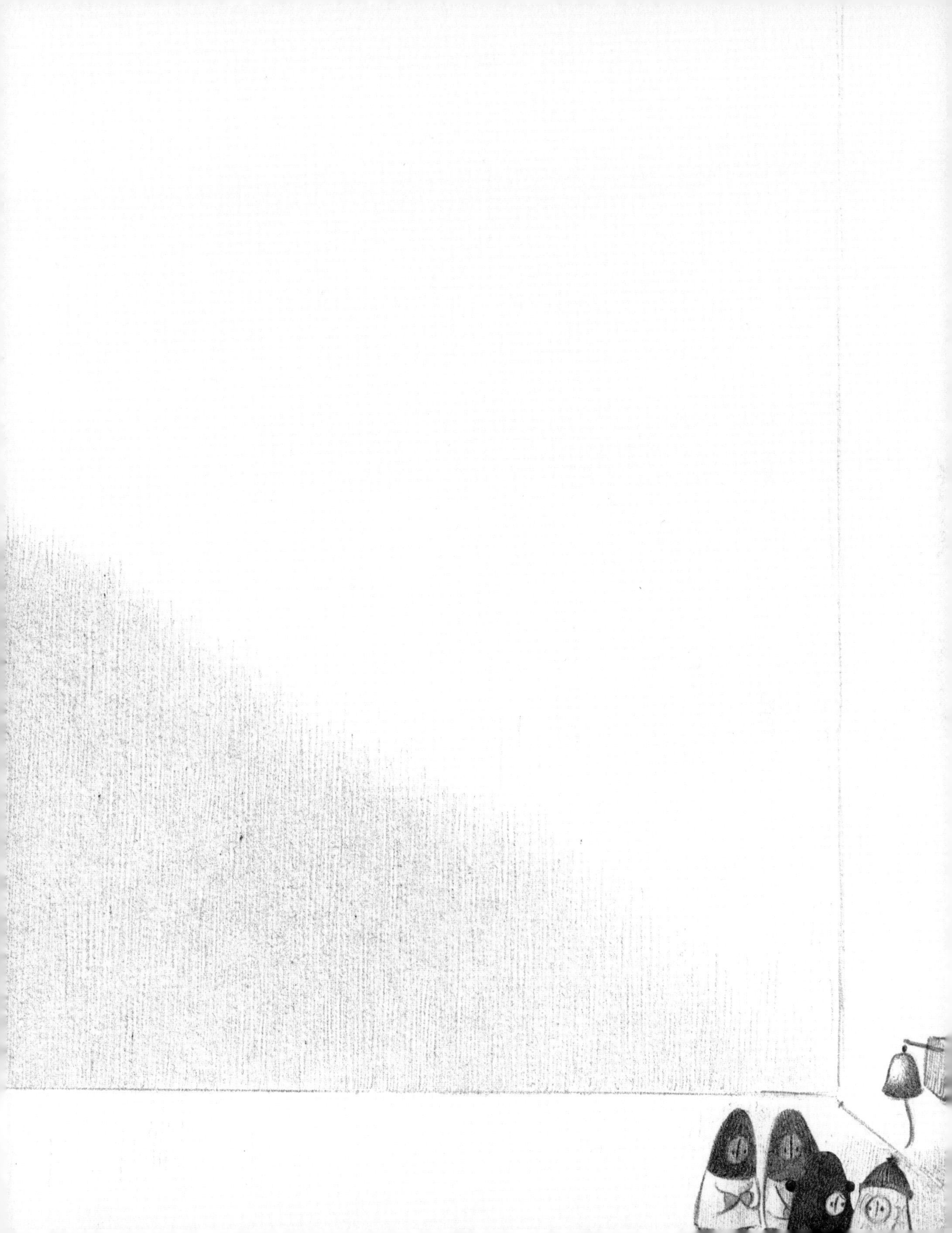

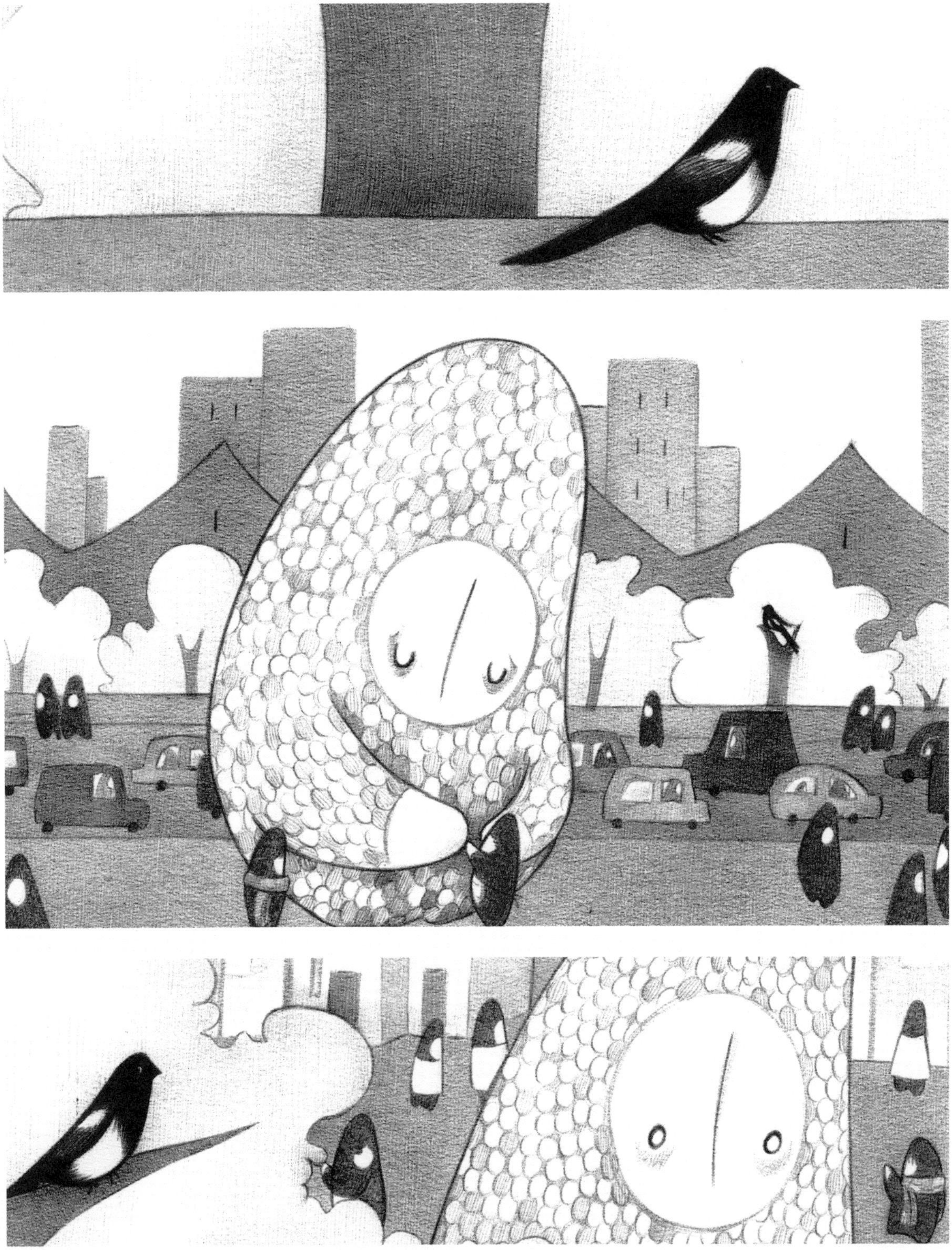

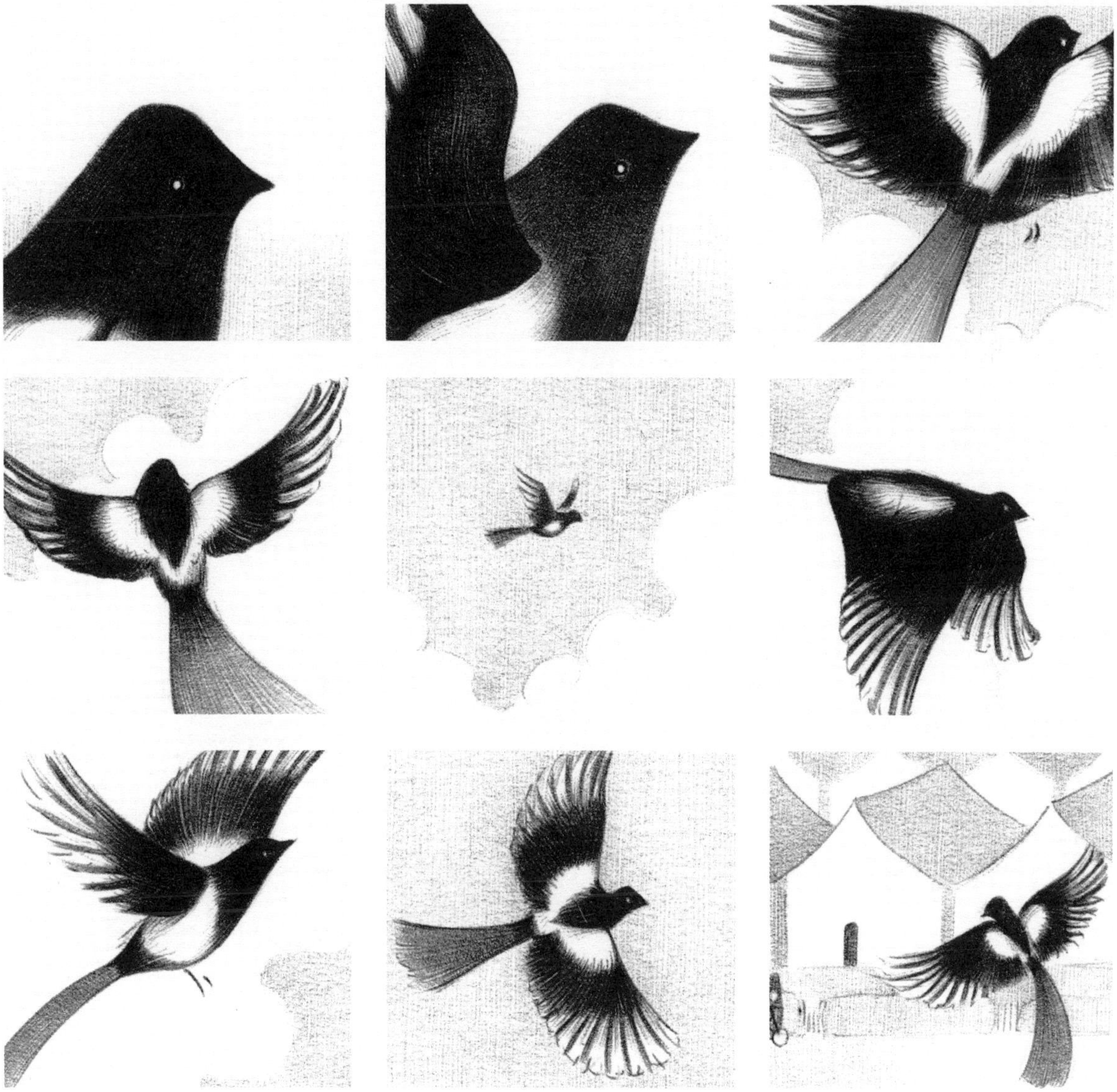

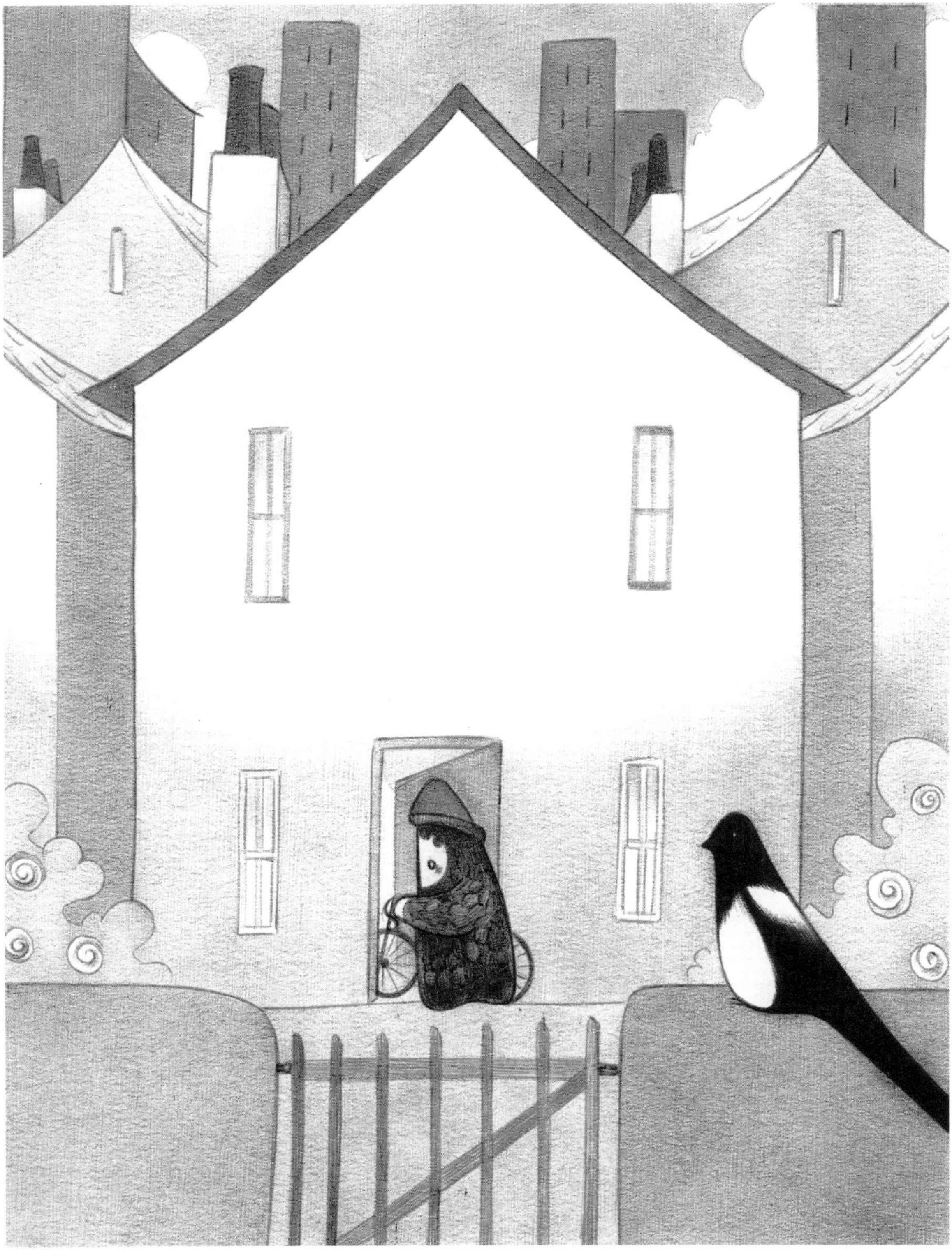

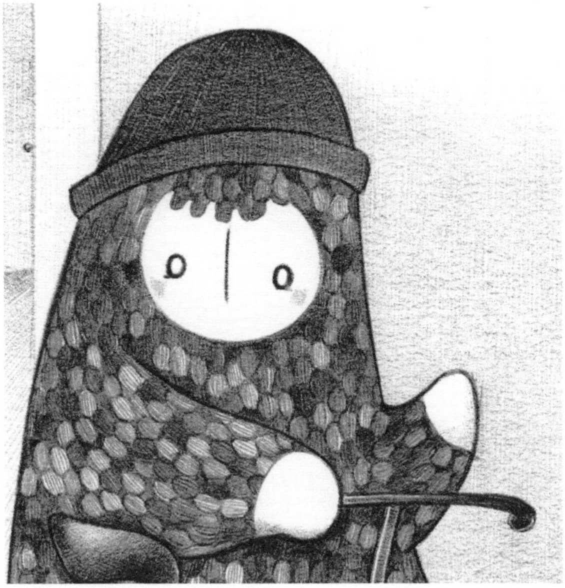

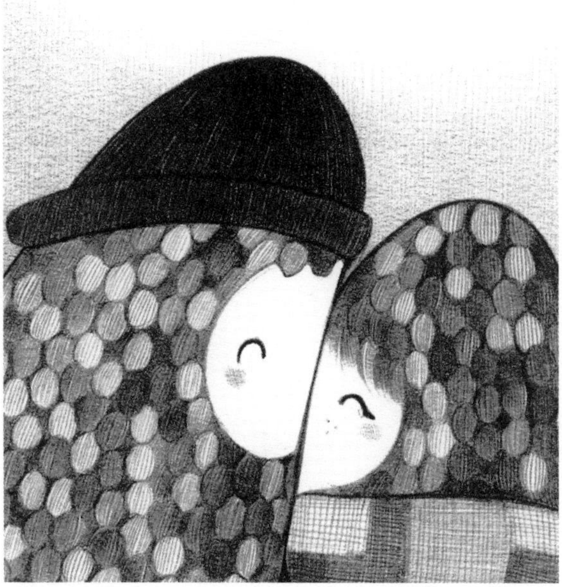

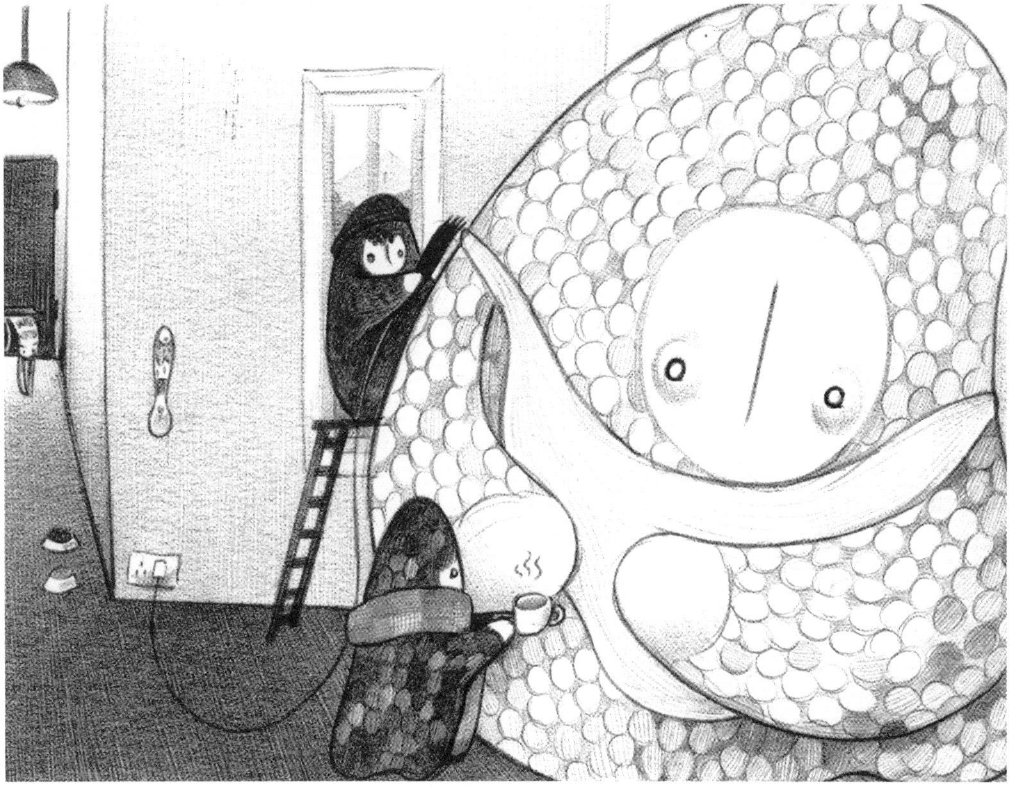

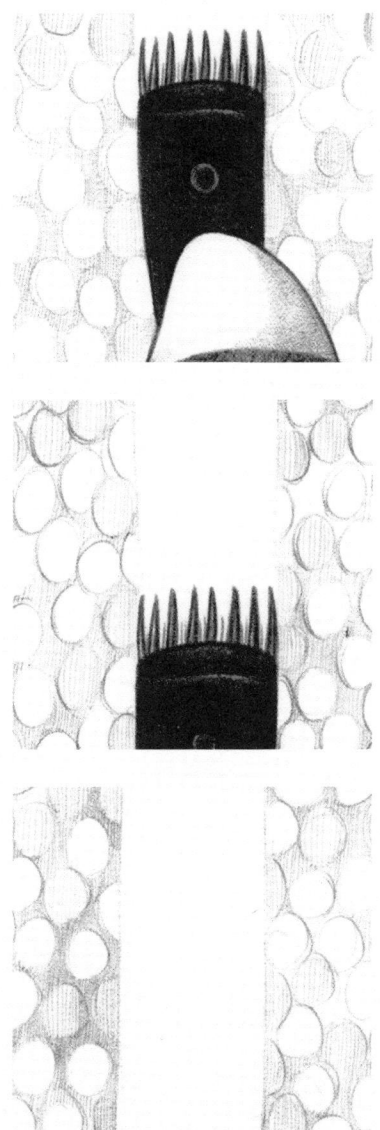

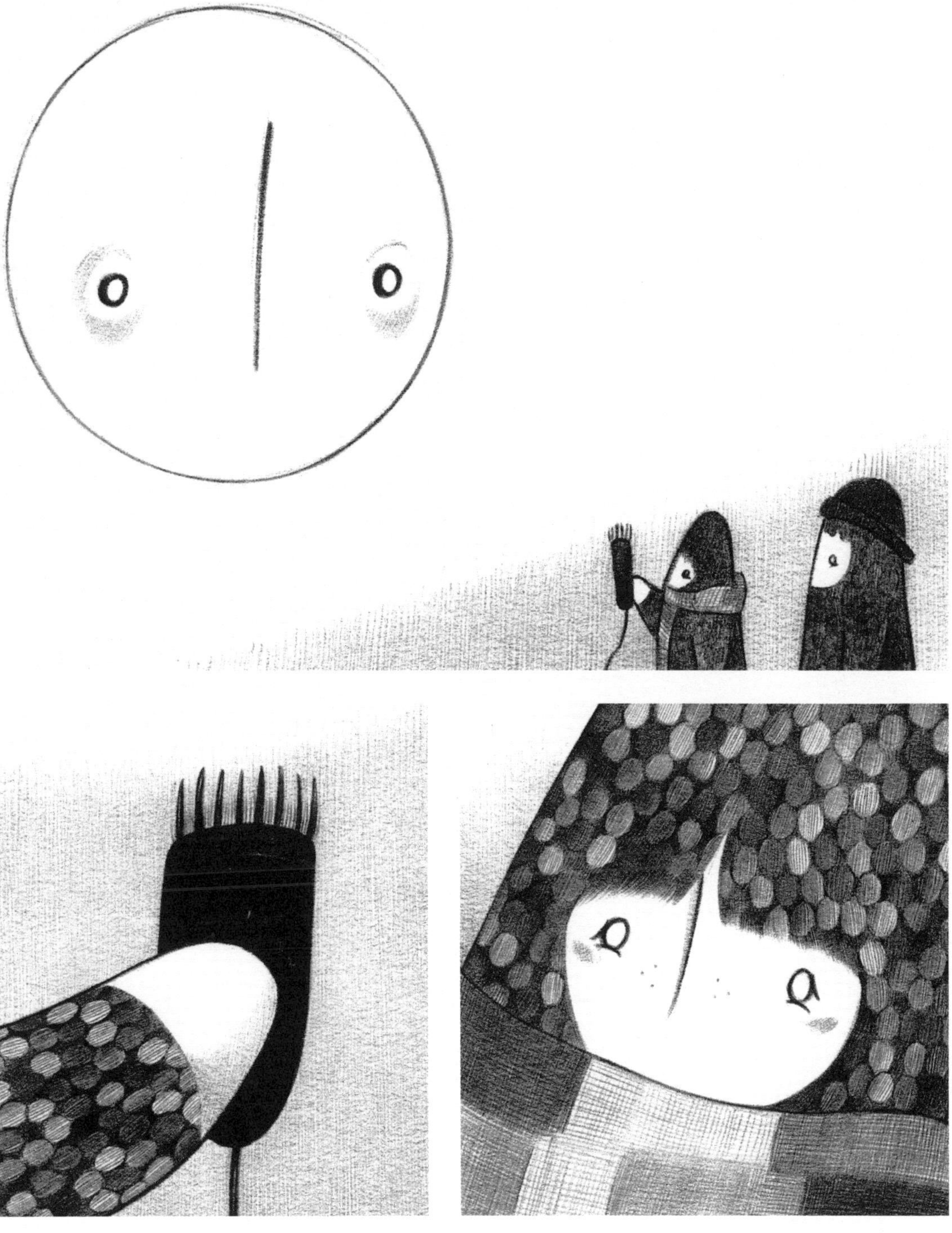

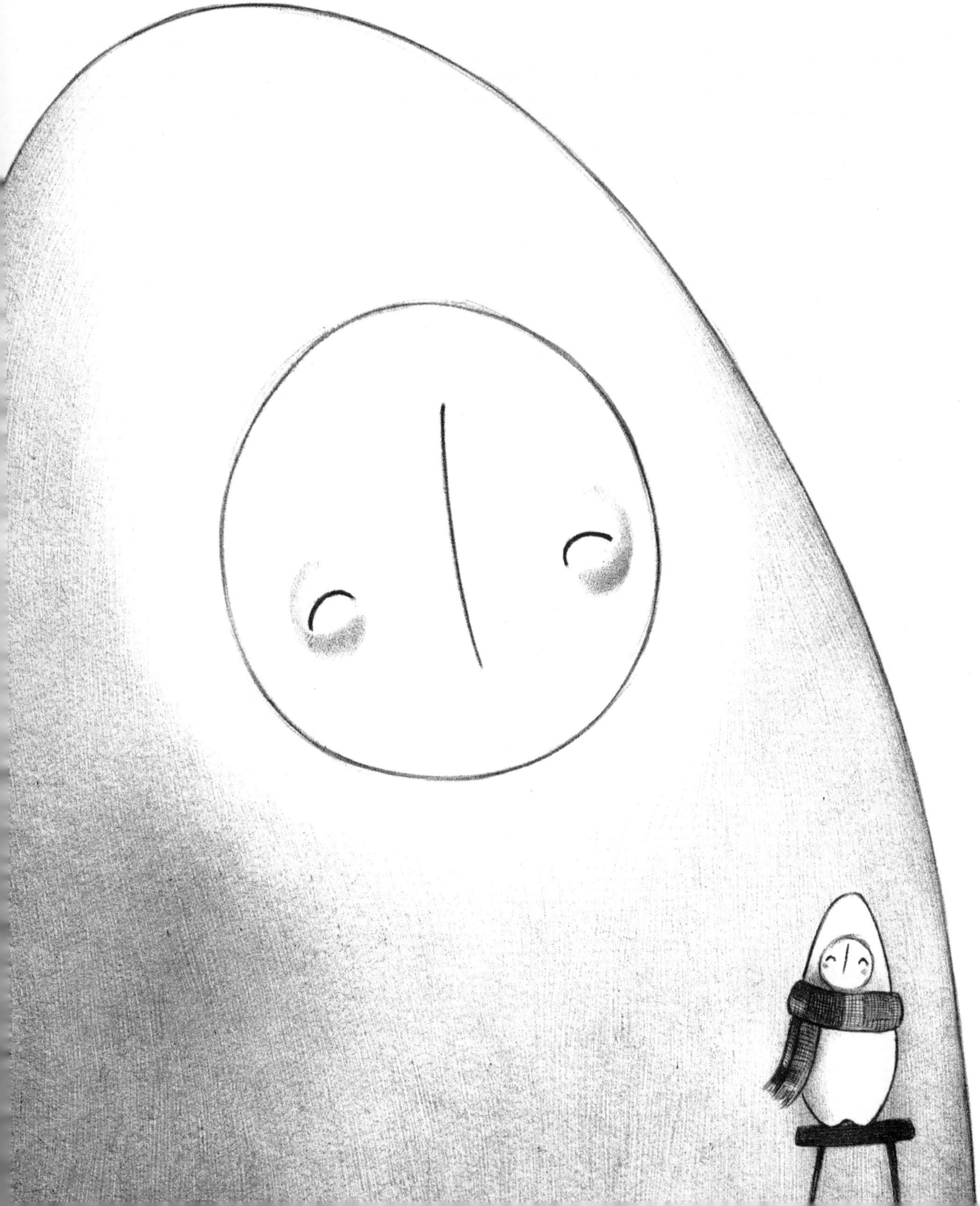

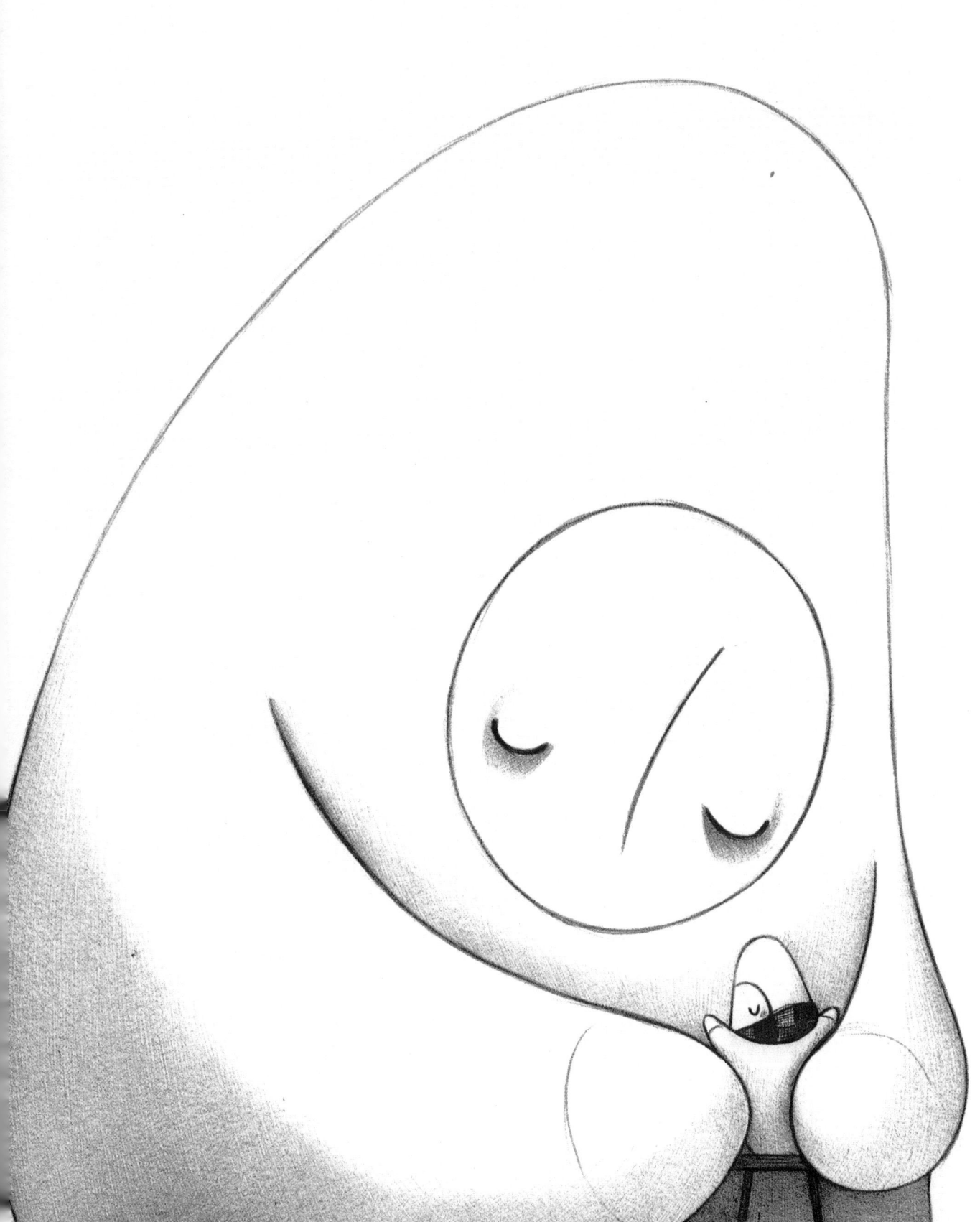

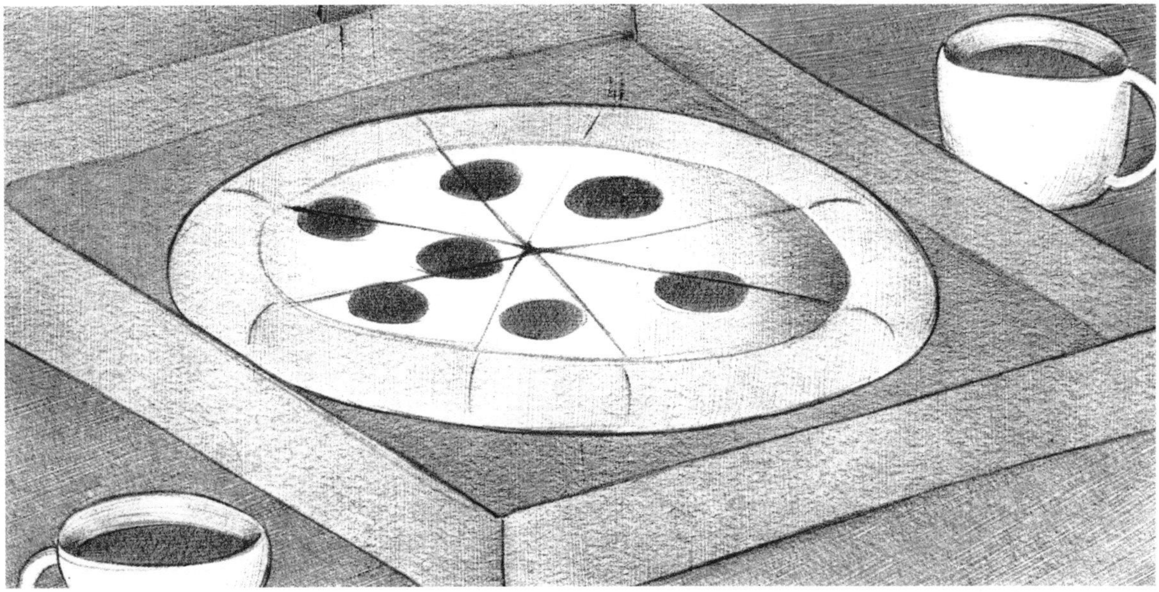

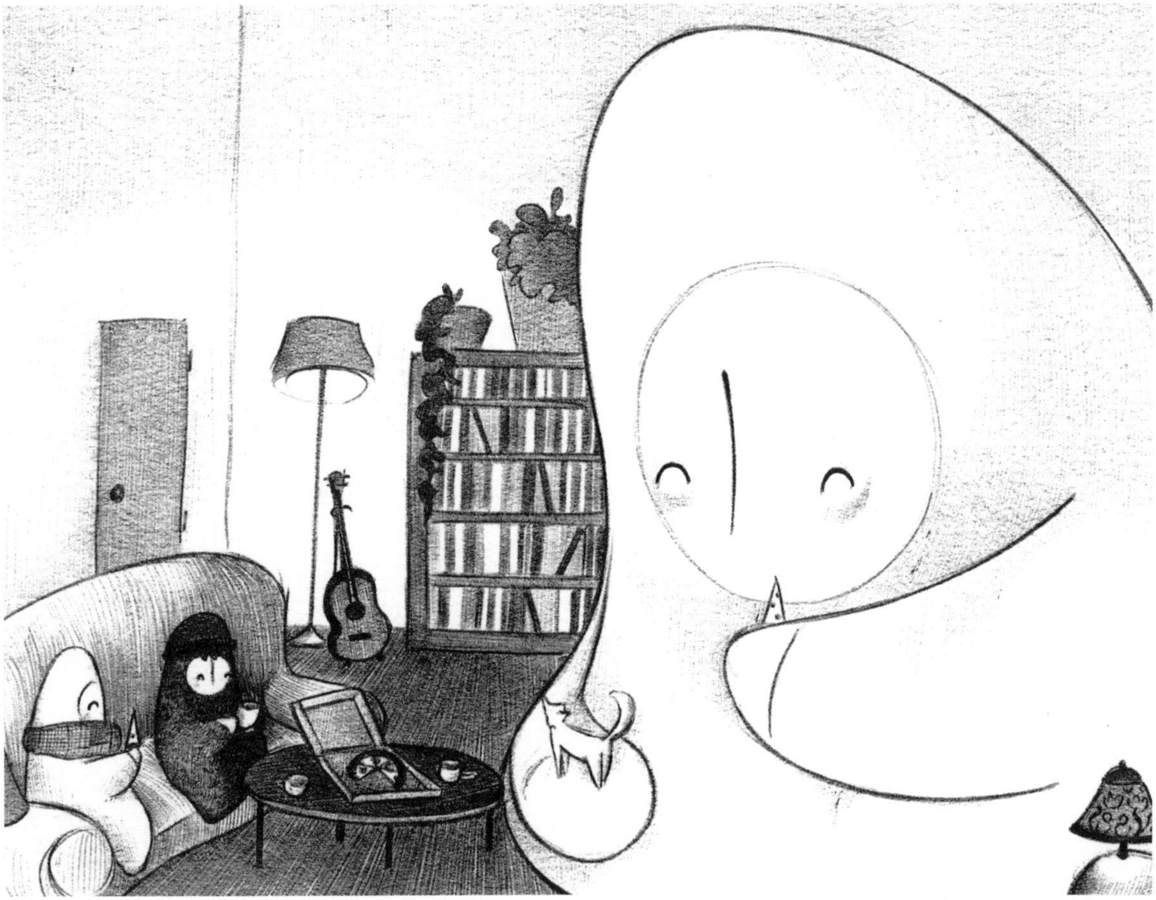

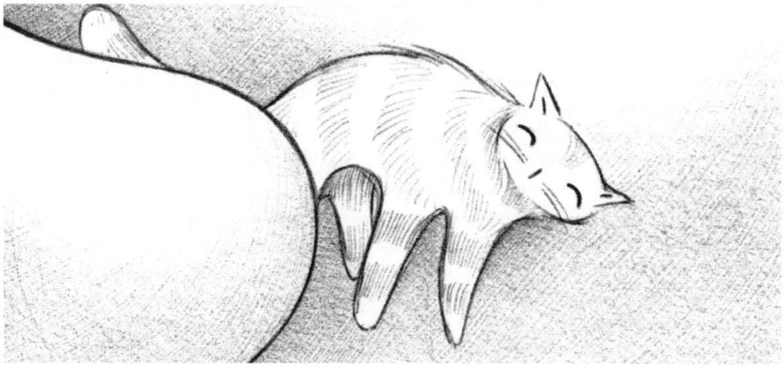

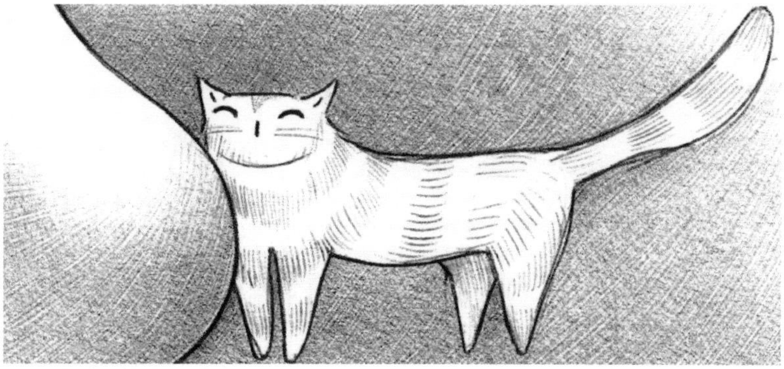

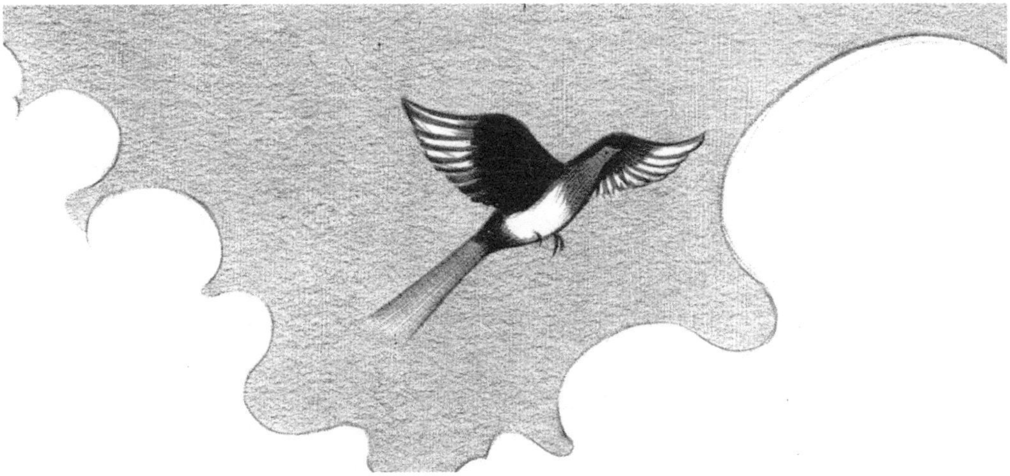

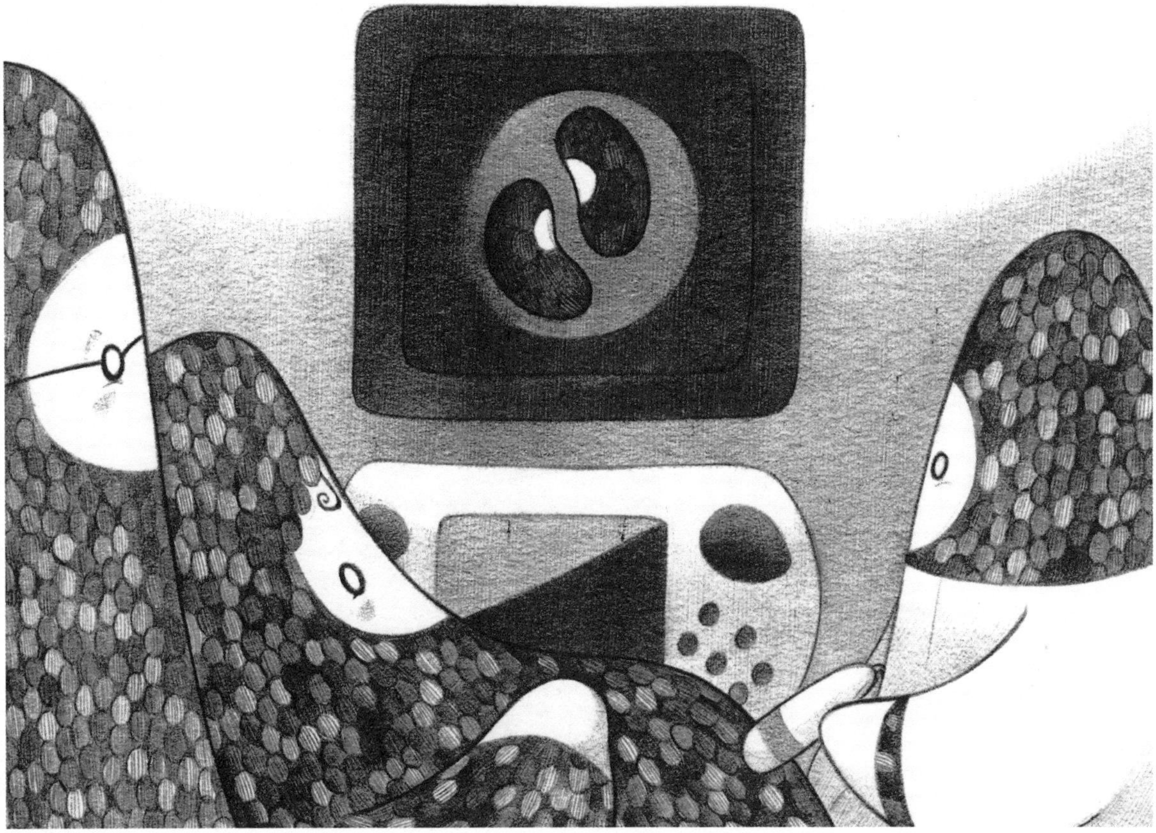

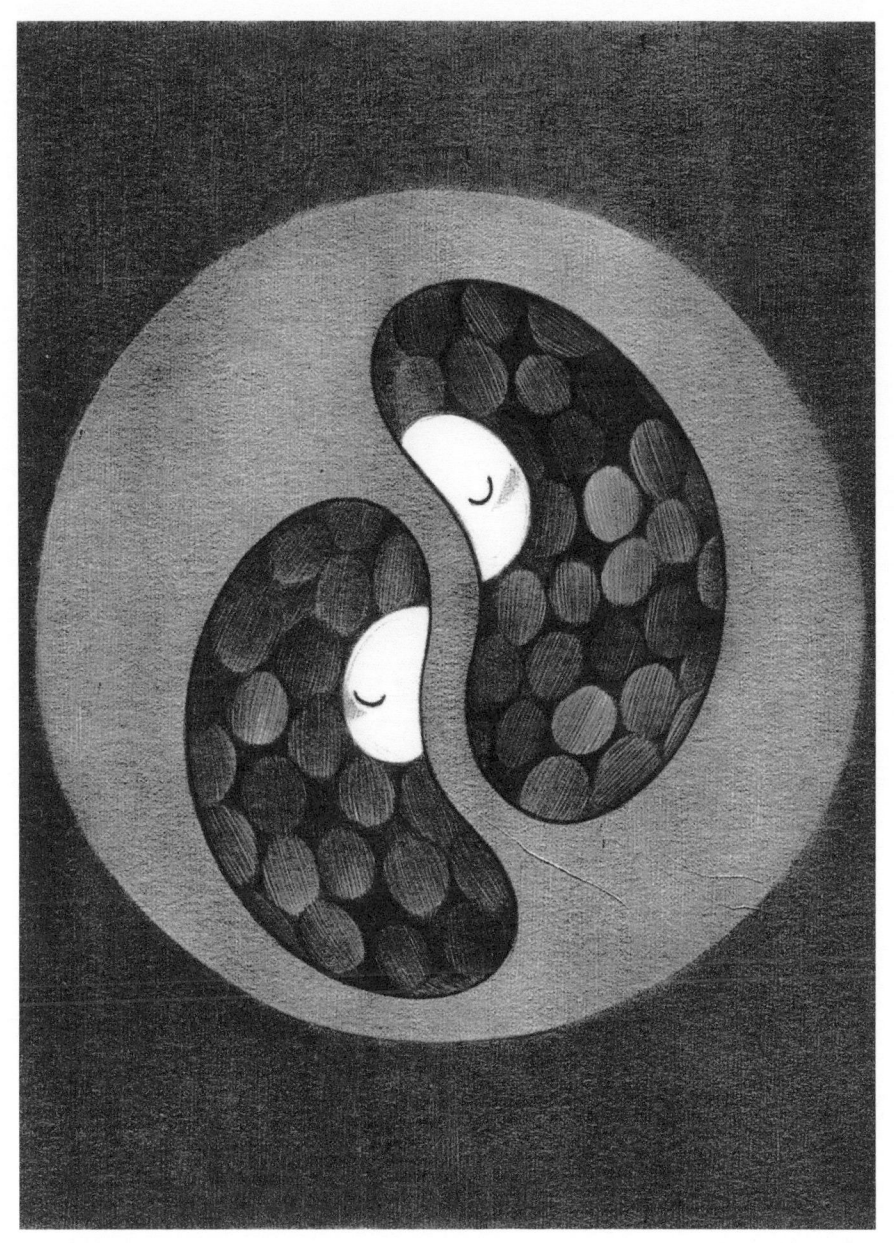

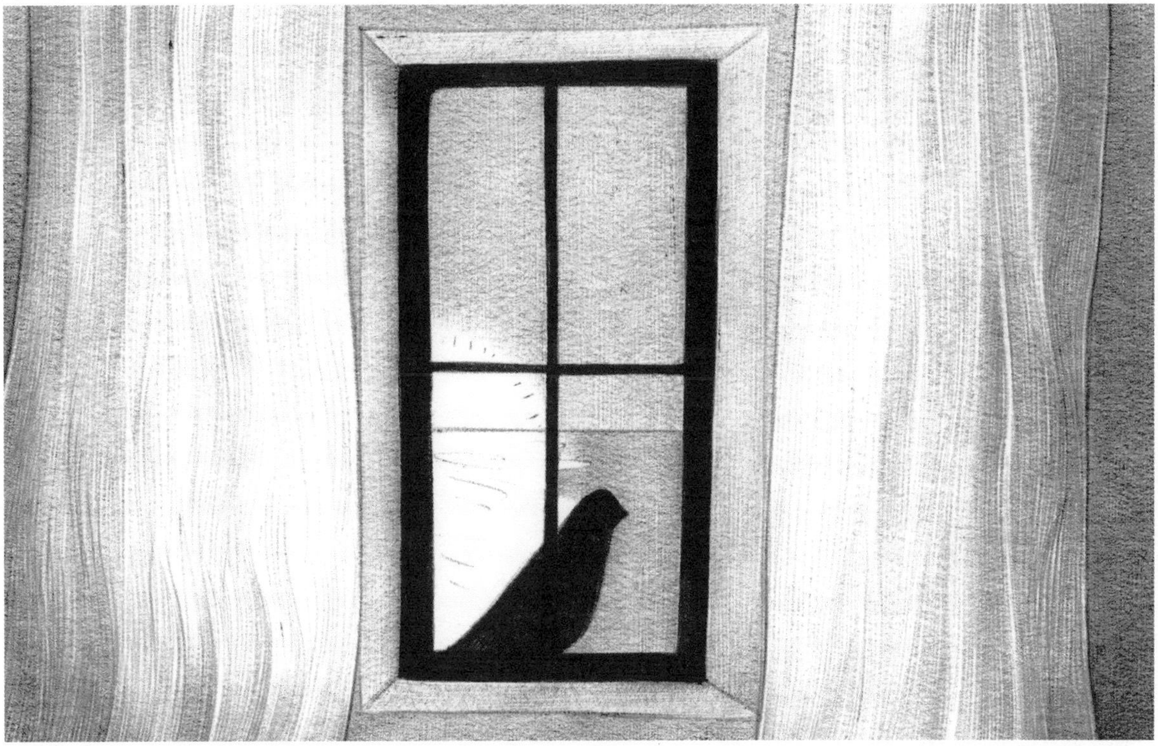

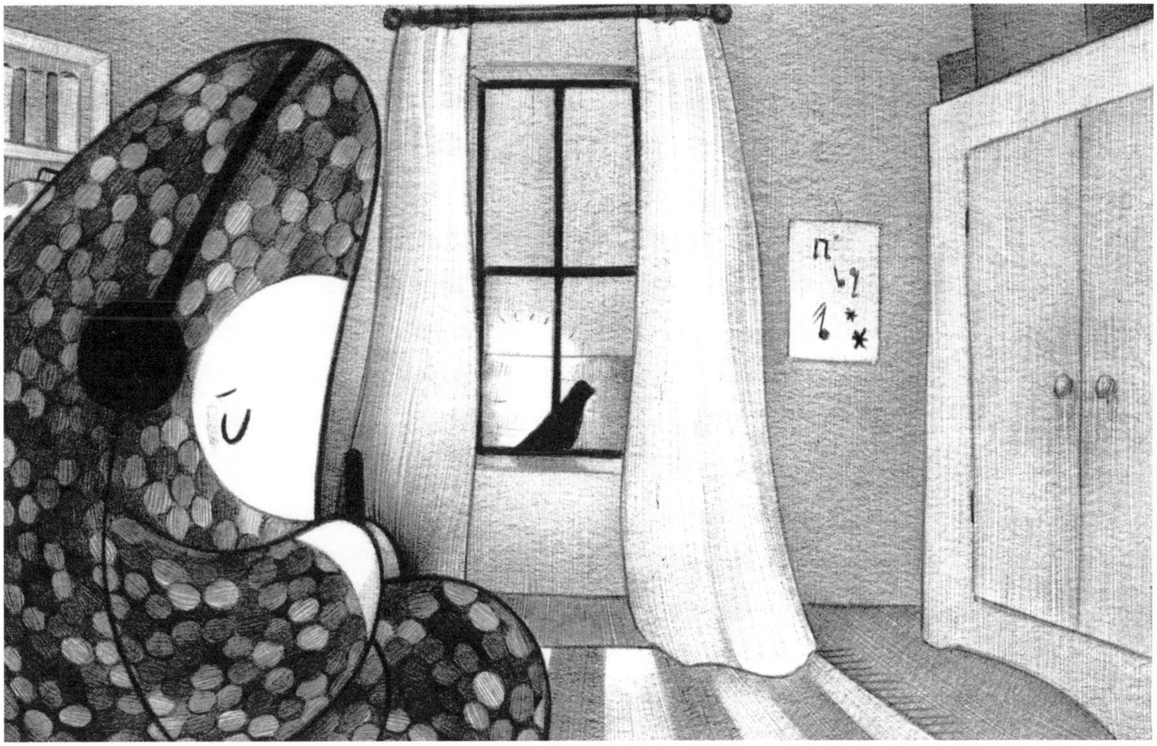

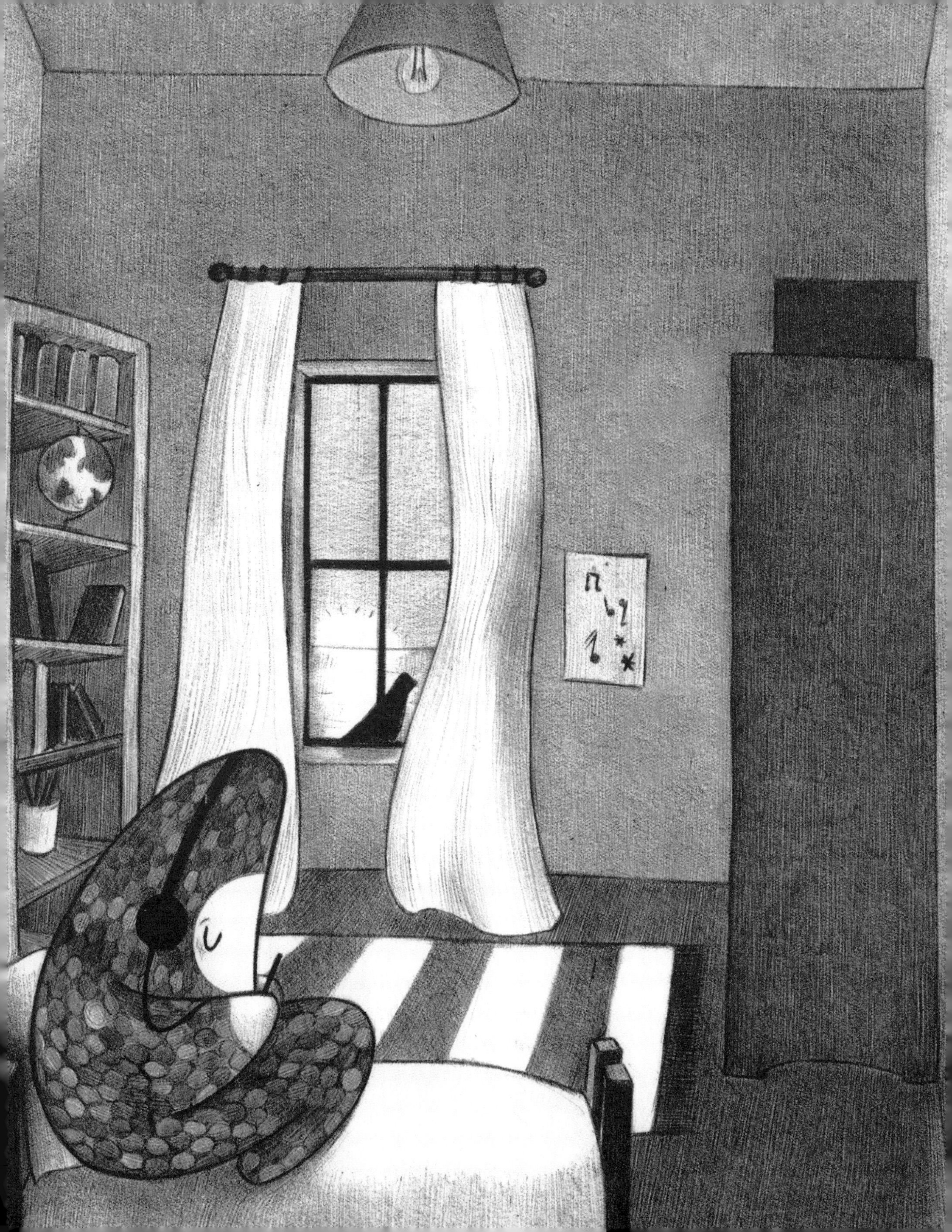

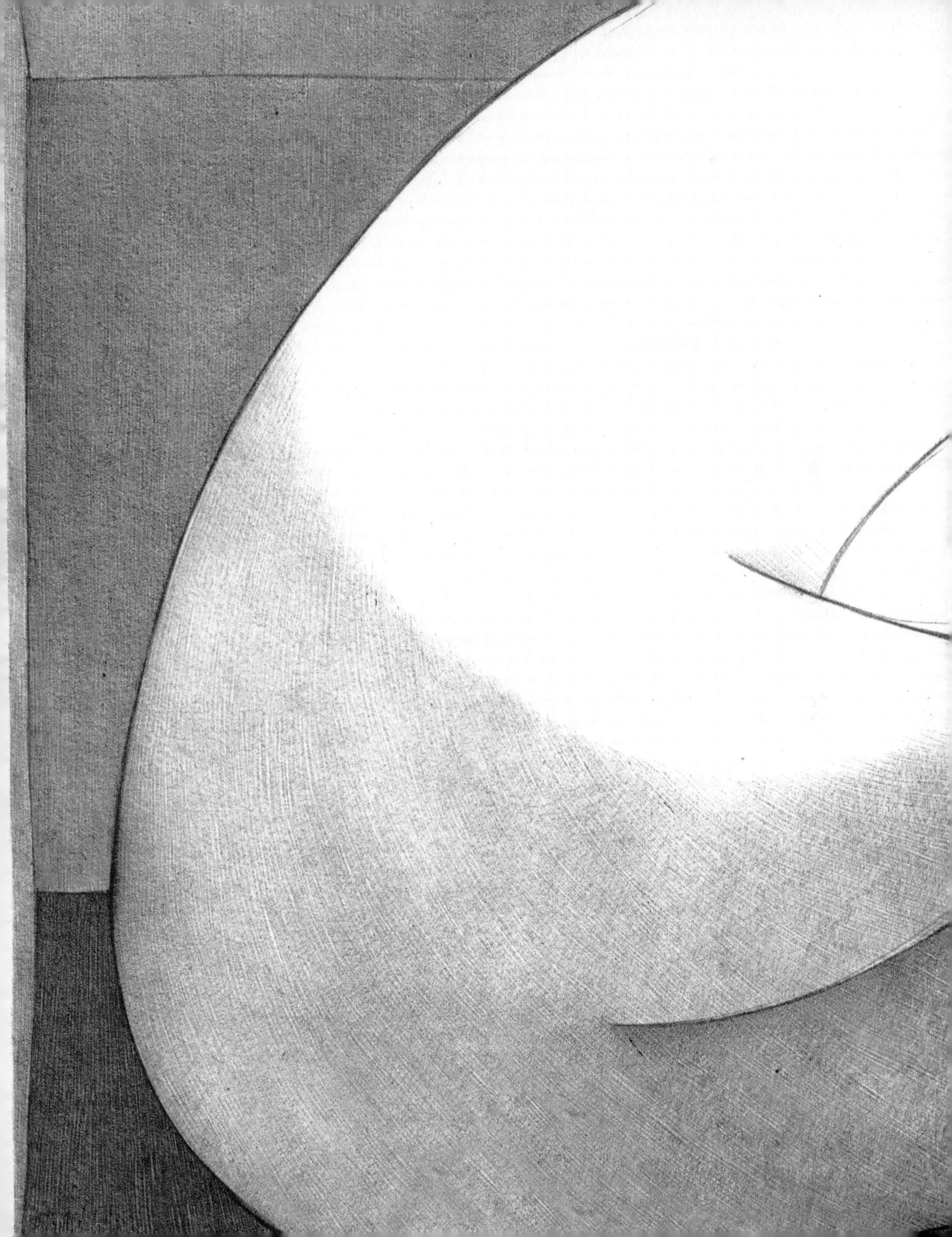

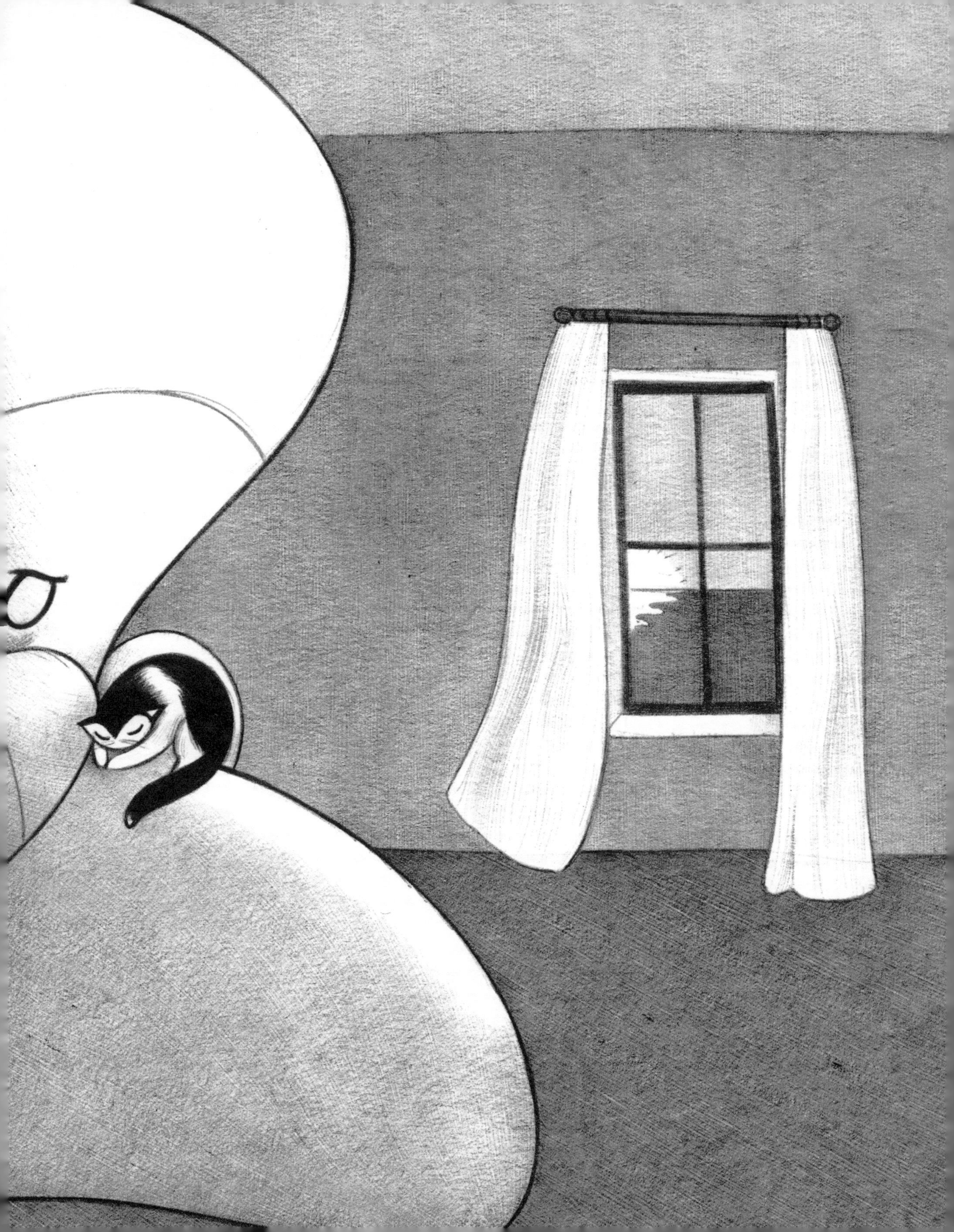

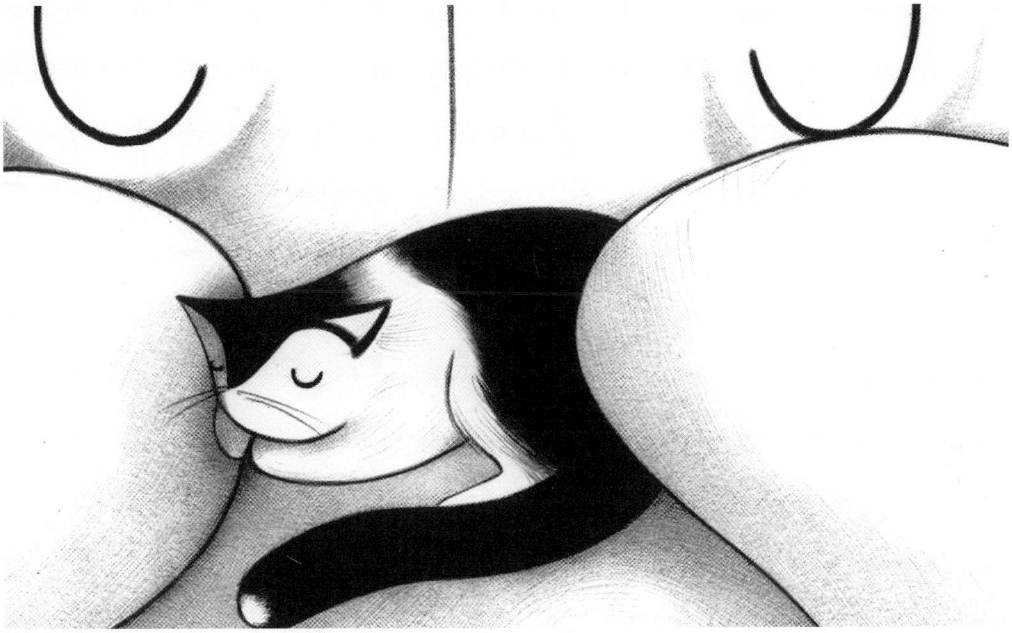

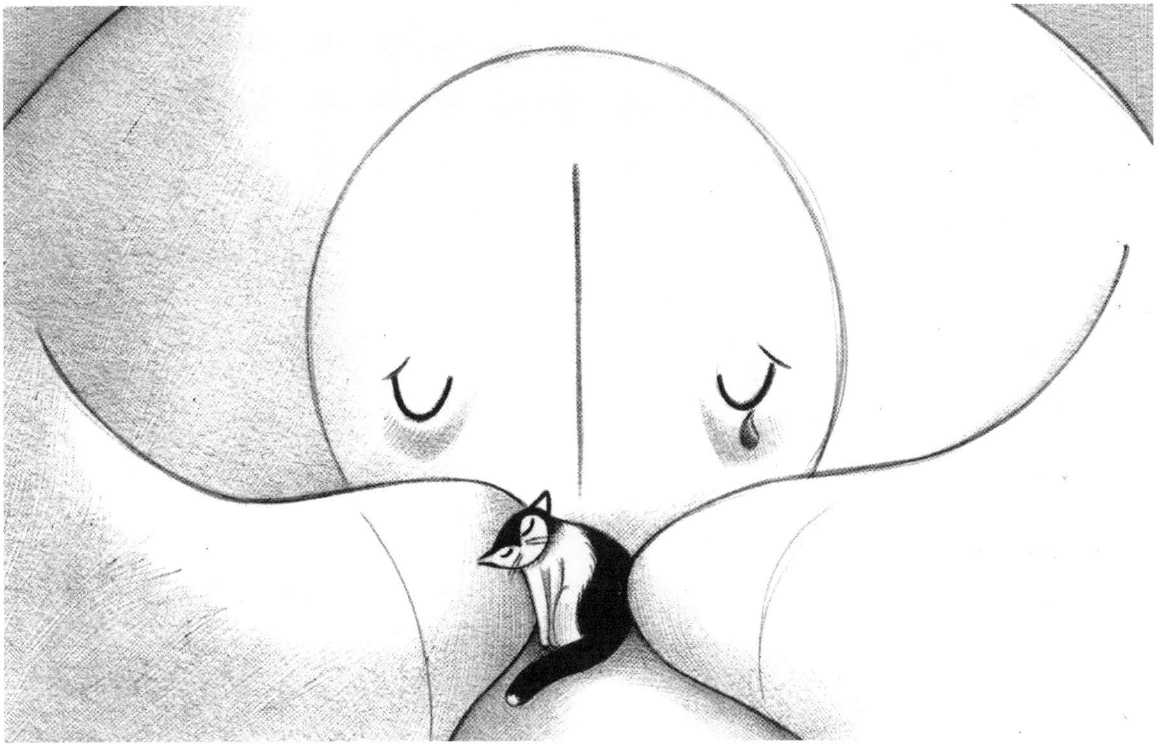

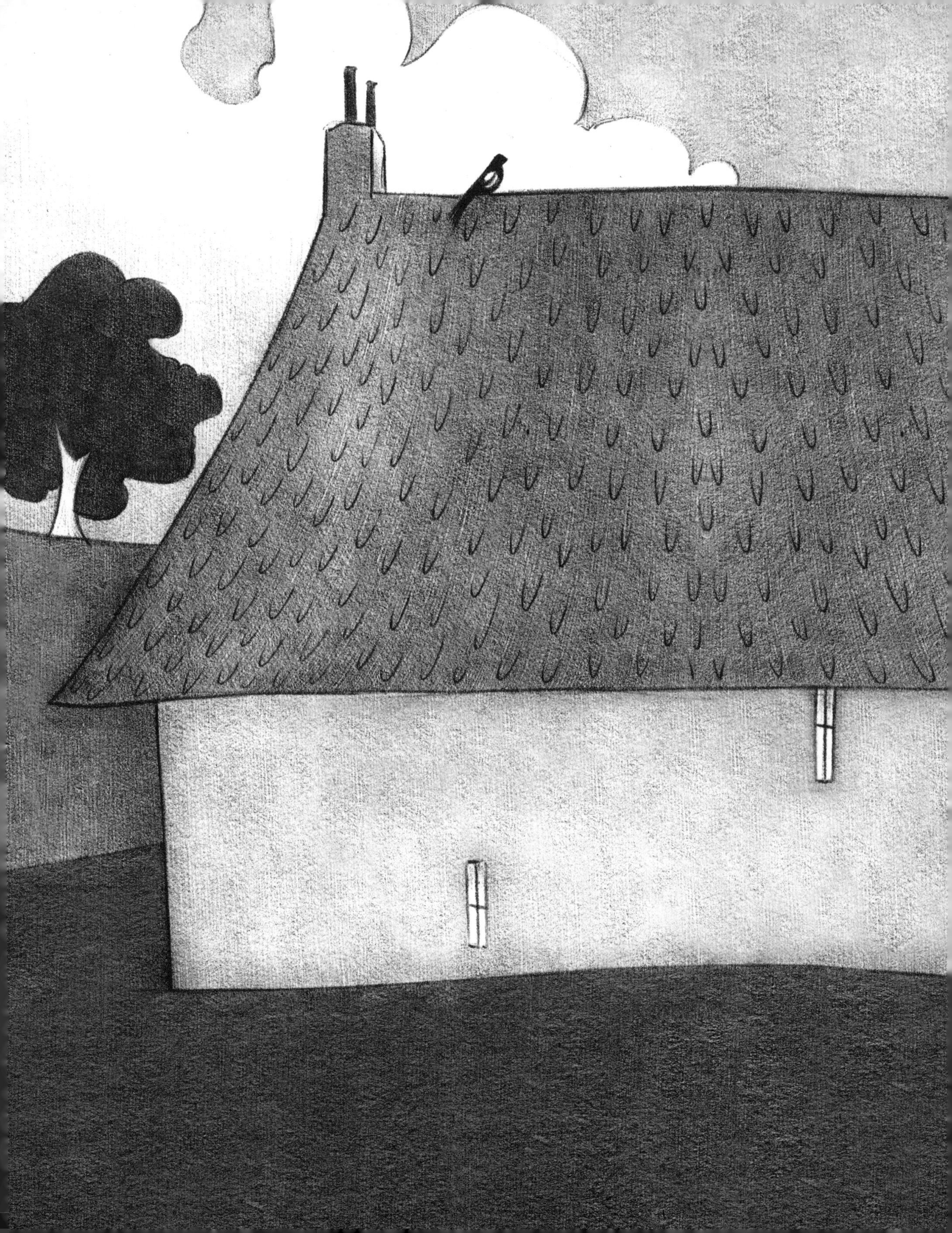

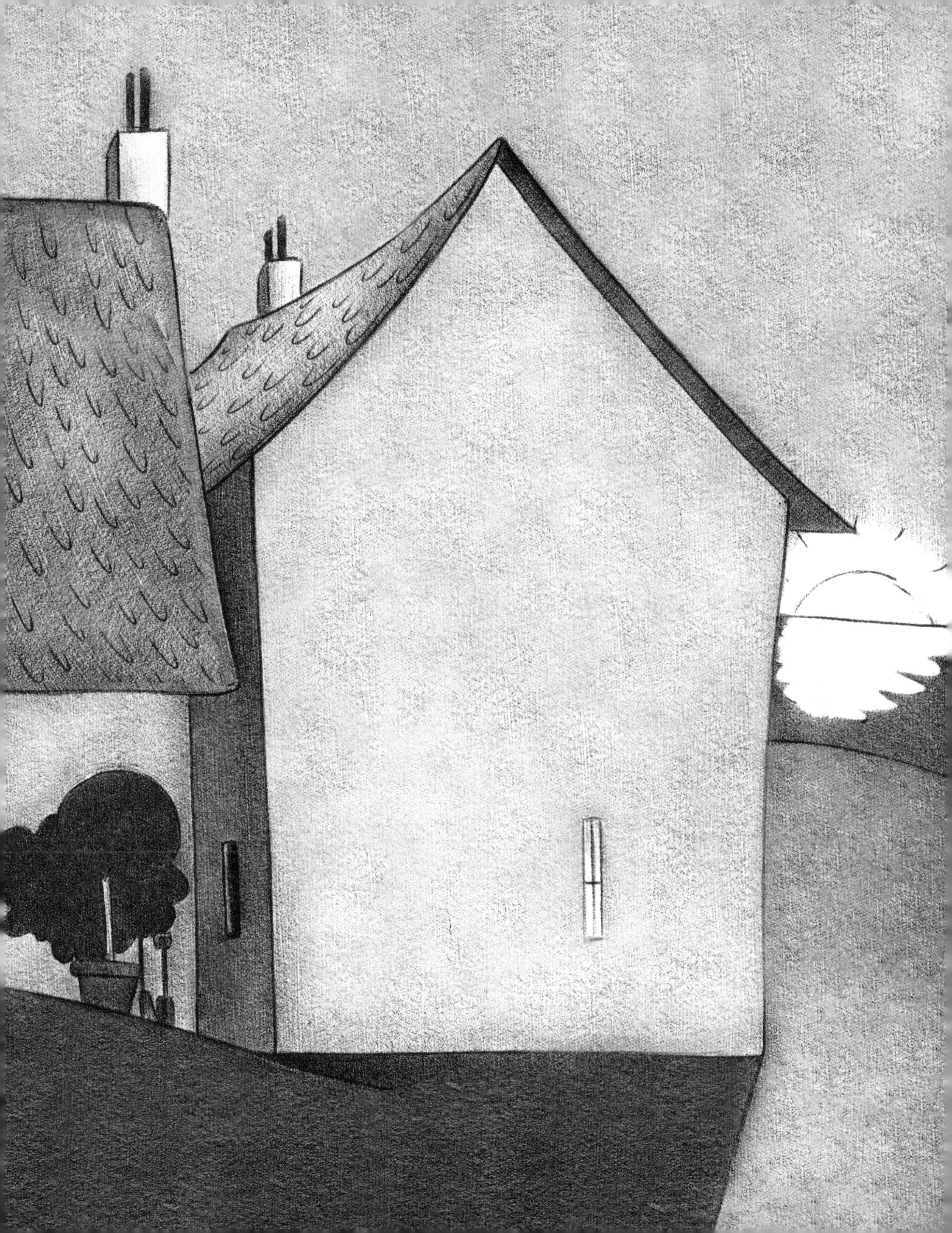

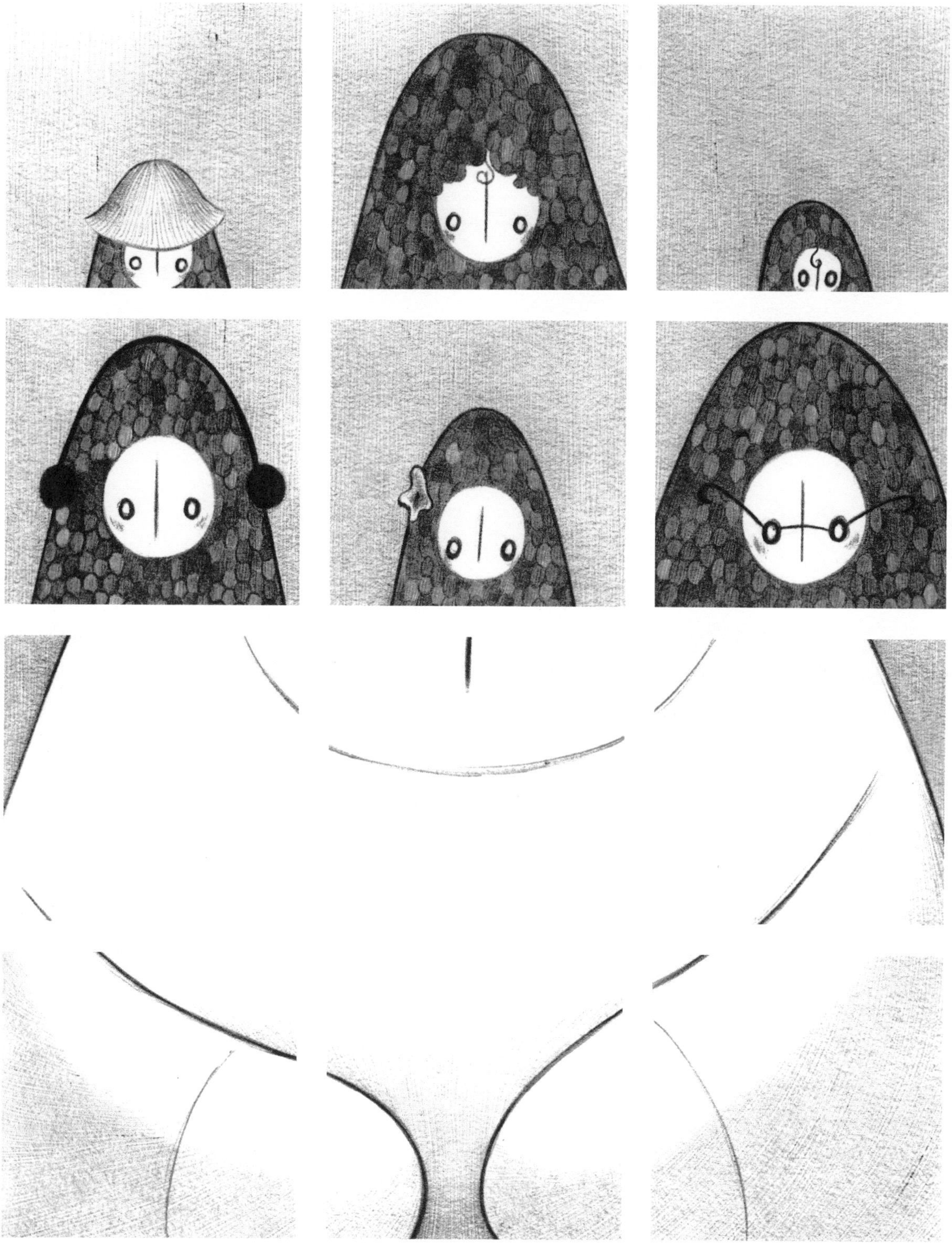

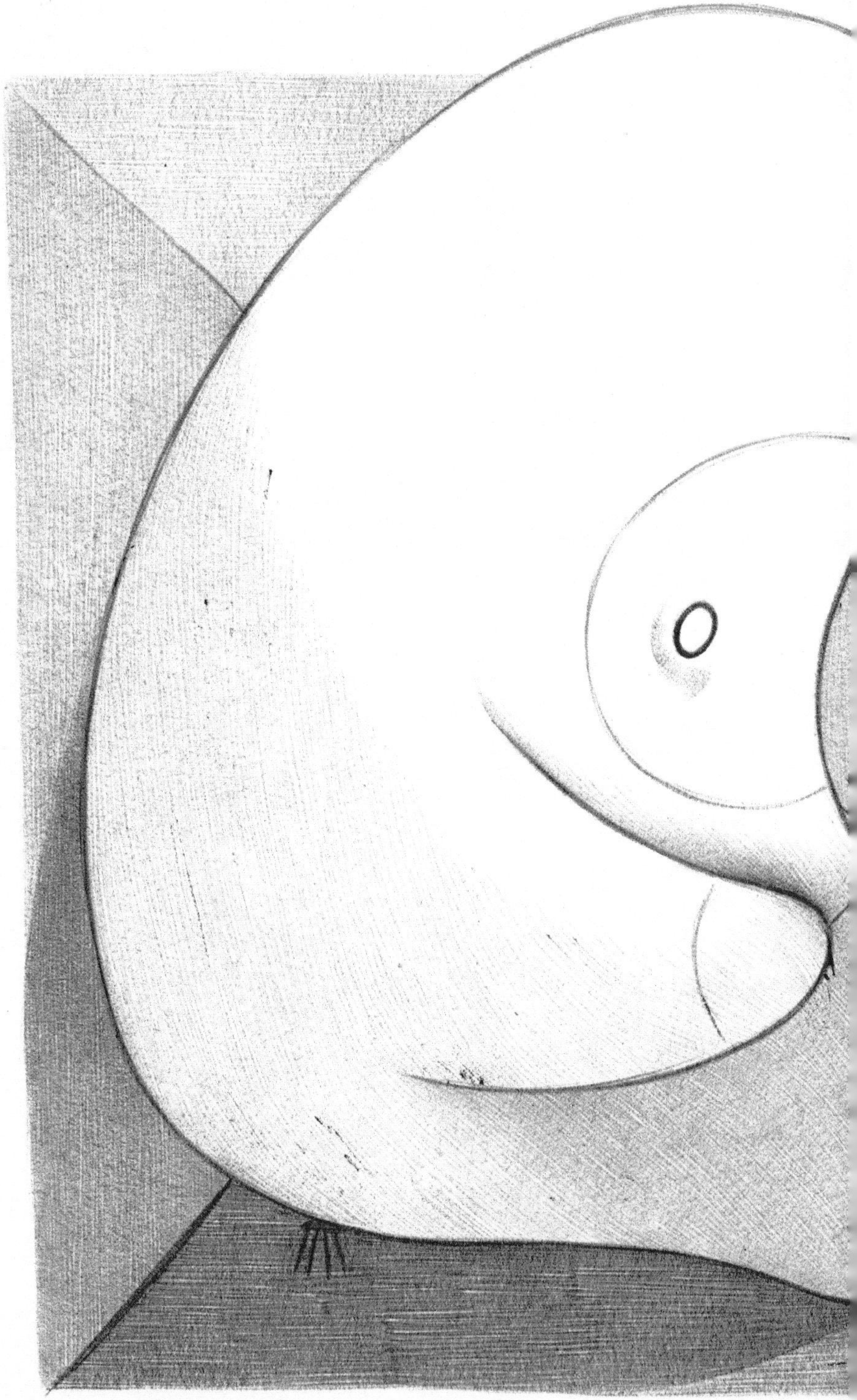

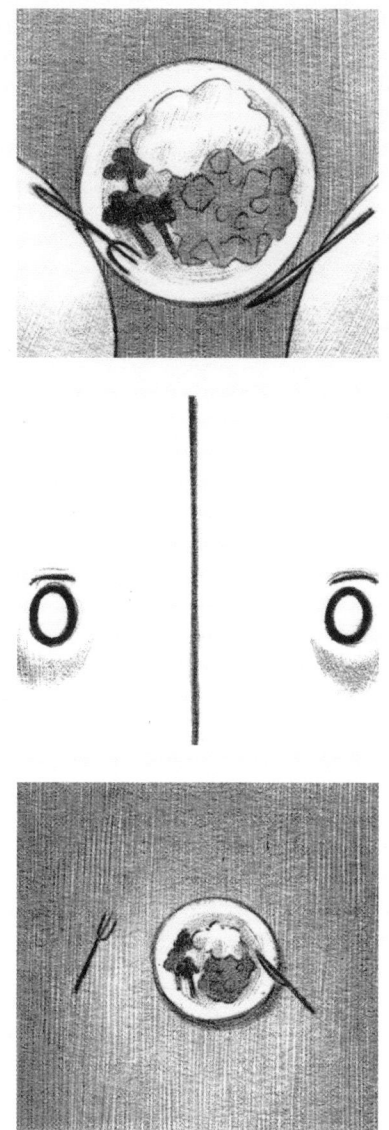

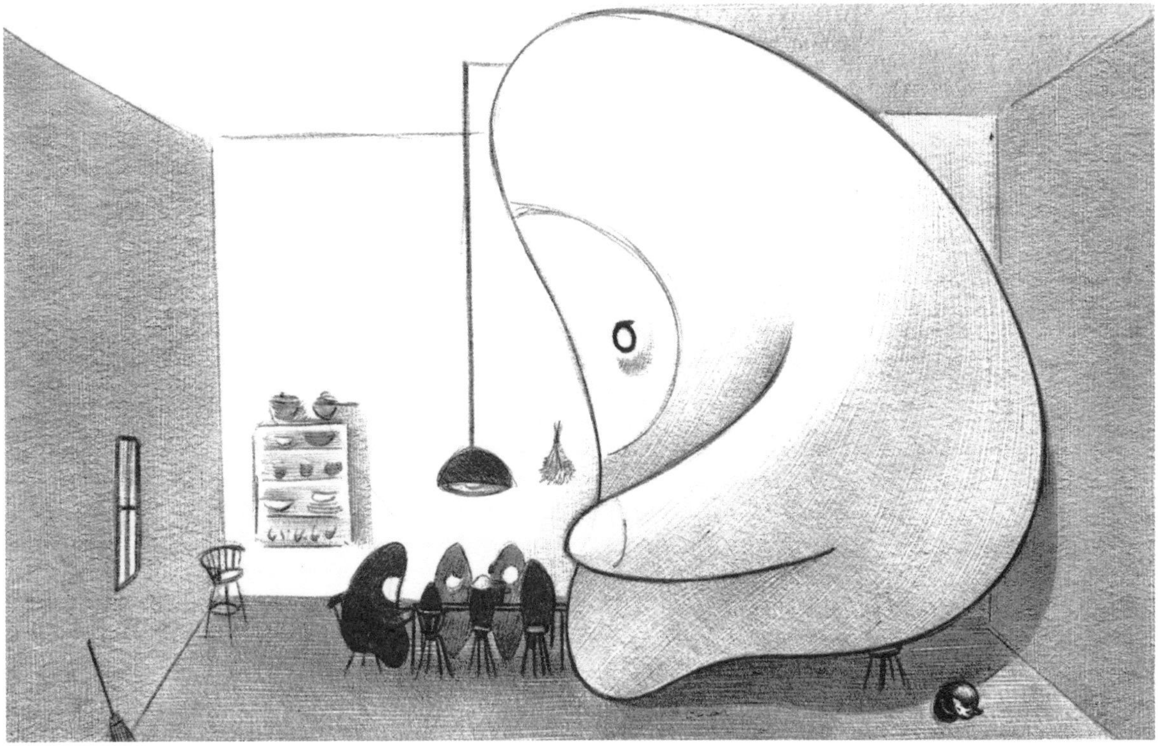

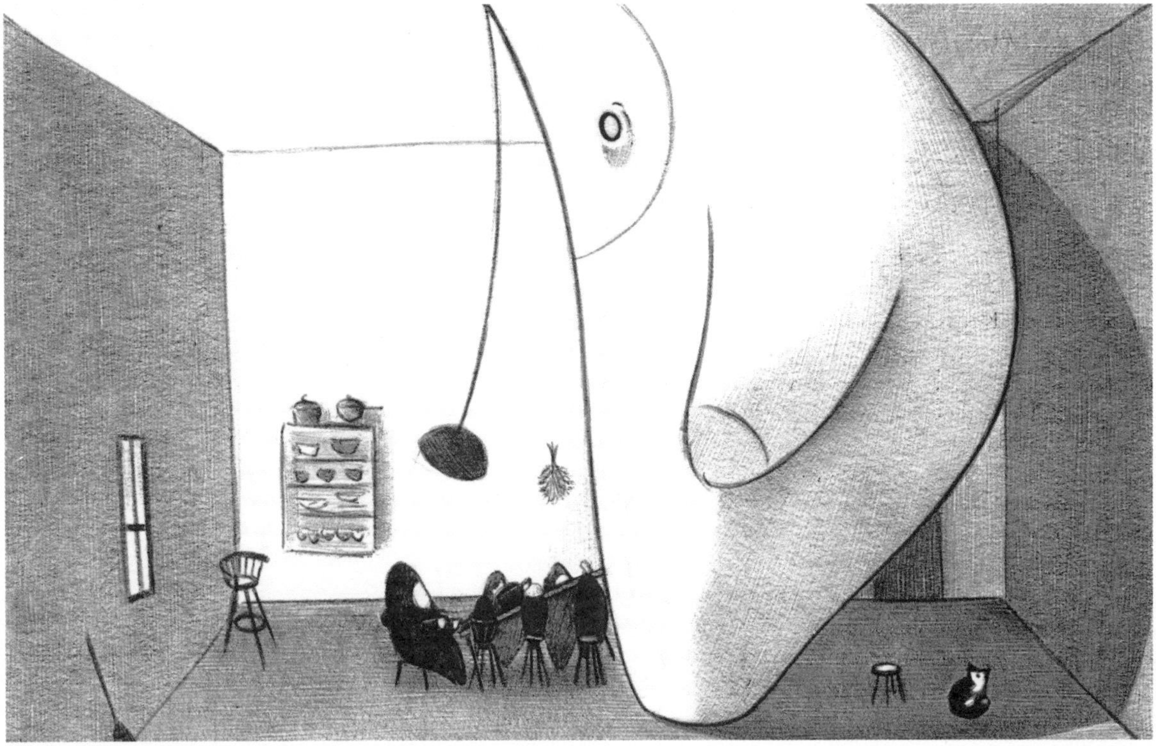

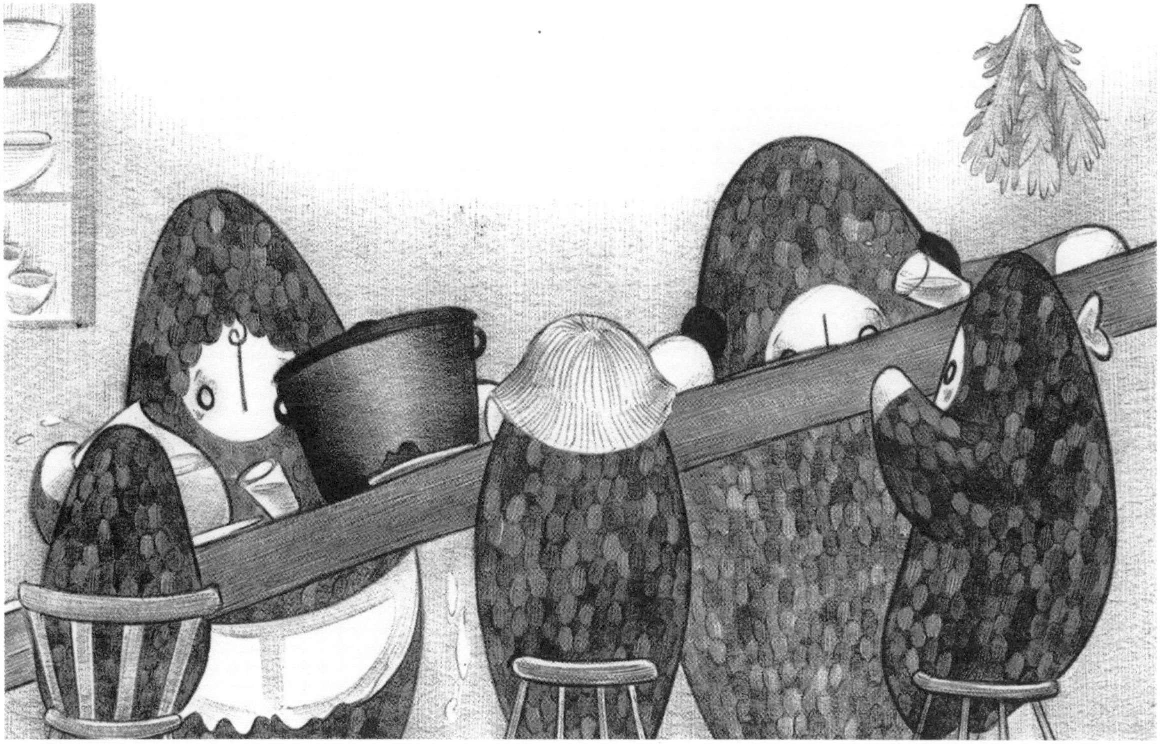

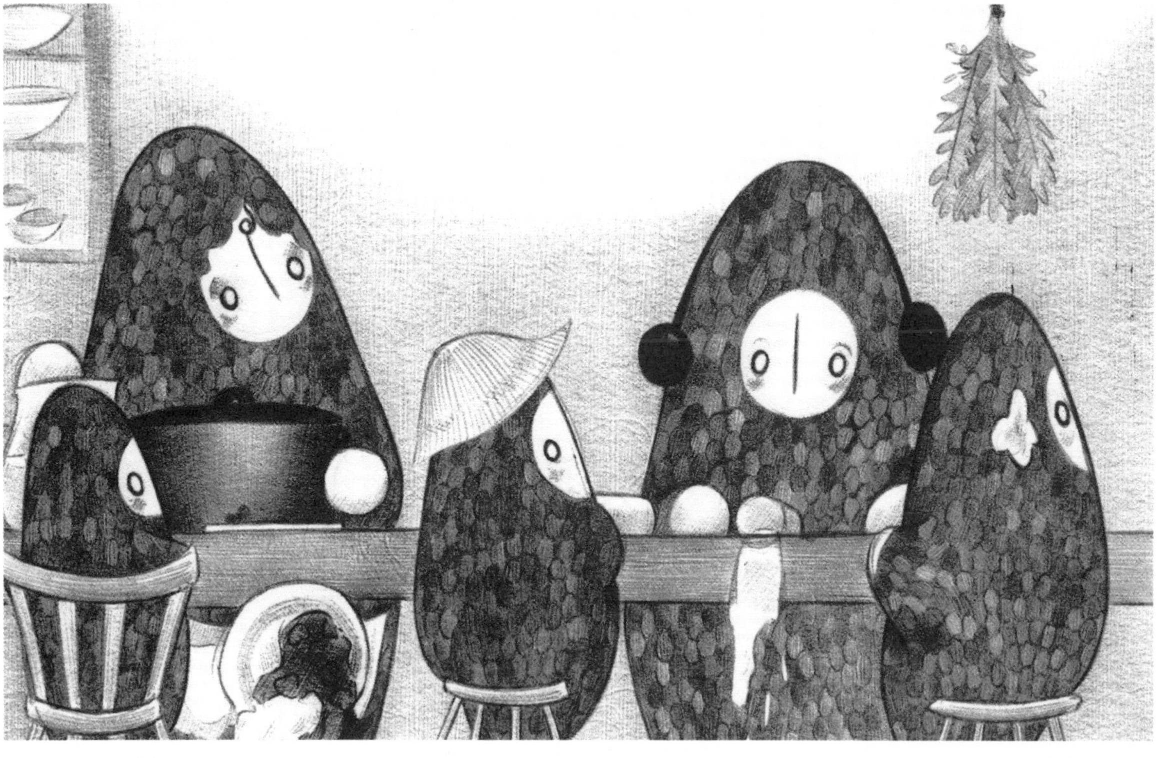

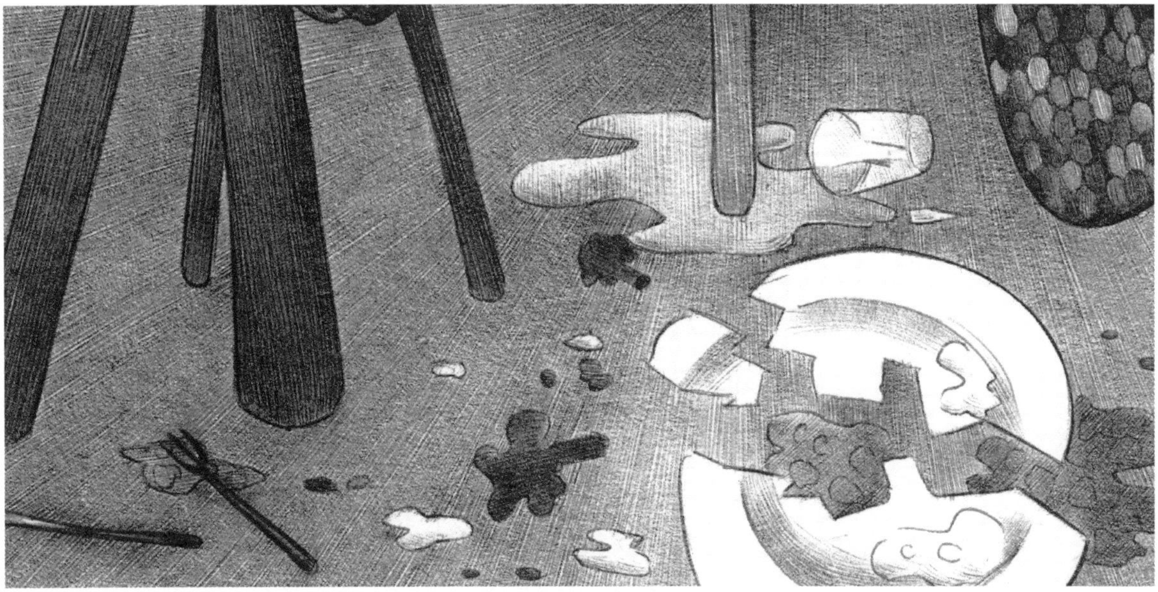

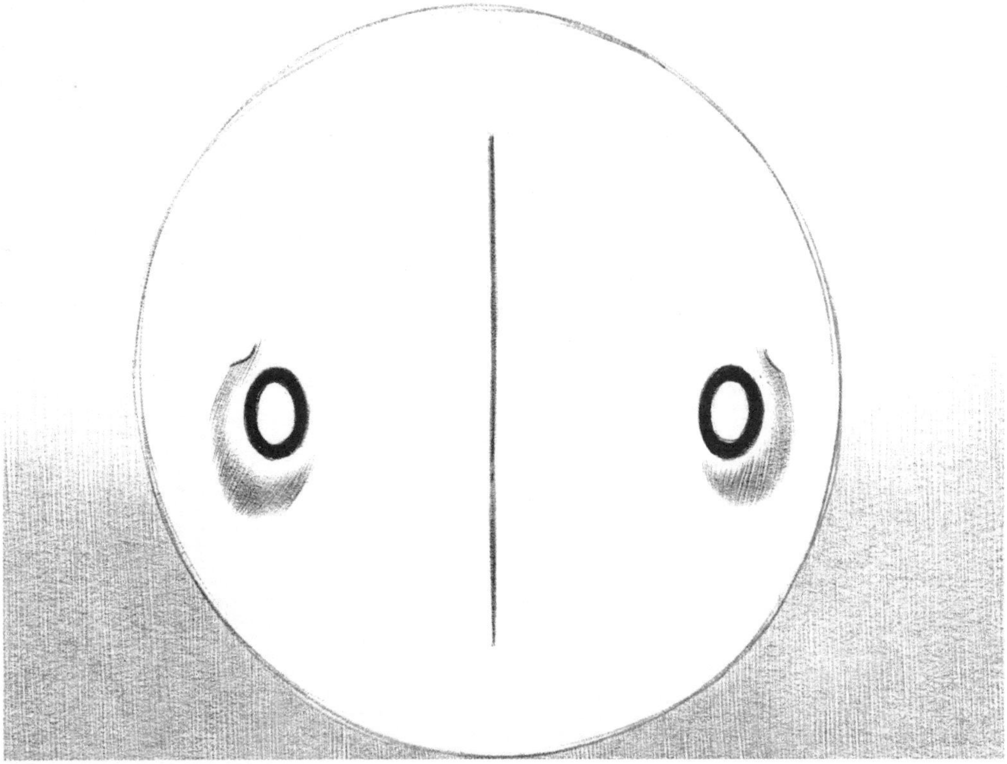

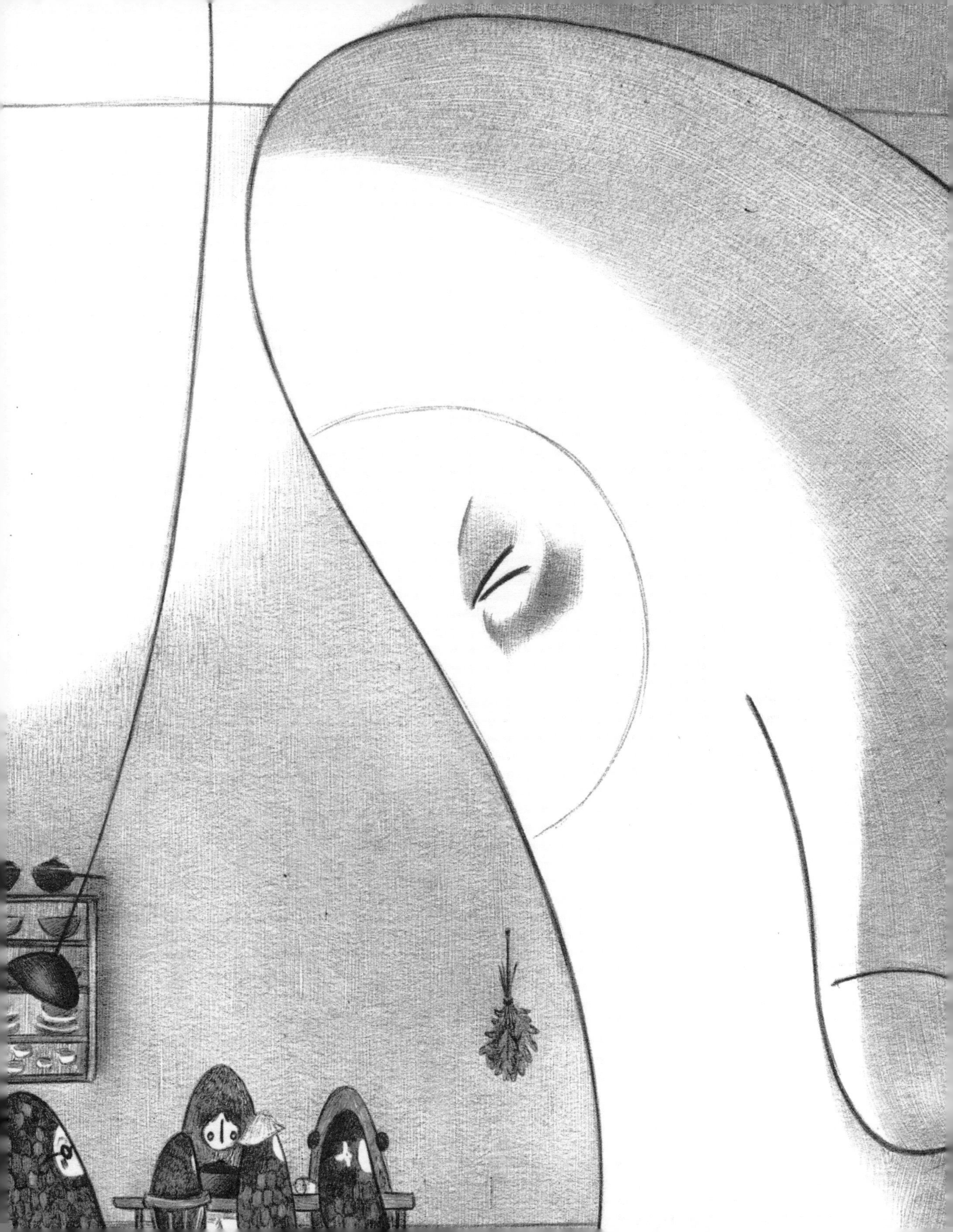

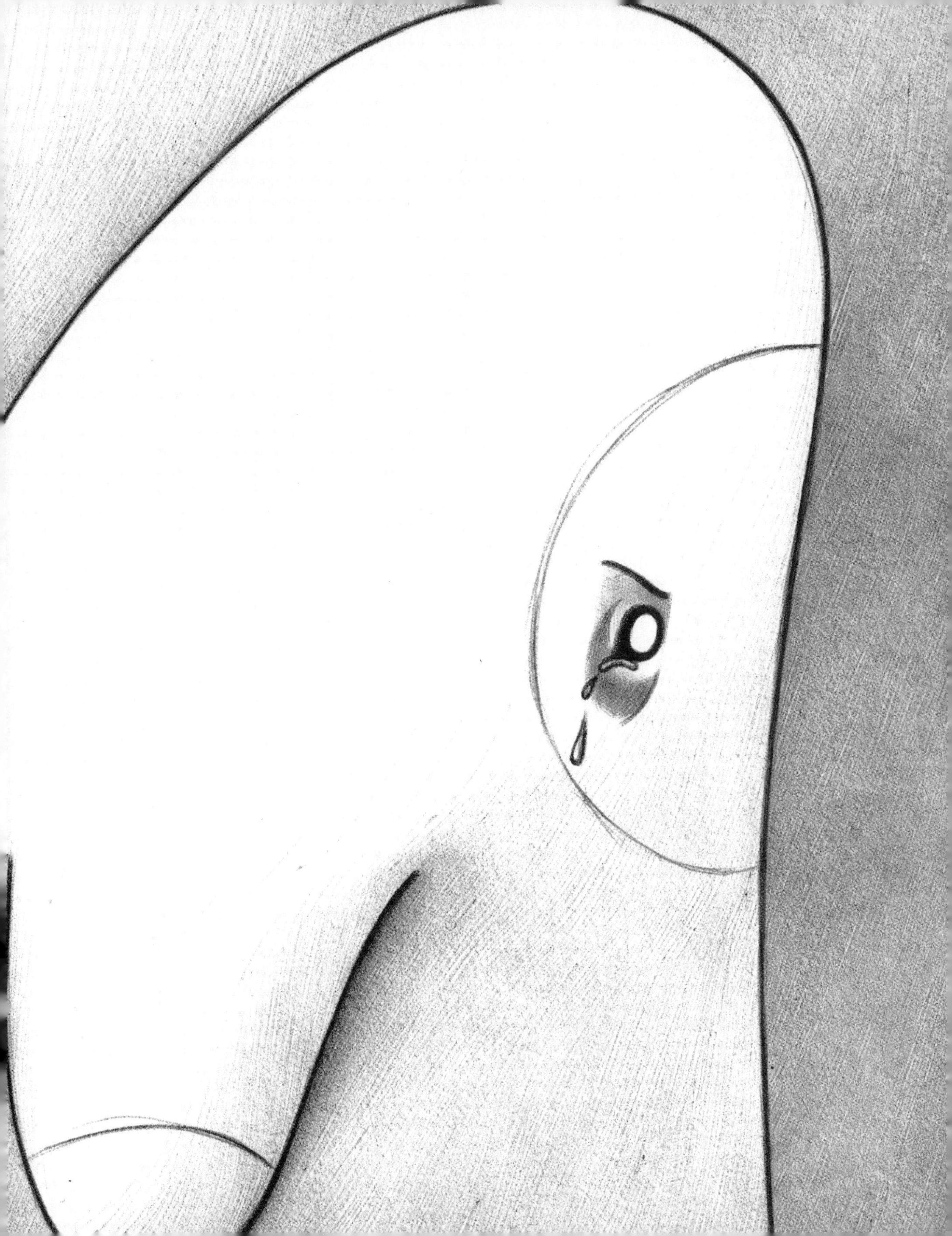

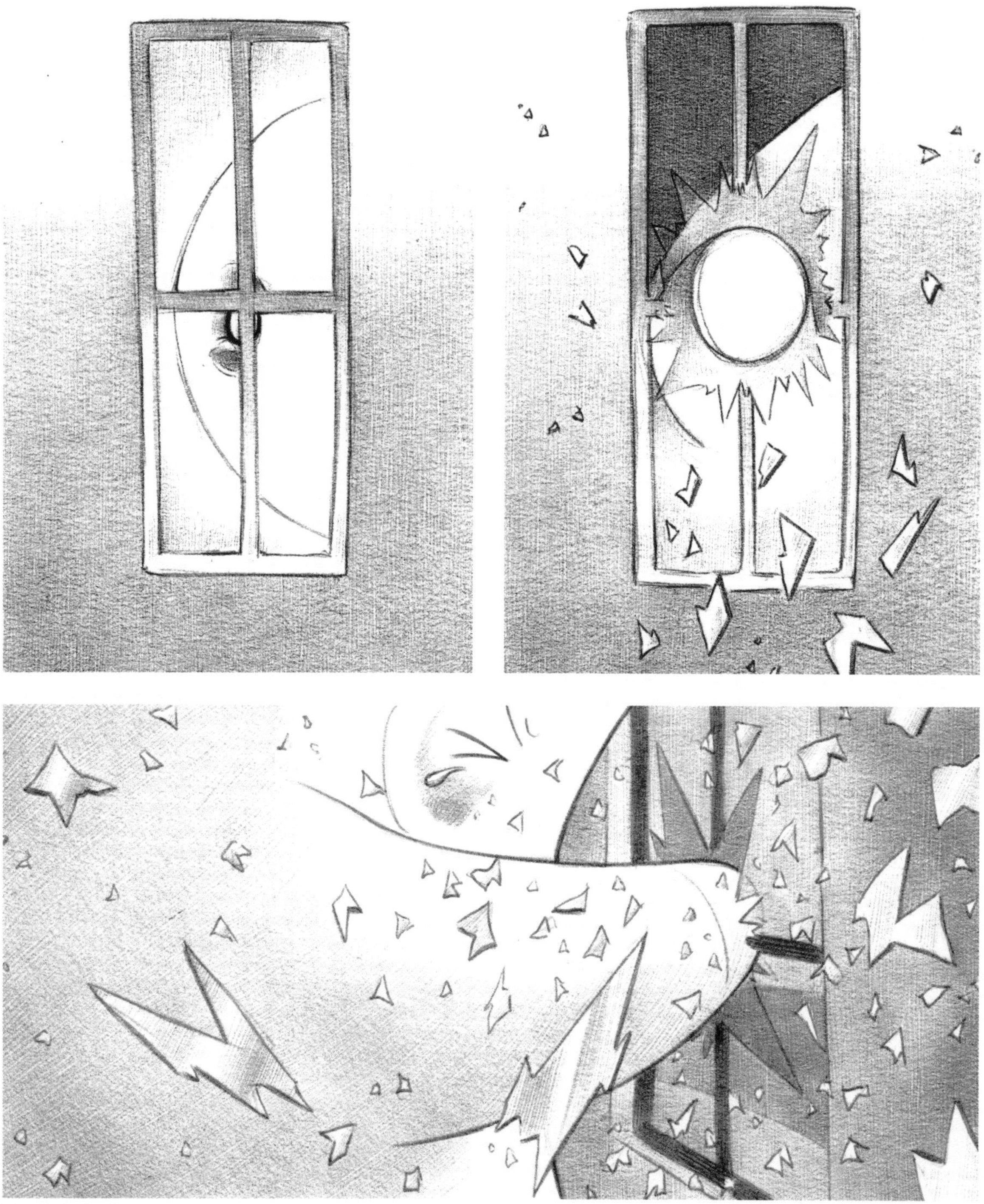

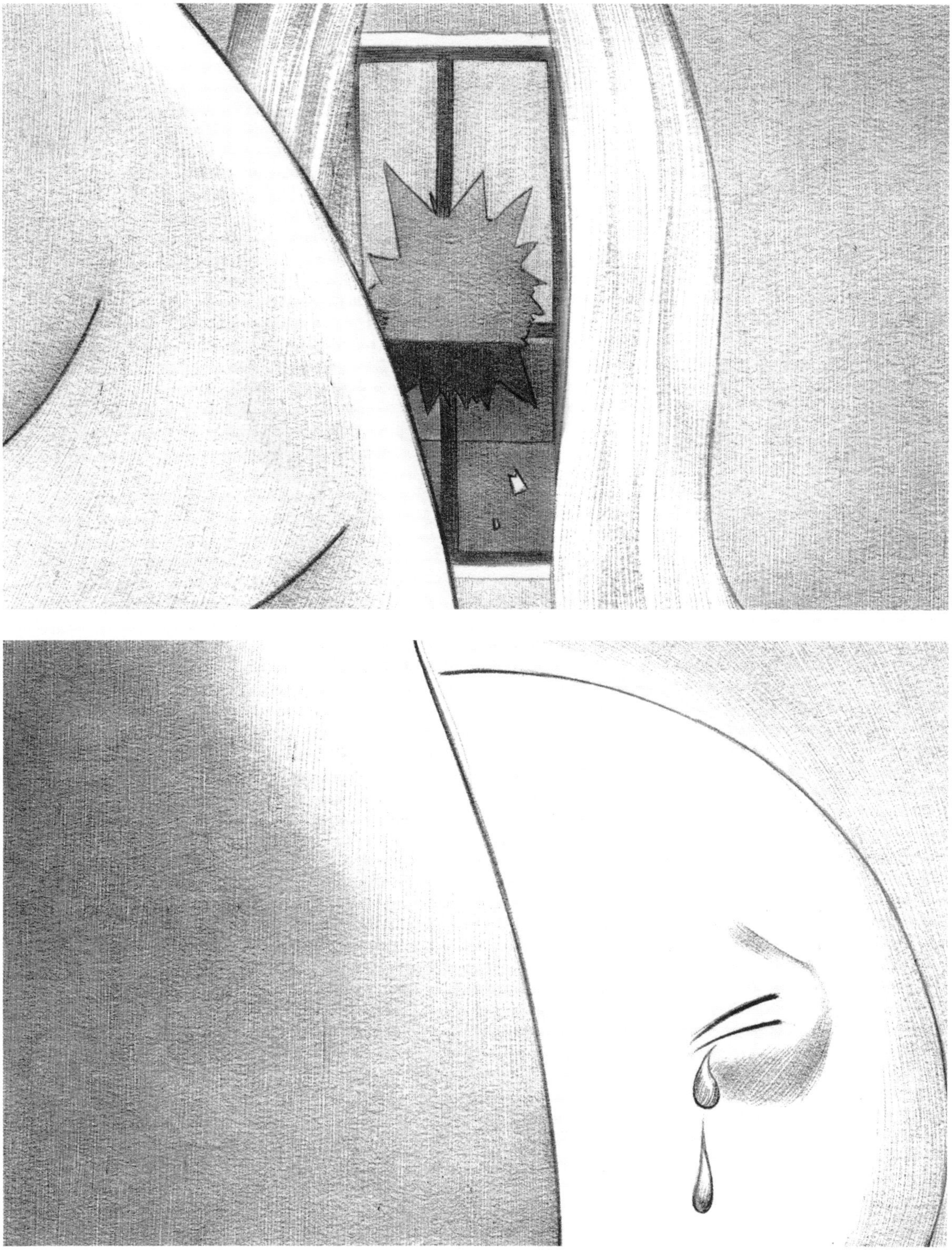

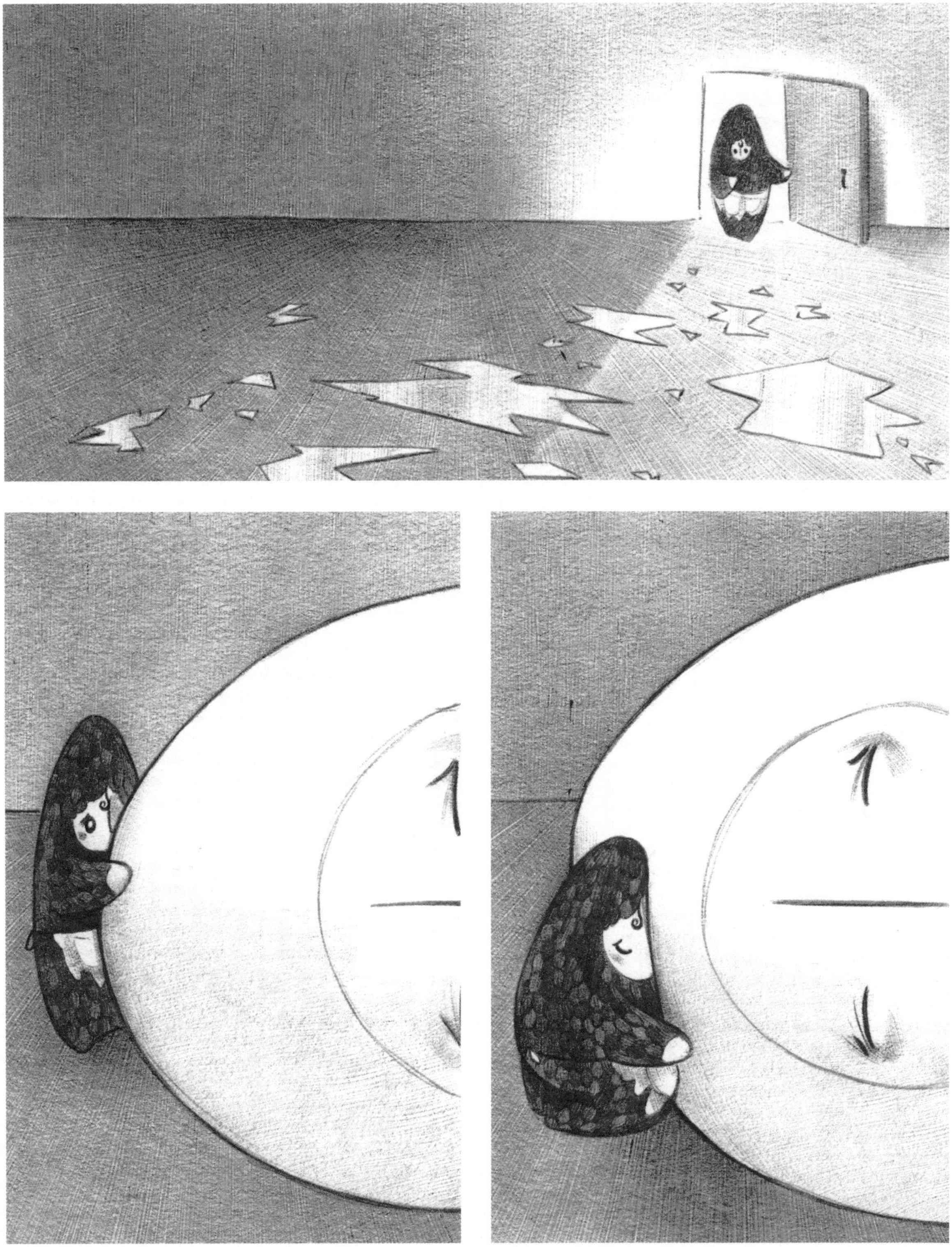

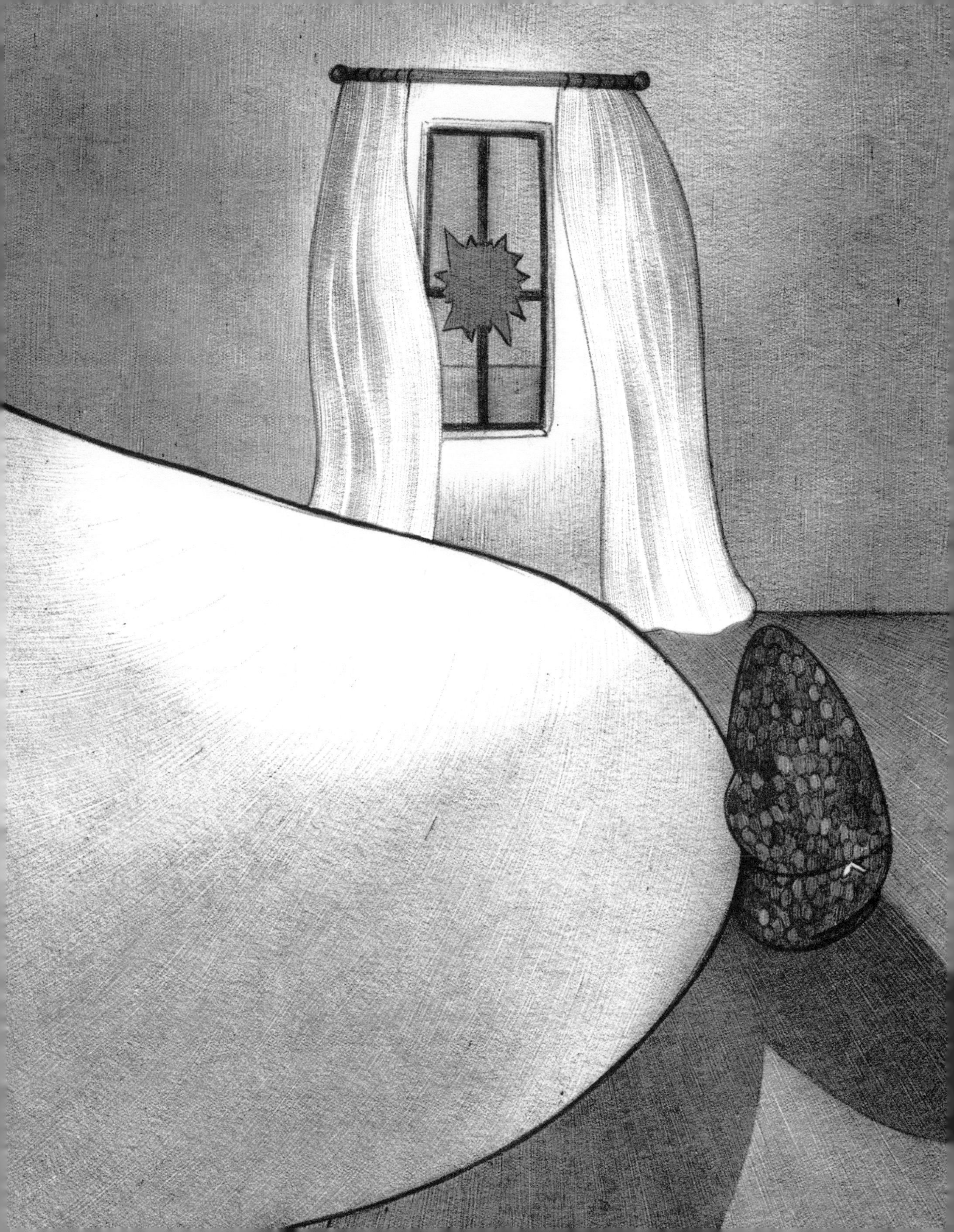

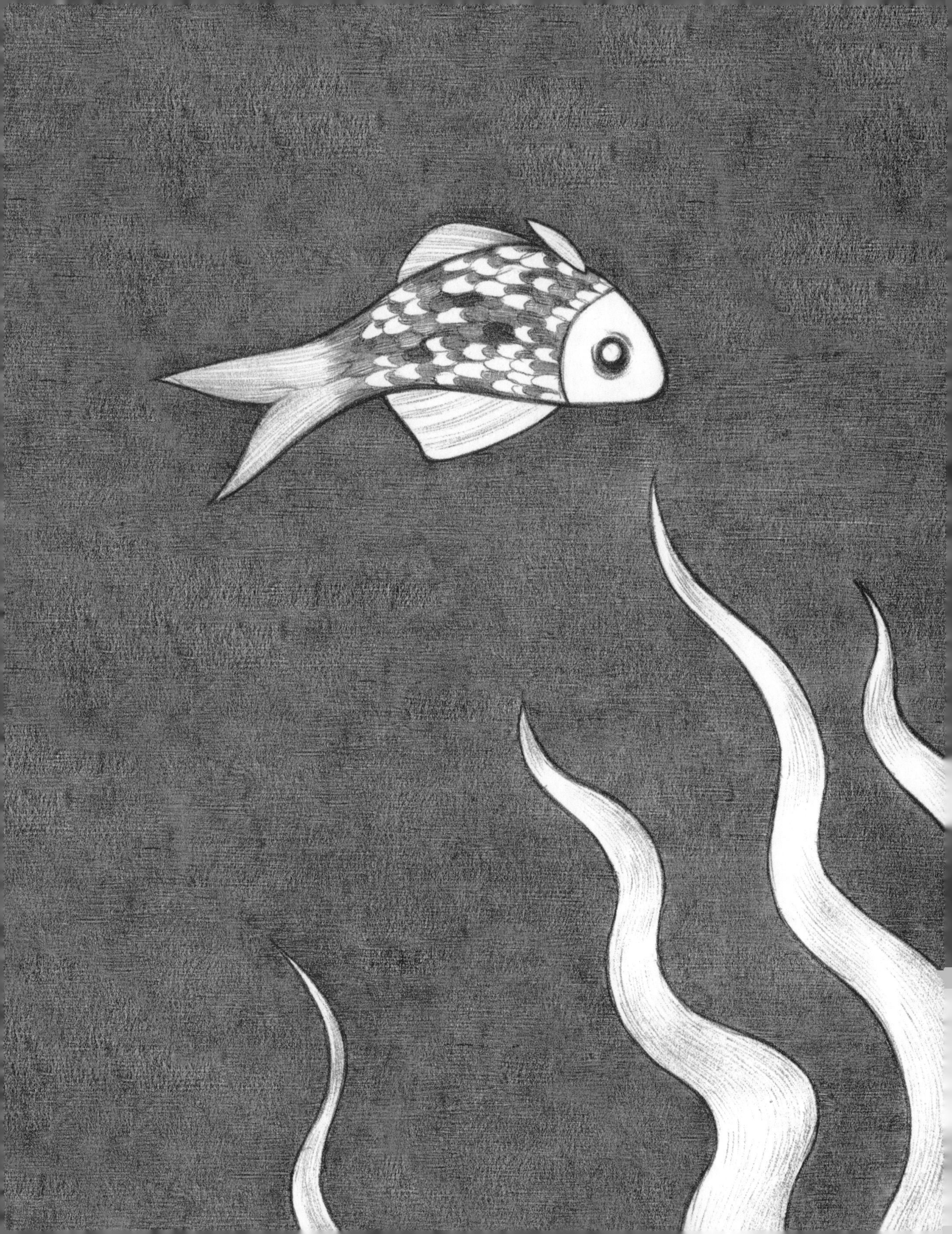

CHAPTER FOUR

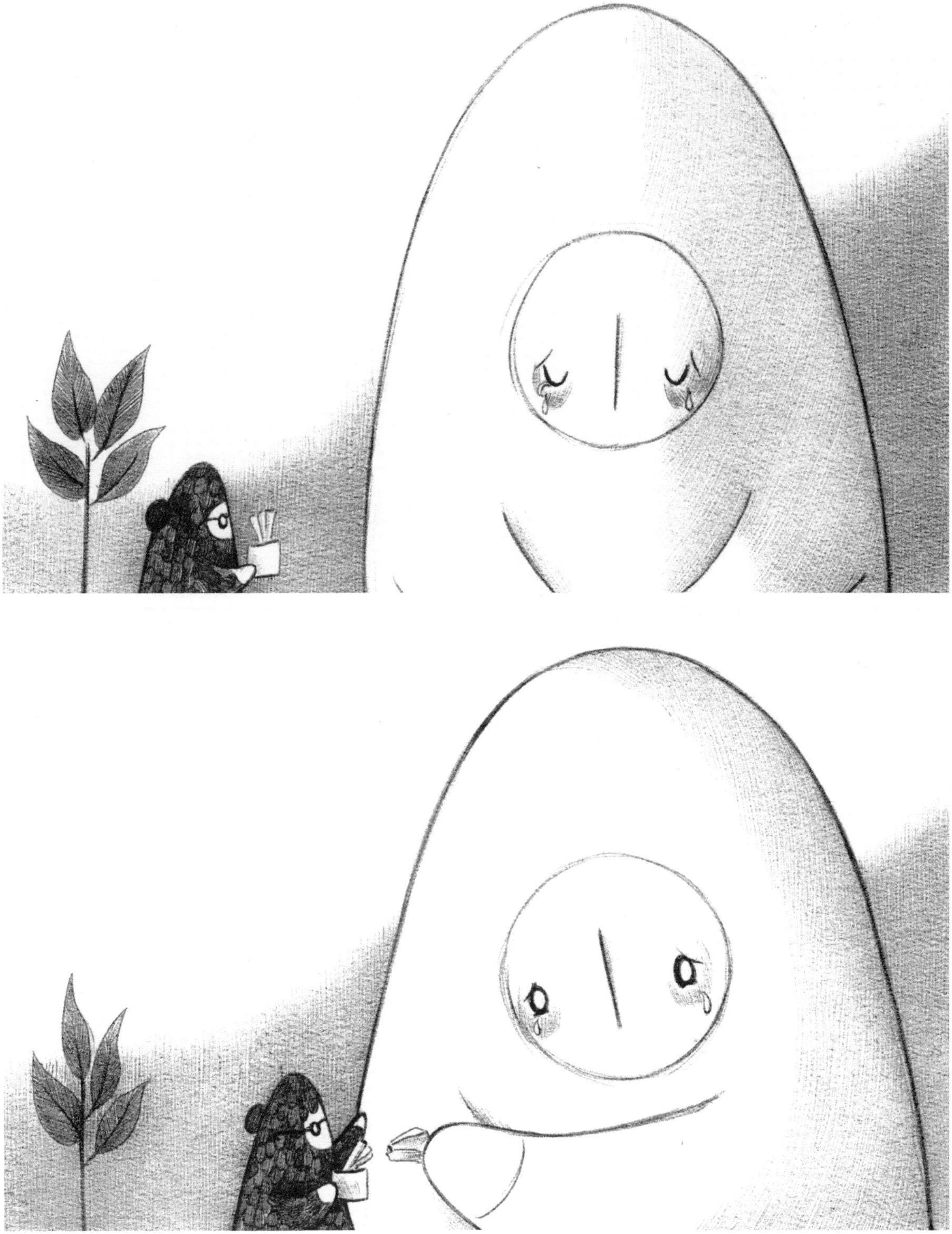

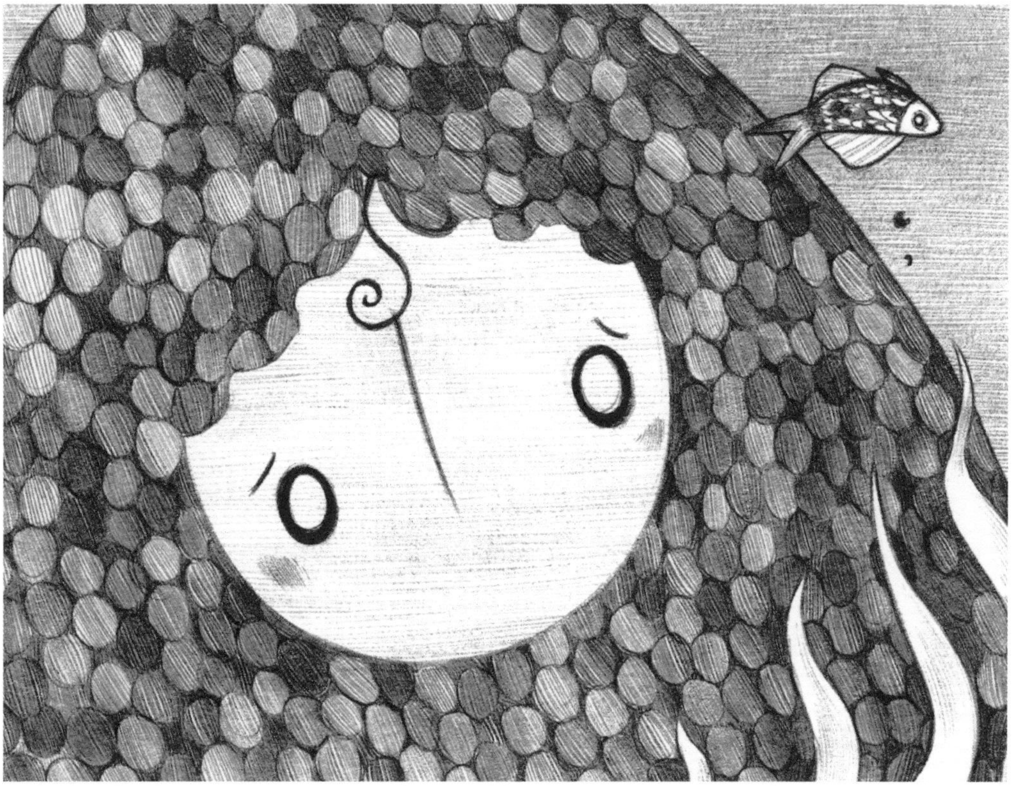

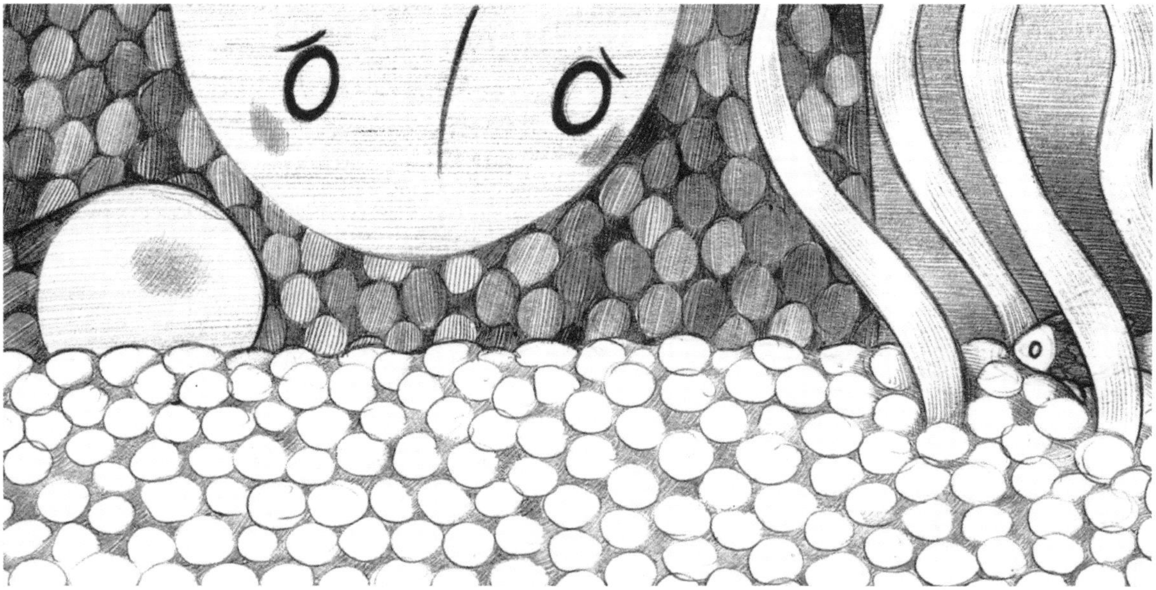

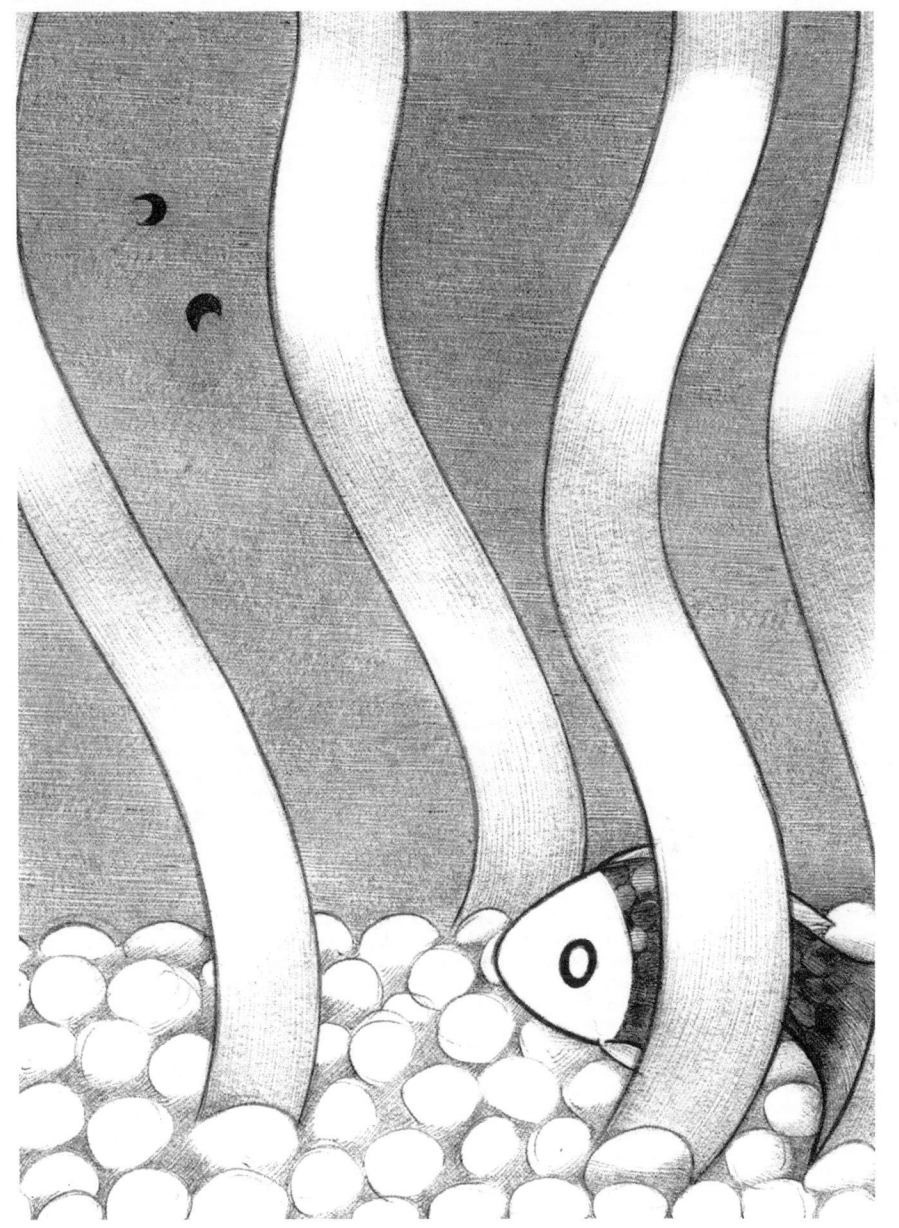

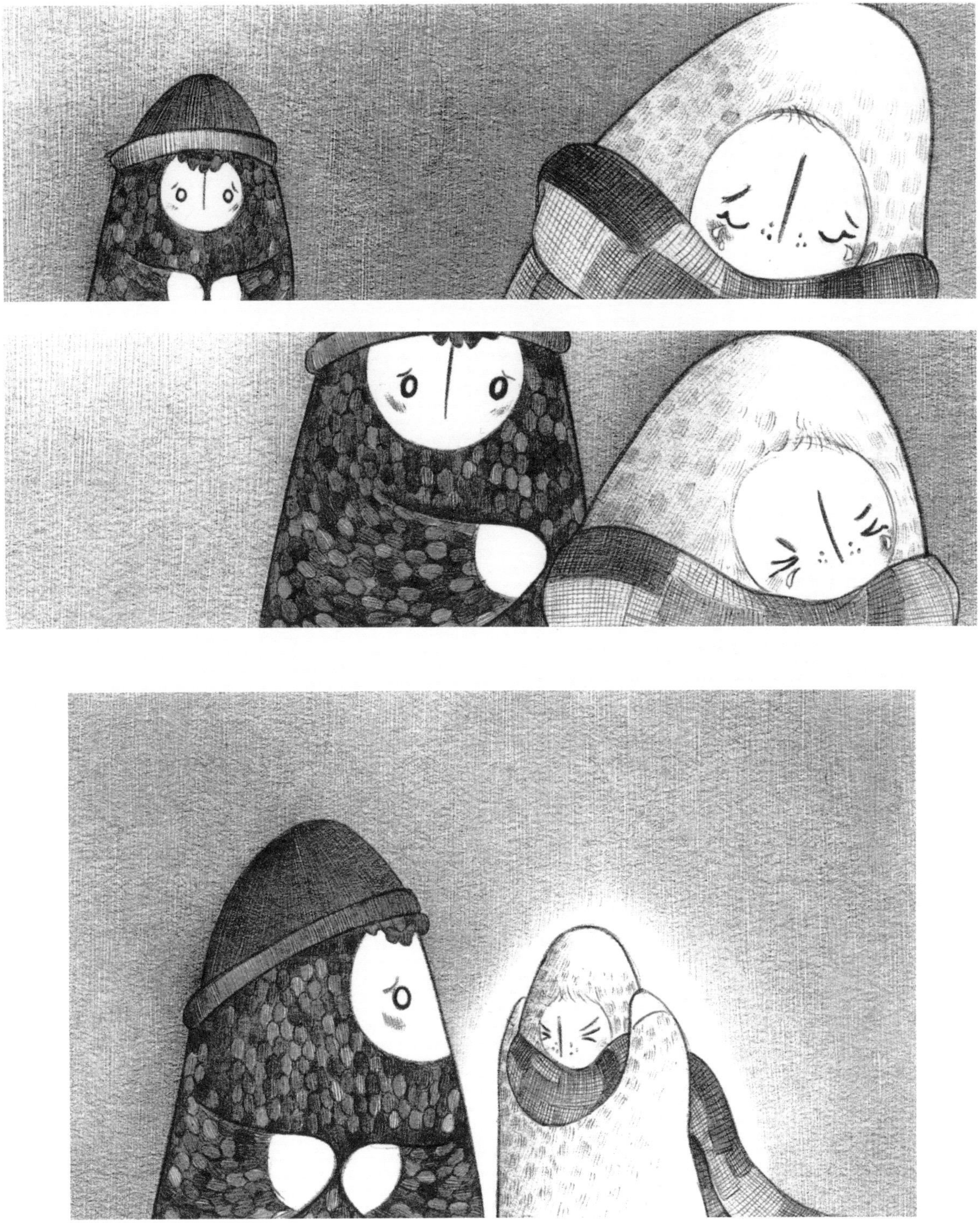

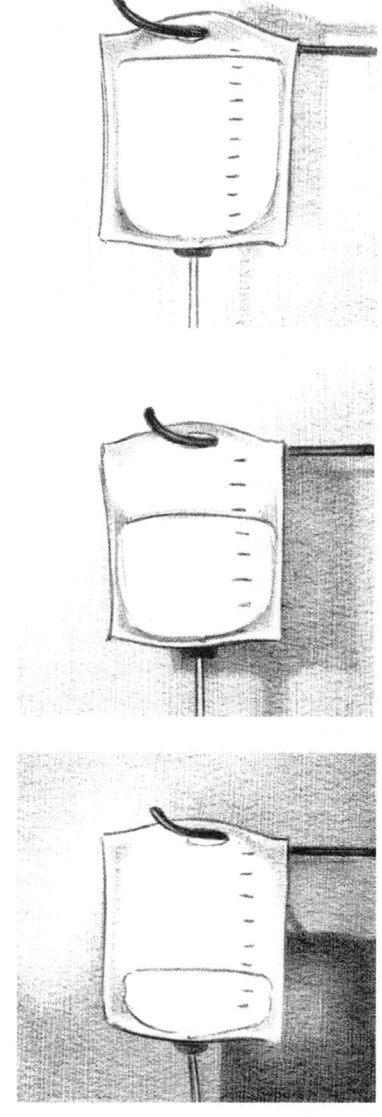

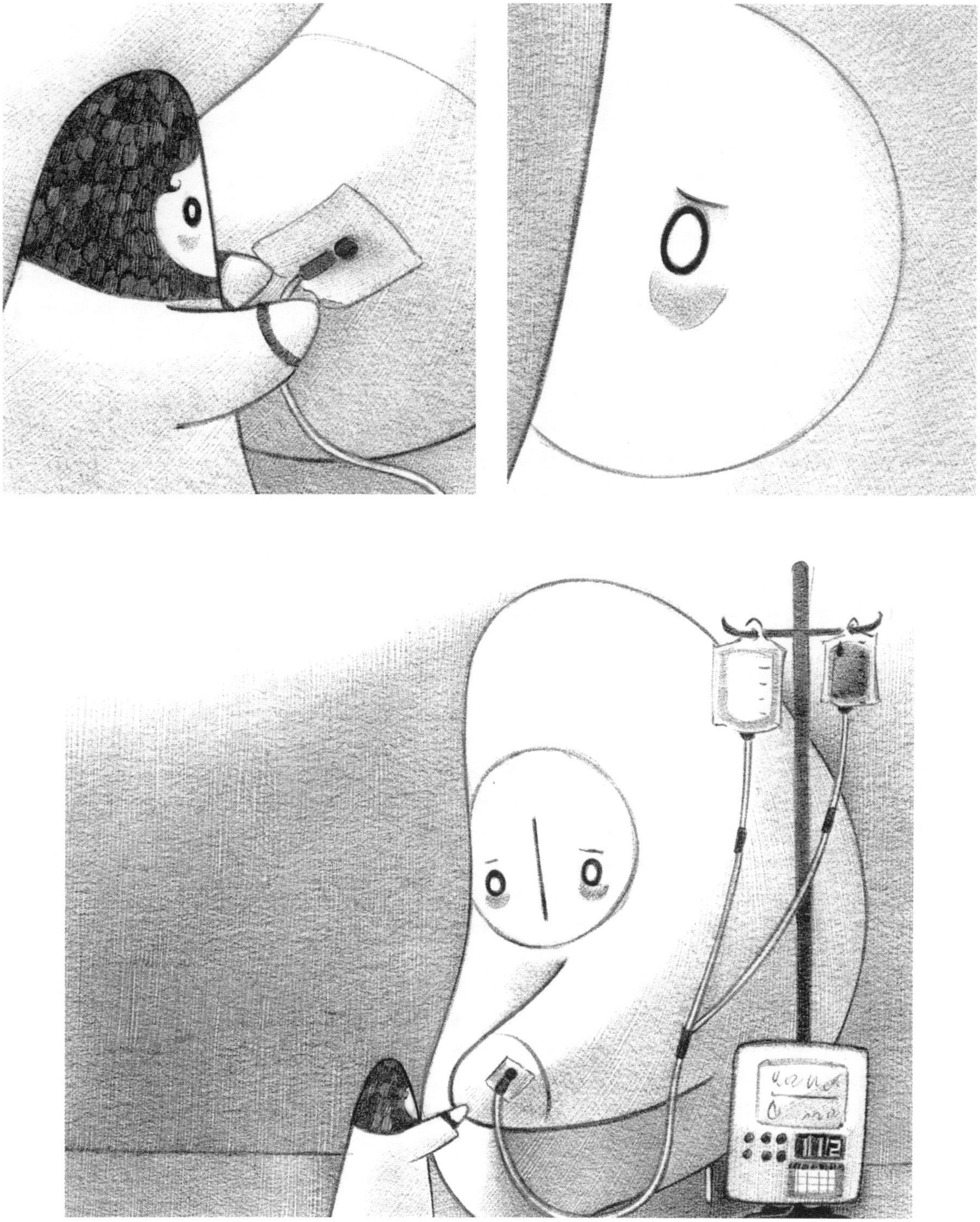
112

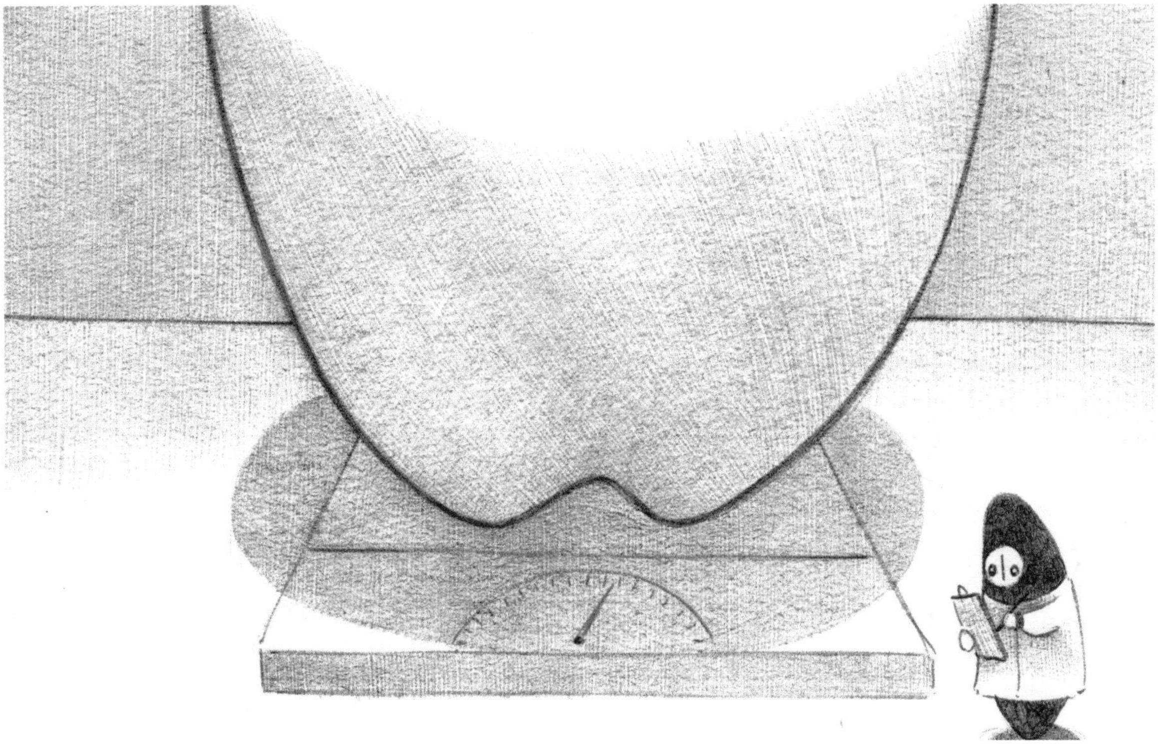

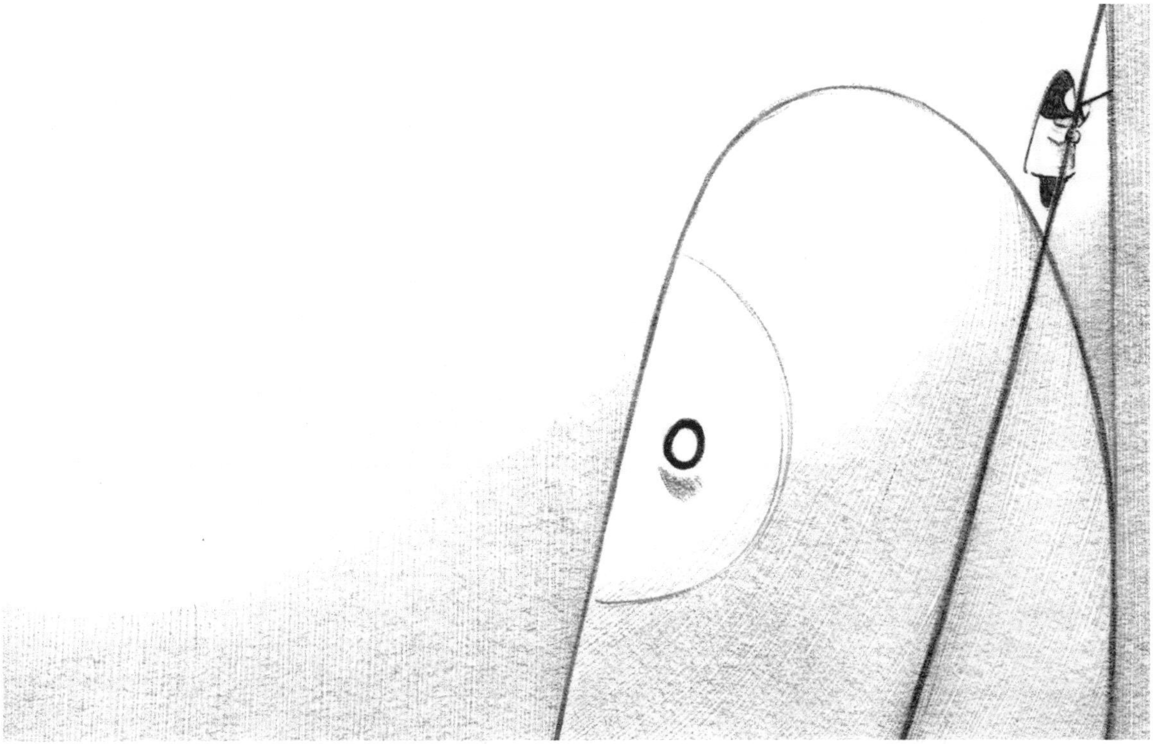

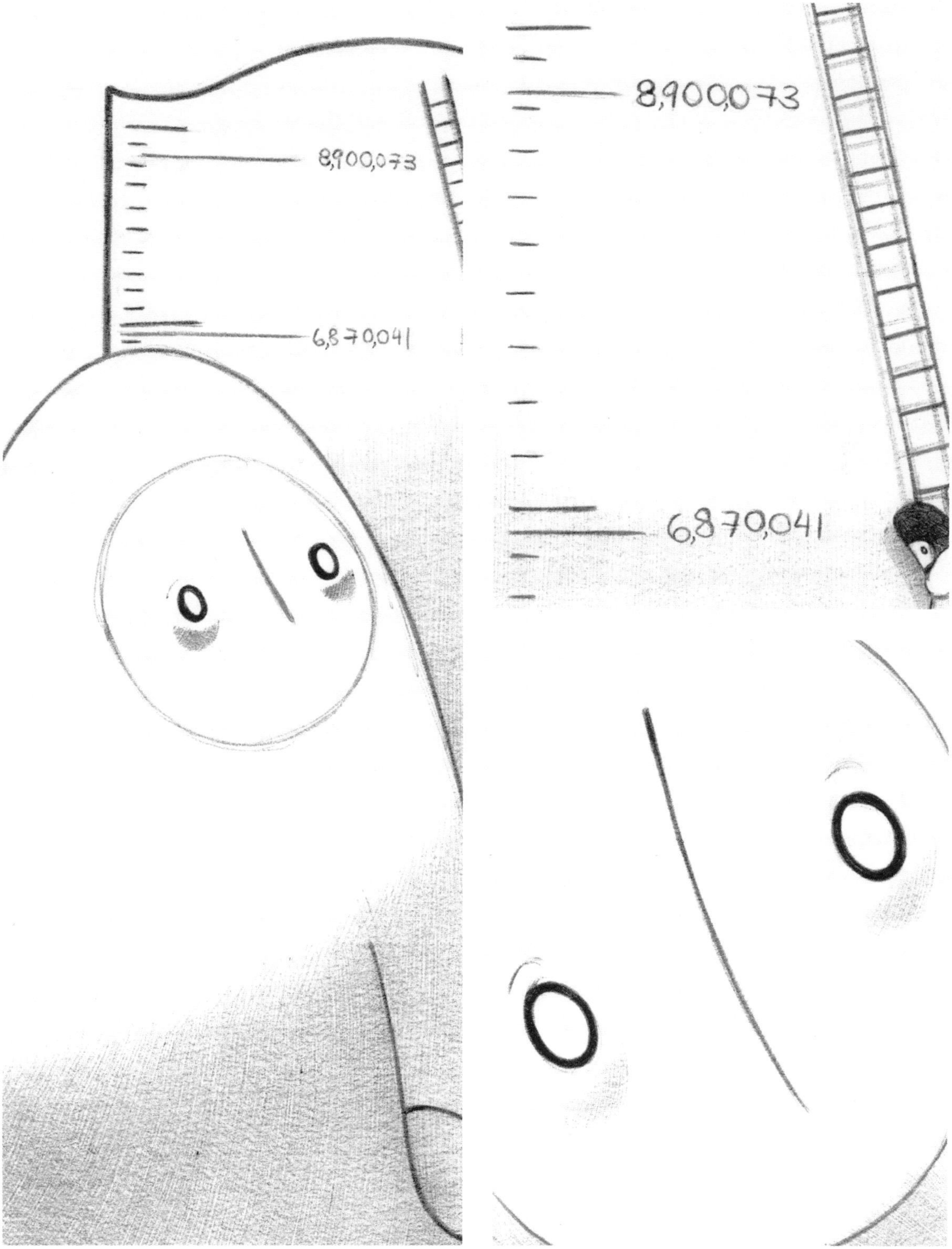
8,900,073
6,870,041
8,900,073
6,870,041

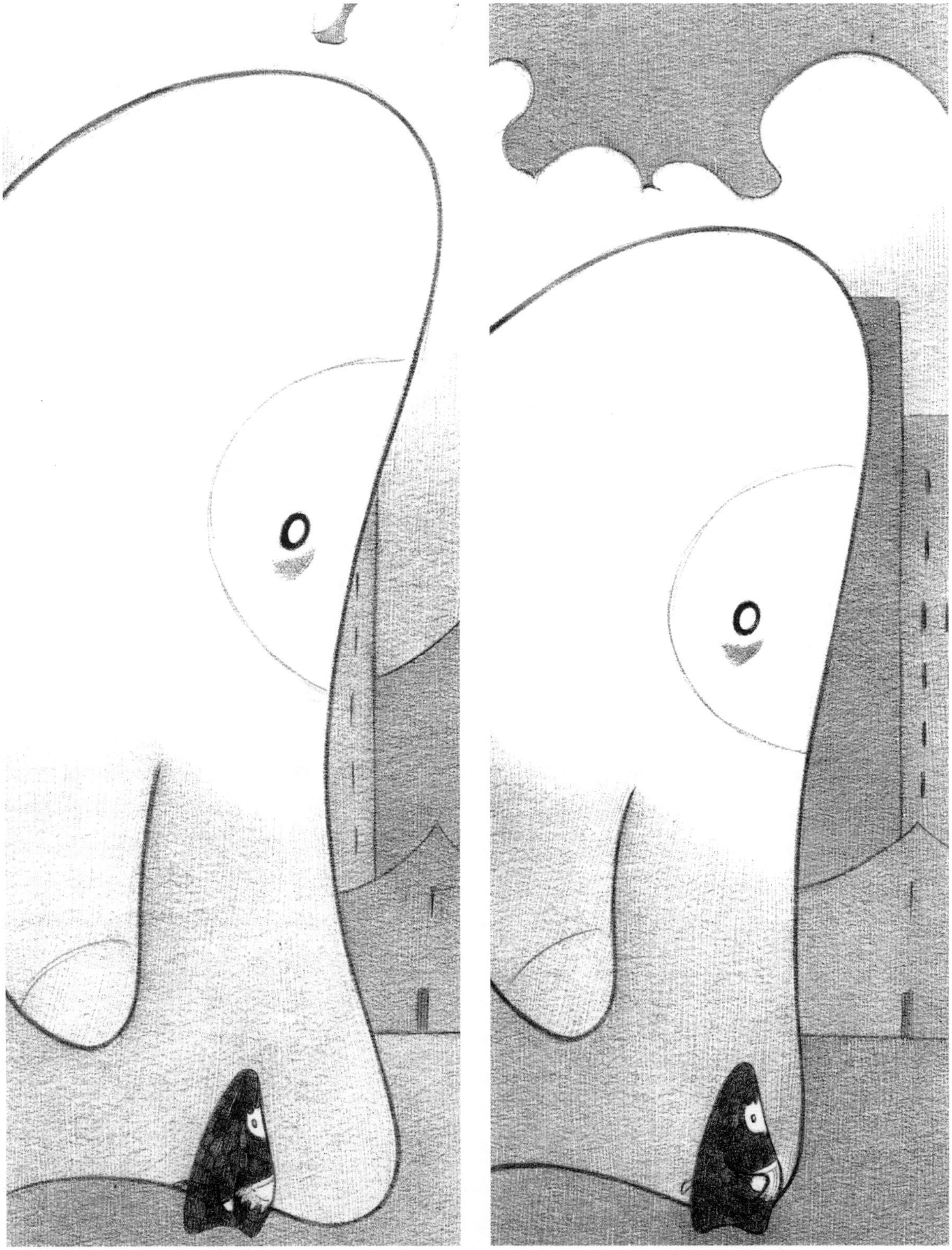

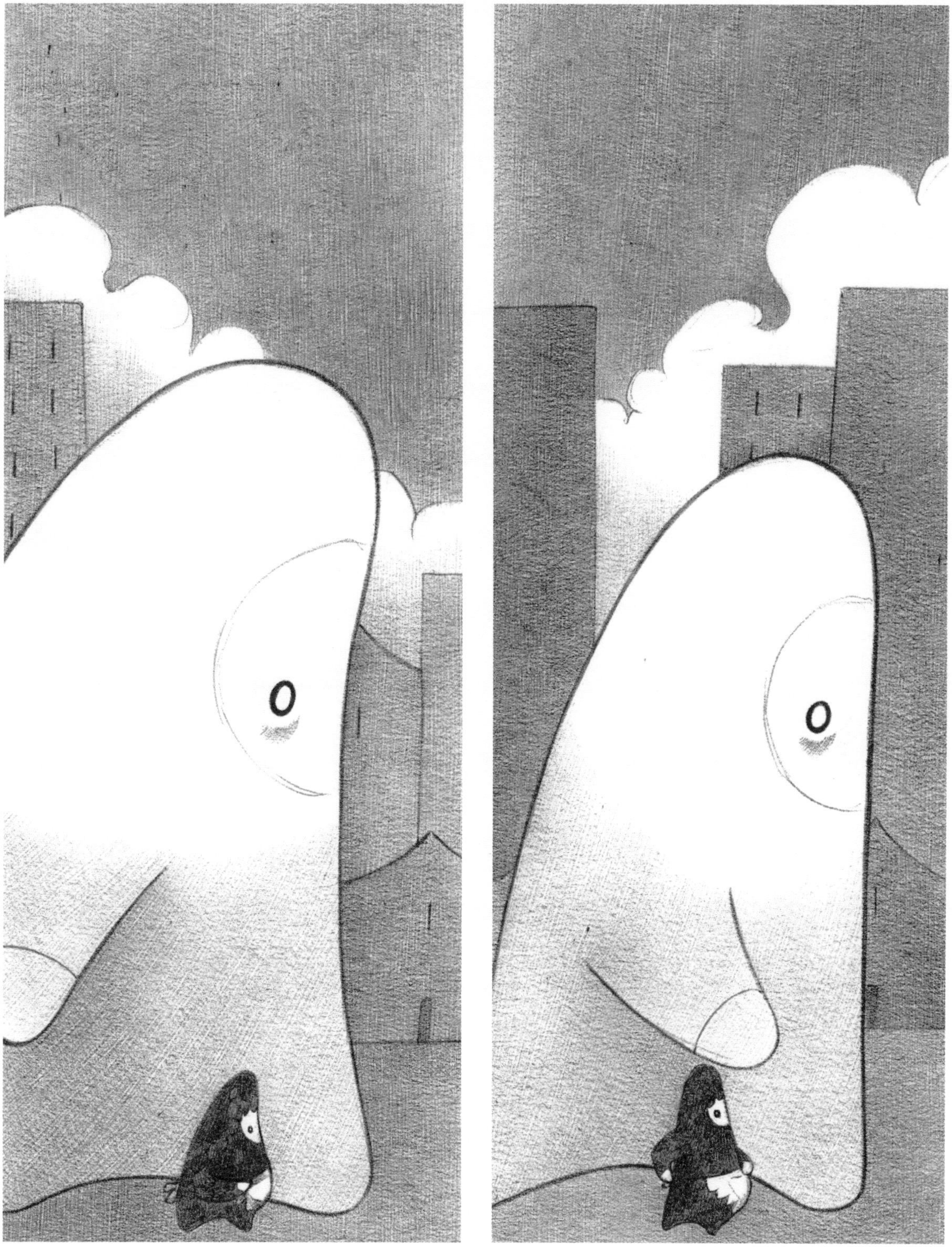

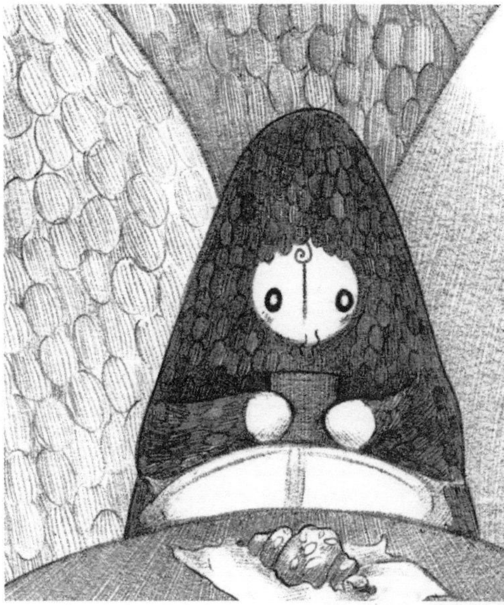

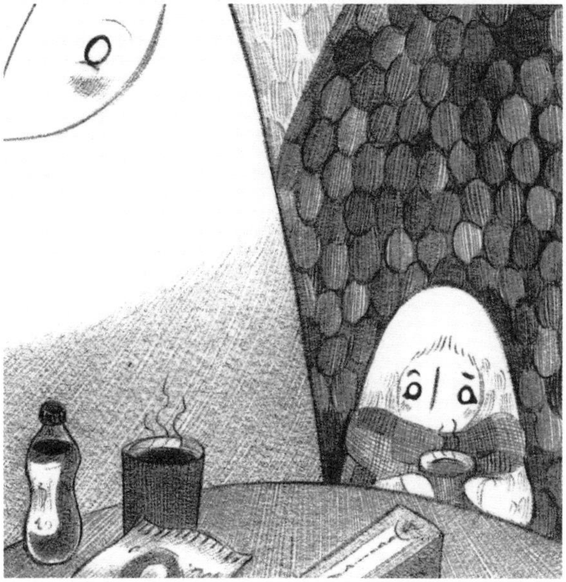

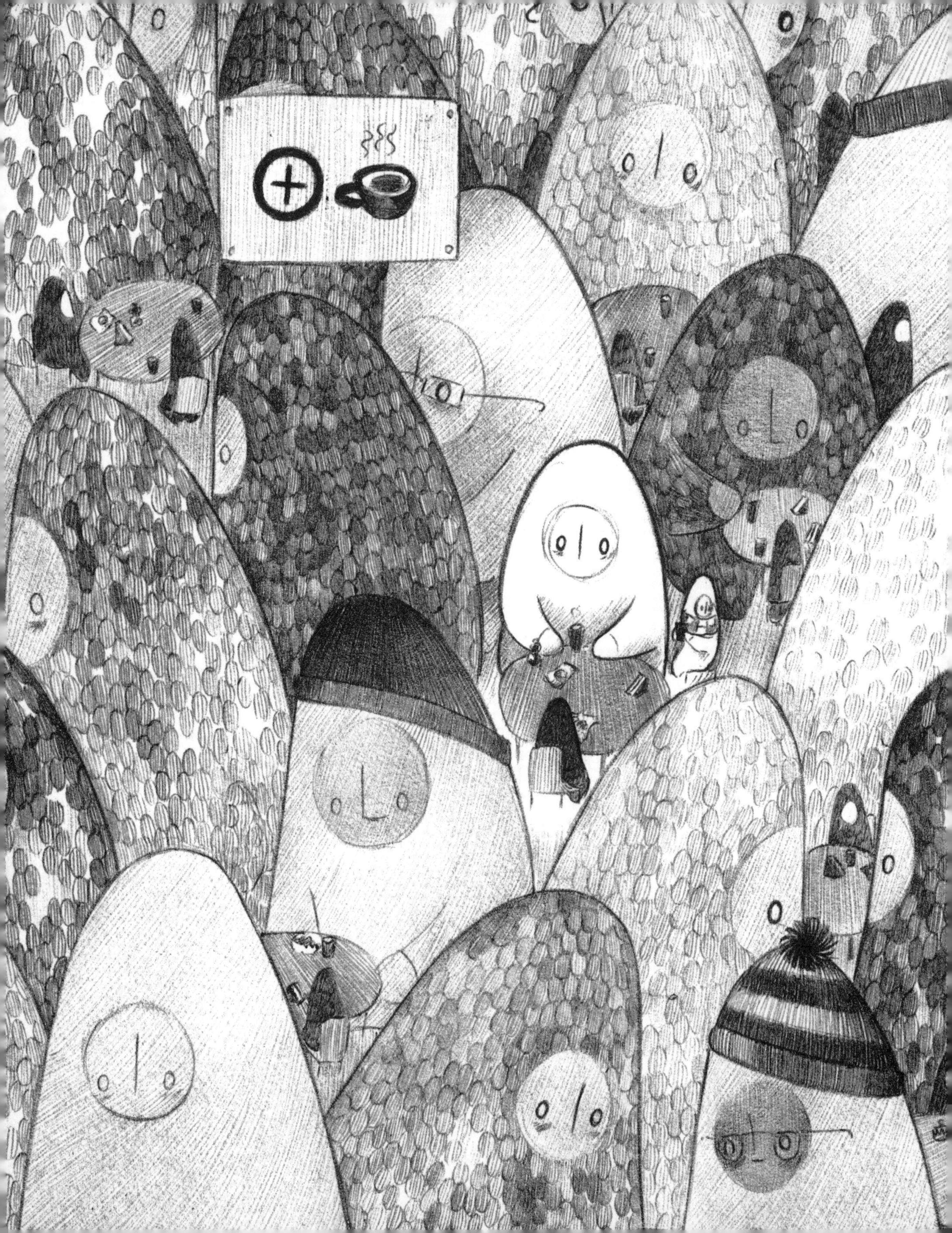

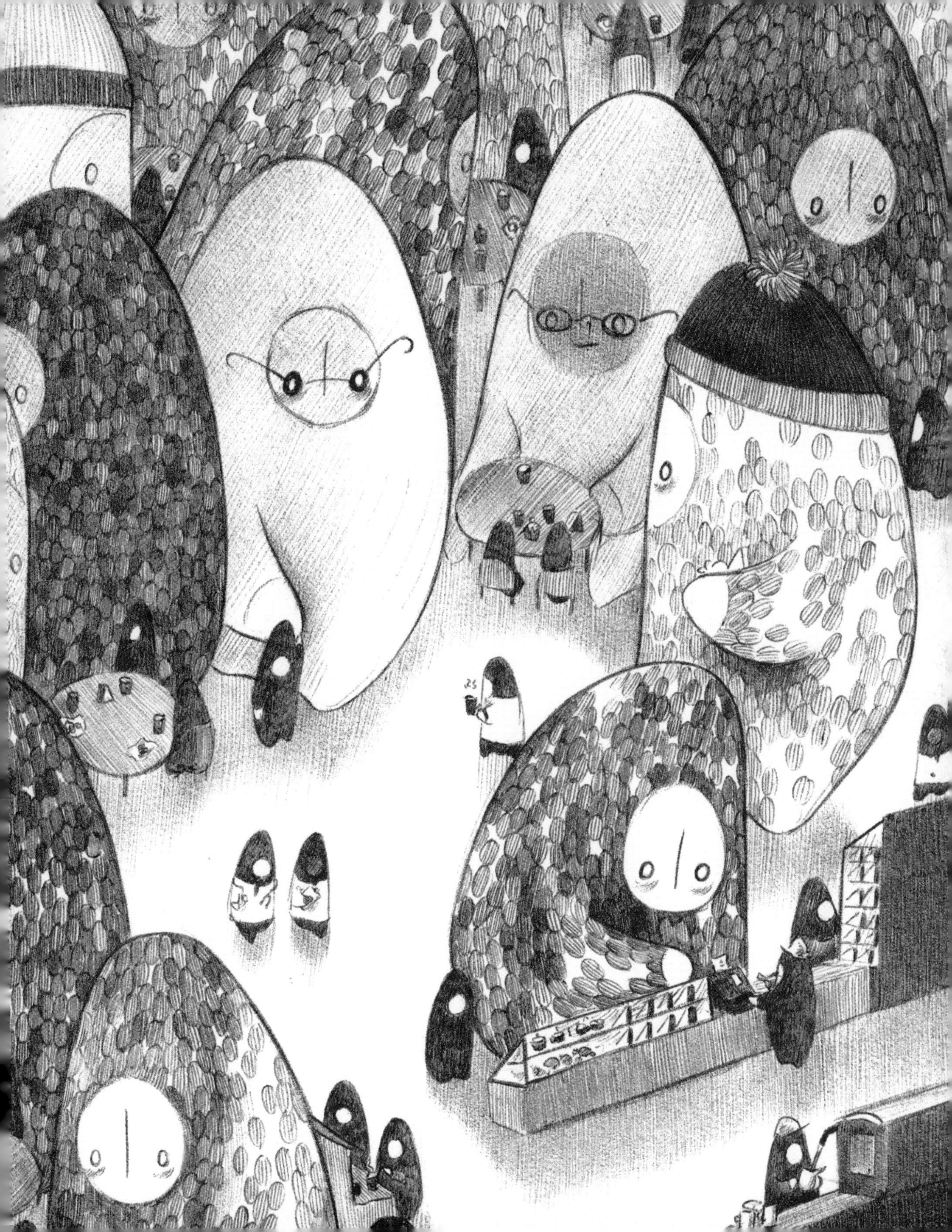

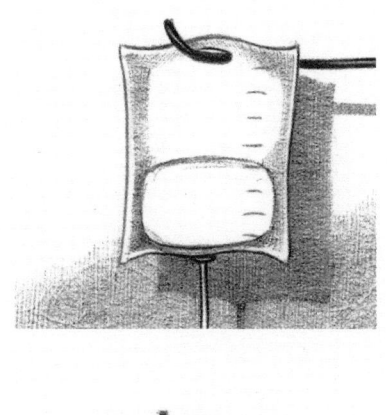
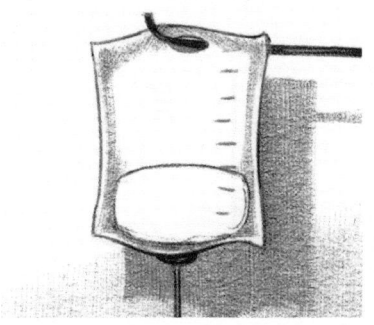
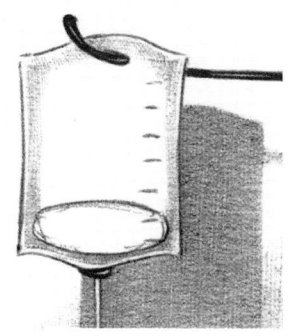

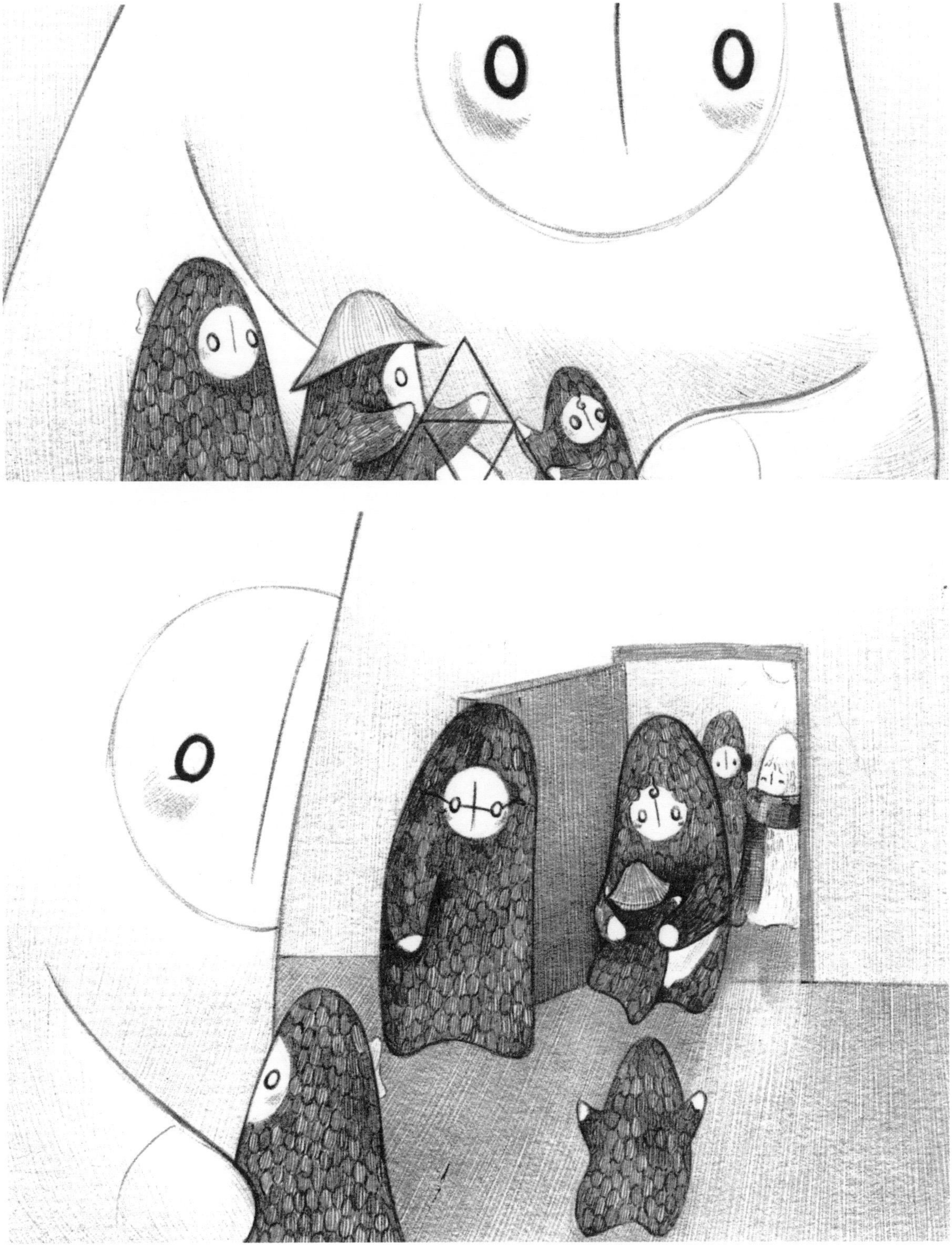

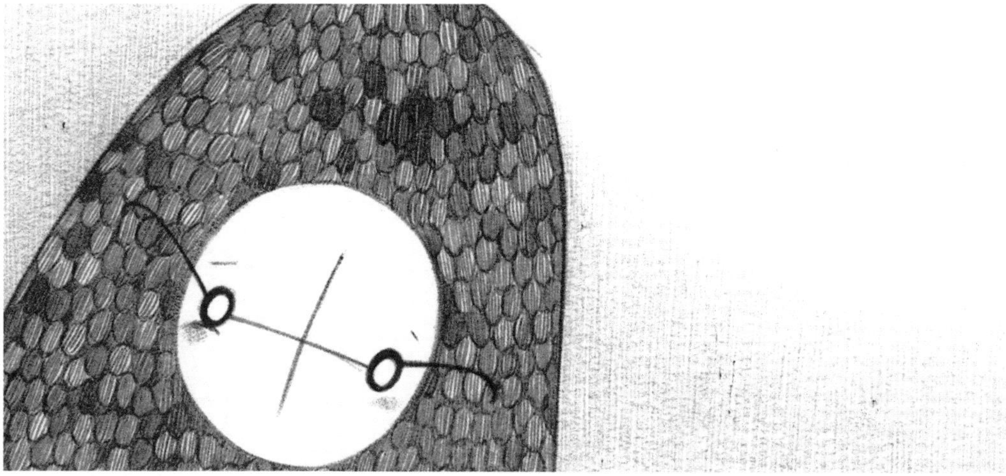

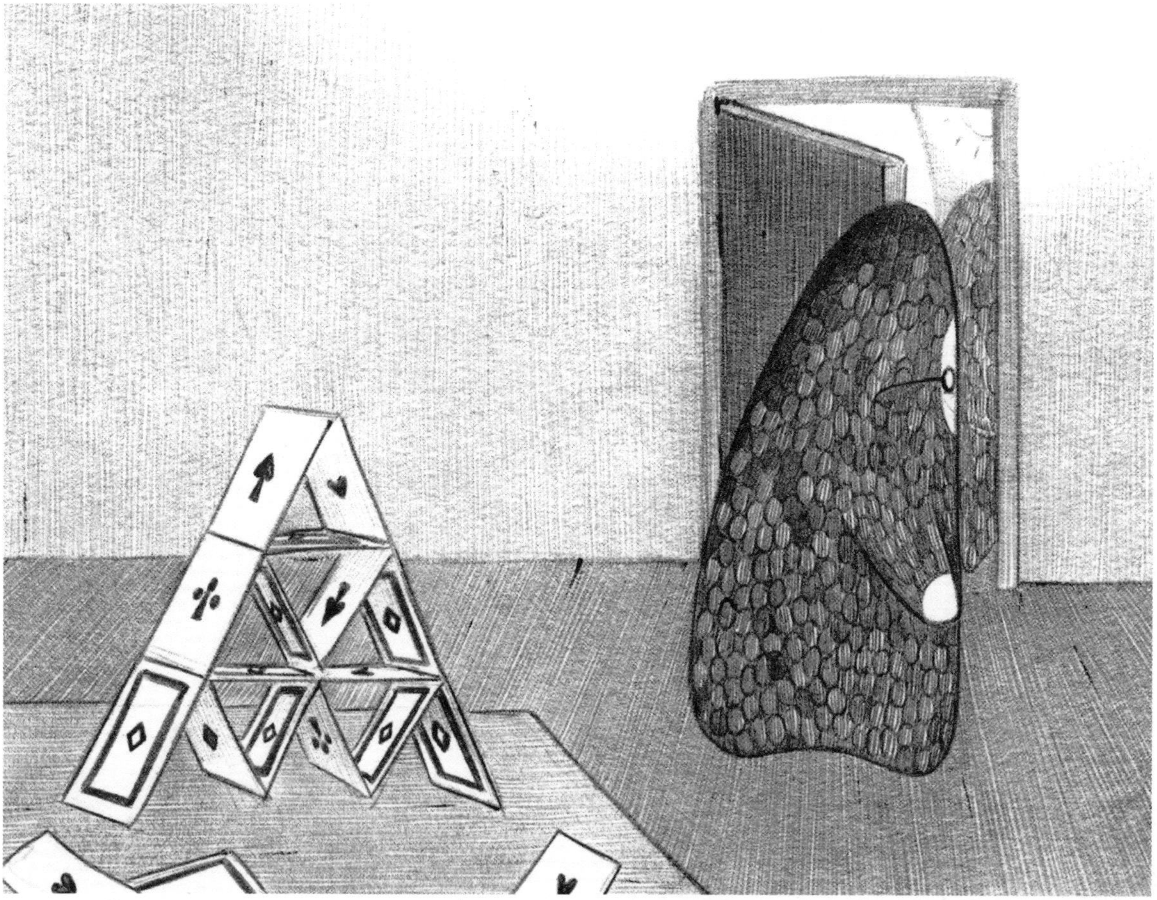

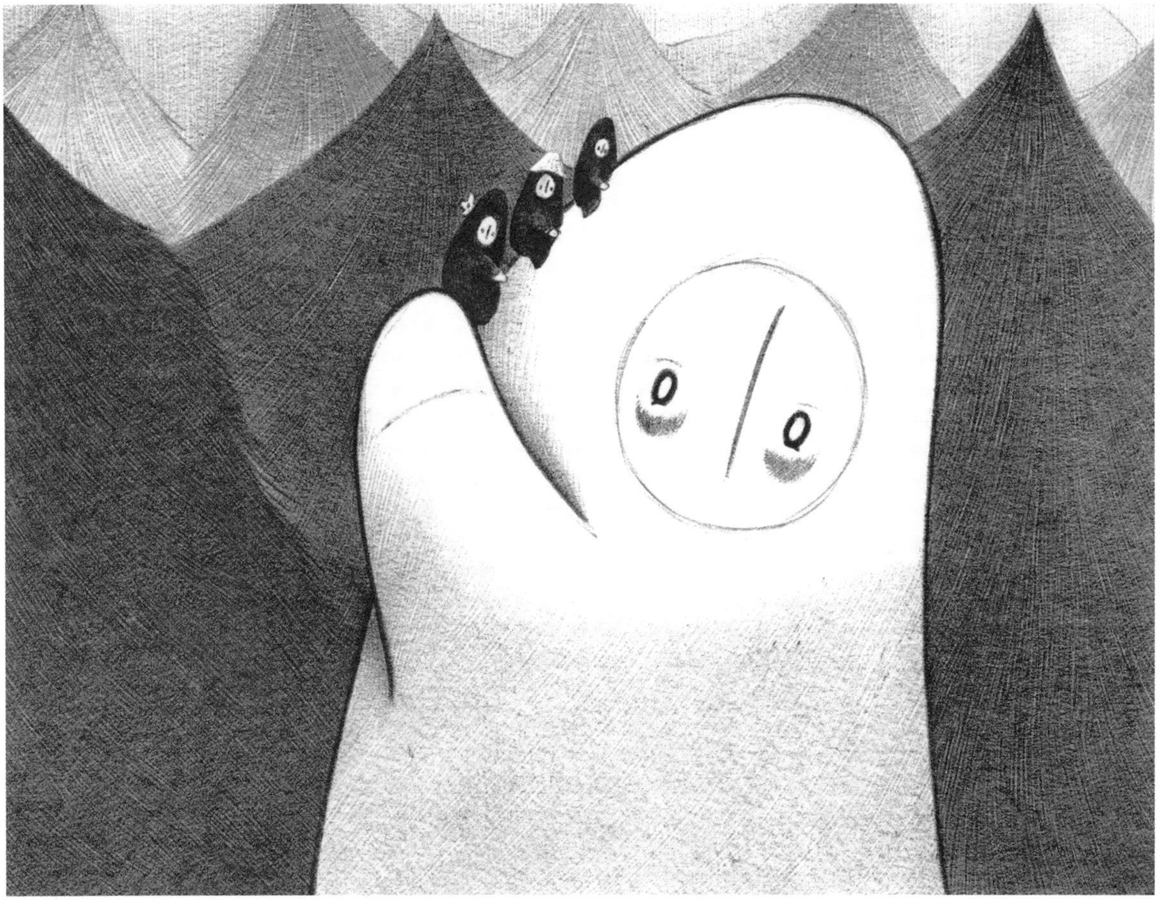

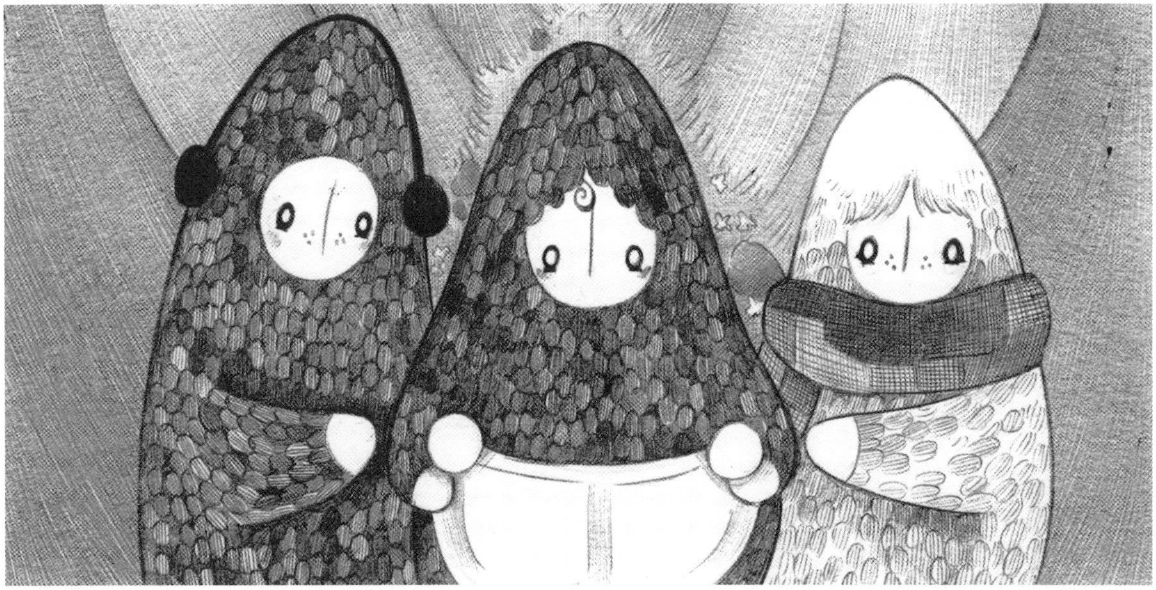

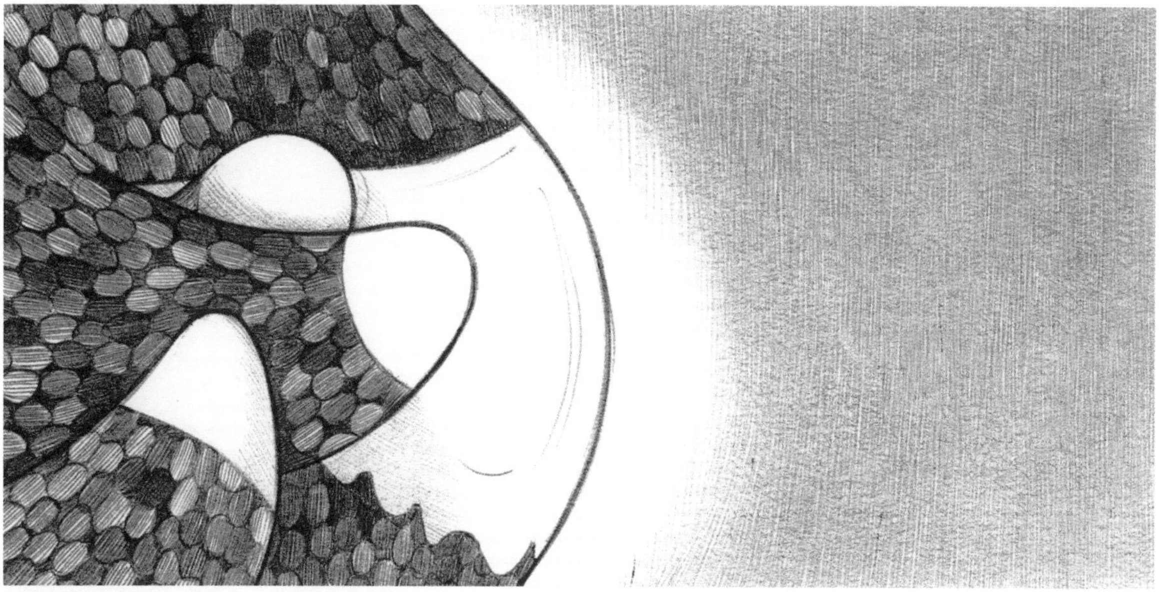

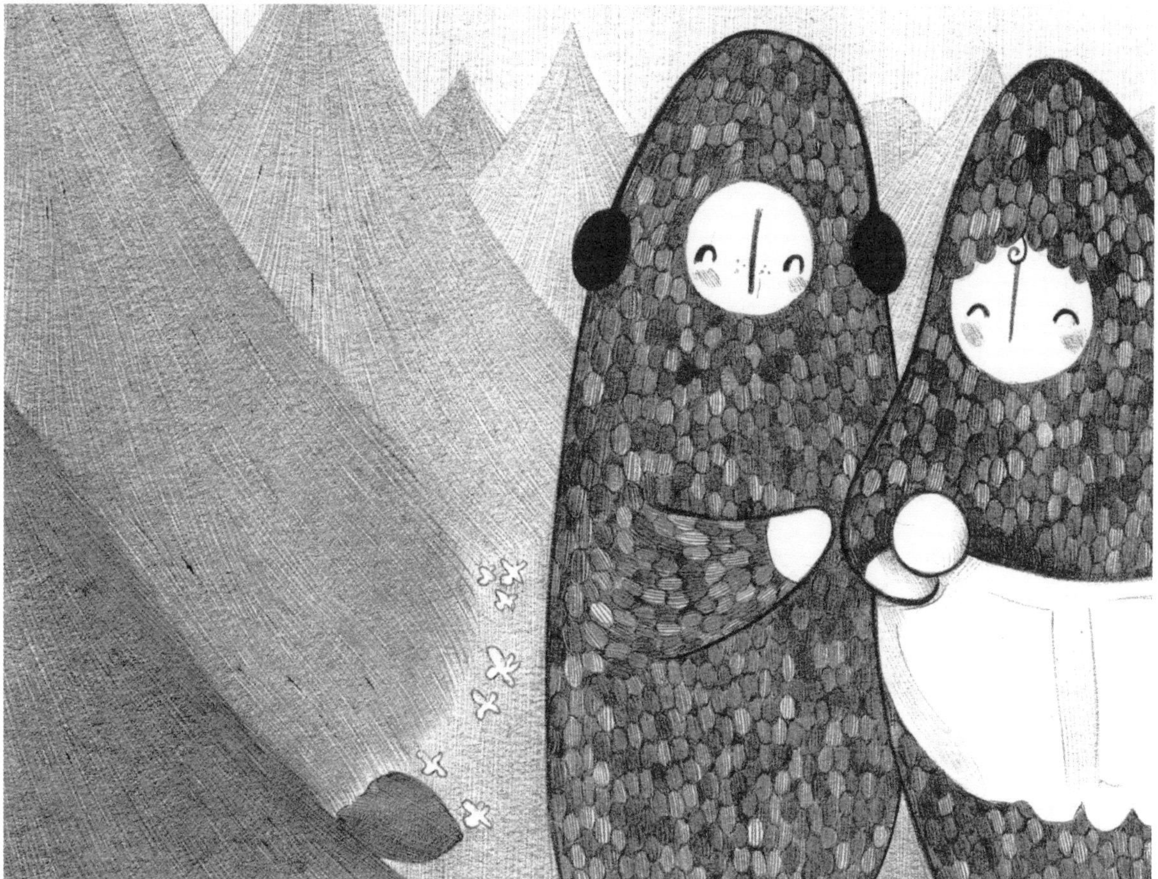

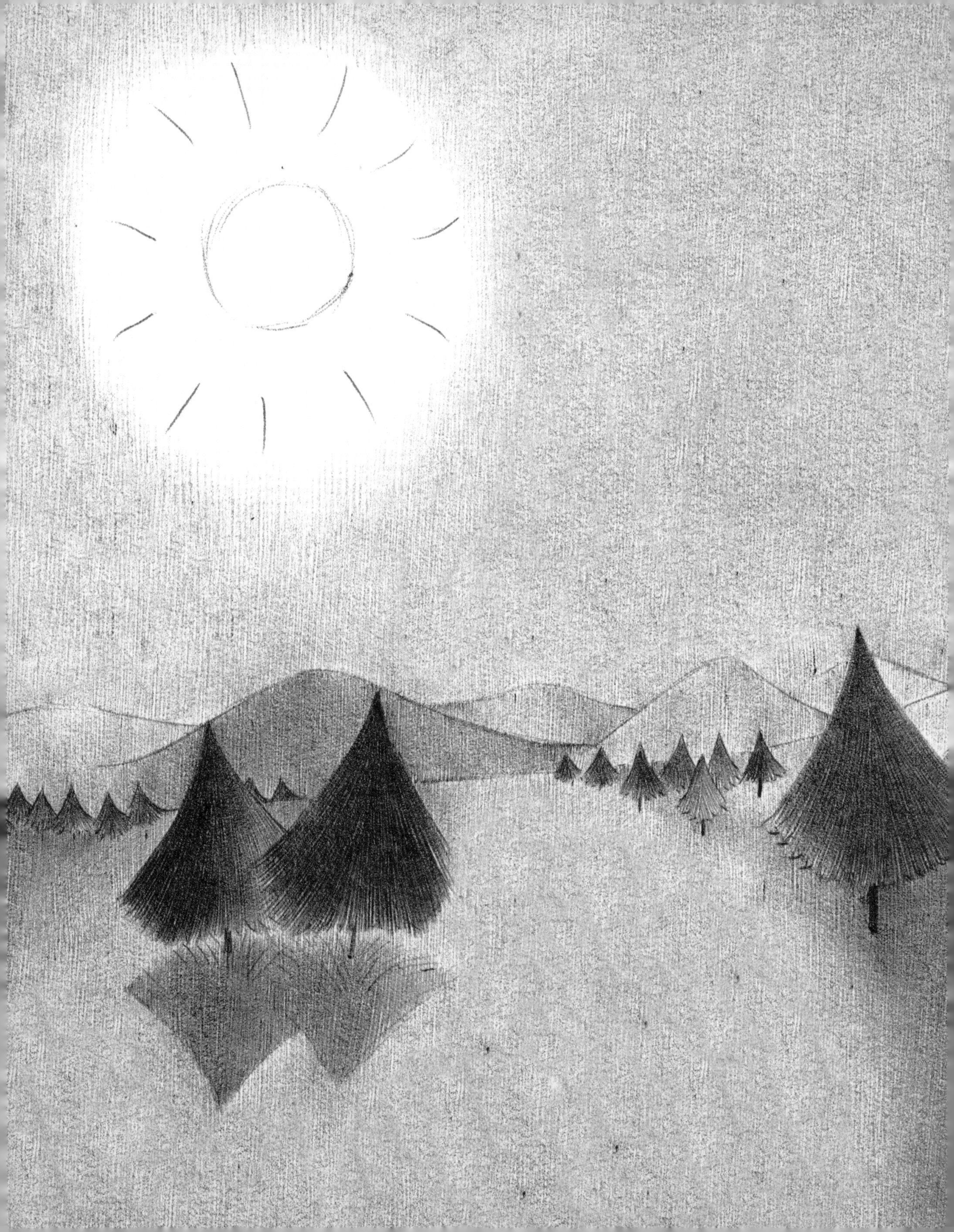

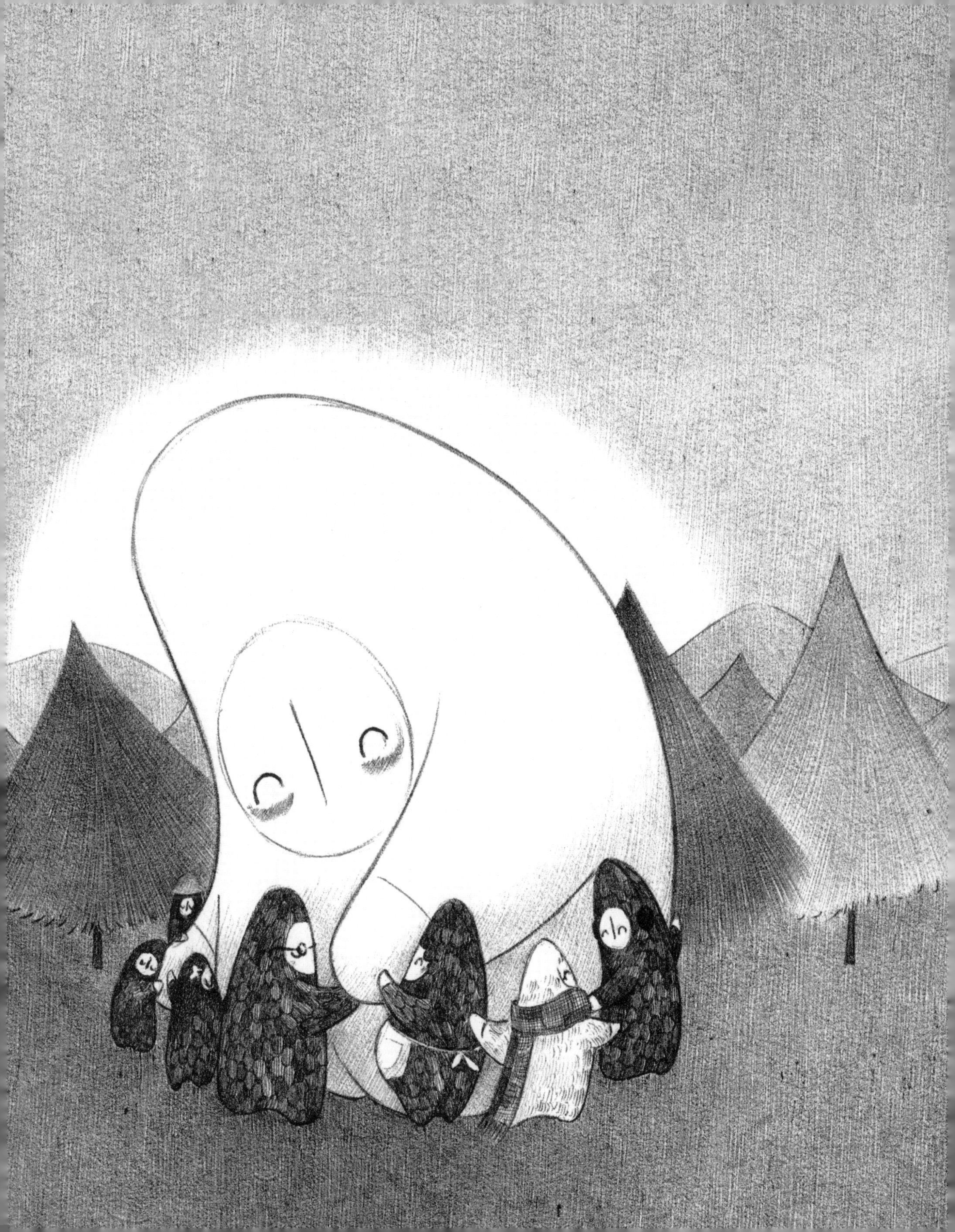

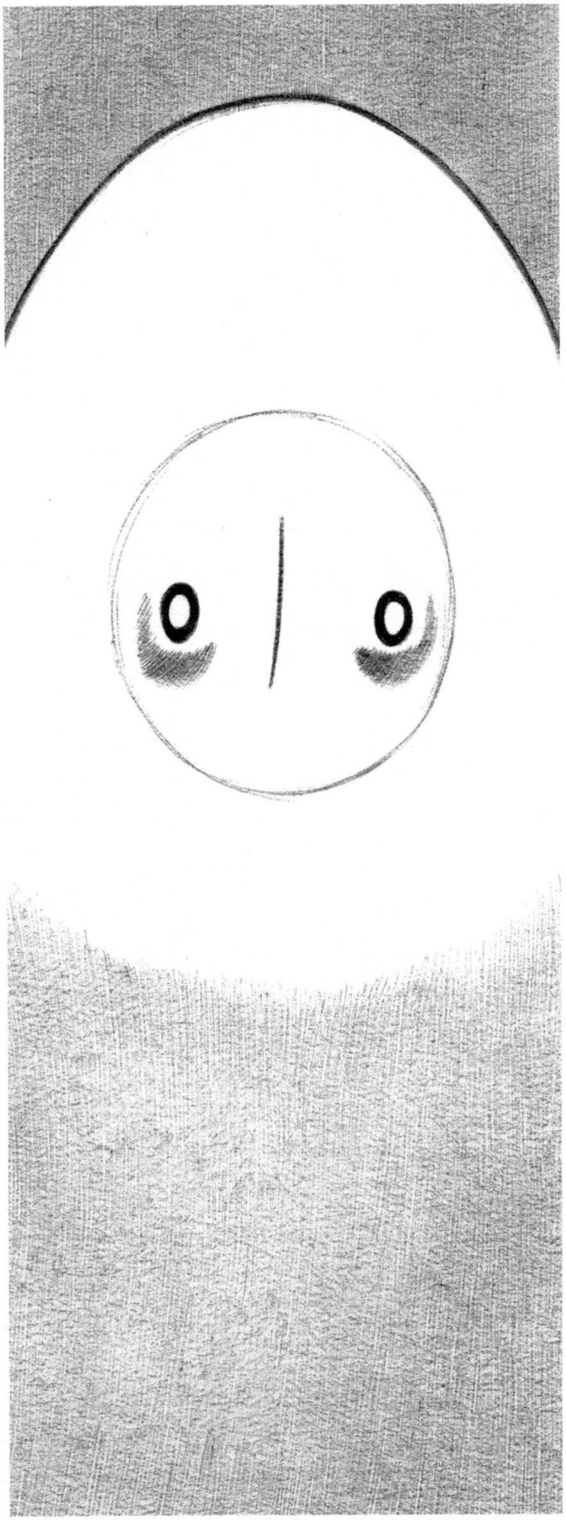

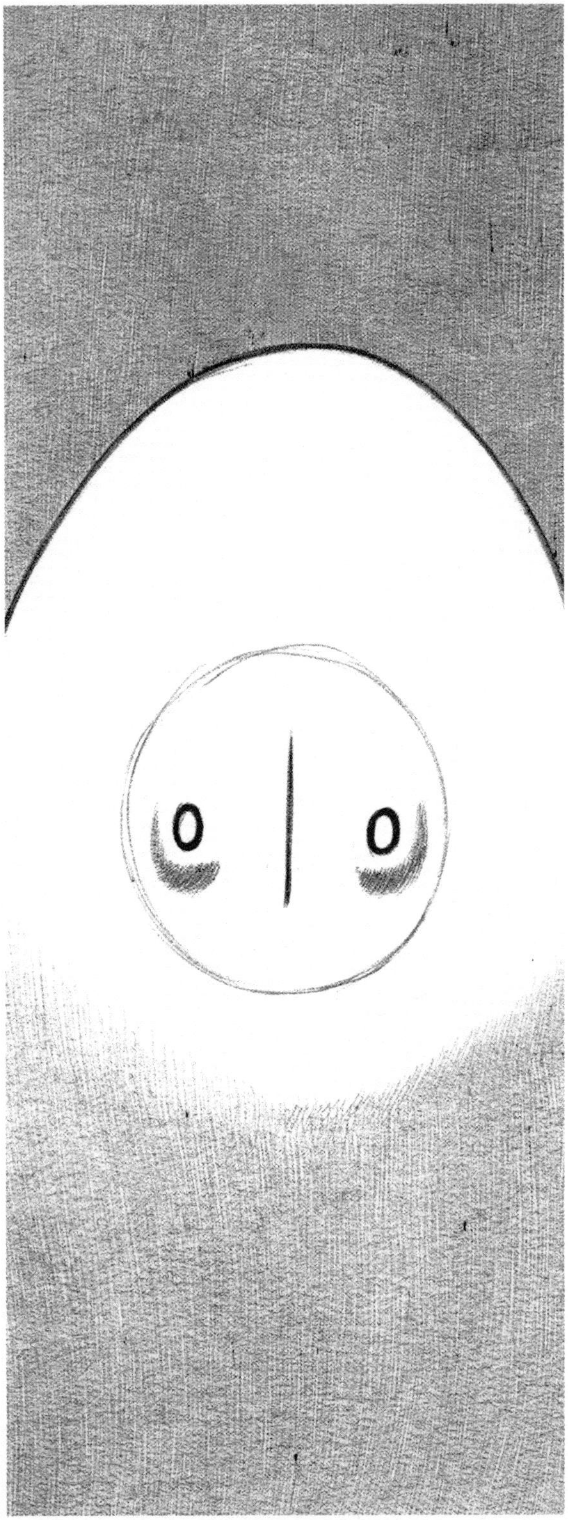

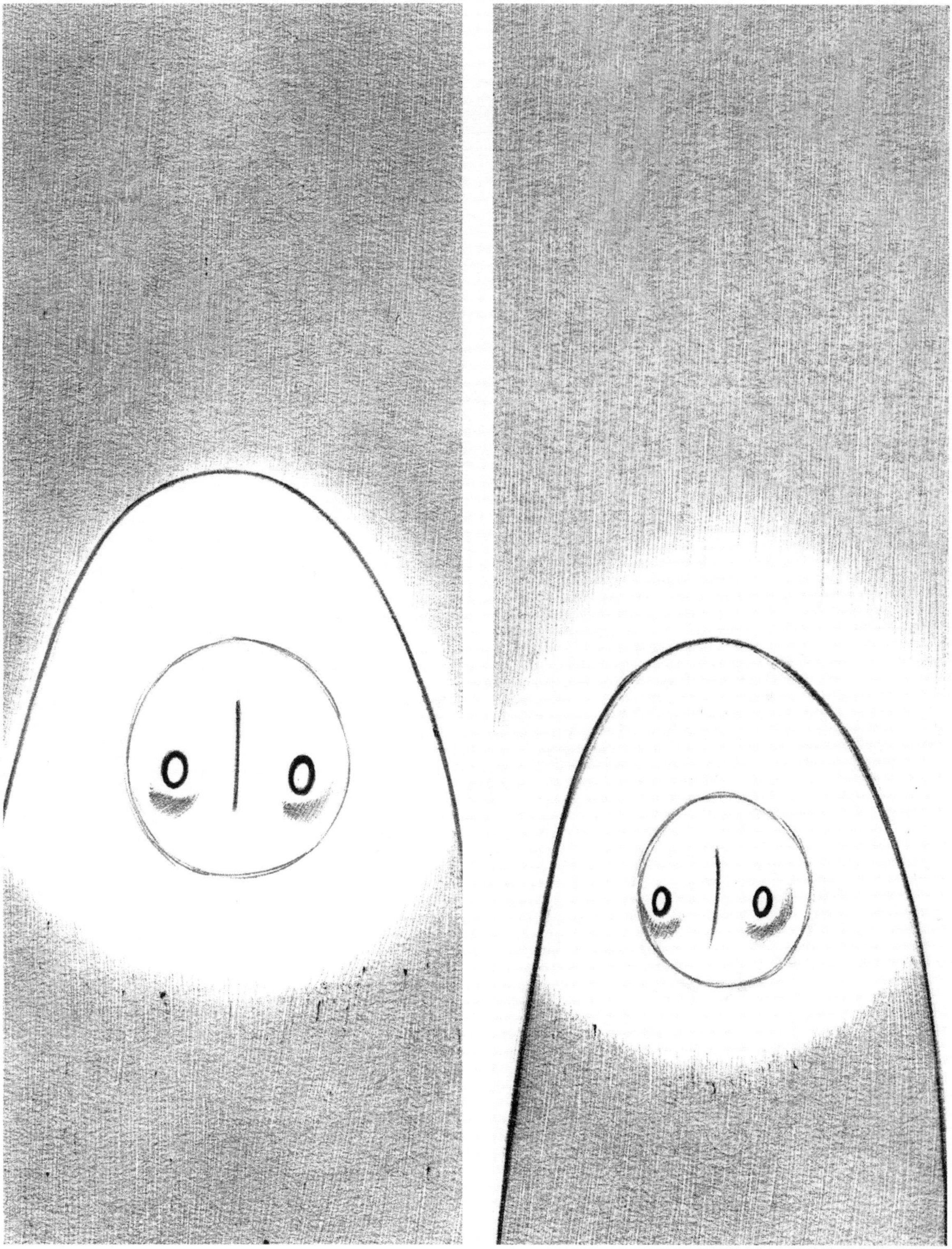

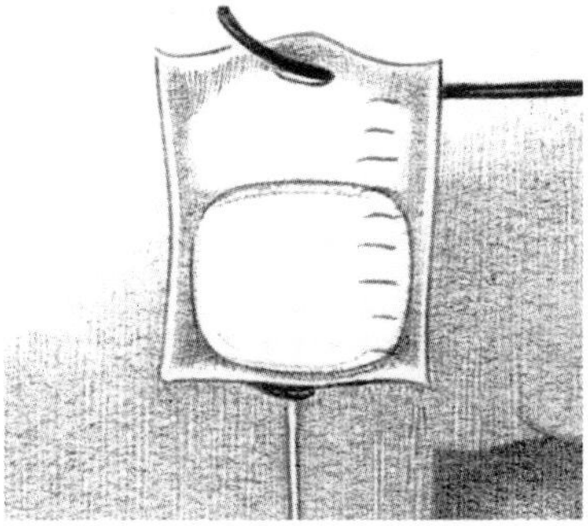

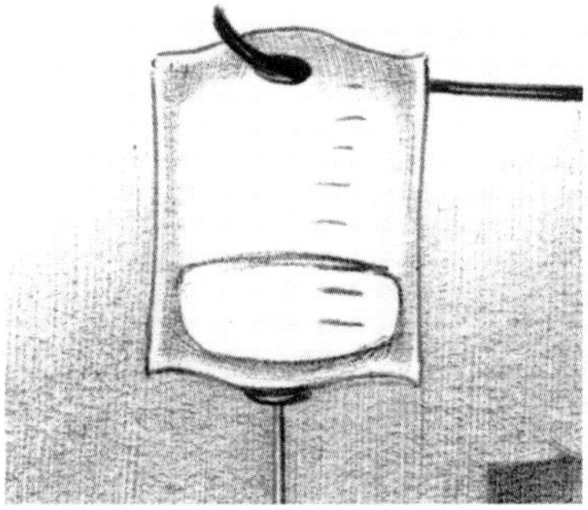

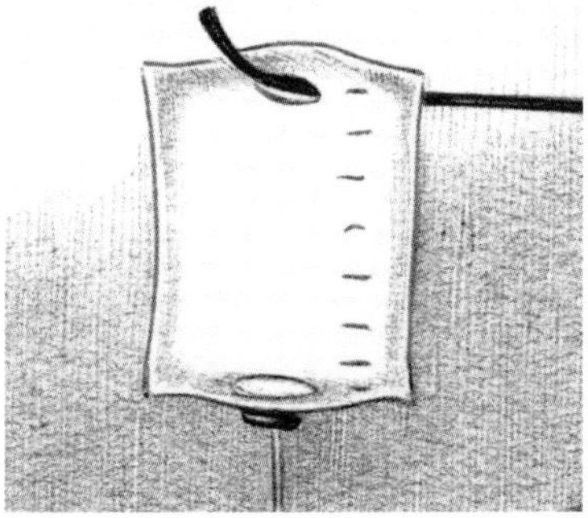

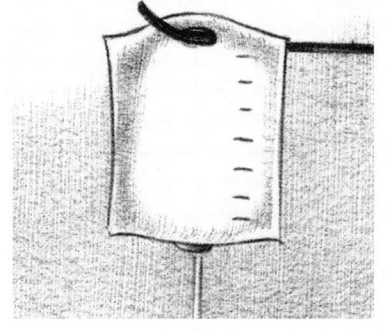

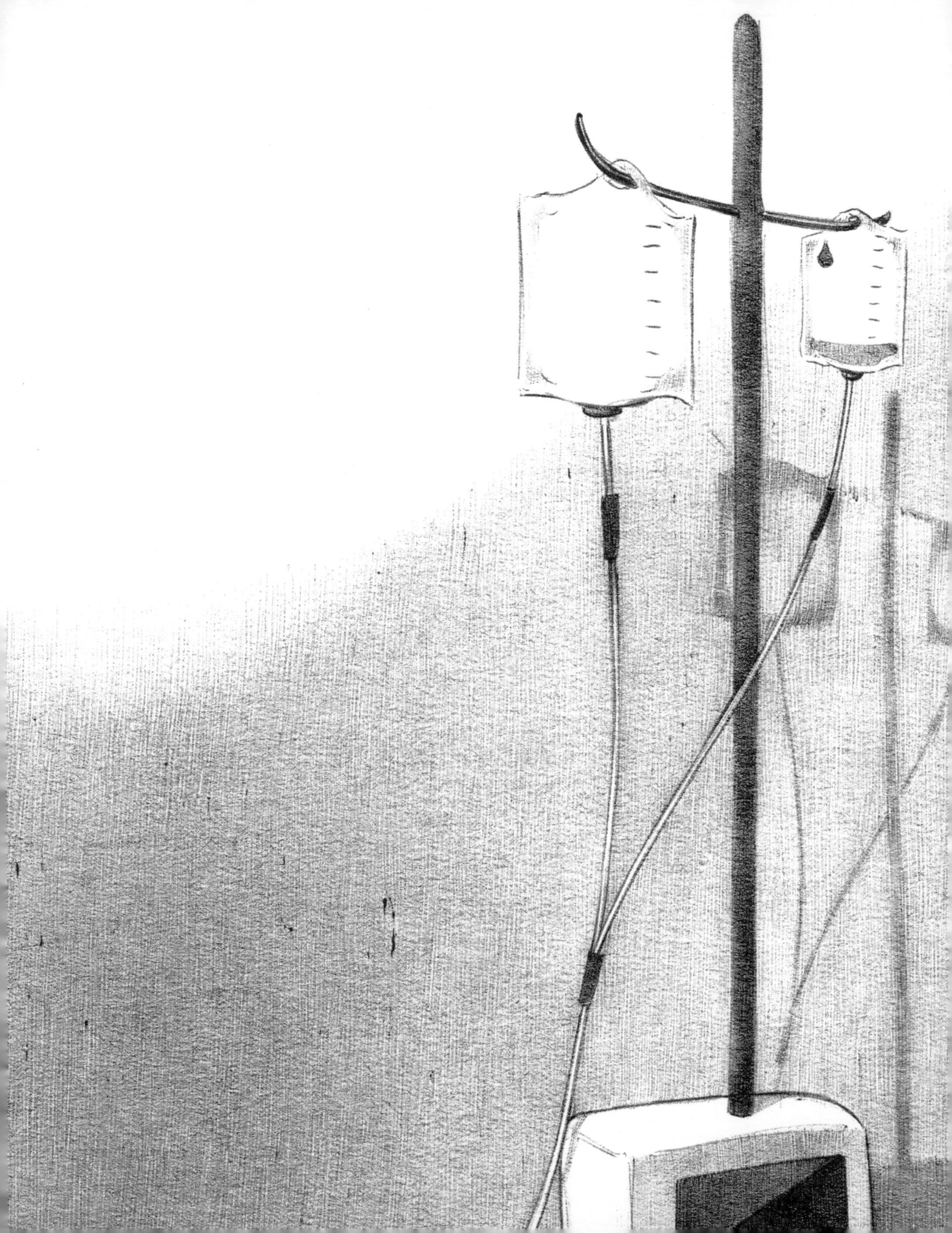

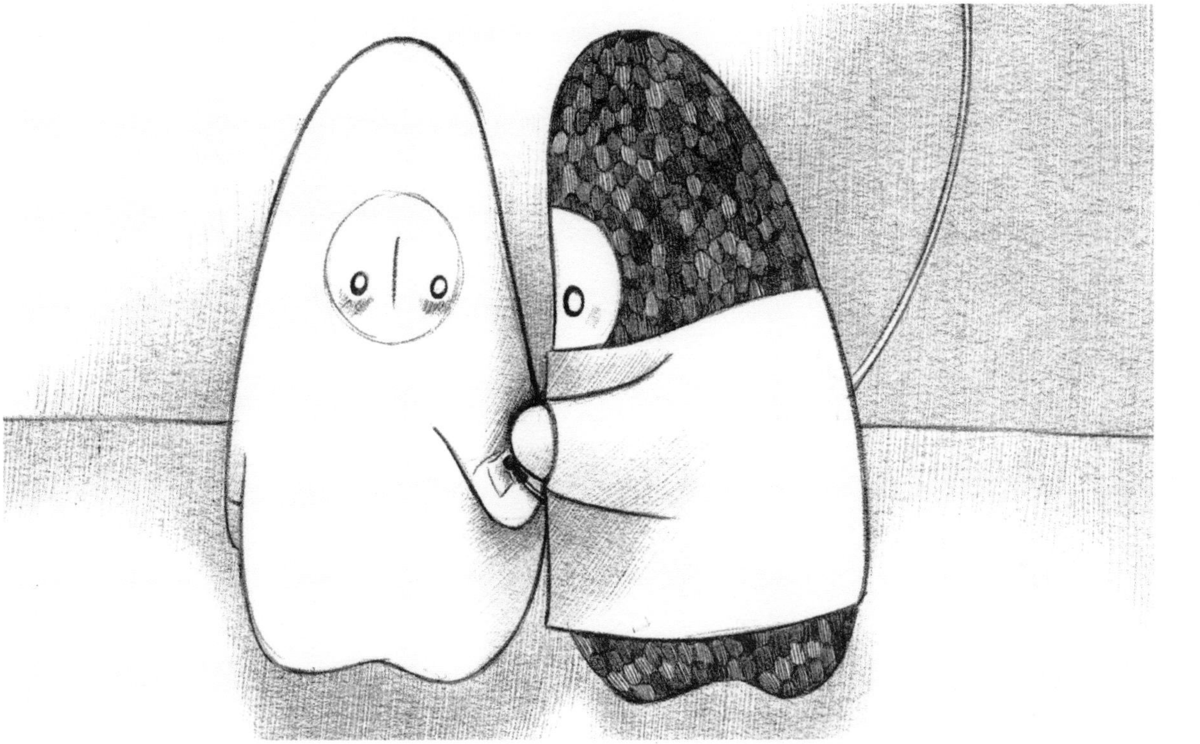

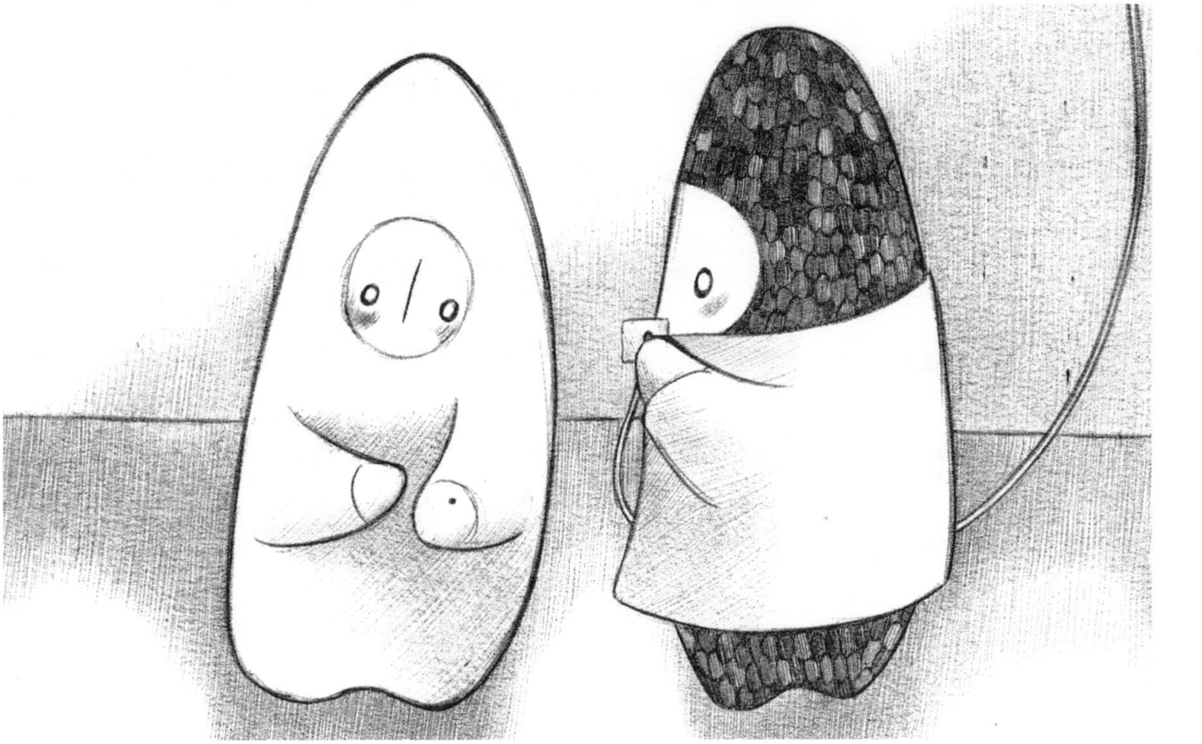

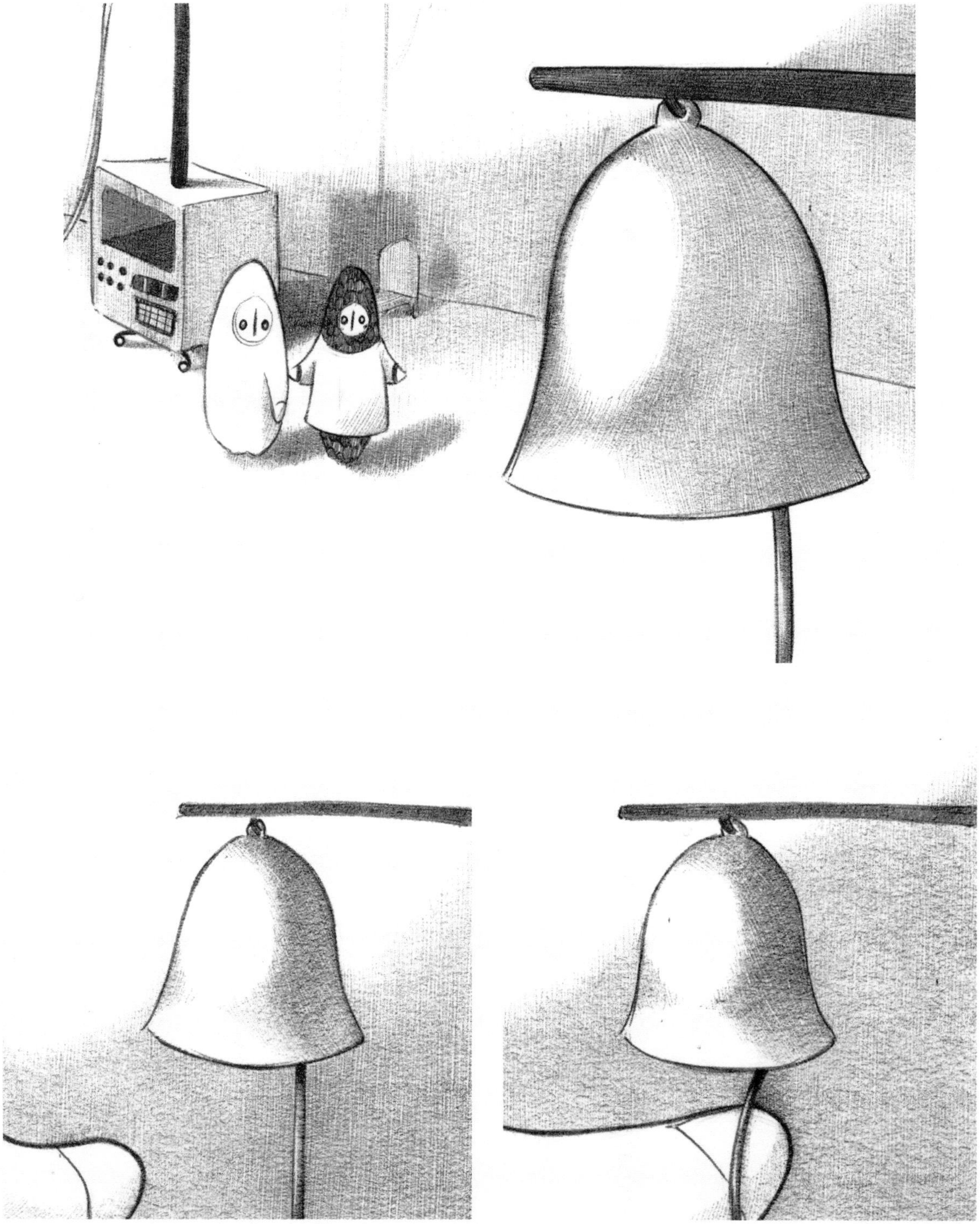

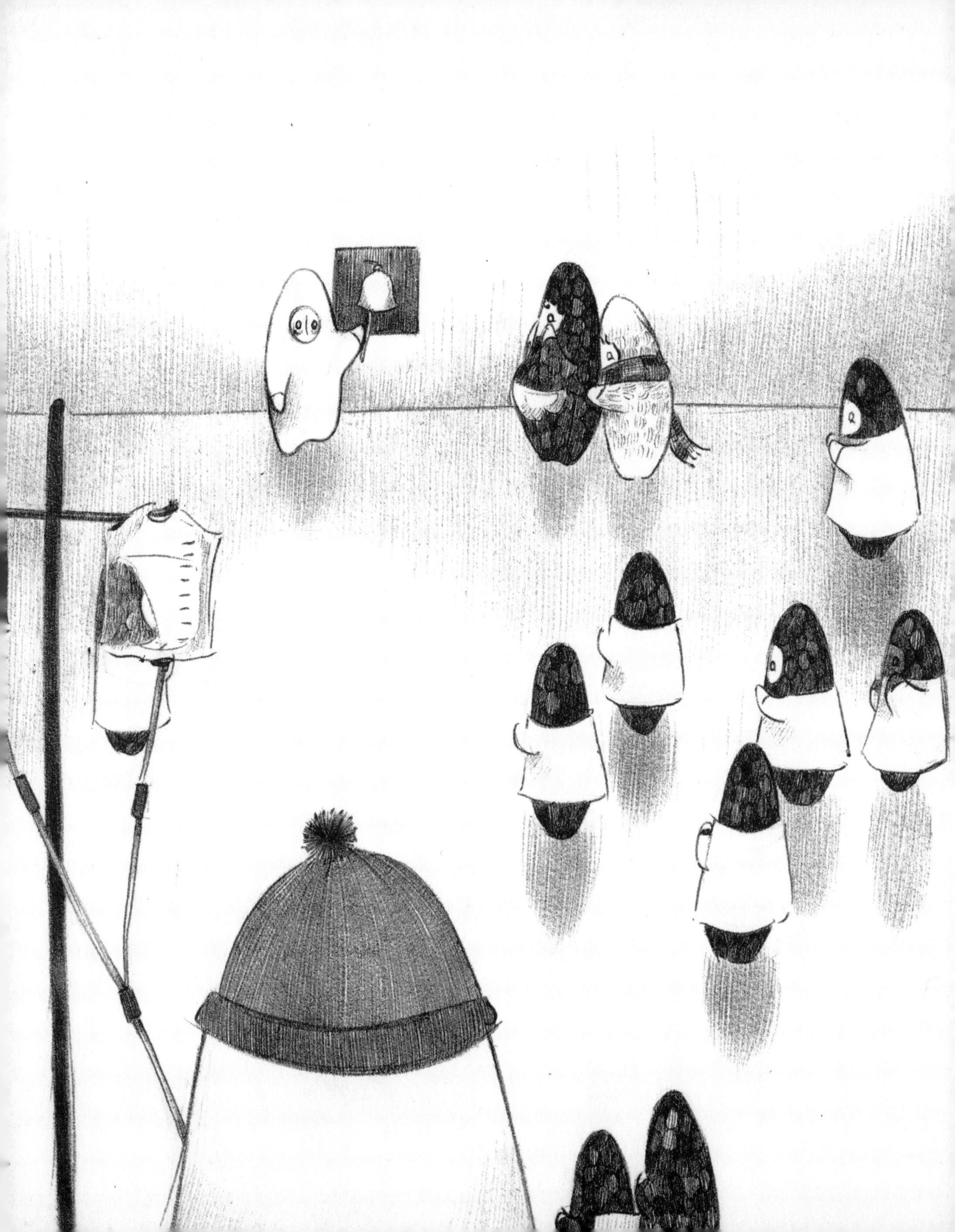

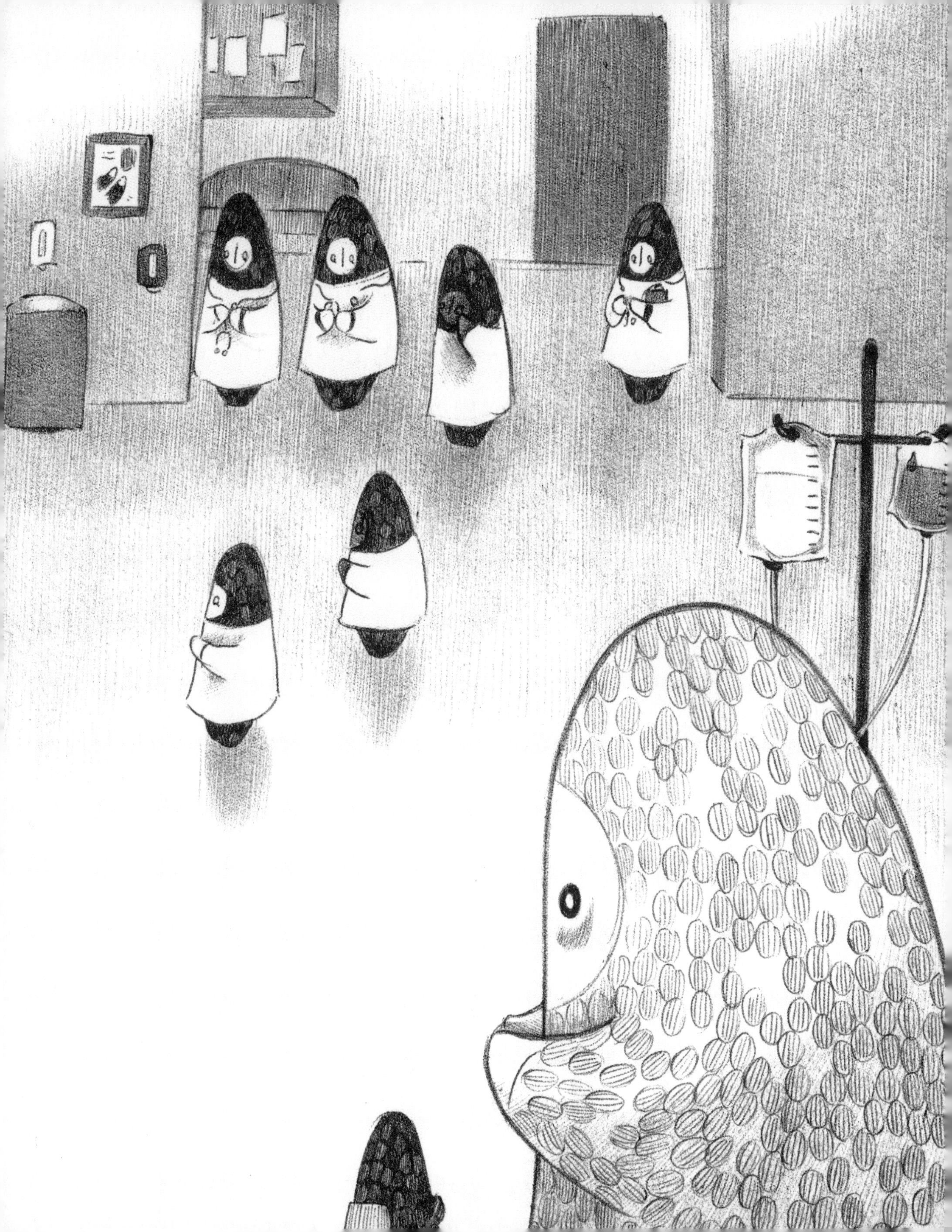

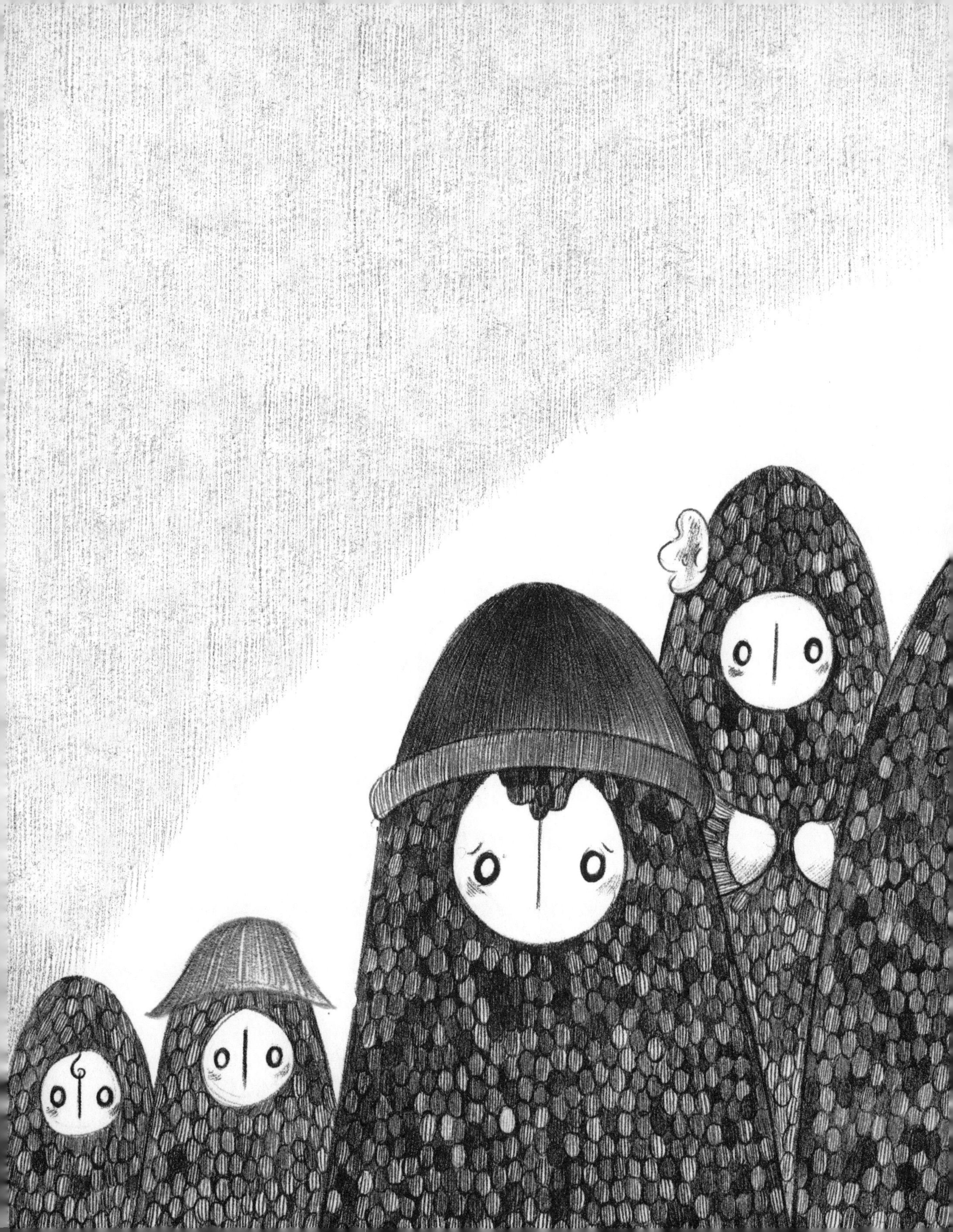

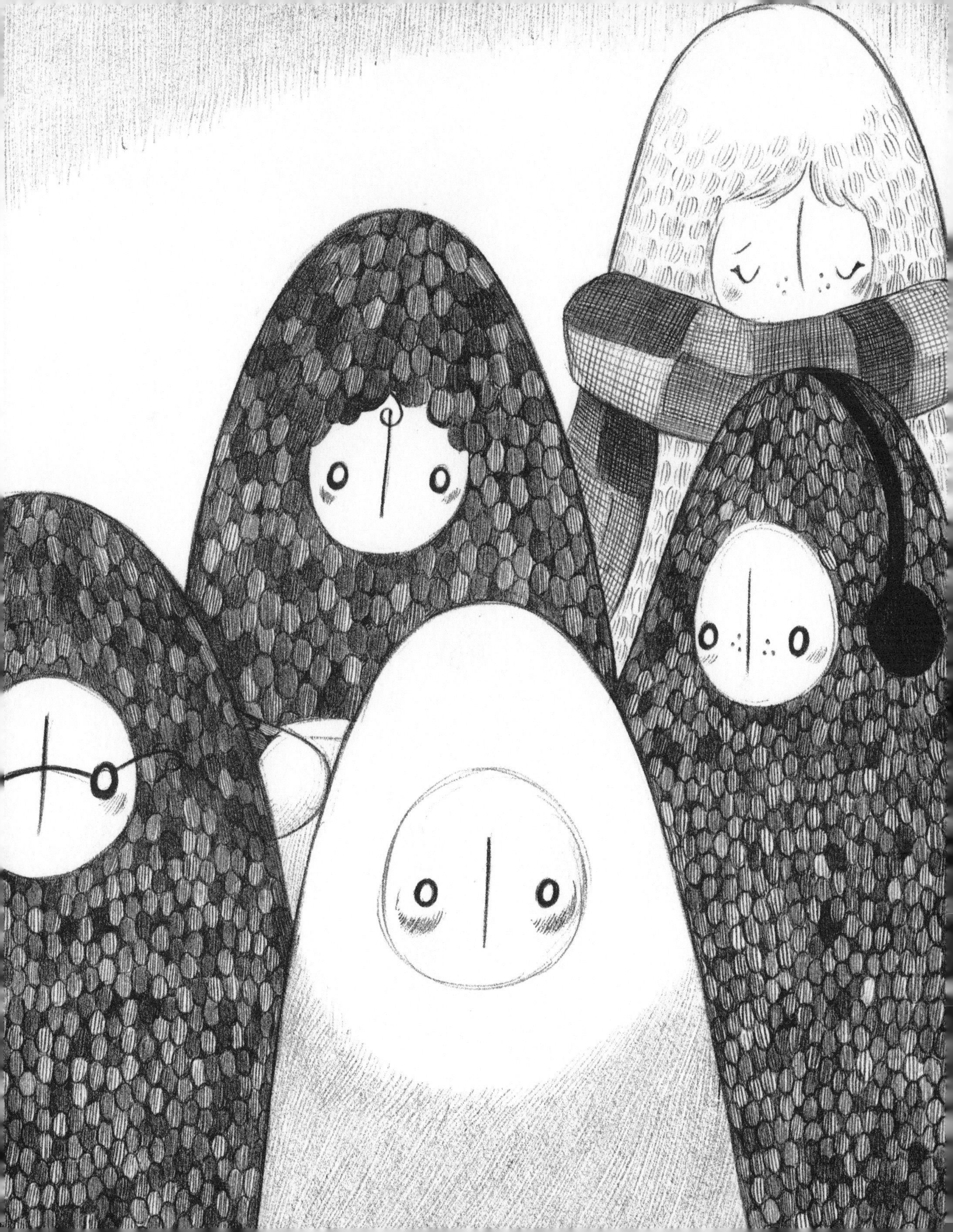

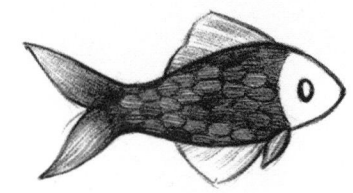

CHAPTER FIVE

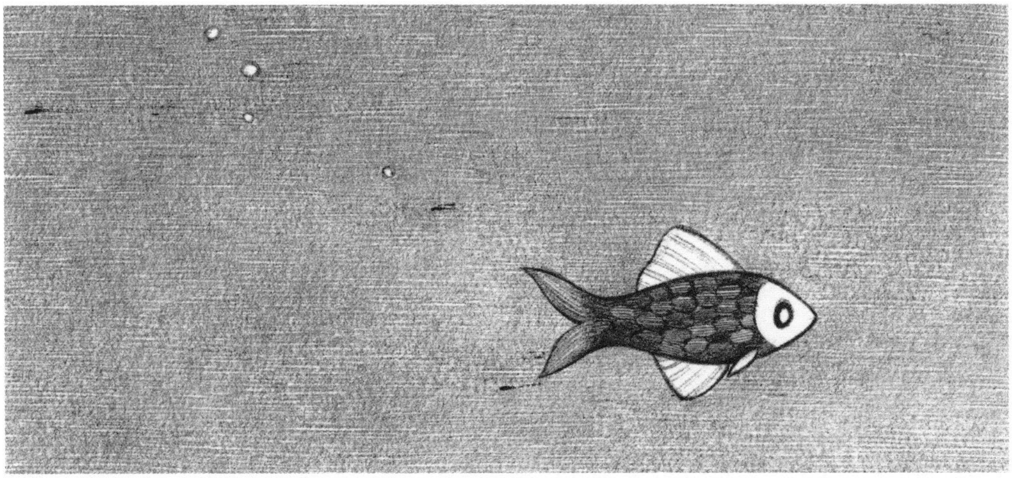

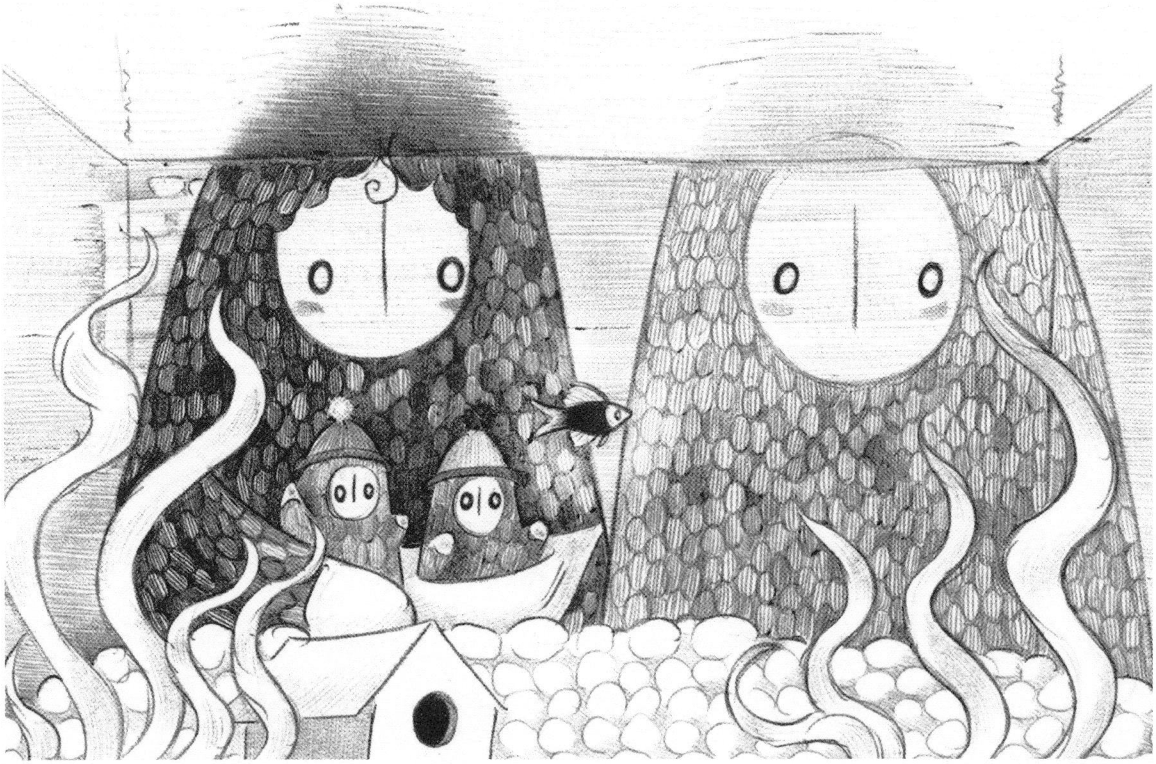

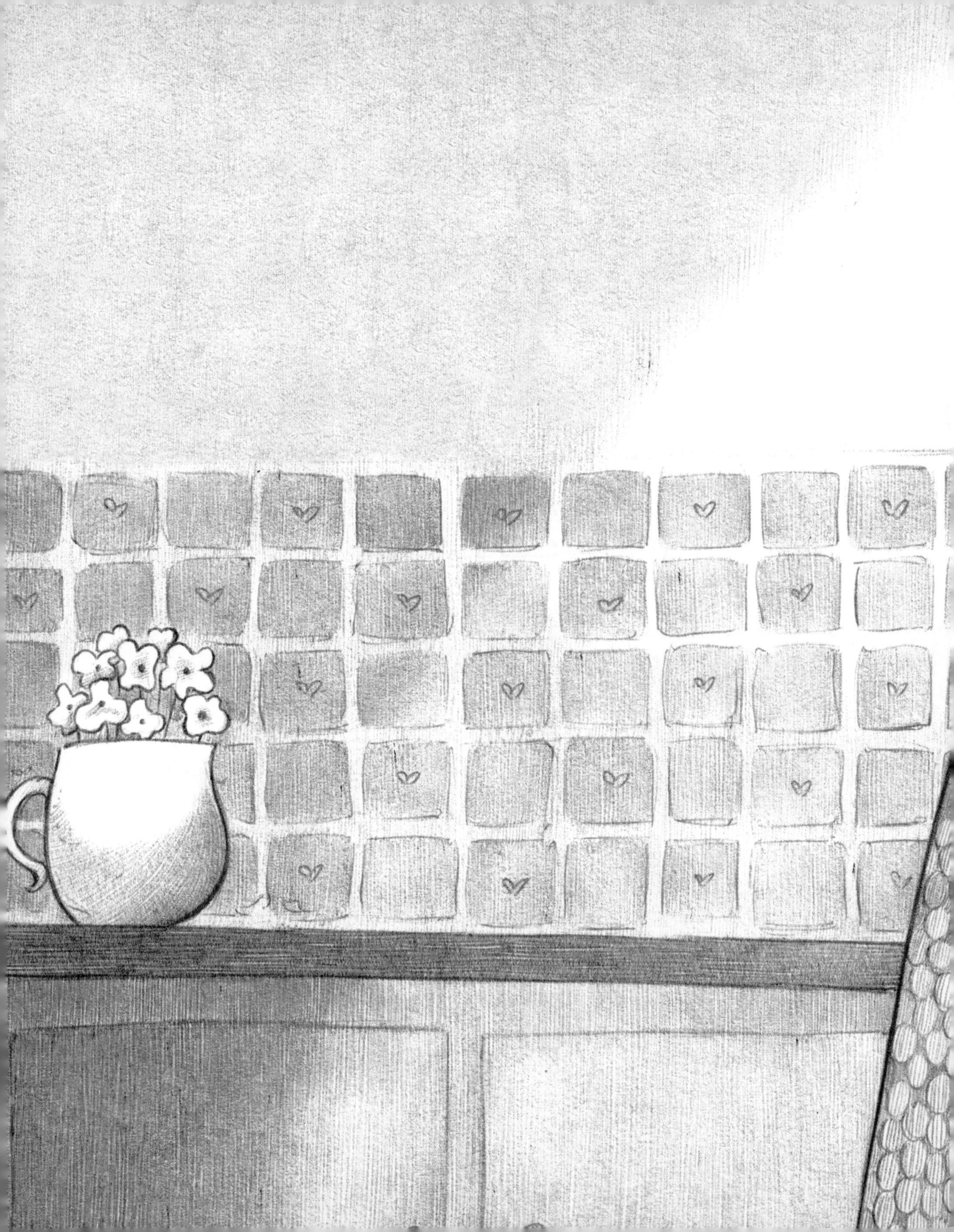

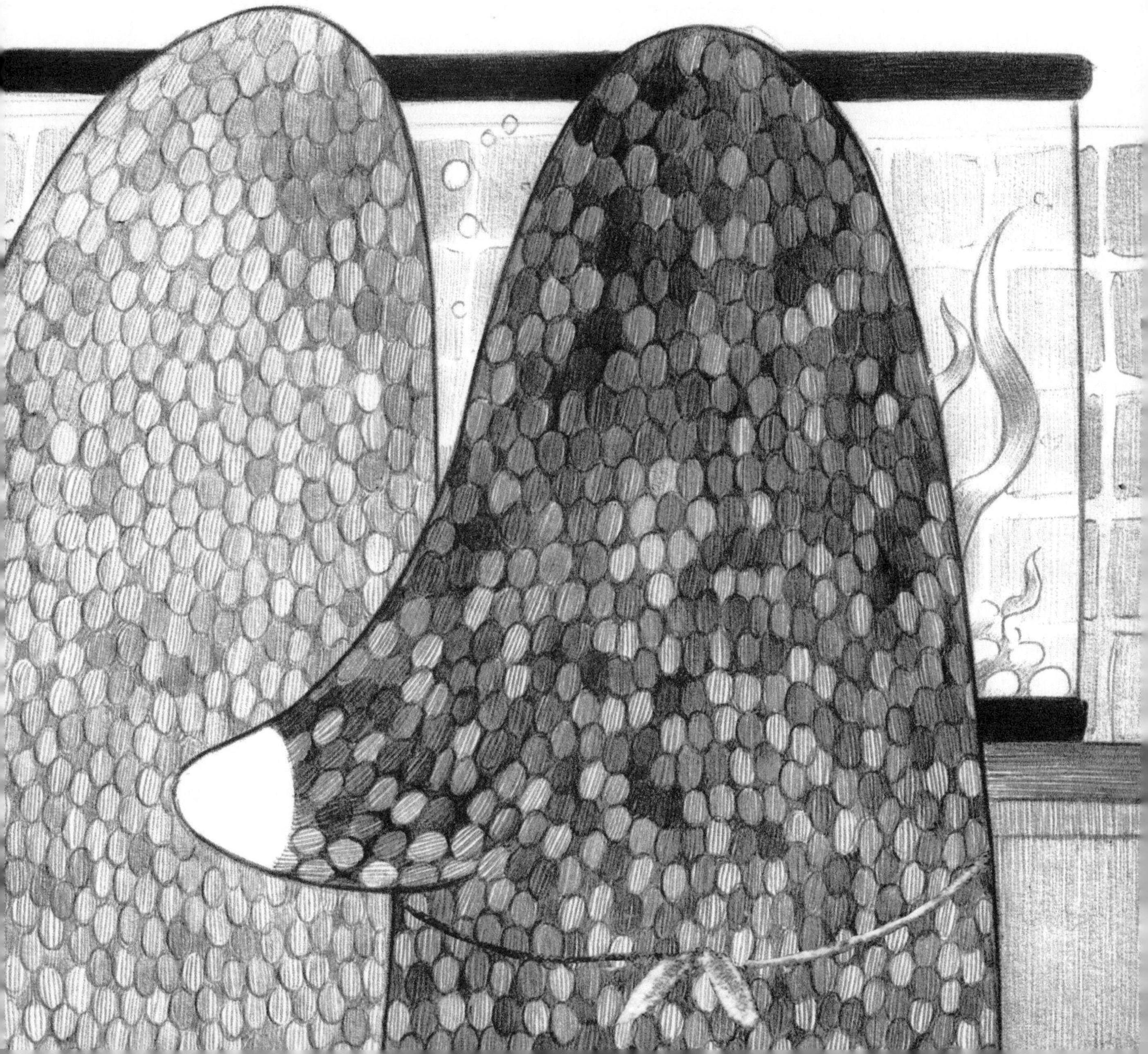

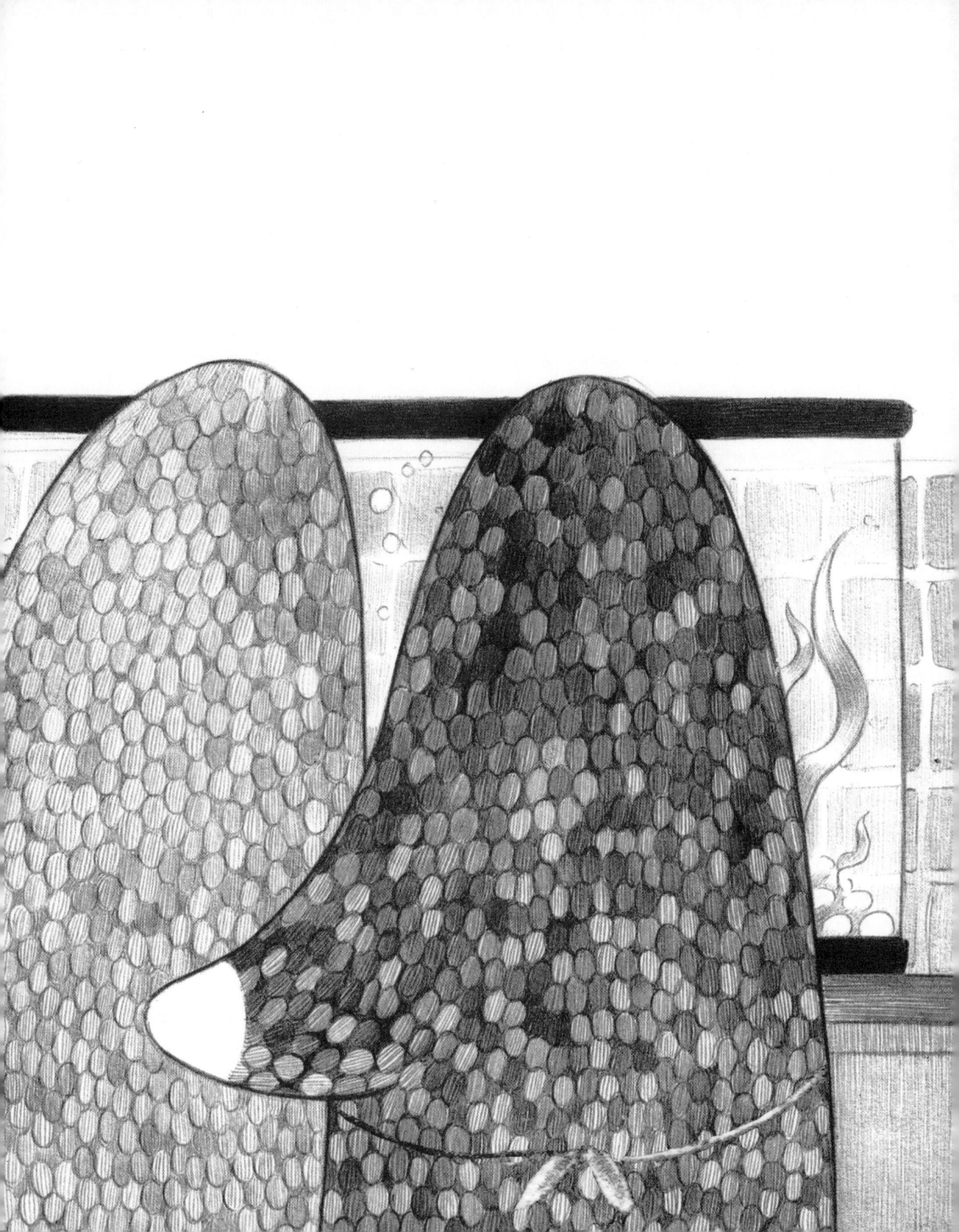

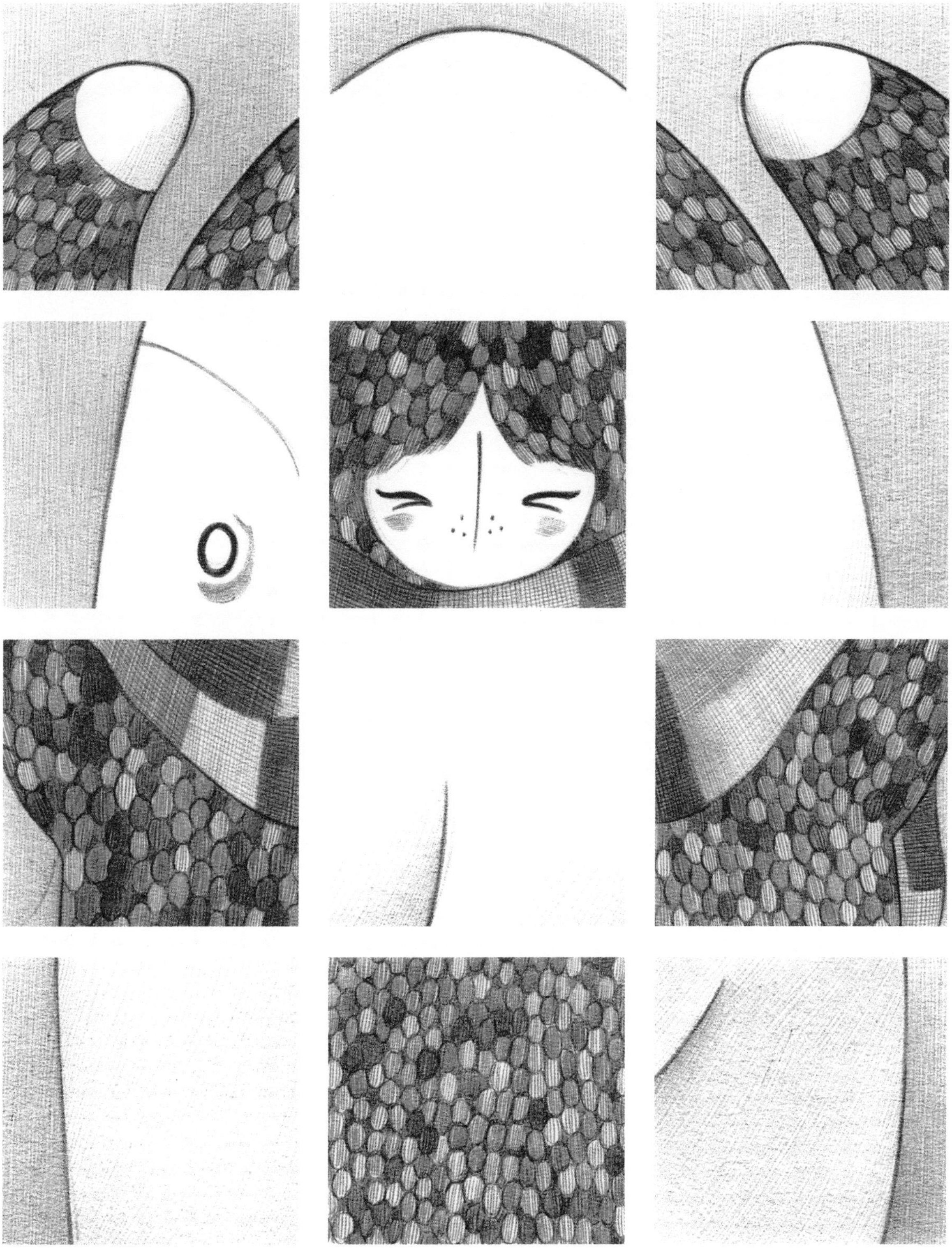

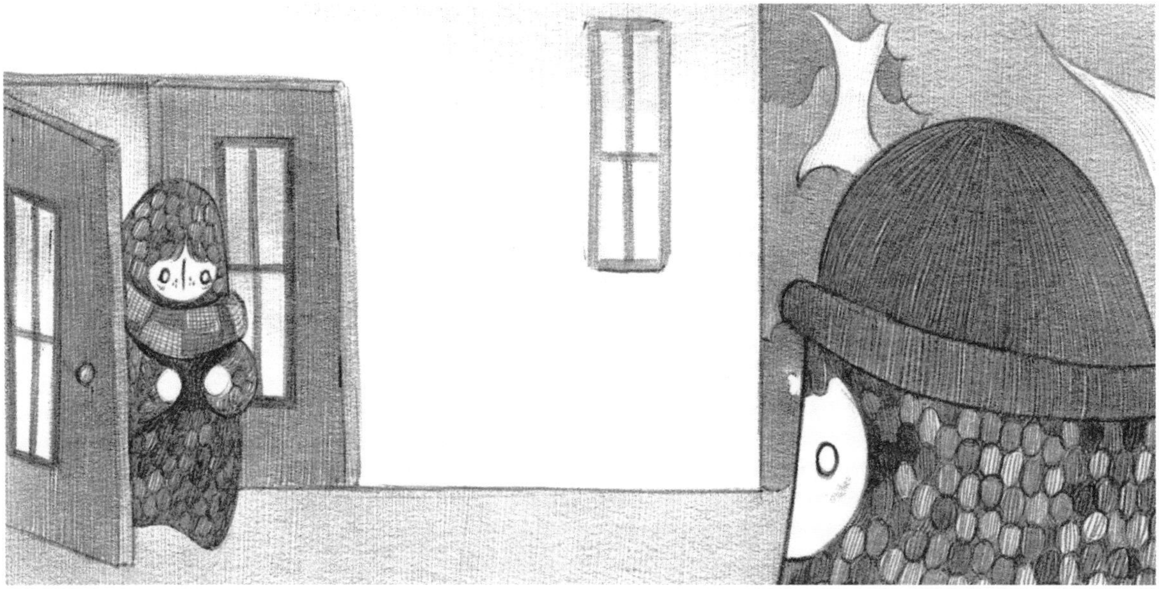

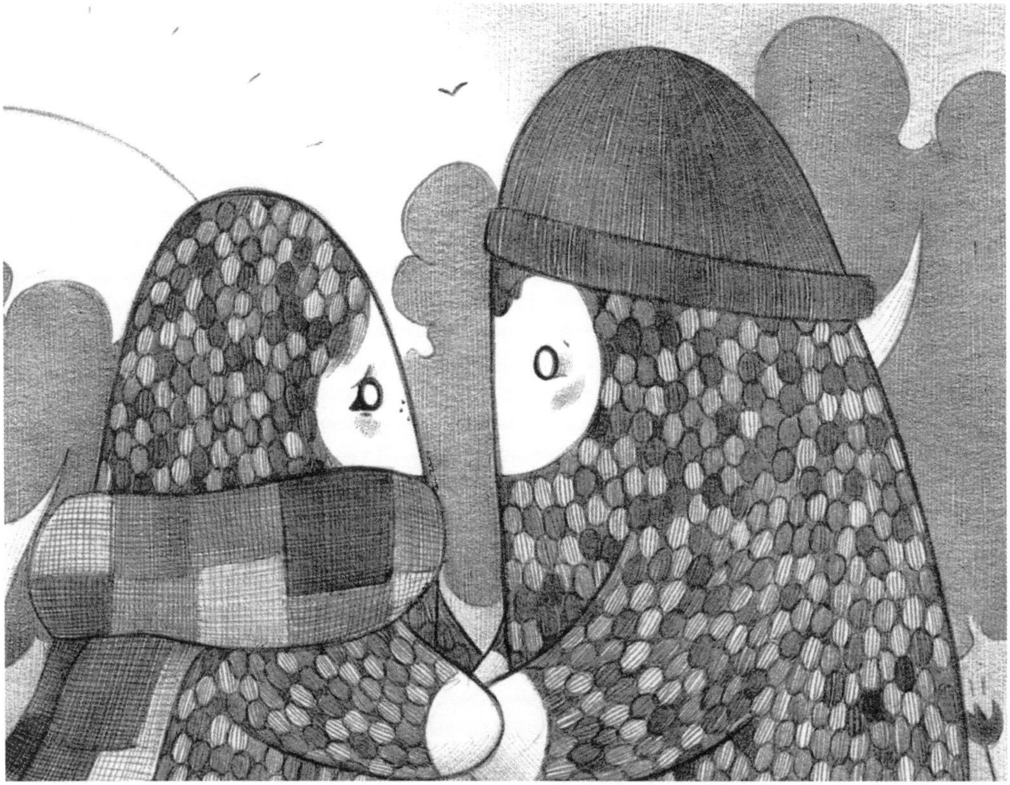

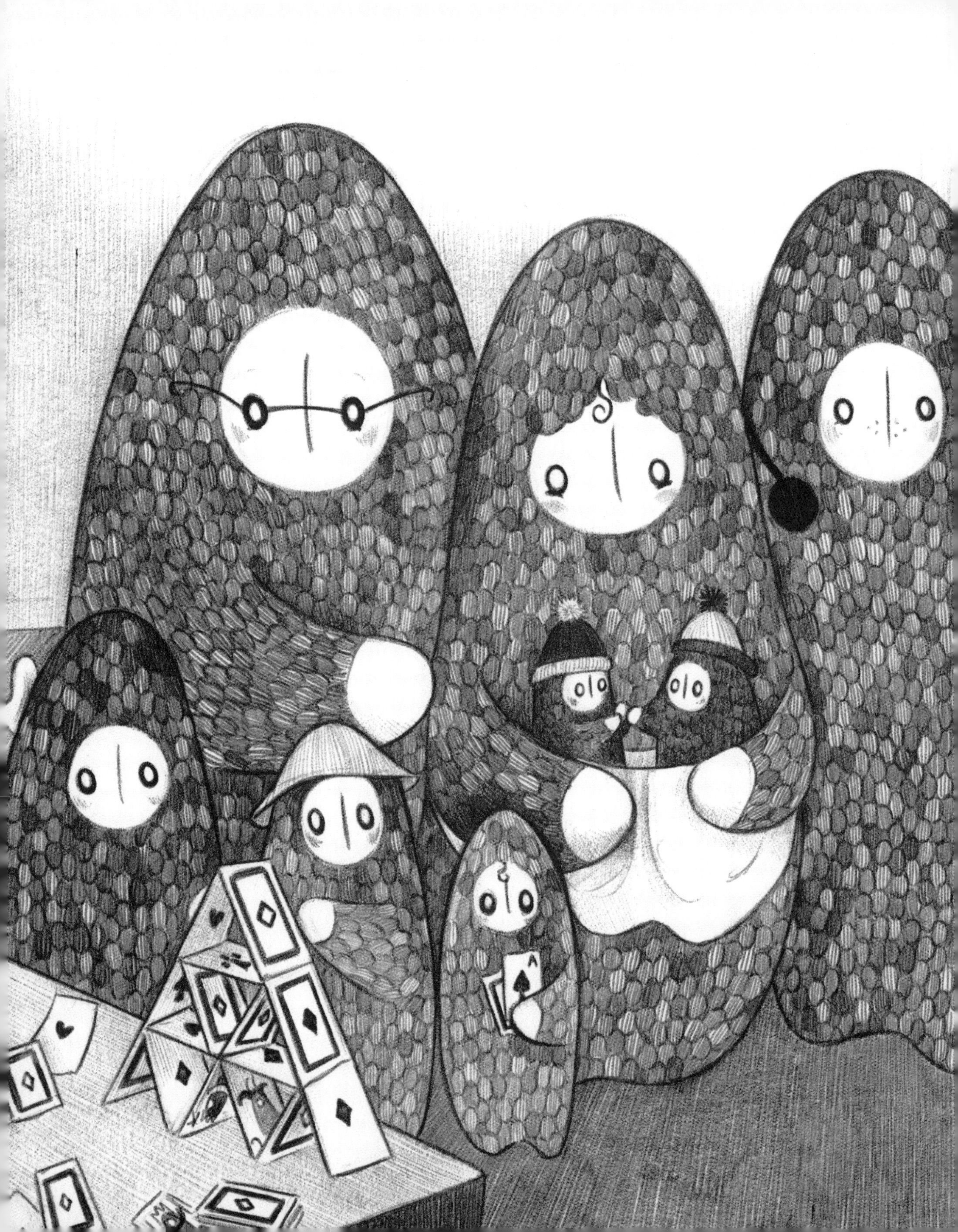

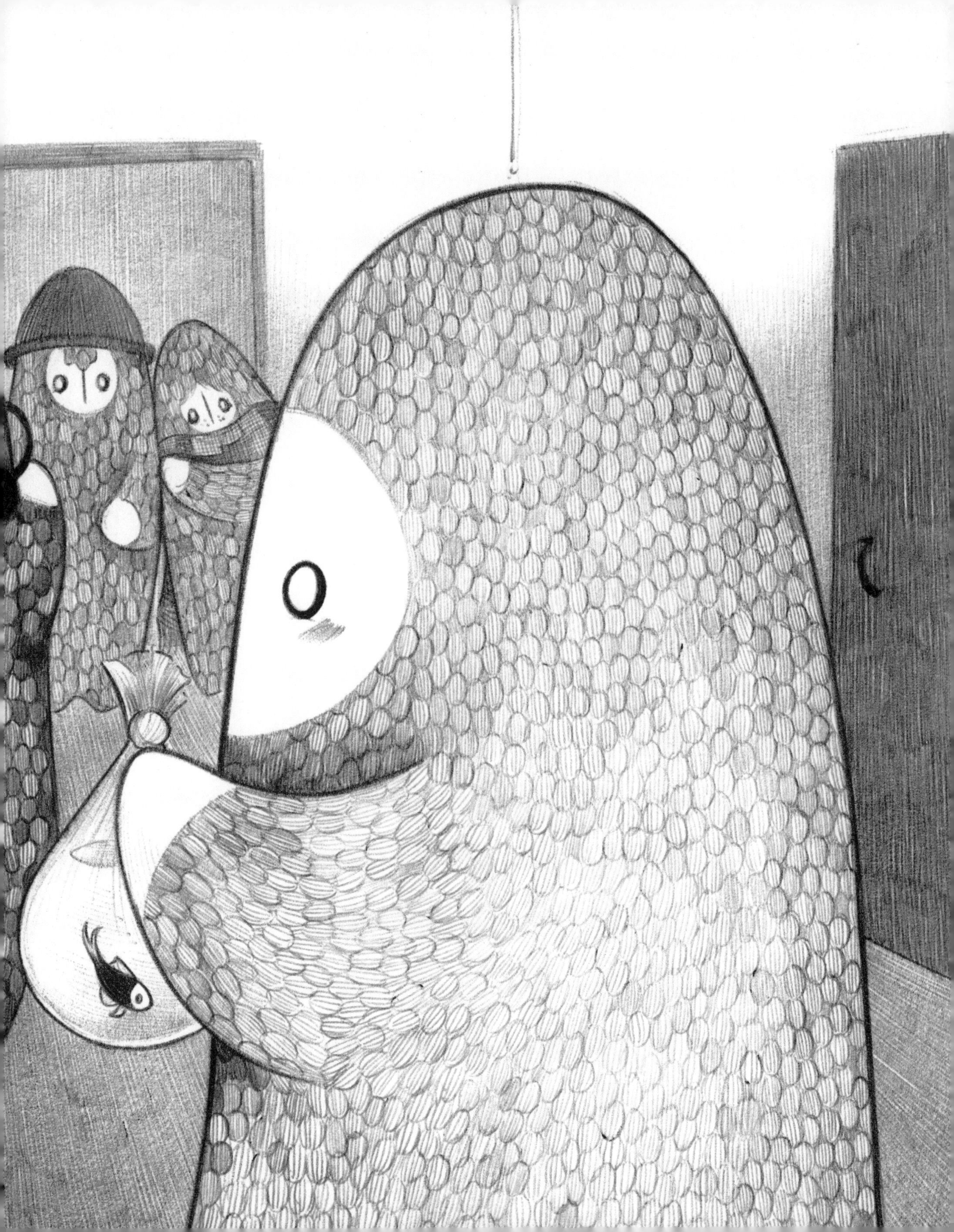

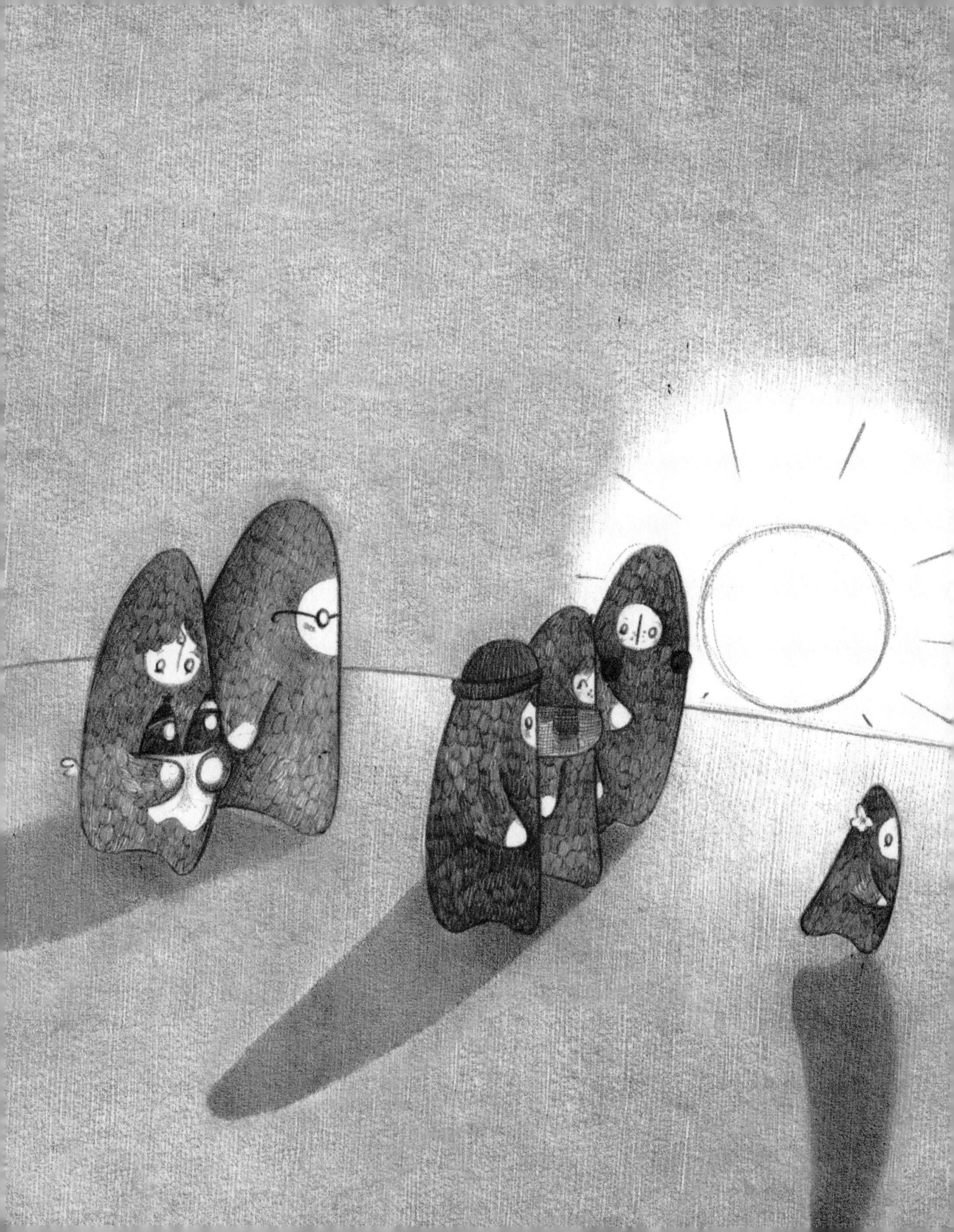

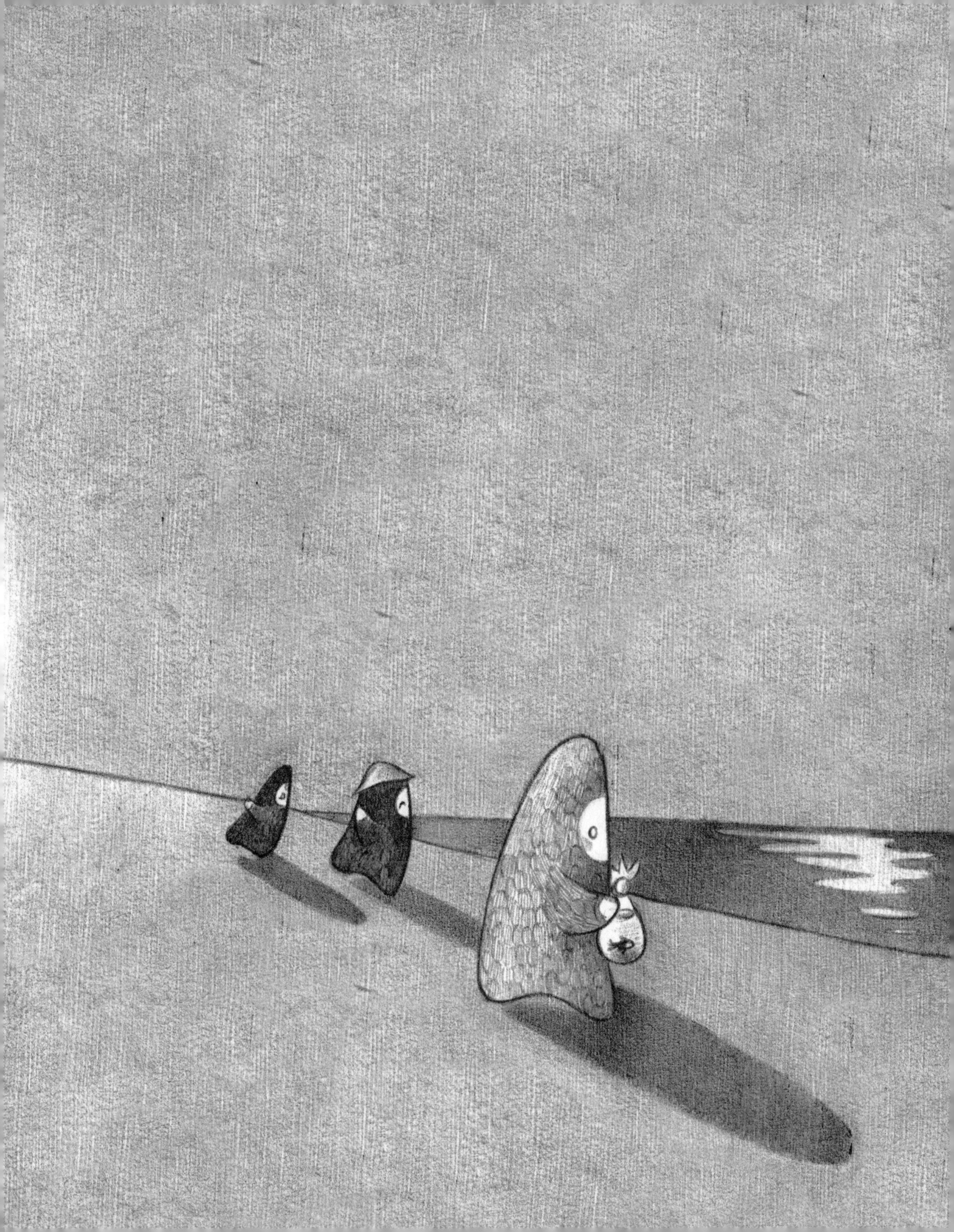

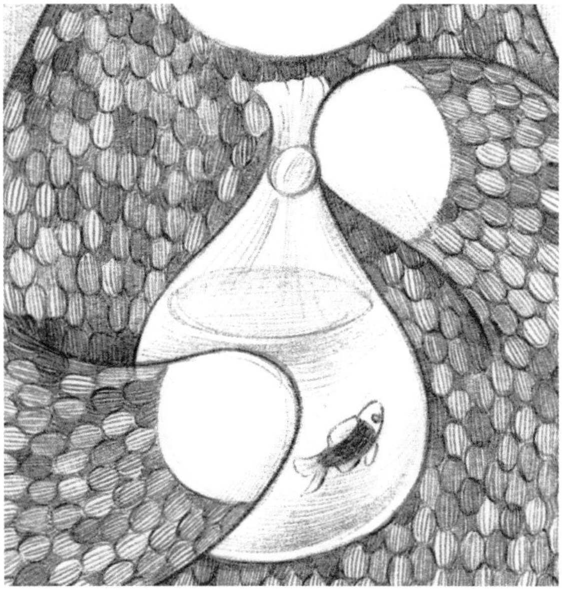

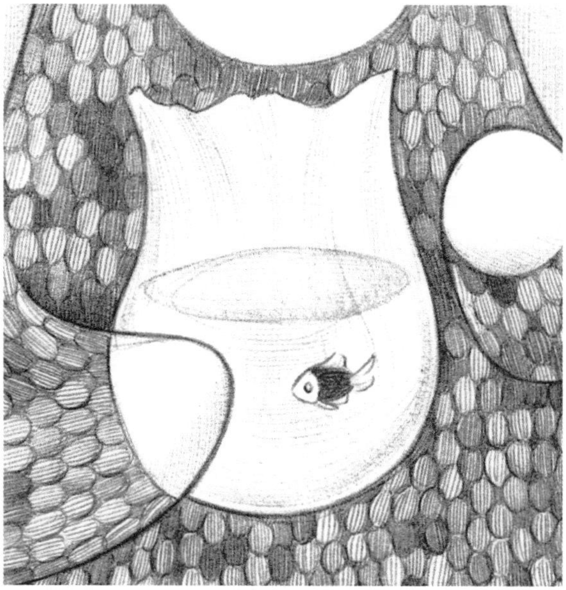

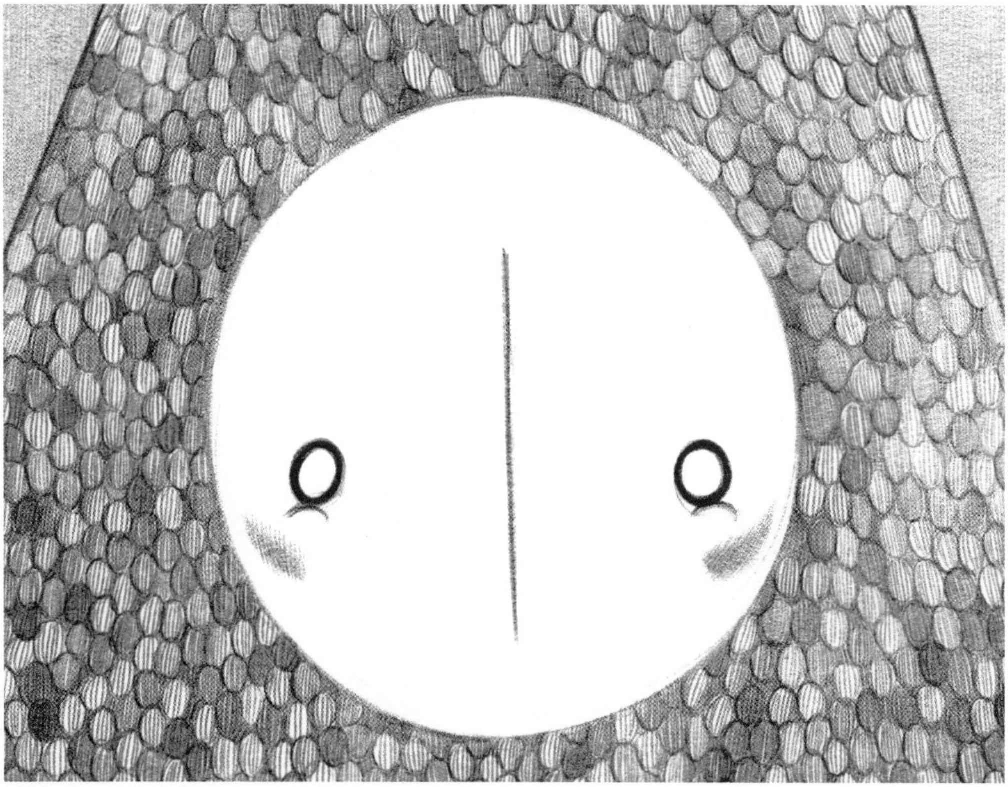

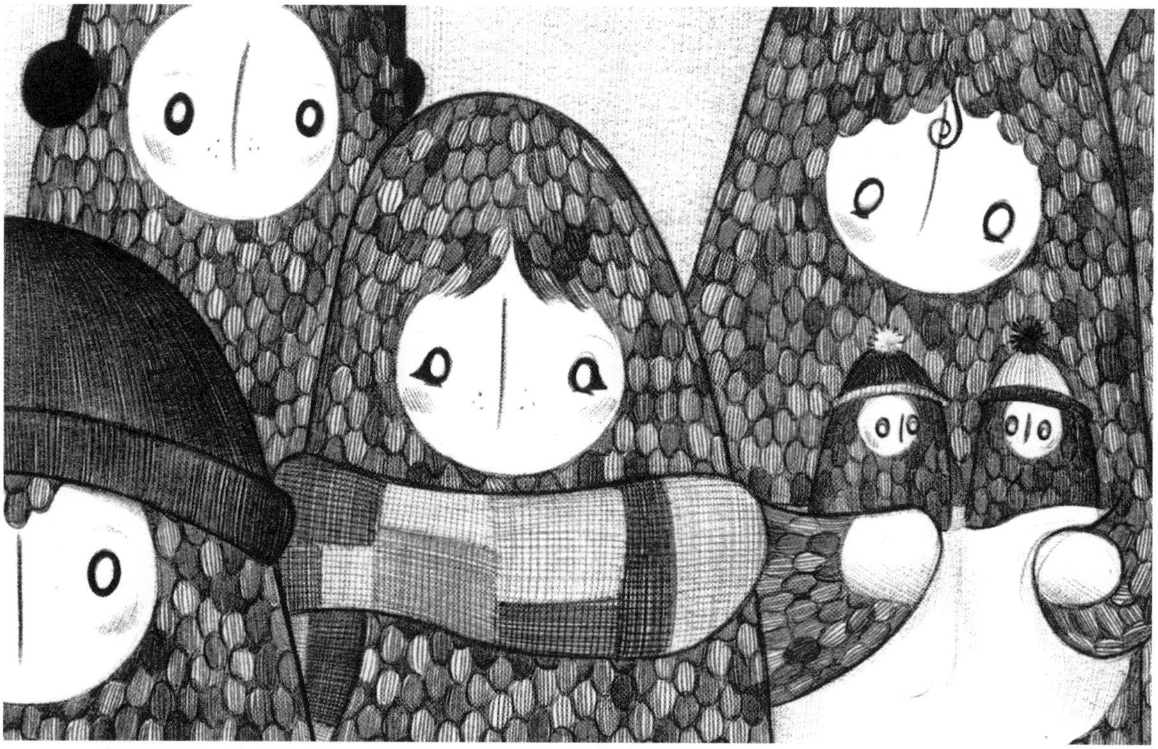

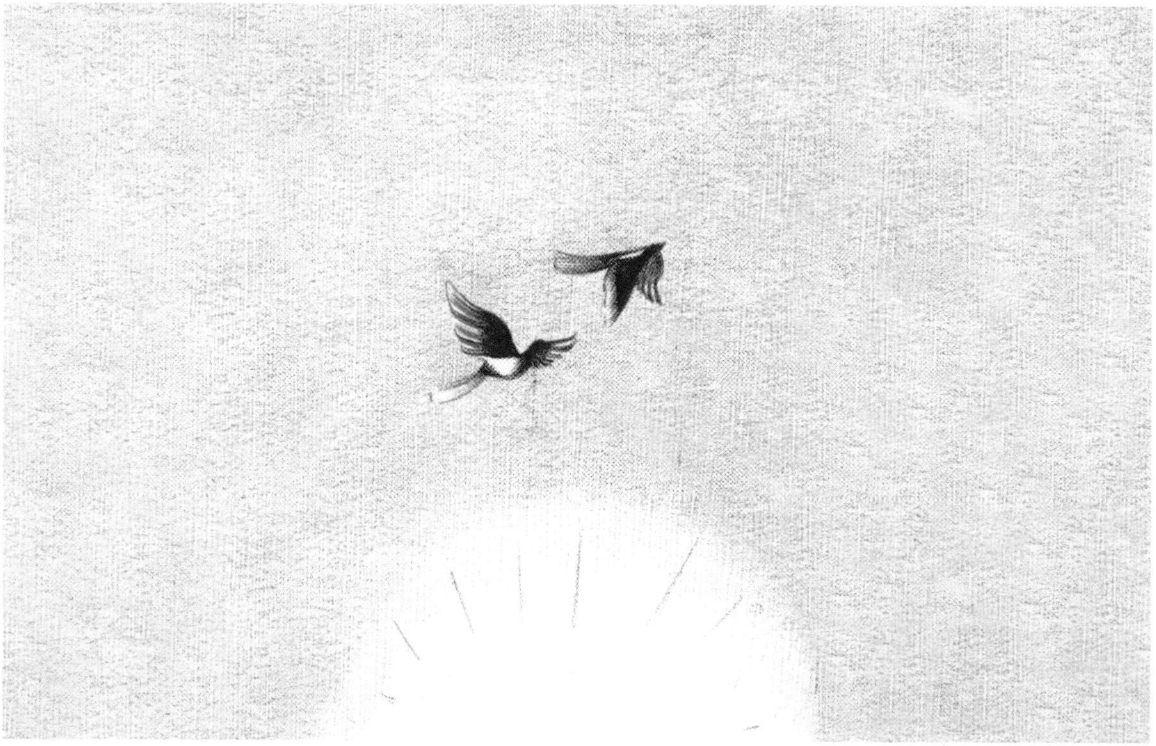

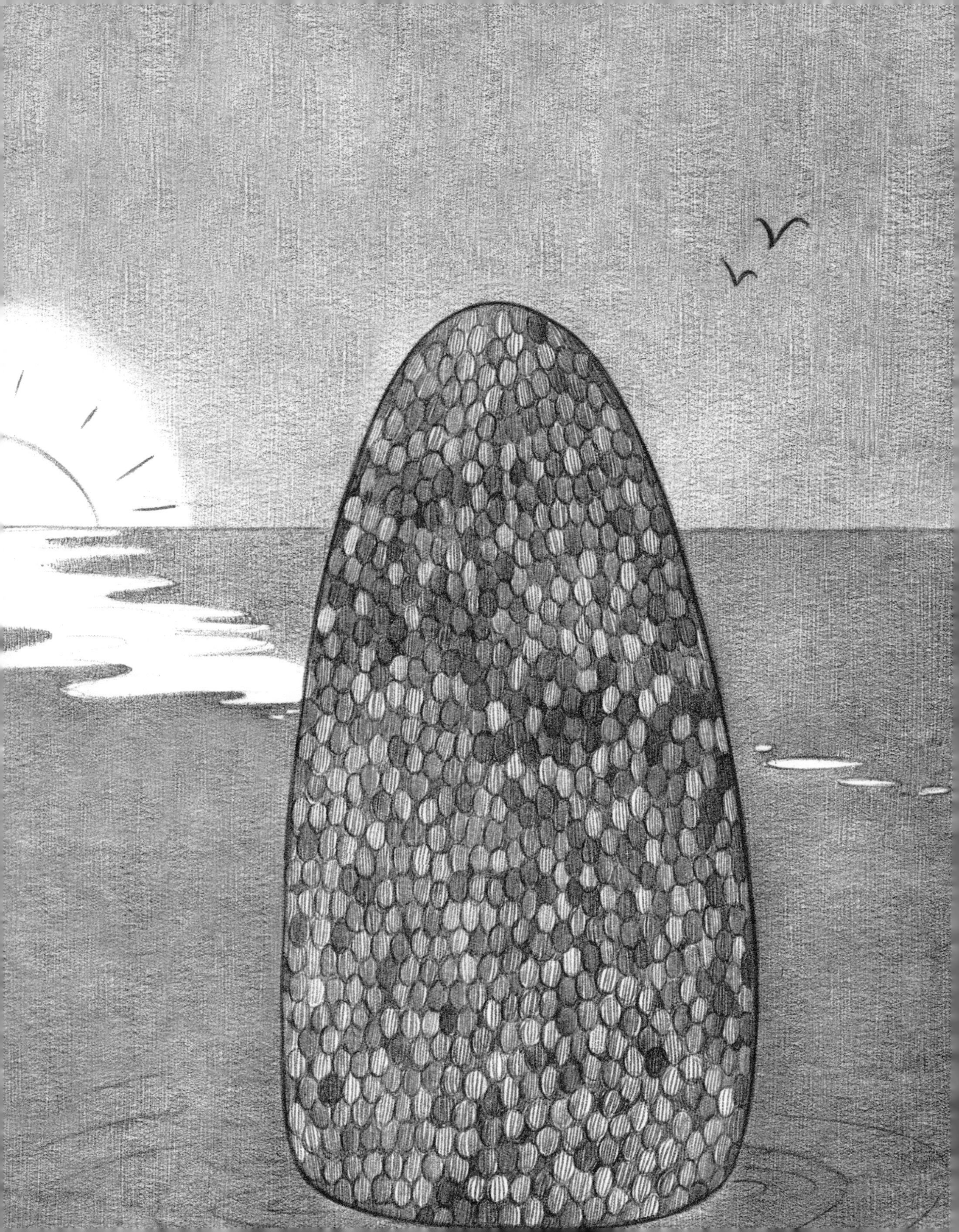

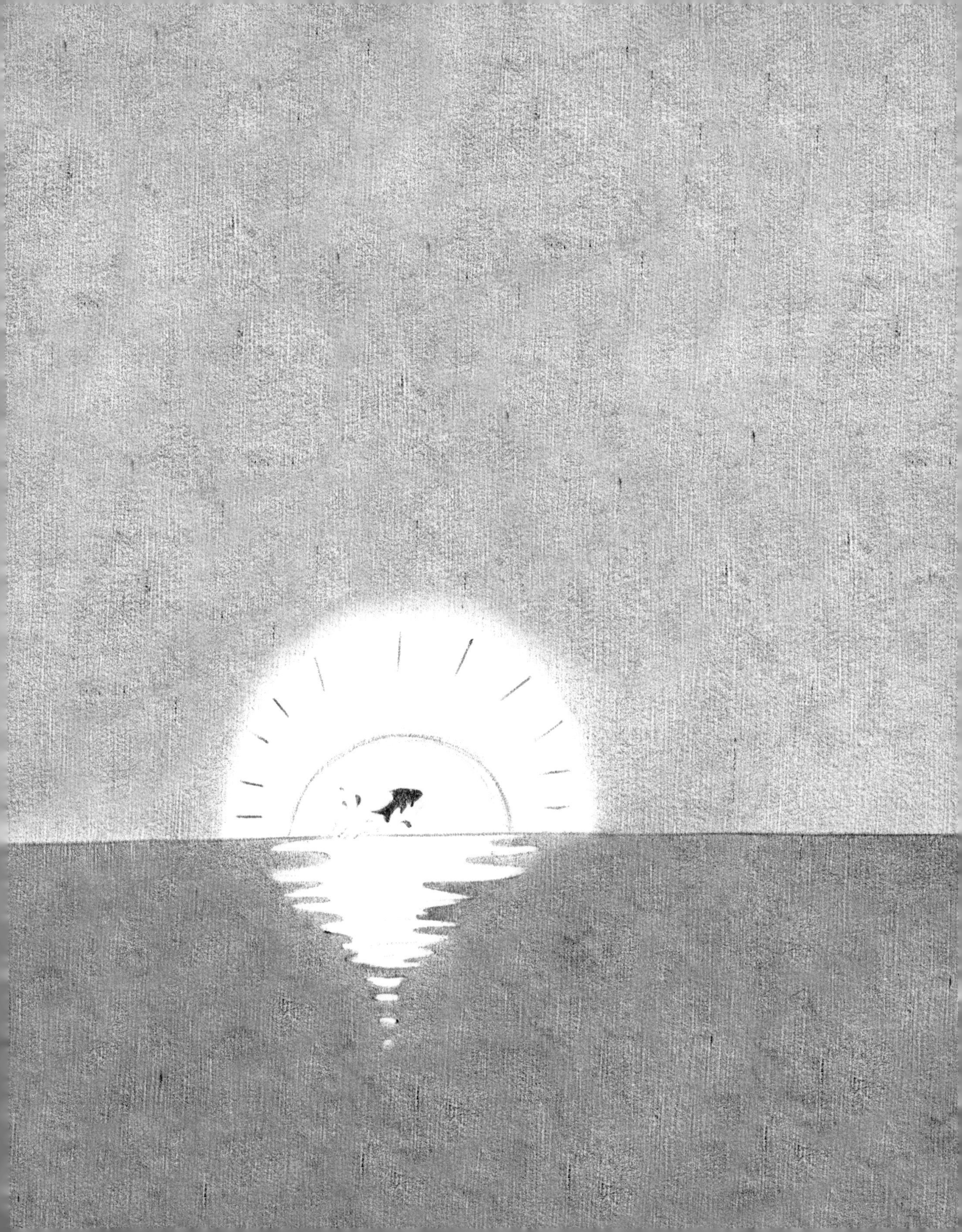

*AND...

MY BRAVE, LOVING MA
OUR BRILLIANT FAMILY: TONY, ARCHIE, ROSIE, HENRY, TEDDY, MONTY AND EIRLYS
MY LOYAL BEST FRIEND AND PARTNER: LIAM
MY SHINY STARS: LEA AND HAYLEY
LOUIE'S SHINY STARS: HARRY THE CAT AND WILL THE HUMAN
THE AMAZING DOCTORS AND NURSES AT THE CHRISTIE
THE WONDERFUL DR WEEKS
TEENAGE CANCER TRUST, CANCER CARE AND THE CRISIS TEAM
MY MENTAL HEALTH SAVIOURS: DR CORLEY, FIRST STEPS AND THE MAGGIE CENTRE
MY 'COMICS ANGEL' AND HONORARY BIG SISTER: GEMMA
MY KIND, PASSIONATE AGENT AND FRIEND: JAMES
MY FABULOUS EDITOR: ANGUS
THE WHOLE FABER TEAM
MY GIANT GUIDING LIGHTS: NICOLA AND KATIE
THE LEGENDS OF LICAF: JULIE, CAROLE, HESTER, SIM AND GEMMA (AGAIN)
BROKEN FRONTIER'S ANDY OLIVER
MY GENEROUS FUNDERS: ARTS COUNCIL ENGLAND AND THE SOCIETY OF AUTHORS

WITHOUT YOU, A WHOLE LOT OF PEOPLE WOULDN'T HAVE PULLED THROUGH AND THIS BOOK WOULDN'T EXIST OR HAVE LEGS. I CAN'T THANK YOU ENOUGH.

AND LOUIE, I COULDN'T BE MORE PROUD OF YOU. YOU ARE SO STRONG AND SO BRAVE —

— YOU ARE A GIANT.

MOLLIE X

LOTTERY FUNDED

Supported using public funding by ARTS COUNCIL ENGLAND

THE SOCIETY OF AUTHORS

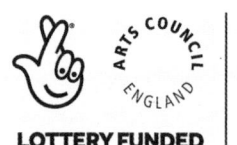

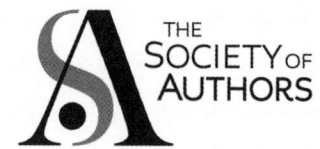

Mollie Ray is a Lancaster-based comic artist and illustrator. In 2019, she graduated from the University of Edinburgh with a first-class honours degree in illustration. Her work has been featured by Creative Boom, the AOI and Broken Frontier's 'Six to Watch in 2021'. She has also done work for the BBC and self-published multiple short-form comics.

This book was drawn in biro.

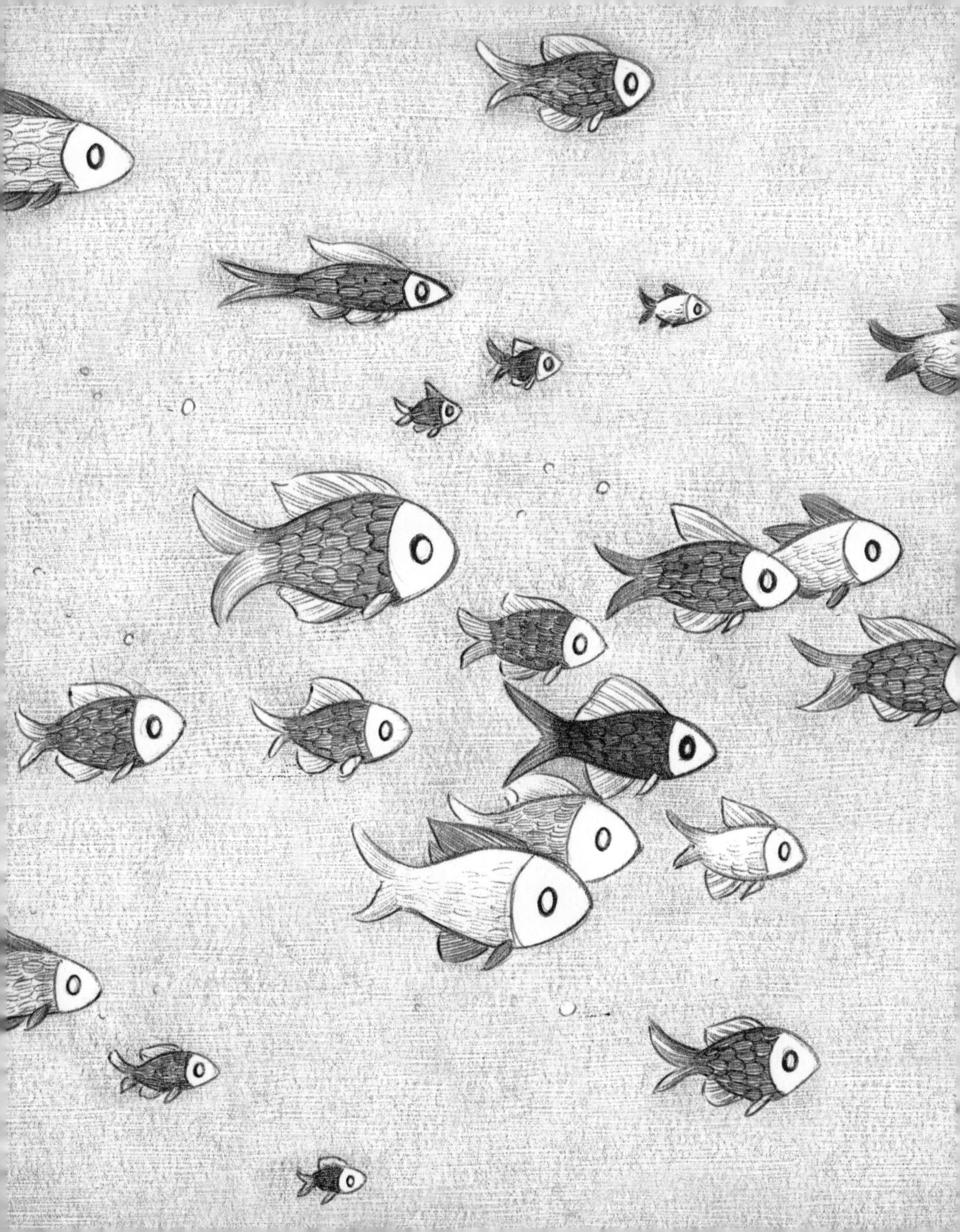